My Daughter's Legacy

My Daughter's Legacy

MINDY STARNS CLARK
and LESLIE GOULD

HARVEST HOUSE PUBLISHERS
EUGENE, OREGON

MY DAUGHTER'S LEGACY
Copyright © 2017 by Mindy Starns Clark and Leslie Gould
Published by Harvest House Publishers
Eugene, Oregon 97402
www.harvesthousepublishers.com

ISBN 978-0-7369-6292-6 (pbk.)
ISBN 978-0-7369-6293-3 (eBook)

Library of Congress Cataloging-in-Publication Data
Names: Clark, Mindy Starns, author. | Gould, Leslie, author.
Title: My daughter's legacy / Mindy Starns Clark, Leslie Gould.
Description: Eugene, Oregon : Harvest House Publishers, [2017] | Series: Cousins of the dove ; 3
Identifiers: LCCN 2017005464 (print) | LCCN 2017011335 (ebook) | ISBN 9780736962926 (softcover) | ISBN 9780736962933 (eBook) | ISBN 9780736962933 (ebook)
Subjects: | BISAC: FICTION / Christian / Historical. | FICTION / Christian / Romance. | GSAFD: Christian fiction. | Love stories.
Classification: LCC PS3603.L366 M93 2017 (print) | LCC PS3603.L366 (ebook) | DDC 813/.6--dc23
LC record available at https://lccn.loc.gov/2017005464

Printed in the United States of America

17 18 19 20 21 22 23 24 25 / LB-JC / 10 9 8 7 6 5 4 3 2 1

For our strong, creative, and devoted daughters,
Emily and Lauren Clark
and
Hana and Thao Gould.
You are our legacies.

Yea, the sparrow hath found an house,
and the swallow a nest for herself,
where she may lay her young, even thine altars,
O LORD of hosts, my King, and my God.

PSALM 84:3

CHAPTER ONE

Nicole

*S*ometimes a lie was the better choice—or at least that's what I'd always told myself. After all, lying was easier, faster, and more efficient than the truth. "I'm sick" was a more prudent option than "I'm sick of working." "I'm busy" was a lot kinder than "I don't want to." But for some, lying could become a habit, the proverbial spider weaving its tangled web. Problem is, once I'd made my own web big enough, I found I was no longer spider but prey, trapped by silvery threads of my own design.

I'd spent the last year and a half—ever since the night I got loaded and slammed my car into a tree at sixty miles an hour—slowly untangling my own threads. Now, after two months of convalescence, nine months in a drug rehab facility, and two full semesters away at college, I was nearly free of all that—save for one big, fat lie that remained.

"Nicole!"

My head snapped left to see the setter knocking the volleyball into an easy arc over my head. Telling myself to focus, I bent my knees, waited for the exact right moment in its trajectory, and then shot up from the ground to slam the ball as hard as I could, spiking it straight through the upraised arms of our opponent and onto an empty space on the court behind her.

Set and game. Our victory, 3 to 2.

My team burst into cheers, jumping and hugging and laughing. When we finally calmed down, we lined up and did the high-five-and-thanks-for-a-good-game thing with the opposing team. Then we gathered for a quick huddle, mostly so our team captain could remind us, yet again, to stay in shape over the summer. Ours was just a local league in a small town in Virginia, but it was important to us.

"Together now," she said, holding out a fist. We circled around and each placed a hand atop until all were in.

"*One. Play.* At a *time!*" We shouted the team motto in unison, and then our huddle was done.

After some quick goodbyes and see-you-in-the-falls, I gathered my stuff and headed for the locker room, eager to grab a shower before all the stalls were taken. This was our last game of the semester, and though I was glad to be heading home to Richmond tomorrow, I knew I was going to miss this over summer break. The court was where I brought everything—happiness, sadness, anger, fear, elation, confusion, frustration—and it had proven to be an almost better outlet than my weekly on-campus counseling sessions. Which was saying a lot, considering what a great counselor I had.

Of course, my teammates were almost like counselors as well, or at least like savvy older sisters, I thought as I snagged a stall, set my little mesh bag of toiletries on the shelf, and turned on the water. We weren't just a sports team. We were a support group, former addicts and fellow students trying to make our way at a very conservative, totally non-partying university tucked away in the Shenandoah Mountains of western Virginia.

I'd come to Silver Lake University specifically because it was a dry campus, even though initially I never would've considered such a thing for fear I might stick out like a sore thumb. But then someone let me in on a secret back when I was fresh out of rehab and trying to choose the right college. My sister's boyfriend, Greg, was a certified addiction specialist, and he'd told me about a small sobriety network that existed here, one endorsed by the administration and geared toward students who had gotten themselves into trouble in the past but had gone through treatment, sobered up, and sincerely wanted to stay that way.

I'd been intrigued enough to check it out and found that he was right. Among the long-haired and long-skirted conservative student body of this all-female, drug-free, alcohol-free Christian university were a dozen or so freaky types like me who were clearly the opposite of conservative—or at least had been at some point in their lives.

My sister, Maddee, and I had taken a weekend trip to see the place, and the young woman who led our campus tour told us, straight out, that despite such differences in the student body, there wasn't much in the way of divisions or ostracism. According to the college's oft-quoted mission statement, the students here were all "one in Christ and all worthy of acceptance, respect, and a positive, mutually supportive environment in which to learn."

I was skeptical but decided to give the place a shot anyway, and now that I'd reached the end of my first full year, I had to say she'd been pretty much on the mark. I'd never felt anything but accepted and respected here, which in turn had made me a lot more open to the other side, to the kinds of girls I used to consider hopelessly naive, over-protected, and repressed.

I always figured kids like that were just time bombs waiting to go off, ready to turn wild the moment they were out from under their parents' thumbs. Instead, with few exceptions, they'd turned out to be intelligent, mature, thoughtful women who seemed perfectly happy with their theology and their life choices. They were actually comfortable wearing conservative dresses, dating only in groups, and saving their first kisses for their wedding days. And though I didn't hang with them often, I liked and respected them, something the old me would never have seen coming.

The locker room grew louder as more and more players got in line for the showers, so I finished up, quickly dried off, and wrapped myself in a towel. Then I made my way back to the locker, flip-flops slapping against the damp tile as I went.

My friend and sponsor, Riley, was on the bench, already fully dressed and tying her shoes, so I plopped my things next to her and stepped to my locker, which was at her back.

"Hey, Rocket," she scolded, "I thought you needed a ride."

"I do," I replied, quickly pulling on my clothes.

"Why'd you take a shower, then? I told you I don't have a lot of time."

"Yeah, me neither." Once dressed, I reached for my brush and ran it through my shoulder-length blond hair, gave my head a good shake, and then slipped my feet back into my flip-flops. "So let's go."

She turned, startled to see that I was as ready as she was despite the fact that she had simply changed clothes while I had gotten in a shower as well. She shook her head.

"You know me. I'm all about low maintenance." I grinned, gesturing toward the line of women at the mirrors, busy with lip gloss and mascara and hair straighteners. I wasn't averse to fixing myself up, but not on an evening when my agenda consisted of some final packing followed by a good night's sleep.

"Low maintenance," she repeated skeptically, waiting as I scooped everything into my tote bag and closed the door on the now-empty locker.

"Yep," I said, swinging the bag over my shoulder and gesturing toward the exit. "That's me. No drama, no muss, no fuss."

"Uh-huh."

Together we walked out of the locker room and down the hall. We both knew that drama and muss and fuss almost always came part and parcel with addicts. And though I was only teasing about the low-maintenance part, I really had worked hard this year to cut as much of that stuff down to a minimum as I could.

We headed to the parking lot—me feeling even shorter than usual next to my extra-tall friend—and got in Riley's car, a rattletrap piece of junk held together by duct tape and prayer. She started it up, and we chatted as she drove the familiar route across town to the sleepy little campus we called home. At first we were just reviewing some of the highlights of tonight's game, but eventually, as often with Riley, the conversation turned toward matters of the heart.

"So you're really gonna be okay near your old stomping grounds for an entire summer?"

I knew what she was talking about, but I waved off her concerns, wishing I felt as confident as I pretended to be. Tomorrow morning I would get on the bus for Richmond, where I would spend the next three months living with my sister and working at a job in my field, one that would provide some pocket money and a college credit besides. These were positive things, happy things, and I refused to let my insecurities bring me down even if I would be in closer proximity to old temptations. I'd been sober for a year and a half, and I intended to stay that way.

"I have safety networks in place, including plenty of meetings to choose from. Plus, I have all my positive experiences from this past year to build on."

"Good." We were quiet for moment until she added, "You're totally up to this, you know. You've come so far that a few months back home will be a good thing. I'm not worried about you at all."

"That makes one of us."

Riley chuckled as she turned into the parking lot for my dorm and rattled to a stop near the front steps. Before getting out, I gave her a big hug and told her I would miss her over the summer. "I don't know how I could've made it through the school year without you."

"Yeah. Well, just remember. What is this? The summer of..."

"Truth," I responded. "The summer of truth."

I grabbed my stuff and climbed out, and then I shut the door with a wrenching squawk. She started off again, her car chugging and clanking its way across the parking lot toward grad student housing, and soon she was out of sight, if not sound. I turned and headed up to my room, anxiety surging in my throat.

The summer of truth, including the truth about the secret I'd been holding inside since I was six years old, which I was going to share with my family at last. I loved my grandfather deeply and would always cherish his memory, but I knew that these truths—both what I'd witnessed back then and the fact that Granddad had sworn me to secrecy about it afterward—must finally come to light. At the time, he'd made me promise I would take our secret to the grave. Now that I'd decided to renege on that promise, I only hoped it wouldn't be the biggest mistake of my life.

Forcing my mind away from such thoughts, I concentrated on the rest of my packing and was just zipping the last bag shut when I got a call on my cell. It was my grandmother, no doubt wanting to touch base yet again about my trip home. Lately she'd been a broken record on the subject.

"Hi, Nana." I took the big duffel from the bed and set it against the wall.

"Hello, Nicole. I thought you said you were coming home via the train."

I flopped onto the mattress. "I'm fine, thanks. How are you?"

Nana rushed ahead, ignoring my sass. "I'll have you know that there is no train between there and here," she said, almost triumphantly. "I checked."

I bristled. Was she kidding me? I understood we still had a ways to go before she could trust me implicitly, but since when did she feel the need to verify things like this?

"Well?" she prodded.

"Are you serious right now?" I rolled my eyes with great exaggeration. Too bad Nana couldn't see me because it was an excellent eye roll. "I wasn't lying," I said, forcing my voice to remain calm. "They take you by bus as far as Charlottesville, and then they switch you over to a train for the rest. It's one ticket for the whole thing." I didn't add that I hadn't yet bought that ticket. I would do it in the morning once I got to the station.

"No, no, no. I can't have you taking a bus even if it's just for part of the trip. It's too slow, and the people...Well, I just don't like the idea. I'll arrange for a car and driver instead."

"Nana! No. The bus is fine. Don't be such a snob."

"A car would be quicker."

"For your information, I'm actually looking forward to the long ride. I need time to think, to be alone. To process the transition from school back to home."

Nana huffed. "Well, at least let me arrange for a ride from your dorm to the station."

I sighed heavily, making sure she heard it, and then agreed. I'd been planning to call an Uber, but whatever. With Nana, you had to pick your battles.

"Oh, and Nicole?" she added before hanging up. "I just want to acknowledge that you met all of my requirements this year. Good job."

"Thanks," I replied through gritted teeth. Then I added a quick "Bye" and hung up before I exploded.

Met all of her requirements? I'd done a lot more than meet them. I'd *exceeded* them by far. I'd slam-dunked the suckers. How dare she?

The deal we'd made last summer had been straightforward and simple. She would pay for everything—tuition, room and board, expenses, and more—and in return I was required to maintain a 3.0 grade point average, not miss more than two counseling sessions per semester, submit to four random drug tests during the school year, and keep her in the loop regarding how things were going.

Instead, I'd gotten a 4.0, never missed a single counseling session, and passed all four drug tests with flying colors. Better yet, not only had I kept her "in the loop"—I'd texted and emailed her regularly.

I knew I wasn't an accomplished scientist or artist like my cousins Renee and Danielle, nor was I an up-and-coming psychologist like my sister, Maddee. But that didn't mean our grandmother had to treat me like a poor stepchild. What was her problem? Now that I was sober, I was trying hard to believe I could accomplish anything I set my mind to, but Nana's doubts didn't help things.

Worse, our relationship was about to face a new challenge once I revealed my secret. With another heavy sigh, I got ready for bed, telling myself I could handle whatever lay ahead so long as Maddee stood beside me and believed me. The trick would be getting my sister to trust this recovered addict who used to lie as a matter of course and had proven over and over through the years that she could not, in fact, be trusted.

The next morning, I was sitting on the front steps of the dorm, waiting for Nana's ride to show, when a shiny blue mini SUV pulled to the curb in front of me. The driver turned it off, climbed out, and looked my way. "Nicole Talbot?"

"That's me." I stood and grabbed the handles of my various bags and lugged them toward the back of the car, where the man popped the hatchback and helped load everything inside. Then, to my surprise, he gestured toward the driver's door and offered me the key.

I looked at the gray fob dangling between us and then back at him. "Um, excuse me, but aren't you supposed to be the one at the wheel? I think that's why you're called the *driver*?"

He responded by reaching into his suit jacket and pulling out an envelope, which he handed over to me. Puzzled, I opened it up and slid out the contents. First was a printed note, like the kind that might come with a mail-order fruit basket.

> For going above and beyond in every way this past year.
> I'm so very proud of you.
>
> Love, Nana

There was a second page, and I turned to it, realizing it was the title to the car in front of me—with my name on it.

"This car?" I asked in disbelief. "It's mine?"

"Straight from the lot and loaded with every bell and whistle we've got."

"Is this some kind of prank?" I knew I was staring at him stupidly, but I couldn't help it.

"Nope. It's legit." He turned and walked to the passenger side. "Get in. I'll show you everything you need to know."

With shaking hands, I took my place behind the wheel, still too stunned to speak. I listened in a daze as the man gave me a quick orientation, pointing out the touchscreen navigation system, keyless ignition, and a bunch of other stuff I knew I wouldn't remember.

He asked for a lift back to the dealership, and somehow I managed to get him there. But as soon as I was alone, I pulled into a parking lot, took out my phone, and dialed Nana's number. She answered on the second ring.

"Are you crazy?"

To my surprise, my grandmother actually giggled, a sound I'd never heard from her before. "Do you like it, dear?"

"Are you kidding me? How? Why?"

"You earned it, Nicole. Now come on home, will you? I can't wait to see you tomorrow."

I shook my head in wonder. My exacting, critical, demanding, crazy-making grandmother, of all people, trusted me enough to give me this? Tears filled my eyes, and I grabbed a tissue from the complimentary packet in the cup holder to wipe them away.

"Nana, I—"

"Hush, now. I know. Just be sure to wear your seat belt. Drive safely."

With that, she was gone.

Between the high of my grandmother's approval and the smooth ride of my new—*my* new—car, I was in heaven as I headed out on the two-hour journey to Richmond. It took a while before I came down from the shock of it all, but by the time I reached the halfway point at Charlottesville, I was fully in the zone and doing what I'd told Nana I would, using the travel time to process the transition from school to home.

I'd learned a lot in the course of my first successful year back in college, and not just academically speaking. I'd learned I could stay sober even out of rehab and on my own. I'd learned how to make friends in places other than bars. I'd learned that I actually enjoyed myself a lot more without the fog of drugs or alcohol dimming every experience. In a way, this had been a year of narrowing down, of figuring out what I did and did not want. I wanted to stay sober, and I wanted to tell my secret. I wanted to be completely honest from here on out. I was pretty sure on all of that.

Unfortunately, in other areas, mostly what I'd managed to figure out thus far was what I *didn't* want. I wanted to try dating for the first time since the accident, but I didn't want to end up with the kind of guy I'd always gone for before—the tough, sexy, dangerous sort. I wanted some kind of career in psychology, but I was pretty sure I didn't want to be a therapist who just sat in a room all day, working with people one on one.

In both of these things, I knew what I didn't want, but what did I want? Growing anxious at the uncertainty of it all, I reminded myself to take it one day at a time. I simply had to trust that God would reveal each of these things to me according to His will, His plan. When it came to church and men and career, I could simply trust and wait.

But then there was the police investigation, which was a bit more...complicated.

Twenty-two years ago, when I was just six years old, a man had been stabbed and killed in an old hunting cabin in the woods next door to my grandparents' estate. My sister, who was eight at the time, our two nine-year-old cousins, and I had gone for a hike soon after it happened and accidently stumbled upon a lifeless, bloody body with a huge knife protruding from his chest. We'd run screaming back to the house, but by the time police arrived and made it out to the cabin to investigate, the body was gone and all traces of the crime had been cleaned away. Not one person—not even our own parents—believed our story. Some of the boy cousins taunted us, laughing behind our backs and naming us "the Liar Choir."

All four of us had been traumatized by the incident, albeit in different ways. My cousin Renee had been hurt most by the mistrust and doubt of those who said we'd simply imagined it or made it all up. My cousin Danielle suffered primarily from the visual assault. As an artist, she saw the world differently than others and retained it all too well. As she'd said many times since, she hated that she could never unsee that body. That knife. That blood. It hovered in her dreams and sometimes even made its way into her artwork.

For my sister, Maddee, the worst part had been me. Older by two years, she'd always been deeply maternal, and the fact that she hadn't protected me from such a horror weighed heavily on her. It was even worse afterward, when she had to sit helplessly by for years as I struggled first with night terrors and, later, with addiction. She hadn't understood the full cause of my trauma, however, because she hadn't known the whole story.

My own scars were different than theirs because they included seeing a man I loved and idolized do something wrong, and when I told him what I'd seen, he made me promise not to tell anyone else. According to my counselor, we'd never know how much of my addiction was rooted in that mess, but it definitely played a part. Now that I was sober and stable and ready to reveal the truth, I could only hope I would find healing in the same way the others had.

Fortunately, both Maddee and Renee had managed to work through much of their trauma and were doing much better, starting nearly two years ago when Renee had used her skills as a scientist to prove our tale was true, that there really had been a dead body in that cabin when we were children. In response, the police had reopened the case, and though they still didn't have all the answers, they certainly knew a lot more now than they had before. Once I shared my secret, would it help them figure out the rest?

Or would it serve only to smear my grandfather's good name and muddy the waters even more?

CHAPTER TWO
Nicole

I reached Richmond's Fan District shortly after eleven and managed to find a parking spot directly across the street from the carriage house where my sister lived. She rented it from a lovely older woman we called Miss Vida, who resided in the much larger and quite beautiful home in front of it. During my convalescence here after the accident, Maddee had talked Miss Vida into helping out as an ad hoc caretaker, but she and I had hit it off so well that we'd become fast friends.

Maddee must have been watching for me, because by the time I'd climbed from the car, she was practically at my side and throwing her arms around me for a big hug.

"Where'd this come from?" she asked as we pulled apart, eyeing my new vehicle.

"One guess." Suddenly I felt embarrassed that I'd been the beneficiary of such generosity. But before I could say anything else, Maddee flashed a knowing grin. "Ah, yes. The Nana graduation car."

My embarrassment turned to relief. "You got one too?"

"Oh yeah. And Renee and Danielle when they graduated. Looks

like yours came early, probably because she's so proud of how well you've been doing."

I shrugged, but on the inside I was beaming. "I always wondered why you drove a Mustang."

Maddee laughed. "I know, right? She tries to choose something appropriate, and I guess because I'm so into fashion she thought I'd want something sleek and sporty, but that car wasn't me at all. I was so happy when I finally got to trade it in for the Prius, which is so much more—"

"Boring?"

"I was going to say sensible."

We shared a smile and then grabbed my bags and headed to the carriage house, a small brick building with just enough space for a kitchen-living room combo and bathroom downstairs and a single bedroom upstairs. When I'd stayed here after my accident, I'd been in a hospital bed that pretty much took up the entire living room area. But this time around I would be using Maddee's pullout sofa at night, which would leave us with a bit more room during the day.

"Oh, boy. I see the curtain's back," I said as I caught sight of the familiar fabric that she'd used to give me a semblance of privacy. At the moment, it was pulled to the side and tied in place to the banister.

Maddee's home was so tiny that everyone thought we were nuts for rooming together this summer, especially our parents. Before, they argued, I'd been in a bad way, limited to the bed or the wheelchair in the weeks following my accident, so space hadn't been an issue. But this time around, I was perfectly healthy and fully mobile, which would mean a much greater need to work around each other.

We assured them we knew what we were doing. We'd been close as children but then drifted apart once I started using. After the accident, however, Maddee really stepped up to the plate, taking me in and nursing me back to health, and in the process we had discovered a new sister dynamic that really worked. She might get on my nerves now and then, and we were about as different as two people could be, but she was also my best friend in the world, and I knew her well enough now to know that there would be a lot more laughs this summer than arguments.

Not surprisingly, the moment we got my bags into the living room area, Maddee headed for her trusty whiteboard, which hung on the wall of the kitchen near the spiral staircase. Glancing at it, I saw that this was a new and much bigger version of the old one, divided into three sections labeled "Schedule," "To-Do," and "Calendar." Good grief. Then again, why was I surprised? Throughout our childhood, every Christmas I begged for a pony while Maddee consistently requested a leather-bound Franklin daily planner.

"Let's talk schedules!" she said excitedly.

"Can't a girl freshen up first? I've been in a car for two hours."

"Sure, sorry. I'll make coffee."

I headed for her little bathroom, stifling a smile. My sister truly was one of a kind.

Soon I was settled at the kitchen table, cup of joe in hand, and Maddee was back at the board, explaining that she thought we should establish some basic rules so things would run as smoothly as possible this summer.

"We can divide the shopping and cooking fifty-fifty," she said, pointing to the fridge, where she'd tacked up the week's meal plan and shopping list. "We do have one problem. We need to find a way to avoid conflicts with the shower in the mornings because our schedules are fairly similar."

"I think there's a locker room at Dover Creek Farms. I can shower there at the end of the day. If this job is as dirty as I think it is, I'll need it—especially with my new car. I don't want to create a manure mobile." Originally, my dad was going to loan me his old truck for the summer so I'd have a way to get back and forth to work. But how could I drive that thing to the farm now that I'd seen Paree?

Maddee continued working down the list, and then she turned her attention to the big calendar across the lower half of the whiteboard. "Note that we have church tomorrow with Nana, followed by lunch at her house, and then we'll head to the Virginia Museum of Americana for a special exhibit."

"A museum?" I asked skeptically.

"Oh, I think you might be interested in this one. The exhibit is called 'Civil War Richmond: Through the Camera Lens,' and it features Civil War–era photography and memorabilia."

"And this interests me why?"

"Because some of the pictures came from our own family. They feature our Talbot ancestors."

She was right. She had my interest now. I wasn't as big on ancestry and family trees and stuff as she was, but after the accident we'd had the chance to read a series of letters written by one of our forebears back in the early 1700s, and I had found them fascinating. Somehow, learning about those who came before made me feel so *connected* to time and space and family in a whole new way.

"Aunt Cissy is the Civil War buff and keeper of the photos," Maddee continued. "She's the one who loaned out the items for the exhibit."

I rolled my eyes. We weren't proud of it, but Aunt Cissy was sort of the family joke—at least among the younger relatives. She was sweet and always upbeat, but she lived to sing, much to the detriment of anyone who had to listen. Maybe she'd had a nice voice when she was young, but in my lifetime I'd never heard anything come out of her that didn't curl my toes and threaten to shatter the nearest glass.

"Come on now," Maddee scolded. "She is family."

"Fine. I won't make fun."

"And of course keep in mind that the annual Talbot family reunion will be at the end of June."

"Um, Maddee? It's the sixth of May. Why are we even talking about this now?"

"Just thinking ahead." Without missing a beat, she continued to update me all the way through August 5, which she'd circled in red and written *Nicole—Back to school*. It was moments like these that made me want to grab the eraser and go to town on her entire system. I liked to take time as it came, not plot everything that lay ahead to the minute. Yes, she was right, I would be moving out August 5. But looking at the board in its entirety made me depressed, as if it were almost time to turn around and go back to college now.

"And that's that," she ended, capping her pen, oblivious to my irritation.

"Not quite," I said. I rose and retrieved from my backpack a single page I'd printed up, after much thought, just yesterday. "Tape?" I asked, holding out a hand until my sister complied, tearing a piece from the roll on the counter and handing it over. "Thanks. Have a seat. It's my turn now."

Surprised but curious, she took the chair I'd been using and gave me her full attention.

"Remember when I moved in the last time, after the accident, and you laid down a list of ground rules about what you expected from me?"

She nodded.

"Well, this time I have some rules for you." With that, I taped my list next to the whiteboard and went through it point by point. "No mothering, no monitoring, give me the benefit of the doubt, remember that I made it through two full semesters far from home and did great. Be my sister and friend, not my nursemaid or my mother or my enforcer or my accountability partner or anything else." I let out a long breath and met her eyes. "Deal?"

Maddee paused for a moment, considering, and then she smiled. "Deal."

"Oh, yeah. One more thing." Pulling out my phone, I opened up a playlist and waved it at her. "Remember how you held me prisoner here and tortured me with your '50s music? Well, it's my turn now. Get ready to rock."

Maddee and Greg gave me a welcome home cookout that afternoon, and it ended up being a really nice way to ease back into things. Later that night, once Maddee and I were alone, she was planning to update me on the investigation. I'd intentionally kept myself out of the loop this year, not wanting the added pressure of dealing with that on top of sobriety and school and everything else, so I had some catching up to do. But I wasn't exactly looking forward to it—nor of telling her my big secret in return—so the barbecue made for a great distraction in the meantime.

Because the temperature was pleasantly cool, we decided to dine on the front patio, which sat between the carriage house and Miss Vida's back fence. Maddee and I had just finished setting the table when we were joined by Miss Vida, who came bearing a heavenly-smelling kugel. With her was a man she introduced as her boyfriend, Lev Sobol, and I tried not to act as surprised as I felt. Why hadn't Maddee warned me?

Lev wasn't a bad-looking guy for his age, I supposed, with thick silver hair and a nice smile. When I asked how they'd met, the two of them answered together, like a storytelling tag team. Miss Vida started by explaining that theirs had been a "telephone only" relationship at first.

"To tell you the truth, I was a cold call," she said with a giggle. "Lev dialed me up out of the blue to talk investments, but we had such a good time chatting that he asked if he might call me again sometime—and not in a business capacity."

"Which I did that very night," he said. "And the night after that, and the night after that..."

"Finally I said, 'Lev, it's time to step up your game. We doing this or what?'"

They smiled at each other and then back at me.

"So I took her to dinner..."

"I had the clams casino..."

"She was, of course, even more lovely than I had expected..."

"And he was so handsome and debonair..."

"And we really hit it off..."

"So, long story short, he hasn't been able to get rid of me since."

"As if I'd ever want to," he scolded fondly, leaning toward her and, to my surprise—not to mention dismay—actually rubbing noses with her.

No wonder Maddee hadn't said anything. This was just one of those things that had to be seen to be believed.

Still, we ended up having a fun afternoon—though once the food was served and we all dug in, it was kind of hard not to feel like a fifth wheel. Between Lev and Miss Vida making goo-goo eyes at each other, and Greg and Maddee acting like a happy old married couple, I really was the odd man out. Greg had cooked for us on the grill, and when

Maddee took the first bite of her burger, she cried, "Oh, Greg! This is marvelous. What would I ever do without you?"

Of course, I couldn't resist the urge to tease my sister throughout the meal, saying, "Thanks for passing the ketchup, Greg. Thanks for the napkin. What would I ever do without you?"

Maddee nudged me in the ribs playfully and tried to hide her blushing face. According to her whiteboard, later this month they would celebrate their year-and-a-half anniversary, and clearly things were going well. I couldn't have been happier for her, even if I did make fun.

We called it a night once the mosquitoes came out at dusk, parting on the walkway with a hug from Miss Vida and a handshake from her beau.

"It's a real shame, your grandfather's passing," he said, growing serious as he looked from Maddee to me. "He was a good man."

"You knew him?" I asked.

He nodded. "He and my dad were hunting buddies. Occasionally they let me tag along. I was even out at that cabin of his a couple of times." With a glance at his girlfriend, he added, "Sorry, maybe I shouldn't have mentioned the cabin. Vida told me about what happened out there, and about the investigation and everything. That's a real shame all the way around."

Surging with anxiety, I wrapped up my goodbyes and headed into the house, startled at how strongly I'd just reacted to Lev's words. My hands were shaking, and I could barely breathe. So much for telling Maddee my big secret tonight. I clearly wasn't ready yet.

Greg stuck around to help with the dishes. Before he left, he asked about my old injuries from the accident. Besides two cracked ribs and lots of cuts and bruises, I'd sustained multiple fractures in both legs, with one messed up so badly that it had required surgery. I'd needed tons of physical therapy, starting when my legs were still in casts and continuing for a good while after those casts had come off. Greg had been my PT until I went away to rehab, and he'd done a great job. Nowadays, except for some small residual scars here and there—plus the big one from my surgery—you'd never know by looking at me that the accident had ever happened.

I told him about volleyball and how it had strengthened me all over but especially in the legs. "My team nicknamed me 'Rocket,' because even though I'm the shortest one, I have enough thrusting power in my legs to play attack."

"Attack?" Maddee asked.

"Yeah, you know. The setter sends the ball to the attack, and then she jumps up and smashes it into the opponent's court."

"Wow, impressive," Maddee said. "Considering that Greg's gotten me into P90X, maybe you and I can have a Sister Cage Match."

We all laughed, and with that, Greg said it was time for him to go. Maddee offered to walk him out—probably so she could give him a big, fat goodbye kiss in private—but before they left, he patted me on the shoulder and said to keep up the good work. "I'm really proud of you, kid."

Warmth spread through me at his words and stayed long after he was gone. Besides being my sister's boyfriend, my former physical therapist, and one of my wisest advisers, Greg was like a brother to me, and I truly valued his opinion.

Once Maddee came back inside, she served up ice cream for the two of us, and we settled down at the kitchen table so she could bring me up to speed on the case. She began, however, by saying it was really complicated, and she might not get through the entire story tonight. "But at least we can get started, right?"

"If you say so."

With a nod, she launched into her update, sounding like an elementary schoolteacher carefully laying the groundwork to lead her class through a complex concept. "The man we found dead in the cabin, as you know, was named Taavi Koenig, and he was from Cleveland, Ohio."

"Right." I remembered that much. "So do we now know why he was there?"

"Yes and no. We don't know why he was in the cabin, but we do know why he was in Richmond. He was trying to track down a valuable family heirloom stolen from his great-great-grandfather."

"His great-great..." My voice trailed off as I took a bite of ice cream.

"Yeah." Maddee twirled her spoon around in her bowl, just as she

did when we were little. "Bottom line, Taavi's family and our family
had a connection, one that began back in 1864."

"Get out."

"Yep. Do you know what an illuminated manuscript is?"

"I'm not sure..."

She put down her spoon to pull up a few images on her phone and
then handed it over. I scrolled through photos of old, hand-lettered
books decorated with elaborate borders and tiny illustrations—very
colorful, some with gold and silver leaf.

"Those are cool," I said, returning her phone.

"I know, right? So back in the 1800s, a Richmond rabbi owned a
valuable illuminated manuscript that had been passed down through
his family for generations. That rabbi's name was Elias Koenig, and
he was Taavi's great-great-grandfather." Her eyes grew serious. "Tragically, in 1864, a con man tricked Elias and managed to steal the manuscript from him."

"Tricked him?"

"Yeah. It's kind of complicated. Apparently, the guy pretended to be
a reporter from a big magazine doing a story about illuminated manuscripts. That's how he got a foot in the door. Then, in his 'interview,' he
gathered a bunch of information, including the fact that the rabbi was
friends with the owner of a local company, Talbot Paper and Printing.
The con man didn't know the Talbots, but that didn't matter. He lied
and said he did, and then he came back a few days later with a 'message' from the Talbots, saying they'd learned of a group of thieves plot-
ting to steal the manuscript. The Talbots supposedly offered to keep it
in their company safe, where no one would ever think to look for it."

"The rabbi bought his story?"

Maddee nodded. "It was a well-done con involving an old safe and
some faked documents and stuff. But the important thing is that the
con man stole the manuscript, and that part of his trickery involved
the Talbots through no fault of their own."

"So what happened?"

"The con man took the manuscript to New York City, where he'd
already lined up his mark, a merchant from San Francisco who was in

town on a buying trip for his store and for a new synagogue that was going up out on the West Coast. That guy purchased the manuscript, which he thought was legit, and then he sent it off to San Francisco with some other cargo aboard a ship called the *Tycoon*."

By now I'd finished my ice cream, but Maddee still had a few bites left.

"The rabbi didn't realize right away that the manuscript was gone, but once he and the Talbots figured it out, there wasn't much they could do. Feeling bad for their friend and how they'd unwittingly been connected to the theft, the Talbots hired a private detective to recover the manuscript."

I was surprised to hear there had even been private detectives back then.

"The detective did finally track it down, but by then the con man was long gone, the poor merchant was appalled to learn he'd purchased stolen goods, and the *Tycoon* was out to sea." Maddee took a last half-melted bite and then kept going. "One of the Talbots' sons, Michael, was over in France at the time, learning about new methods of paper-making, and not long after this happened, his dad wrote and told him all about the poor rabbi who lost his treasured book and how the Talbot name had been dragged into it and so on. In the letter, he said that he felt sorriest of all for the poor merchant, who was out a bunch of money, because once the *Tycoon* got to San Francisco and the book was delivered, he would be legally required to ship the manuscript back to its rightful owner in Richmond."

"Well," I said, wondering where this was all going, "except for the merchant, it sounds like everything turned out all right in the end."

Maddee shook her head. "Nope. In fact, the real troubles had just begun."

CHAPTER THREE
Nicole

I dished up a second helping of ice cream as Maddee continued the story of the stolen illuminated manuscript.

"This all took place during the Civil War, and if you remember your lessons from history class, the *Tycoon* never made it to San Francisco."

I rolled my eyes. Really? She thought I'd remember something as obscure as a ship never making it to its destination in 1864?

Maddee didn't seem to notice. "Instead, it was captured by the *CSS Alabama,* which was the South's most successful commerce raider."

"What's a commerce raider?" I asked as I put the ice cream away.

She explained that they roamed the seas during wartime and captured shipments of goods that belonged to the other side in an attempt to impact trade and damage the economy of the enemy. "Whenever they would capture a ship, they'd take on all the passengers and crew, confiscate any valuables they wanted, and then either burn the other ship or sell it for ransom. After that, they would drop off the passengers at the nearest port and sail away to their next conquest, keeping the booty for themselves."

I sat back down at the table, cradling my bowl. "Sounds like pirates to me."

"Yeah, but legally sanctioned ones." She folded her hands together. "Anyway, to get from New York City to San Francisco back then, the *Tycoon* had to sail all the way down and around South America. But a little more than a month into its voyage, when it was off the coast of Brazil, the *Tycoon* was caught and confiscated by the *Alabama*. Among the valuables taken from the ship was the illuminated manuscript, although you have to wonder if anyone on board really knew its value. Regardless, one of the officers—we don't have his name, so let's just call him Fred—kept it for himself and tucked it away with his things. Whether he was aware of what it really was or not, we'll never know—"

"Wait." I couldn't help but interrupt. "One question. How do you know *any* of this? It's a lot of detail for something that happened a hundred and fifty years ago."

Maddie nodded. "I was getting to that. When all was said and done, the Talbots sat down and documented everything, at least to the extent of their own knowledge. It makes it easy to learn the details when it's all written out for you."

"Cool." I took another bite of ice cream, nodding for her to continue.

"After the commerce raider finished with the *Tycoon*, it headed to France, where the plan was to put it in dry dock for a few months so it could undergo extensive repairs by master shipbuilders there. At this point, the *Alabama* was notorious around the world, and once it reached the port city of Cherbourg, France, in mid-June, word of its arrival was telegraphed to Paris, and that news quickly spread all over Europe. One person who heard the news was Michael Talbot, who was still in Le Chambon at the time."

"And Michael was the Talbots' son, the one who'd gotten the letter from his dad telling him all about what had happened, right?"

"Right. So Michael learns that the *Alabama* is in France, and he's all like, 'Whaaat?'" Maddee's excitement was palpable. "This thing that was stolen from Richmond got put on the *Tycoon*, and then the *Tycoon* was captured by the *Alabama*, and the *Alabama* was now in France? If that manuscript was among the items seized from the *Tycoon*, then it should still be aboard the *Alabama*." She paused for a moment as if I might have a question.

I smiled to encourage her to keep speaking and took another bite of ice cream.

She continued eagerly. "On the chance he was right, Michael raced to Cherbourg, hoping to reclaim the stolen manuscript for the rabbi. Michael would be heading back to America in about a month, and he could bring it with him." She explained that, meanwhile, once the *Alabama* reached the port, anchored in the harbor, and its captain asked permission to come ashore, he was told that permission would have to come from Napoleon III, who was currently out of town and unavailable.

Maddee leaned toward me. "Thus, the crew was forced to stay aboard, though the captain and some of his officers ventured into town several times over the next few days as they waited for official permission to dock. On one of these trips, the officer who had the manuscript—"

"Fred." I smiled, happy to show I was keeping up.

"Right. Fred connected with a cousin of his who lived in the region. Unfortunately for the *Alabama*, word of its location reached the Union, which sent a ship to attack it once it headed back out into international waters. Aware of the Union's intentions, the captain of the *Alabama* decided to go ahead and fight things out right away while they were still waiting for Napoleon to come back from out of town and give them permission to land."

I finished the last of my ice cream as Maddee said, "Everyone on board the *Alabama* made preparations for battle, including sending their valuables ashore. Fred was able to entrust the manuscript and his other valuables to his cousin before reboarding the *Alabama* for the battle."

Clearly my sister loved all this history. She really had the story down. Her voice rose as she gave me a blow-by-blow of how the situation unraveled from there. "Thousands of spectators watched the battle from the French coast. The fighting lasted about an hour, until the

Alabama sank. Although the majority of the crew survived, more than forty died—including poor Fred."

"Of course."

"Yeah, really, like what else can go wrong? Okay, so Michael reached Cherbourg the day of the battle, late in the afternoon, and was devastated to learn that the *Alabama* had been sunk off the coast by a Union ship. He thought the manuscript was now at the bottom of the sea, but then he heard that some crewmembers had sent valuables ashore first. Encouraged, he put the word out that he was looking for an old book, an illuminated manuscript, from among those valuables. Eventually, he was approached by Fred's cousin, who had found one in Fred's things and was willing to sell it to Michael for the right price."

Maddee explained that Michael paid the guy what he asked, which was a fraction of the manuscript's true value, and then he returned to Le Chambon. When his time in France came to an end a few weeks later, he brought the manuscript home with him, intending to deliver it to the rabbi.

"That must've been one happy *mensch*."

"Yeah, except by the time Michael reached Richmond, the rabbi was off fighting with the 25th Virginia Infantry regiment in the Shenandoah Valley. So Michael and his father hung on to the manuscript for him, tucking it away in a safe with the family's other valuables."

I did my best to stifle a yawn but without success.

"Still with me?" Maddee asked.

"Yeah, keep going." I rose and carried both of our bowls and spoons to the sink. "This is interesting and all, but I'm waiting to hear how any of it ties in with a dead body in a cabin some hundred and thirty years later."

Maddee retrieved a clean hand towel and then joined me at the sink, where she stood expectantly. Taking the hint, I reached for the dish soap and started washing.

"That will come," she said. "For now, I'm almost done. Let's wrap up this first part so you can get to sleep. I'll tell you the rest tomorrow, after the museum."

I wanted to keep going now, but it had been an exhausting day, and there was a sofa bed across the room with my name on it.

"Just one last thing, and then we'll stop for the night." As Maddee continued, she took each clean item from me, dried it, and put it away. "Believe it or not, after all of that, the thing was stolen."

"No!"

"Yes, taken right from their safe—along with other items of their own. So unfair. It wasn't as though they'd buried their valuables in the ground or something." Finished with the dishes, my sister pointed toward the stack of linens on the end table.

"What do you mean?"

"Well, theft wasn't all that unusual during the war. People were starving, desperate, and driven to do terrible things—plus, there was always the threat of Union soldiers coming in and taking stuff." Together we pulled out the hide-a-bed and began making it. Maddee kept talking. "The poor homeowners didn't know what to do. A lot of them hid their valuables in the walls or buried them in their yards. But the Talbots used a good, solid safe, and they were still robbed."

We finished the bed, and I began gathering my toothbrush and other stuff from my bag. "So that's how it ends—for now at least?"

"Pretty much. When all was said and done, the Talbots wrote out a full account of everything that had happened, which they gave to the poor rabbi, once he made it home from the war, along with some related documents and letters just in case it ever turned up. That's how we know all this, because the rabbi held on to that packet of information and passed it down through his family." Maddee fluffed the pillows on the bed. "He certainly didn't blame the Talbots for any of it. In fact, he added a brief note to their account, something about how they'd tried valiantly to help him, but that the manuscript was destined to find some other home. He was sad about the loss, but what could he do?"

I smiled a little in agreement. It didn't sound as if there was anything anyone could have done. "Unbelievable."

Maddee's expression turned serious. "Well, that, my dear sister, is the historical part of what we know. Tomorrow we'll pick it up in 1984, when the rabbi's great-great-grandson is watching the news one day and learns something that will end up changing his life."

After a night spent dreaming of sinking ships and dead sailors, I was glad when my alarm went off the next morning.

Church with Nana was fine, as was lunch at her place afterward. Our parents, who lived about two hours southeast, joined us, as did Aunt Cissy, who was all fixed up in a brightly flowered chiffon dress, her hair in a bouffant updo, her welcoming hug leaving me in a cloud of lilac-and-rose-scented perfume. Fortunately, we all had a little time to hang before heading to the museum, which gave me a chance to visit with my mom and dad and catch them up on school and stuff. We weren't especially close, but it was good to see them, and I could tell they were deeply relieved that I was still on the straight and narrow.

The reception at the museum was scheduled to begin at four, but thanks to our family's contribution to the exhibit, we were among those allowed to come early for a private viewing, where we could take it all in without crowds or commotion.

Once we got there and headed for the building, it really was kind of exciting, even if our family photos made up just a small percentage of the overall exhibit. According to Aunt Cissy, the Talbot pics wouldn't be all together but instead spread throughout, depending on subject matter.

The first thing I noticed as we entered the stately exhibit hall was the clever spin they'd used for the presentation, framing this collection of Civil War–era photographs in modern-day terms. Glancing around, I could see big headers, proclaiming "The World's First Selfie" and "The World's First Viral Photo."

Curious, I checked out the selfie, which was a somewhat stained and blurry daguerreotype of a young man with thick curly hair and a thoughtful gaze. According to the description, the man was an amateur chemist and photographer who had taken advantage of the long exposure times required back then by running in front of the camera, removing the lens cap, posing for a minute or two, and then putting the cap back on—thus capturing the image of himself and creating what was, indeed, the world's first selfie.

I was smiling at the thought as I moved on from there, but my smile faded when I came to the next one, "The World's First Viral Photo." Talk about a jolt. According to the description, the picture had been taken in 1863 and, using some new technology, turned into a "*carte de visite*," which was a small, mass-produced reproduction printed on cardstock that could be collected, shared, and passed around. The *carte de visite* of this particular image had caught on like wildfire, eventually ending up in the mainstream media and becoming one of the most widely viewed photographs in America at the time.

It featured a man named Peter, who had been enslaved but managed to escape and make his way to a Union camp. That's where, once they saw what had been done to him, they decided to take photographs. In this image, Peter was sitting on a bench, posed with his naked back to the camera.

This horrific display of cruelty was hard to stomach. The man's back was almost completely covered by crisscrossed ridges of scars upon scars, evidence of a lifetime of whippings. Considering its shock value, it didn't surprise me at all that this particular *carte de visite* ended up going viral, so to speak—becoming a tool of abolitionists and sympathizers who circulated copies as proof of the evils of slavery. Gazing at it now, I could barely process all the thoughts and feelings it brought out in me.

I forced myself to move on, though many of the photos to come were equally disturbing—shots of the dead and wounded, of the enslaved, of the degradation of war. Walking through the exhibit and taking it all in, I found myself growing anxious and becoming short of breath. I was waiting for a wave of nausea to pass when I felt an arm around me and knew from the flowery scent that it was Aunt Cissy.

"Come over here, dear," she said gently, pulling me further into the hall to a different section of the exhibit, one about everyday life in the 1860's South. It was a lot easier to take, and I thanked Aunt Cissy for rescuing me.

"You were looking a tad pale," she said. "Which is understandable, of course. This was the first major conflict ever to be captured so extensively in photos. The images are startling, to say the least."

She stayed with me for a few minutes, helping to calm my jagged nerves by pointing out some of the pictures and objects in this section that had come from our family's collection. Just as I'd finally begun to calm down, the hall began to fill with people, and I realized it must be four o'clock, time for the opening reception to begin.

Aunt Cissy noticed it too, and after making sure I was okay, she excused herself to go greet friends and mingle with the throng. I stayed where I was, turning my attention to a display about the children of Jefferson Davis, president of the Confederacy. It featured photos along with some of their toys—a porcelain doll in a green velvet dress and bonnet, a little china dog, a pink-and-white tea set—on loan from a museum in Louisiana.

As the minutes ticked by, I couldn't believe the number of people who were filling the space around me, brushing against me, laughing and talking and sporting complimentary glasses of wine given to them by tuxedoed waiters circulating through the crowd.

A woman wearing a large diamond necklace nearly bumped into me, her loud laughter reverberating against the case, red liquid nearly sloshing over the rim of her glass.

I had to get out of there.

My heart racing, I looked around for an exit and began moving toward it, nearly colliding with Maddee on the way.

"What are you doing," she hissed, gripping my forearm. "Can't you at least *pretend* this stuff interests you? For Aunt Cissy's sake?"

"It does interest me," I said, my voice tight. "I just— I need to leave."

She huffed. "So like you."

"Hey," I replied too loudly, jerking my arm free. A few heads turned to look. I lowered my voice. "Don't jump to conclusions. I hate that."

Without another word, I pushed through the exit and found myself standing in the museum's inner courtyard.

The fresh air made a difference almost right away, and I stood there for a long moment, breathing in deeply and looking around at the pretty spring landscaping. I wasn't sure what had bothered me so much in there, but at least I'd known enough to remove myself from the situation.

Feeling the weight of keys in my pocket, I thought about taking off, but Maddee and I had ridden together, and as irritating as she could be, she didn't deserve to be abandoned. I decided to use the time as my counselor might have advised, identifying what had disturbed me so, praying about it, and figuring out how to keep it from happening again.

I made my way farther into the courtyard and sat on a bench facing a small koi pond surrounded by pink and purple blossoms. Ten or fifteen minutes later, I was feeling much better when I sensed someone's presence and realized my sister had come outside and was heading my way.

"You here to lecture me some more?" I gestured to the bench beside me, and she sat.

"No, I'm here to apologize. I am so, so sorry."

I turned to look at her, sure she was being sarcastic, but her expression was earnest as she continued.

"Obviously, I'm a little slow on the uptake. But once I figured it out, I felt terrible."

"What are you talking about?"

"The alcohol? The wine?"

I exhaled slowly, looking away. "Well, thanks for the apology, but that was just a small part of it. I've been sitting here trying to figure out what happened in there, and I think I know. It has to do with self."

"Self?"

"Yeah, like, selfishness, self-centeredness. As my friend Riley says, the only thing more self-oriented then an addict is an addict in recovery."

Maddie nodded thoughtfully. "I hadn't heard that one."

"I'm actually glad we came here today because I need to be reminded once in a while that my suffering is nothing compared to the rest of the world. All those pictures of all those people..." My voice trailed off as I tried to articulate my thoughts. "That man? With the scars all over his back? He had no say in what happened to him, no control over his own suffering. But I did. Most of what I've gone through in my life has been self-inflicted. I had choices. He did not."

"I get what you're saying," Maddee replied. "But you can't keep hanging on to mistakes you've made in the past. That's all behind you now."

I smiled. "I'm not hanging on to it. I'm just saying that for years, everything in my life—both before and after the accident—was all about me, me, me. It's the nature of addiction, but it kind of has to be a big part of recovery too. And that's okay. But I'm in a different place now. I'm supposed to be looking outward. I'm supposed to remember that there's plenty of stuff going on beyond the end of my own nose."

We were both quiet for a long moment.

"At least it's a cute nose," Maddee offered, "and not some giant honker."

We both laughed, and as we stood and brushed off our skirts and decided we'd cut out early, I said a silent prayer of thanks for my sweet sister.

The sun wouldn't set till eight, so after a quick stop at home to change into shorts and sneakers, we headed to one of our favorite places in town, Belle Isle. After a few stretches beside the car, we walked the length of the suspended footbridge, cars thump-thumping overhead, and then jogged the nearly two-mile loop around the island. It felt so good to run, especially when I thought of how different my experience here had been a year and a half ago, when my legs were still healing, and it was all I could do to get up the ramp at the start of the bridge. What a difference time makes.

When we finished the loop, I told Maddee I was ready for the rest of the story, if she felt like telling it.

"You sure you're up to it?" She shot me a concerned glance. "Emotionally, I mean. Last night was the easy part. Now we get into the cabin and the stuff that happened when we were kids."

"I'm ready." I wasn't sure if it was the exercise or my earlier revelations in the courtyard, but I wasn't feeling anxious at the thought, not at all.

"Great. So where did we leave off?"

"Something about a guy watching the news and it rocking his world."

Chapter Four

Nicole

As we jogged toward the bridge to cross back over the river, Maddee returned to the story. "So we stopped with the Civil War having ended, the rabbi coming home from fighting, and the Talbots realizing that at some point over the past month or two, all of their valuables had been stolen, including the rabbi's illuminated manuscript."

"Right."

"Okay, so that would've been in 1865. Now we jump ahead one hundred thirty years to March 1995—just four months prior to us finding the dead body in the cabin."

We started up the concrete ramp to the bridge as Maddee continued with the story. "The rabbi was long gone, but his descendants lived on, including his great-grandson, a man named Taavi Koenig."

"Our Taavi Koenig?" I shivered. "The man we found dead?"

"Yes, one and the same. By this point, the Koenigs lived in Cleveland, Ohio, and Taavi was married with two teenagers. Though he and his wife both worked, they struggled to make ends meet."

I led the way onto the concrete bridge at a quick pace as Maddee kept talking. "One night in March of '95, Taavi was watching the news when they did a story about the *CSS Alabama*. They said the ship was discovered off the Normandy coast back in 1984, and an association had just been accredited as the operator of the archaeological investigation of the ship's remains. Family lore among the Koenigs was that they once owned a valuable old illuminated manuscript, but it had been stolen, recovered, and stolen again—and that it had something to do with Taavi's great-grandfather getting swindled and the *CSS Alabama*. Although he'd heard there was a bunch of paperwork somewhere that explained everything, he'd never read it and didn't know where it was. He was fuzzy on the details, but his assumption was that the manuscript sank on the *Alabama*."

We both walked briskly as Maddee talked. "As the reporter went on about the types of artifacts that the divers were bringing up, Taavi grew excited, remembering the old stories and wondering if the priceless heirloom might have been one of the things recovered from down there and, if so, if there was any way it could've survived underwater all these years."

The breeze picked up off the river as I concentrated on Maddee's story.

"Taavi went looking for the fabled paperwork, finally finding it about a month later and getting a firsthand look at the truth behind the old family lore. The file was quite organized and included an extremely helpful summary that detailed what happened each step of the way."

We hurried around a family with small children, Maddee's face lighting up at the sight of them. "Basically," she continued once we were past, "Taavi learned all the stuff I told you last night and saw that the manuscript wasn't aboard the *Alabama* after all. Curious, he wondered if the manuscript had ever turned up in the years since. It didn't seem like it, but as he researched, he realized how incredibly valuable it would be now if it still existed. Considering that he was financially strapped, the appeal of finding this thing and selling it loomed large in his imagination."

When we reached the halfway point, I increased the pace even more.

Maddee matched my stride and kept talking. "As part of his research, he contacted Talbot Paper and Printing and ended up speaking with

Granddad. This big, unanswered question of what happened to the manuscript has always been a part of Talbot family lore too, but Granddad wasn't much help because he knew nothing more than Taavi."

Maddee's mouth was keeping pace with our walk. "He did, however, put Taavi in touch with a man he knew who he thought could help, Dr. Harold Underwood, who's an academic and scholar specializing in historical documents, particularly those that are diaspora related."

"And what does 'diaspora' mean? Something about migration, right?"

"Yeah. Think dispersion, people groups leaving their homelands and scattering to other places."

My brain lit up. "Like the Huguenots had to do."

Clearly pleased with my answer, Maddee's tone took on that elementary schoolteacher vibe again. "Exactly. Or the Amish. The Acadians. The Cherokee Indians on the Trail of Tears."

"How about African slaves?" I thought of the man with the scars in the photo at the museum. "Is it still diaspora if they weren't forced to flee like the Huguenots but instead were dragged away against their will?"

"Yeah. Diasporas can occur for a lot a reasons. Religious persecution, natural disasters, political oppression, other stuff. Think of the Irish during the potato famine or the Cubans after the revolution. It happens all over the world and throughout the history of the world. In the case of the Koenigs' manuscript, the diaspora depicted in it was an important one, the expulsion of the Jews from Spain in 1492."

"So who is this Dr. Underwood guy?"

"You remember him. He's the one who authenticated the pamphlet Granddad gave to the Smithsonian. He worked with Renee on that. He came to the dedication ceremony at the reunion two year ago?"

I felt heat rush to my cheeks. "I wasn't there that year, remember? I didn't come till afterward."

Maddee seemed startled and slowed her pace a little. "Oh. Right. Sorry about that. Anyway, Granddad suggested Taavi contact Dr. Underwood because, I guess, he figured if anyone might know of the manuscript's reappearance, it would be him."

Now it was my turn to slow and match my sister's pace. Maddee paused and turned, her hands on the railing. I stopped beside her.

"So Taavi got in touch with the guy and told his story," Maddee continued. "Underwood was skeptical but deeply intrigued and agreed to look into it. He had Taavi send him copies of everything and said he would do some digging around and get back to him with whatever he found out."

Maddee explained that in the meantime, Taavi's financial problems were getting worse, and his house was in danger of foreclosure. "His wife said by that point he was totally obsessed with finding the manuscript, like a gambler counting on his next big win to get him out of trouble. Near the end of June 1995, she came home from work one night to find him gone. He'd left a note that said he had to go out of town and would be back soon. She didn't know where he went or why, but he never contacted her, and he never returned. Oddly enough, she didn't suspect foul play. She just thought he'd abandoned her as a way to get out of the marriage and the money issues."

"Wow. What a depressing story."

"I know, right?" Maddee frowned. "But hold on. There's more coming."

I nodded. The murder.

"As we both know," Maddee said, "when Taavi left, he came to Richmond. He was probably getting so desperate to find the manuscript that he decided to poke around for some answers in person. But while he was here, he must've gotten mixed up in something bad, because he ended up paying for it with his life."

"What does Detective Ortiz say?" I asked. Calm and competent, Ortiz was the lead investigator on the case, and over the past two years, we'd come to appreciate and respect her efforts even if she hadn't yet found all the answers.

Maddee shook her head. "She can't know for sure because she hasn't been able to account for a single minute of how he spent his time while he was here. She finally did figure out where he stayed—a cheap motel right off the interstate—and things got really exciting when she combed back through some old databases and located his car—or what was left of it. Apparently, at some point after he died, it ended up in a syndicate-owned chop shop in Norfolk, where it was used for parts. An engine block with that vehicle's VIN number on it was listed among the inventory of items recovered there during a raid in early 1996."

I didn't understand. "Wouldn't the police have tracked the VIN number back then and contacted the family?"

"No. Ortiz says if it didn't flag as a stolen or missing vehicle, the police probably wouldn't have taken it any further than that. They had bigger items from the raid to deal with. In retrospect, however, she now thinks it could be significant that the chop shop was connected with a crime syndicate. That could be one explanation for how the murder scene was cleaned up so quickly. A syndicate would know how to get in, get it done, and get out."

"Are you saying the murder victim had some connection with the Mafia?" I asked, incredulous.

"Not necessarily. But there are aspects of this case that Ortiz hasn't shared with us."

My eyes widened. "What kind of details is she withholding?" As soon as the words left my mouth, I realized I, too, was withholding something, what could be the biggest detail of all. Before Maddee answered, I glanced around. "It's going to be dark soon. We should start back."

As we did, Maddee finished her story, although there wasn't much left to say. She reiterated the main points and then said, "As far as I can tell, the investigation may not be taken any further than this. Once Ortiz came up against the syndicate thing, she's been a lot less communicative. She won't say, but I have to wonder if she's still working on it at all."

We were both quiet on our way home, and I knew it was time to share my secret. But somehow I just couldn't get the words out. I needed to think more about all I'd learned first before I tossed my giant monkey wrench into the gears of this case.

~

The next morning I slipped on my best jeans and a crisp button-down shirt and drove to Dover Creek Farms. Located about fifteen miles west of Richmond, the place offered everything from boarding to lessons to horse training and more. The part I was interested in was the on-site equestrian therapy center. I would be their intern for the next three months—though I'd been warned that "intern" was pretty much synonymous with stable hand.

Regardless, I was excited about the opportunity. It wouldn't pay much, but I'd get a college credit for my efforts along with actual hands-on experience with a type of therapy I'd been curious about for a while.

As a kid, I was horse crazy, and though I'd pushed that aside as a teen to focus on, uh, "higher" pursuits, I never lost my love of horses nor my desire to work with them as an adult. Now I was testing the waters of something that sounded tailor-made for me, equestrian therapist, and my hope was that by the end of the summer I'd have a much better idea if it was something I wanted to pursue or not.

Today was orientation, and though I was the only intern, they lumped me in with a small group of new hires—summer workers who would be doing pretty much the same things I would except for the therapy component.

Our time started with a tour of the huge facility followed by a lecture on rules, safety, and policies, which was followed by another lecture on job duties and expectations. There was also a ton of paperwork to get through: waivers and clearances and insurance matters and such. It wasn't until the very end that we were finally brought out to the stables and introduced to some of the horses. When things concluded at noon, everyone was dismissed except me. I was to meet with the head therapist for a few minutes, so I made my way past paddocks and rings and a broad pasture to the therapy center, which was located at the rear of the farm.

I was eager to meet the woman who would be mentoring me for the next few months, but any hopes of bonding over the warm emotional transformations of our clients evaporated the moment I saw her. She wasn't exactly rude, but she was brusque and straightforward and mostly just wanted to review the rules I'd already been taught and then add a few more, especially the biggest rule of all, that I was never to attempt any sort of therapy without direct supervision.

"That's fine by me," I responded. "I don't even know yet what equine therapy consists of...well, other than what I've seen on YouTube."

I was trying to be witty, but she didn't smile. Instead, she just shook my hand, welcomed me to the team, and said, "You can go now. We'll see you tomorrow."

Dismissed, I decided to stroll the long way around to the far parking lot, just to take in more of the facility and maybe run into a horse or two along the way. Sure enough, I was at the front pasture, walking beside the fence, when I saw a beautiful mare up ahead, a gray Appaloosa. Thrilled at the sight of her—why had I gone so long without having horses in my life?—I slowed and then came to a stop once we were face-to-face.

"Hey, girl," I said softly, reaching up to stroke her muzzle. She was a friendly thing, pressing into my hand and blinking her long eyelashes at me, which I took to mean, *You're going to do great here, Nicole. I believe in you.*

"Freeze!" a male voice commanded sharply.

I turned to see a man standing about ten feet away, arms crossed, an intense expression visible under the brim of his cowboy hat. "You're about three-quarters of an inch away from getting a big shock, did you know that?"

My eyes widened as I turned back toward the horse and saw that he was right. Though the fence itself was a wooden post-and-rail, a single hot wire ran across the top about a foot above the fence. Like an idiot, I had reached in between the top rail and the wire.

Slowly, I withdrew my arm and took a step back. When the horse tried to come closer, the man barked, "Puzzles!" followed by a sharp click with his mouth. In response, the horse backed up, gave out a single good-natured whinny, and then turned and strode away.

"Thank you," I said, feeling like such a fool. I knew enough to check for wires. I'd just forgotten. "That would not have been fun."

He didn't reply but instead seemed to be taking me in. "Can I help you find something?" he asked, implying that where I was right now was not somewhere I was supposed to be.

"Nope. I'm good. I'm headed to the parking lot. I just took the long way around to get a feel for the place."

"Are you a new boarder?" His tone was friendlier now, his arms relaxed at his sides. "Because this area is for employees only. Sorry about that. It's for your own safety."

"Not to worry, I am an employee, or at least I will be starting tomorrow. Today was orientation."

I gave him a friendly smile, though on the inside I was thinking, *No, no, no, no, no.* This man was tall, dark, and dangerously sexy—exactly the sort I used to go for. Lean frame with muscles of steel. Tattoos. Stony gray eyes. Just a hint of a beard on his chiseled face. Bad news all the way around, he was the type I needed to stay as far away from as possible.

As quickly as I could, I thanked him for his help and took off, moving past him to the parking lot and praying that the two of us would be working in entirely different sections of the facility. Surely if that were the case, this place was big enough that we could make it through the summer without interacting all that much.

Full of adrenaline from our encounter and feeling emboldened by my choice to walk away, I made a decision as I got into my car. I hadn't been able to tell Maddee my secret yet, but for some reason I suddenly felt compelled to share it with Nana. She was, after all, the one who was going to be the most upset by it. Why not just get that one out of the way first, like ripping off a giant Band-Aid?

I didn't even call or text to see if she was home. I just drove straight to her house, went to the door, and rang the bell.

A maid let me in and then led the way to the sunroom, where Nana was chatting with a woman. As they turned toward me, I saw the woman was Aunt Cissy. Though my nerve and determination didn't falter, I knew I couldn't reveal my secret in front of anyone else. I'd have to wait until Aunt Cissy left so Nana and I could be alone.

In the meantime, both women seem pleased to see me, and when

I explained I was in the area and thought I'd pop in to say hello, Nana insisted I join them for lunch. They were already on dessert—peach cobbler topped with ice cream, but Nana instructed the maid to prepare a plate for me, and soon I was digging into an ample serving of quiche with spinach salad. Delicious.

"I was just telling your grandmother," Aunt Cissy said, "that I brought copies of all the Talbot photos that are in the exhibit at the museum." She said that the reception was so crowded yesterday that it was hard to see everything. "So, I thought y'all might want copies to go through at your leisure."

I smiled between bites, pleased. I really wanted to see all of them, but I didn't think I'd feel like returning to the museum anytime soon. As Aunt Cissy talked, she retrieved a box from the chair next to her, placed it on the table, and then opened it to reveal dozens of photos inside. "Of course, the museum didn't use everything I gave them, so I have photos here you won't see there." She flipped through the pile, spreading a handful out on the table. Though they were all interesting, my eyes were drawn to one in particular, a photo of a young woman with a large Tudor building in the background.

"Who is this?" I asked, wiping my hands on my napkin and then carefully picking it up to take a closer look.

"Isn't she pretty?" Aunt Cissy beamed. "Believe it or not, that's Therese Talbot, your great-great-great-grandmother."

"Seriously?"

I stared at the image for a long moment, amazed at how crisp and clear the image was. The woman in the photo looked to be around sixteen, and she was lovely, with dark, hopeful eyes and delicate features. She was wearing a gorgeous dress, with lace cuffs and some kind of fancy trim around a narrow waist.

"Do we know much about her?" I asked, suddenly quite curious.

"We know some," Aunt Cissy answered, digging through the box. "I have other pictures of her. Ah, here she is a few years later. This one was taken near the end of the war. On the day Richmond was evacuated, in fact."

I took it from her and saw a somewhat older Therese standing stiffly in a far plainer, rather threadbare dress, with a bustling train station in the background. Looking more closely, I thought I could see pain and suffering and fear in her eyes—a reflection of what must have been a truly terrible time.

CHAPTER FIVE

Therese

August 1864

As Therese Jennings leaned against the splintered handle of the hoe, trying to still her spinning head, a blur of gray fabric startled her. She feared it was a soldier, but then her mother stepped closer to the garden gate, wearing her worn gray housedress instead of her black mourning gown.

"Why aren't you resting?" Therese called out.

"It's too hot," Mother responded. "And it's even worse out here. You need to come inside before you burn."

"I need to keep these weeds from swallowing up our food." Therese didn't add *or we'll starve this winter*. Mother would only twist her words into one more reason they needed to give up on this place and retreat to River Pines, Grandfather's plantation on the other side of the river.

Therese wouldn't do it. She'd promised her father she'd stay true to the family's ideals, protecting Mother as best she could at the same time. The war had been going on now for three long years. Surely it would end soon, her brother would return and take over as the new patriarch of the family, and she could finally step down from the overwhelming role of protector and provider.

Mother opened the rickety gate and motioned to Therese as if she were a child obligated to obey her instead of a twenty-year-old woman.

"Go back in the house, Mother." Therese aimed the hoe at the soil, concentrating on not stumbling as sweat trickled down her temples. "Once I finish this row, I'll come in and make our dinner." It had been a month since their bacon ran out, and they'd butchered their last hen the week before, when it stopped laying eggs. But there was cornmeal she could fry, and greens too.

Mother's thick blond hair half hung from the bun at the nape of her neck, though she still carried herself with the poise and charm of the Southern debutante she once was. These days, she was constantly on edge, and her eyes flashed now as she said, "It's time to go back to River Pines, Therese. Your father would agree with me. Look at you." She swept her hand forward. "You weren't meant to do this kind of work."

Therese dug the hoe into the ground, scraping at the weeds between the rows of sweet potatoes, pretending she hadn't heard. Mother had always been high strung, but Father's death a month ago had nearly undone her. All she talked about was River Pines. The place had never been home to Therese, although her adored childhood friend, Aggie, lived there. But other memories still tormented Therese, including the whipping she witnessed there as a girl. Mr. Porter, the overseer, had whipped Badan, one of the slaves, when he was no more than fourteen, for misunderstanding an order about caring for a horse. It was proof of everything her father had ever told her about slavery.

An etching printed in *Harper's Weekly* a little over a year ago reminded her of that disturbing episode. It was of a recently escaped slave, highlighting the web of horrible wounds across his back. The photo established that slavery truly was a barbaric practice, not the benign institution some tried to present.

Father had procured a copy of the magazine, and later a printed version of the image that was even more shocking than the etching. Therese, even though it was so disturbing, marveled at the advances in photography that allowed multitudes of people both in the North and South and even in Europe to truly comprehend the evils of slavery.

No, nothing could drag Therese back to River Pines. She kept her eyes on the ground, sweat running down her neck. "Please go back inside."

Mother didn't budge. Taking responsibility for their survival hadn't come naturally to Therese. She'd always been timid and sensitive, acquiescing to stronger personalities like her brother Warner's and her friend Polly's and even Aggie's. And Mother's, of course. But she was doing her best now to be as strong as she could in honor of Father. She'd promised him she would.

A small caterpillar crawled across her forearm, and she flicked it away as horses' hooves drummed down the road. She sighed heavily, dreading another band of soldiers eager to take the little bit of food they had left.

But then Mother turned her head and called out, "Badan!"

Therese stood too quickly in the heat. The world darkened a little, and she leaned against the hoe again to steady herself.

Badan was Grandfather's slave—or servant, the term Mother preferred.

"Mrs. Jennings!" he called out from the buggy once he had pulled the two horses to a stop. "Master LeFevre sent me to fetch you and Miss Therese."

Mother shaded her eyes. "Has something happened?"

"Yes'm. He fell off his horse yesterday and was dragged a good bit. The doctor said he has internal injuries besides a broken leg. You're to come immediately."

"Mother," Therese whispered. At Father's funeral, Grandfather had begged them to return to River Pines—and Mother had nearly relented except for Therese's reminder of their pledges to Father to keep standing firm against the practice of slavery, no matter the cost. Now Grandfather was resorting to this sort of trickery to get them there?

"Aggie wanted me to make sure you understand that he's truly hurt," Badan said as if reading her mind. "She's been nursing him herself."

Therese pursed her lips. She trusted Aggie, and Badan too, for that matter. So apparently Grandfather wasn't trying to manipulate them after all.

"Oh, dear. Of course we'll come." Mother lowered her voice and stepped closer to Badan. "However, presently, we don't have the money for the ferry."

He leaned toward her and held out his hand, opening it to show a piece of tied cloth. "He sent along what you'll need."

"Well, then..." Mother took the cloth and swept up the skirts of her worn dress in one quick motion. She turned toward Therese. "Come along. You'll need to get cleaned up, and we have to eat."

"Auntie Vera sent something along for y'all." Badan pulled a packet from a bag on the bench.

Therese's mouth watered. Auntie Vera, who was Aggie's mother, must have guessed they'd be hungry. Maybe she'd packaged up slices of ham and some of her biscuits. The first apples in Grandfather's orchard would be ripening, and the garden, along with the first of the vegetables in the fields, would be producing quite well by now. Therese swallowed.

"We'll hurry," Mother said, taking the packet of food from Badan.

"Yes'm," he replied, "but you got time. The horse needs to be fed and watered before we can start out again."

Both women went inside, and Therese headed straight to the back bedroom to pack, wash, and change into her mourning dress. First she checked her hoops, which she hadn't worn since Father's burial. Her metal ones had long since broken, and none were being imported due to the Northern blockade, so she'd fashioned some out of bamboo. On close examination, it seemed the hoops would hold, so she proceeded to get ready.

The house was really just a cottage that Mother and Father had moved into when Father first began teaching at Box Tree Male Academy. The family had lived in it ever since. When the academy closed, as both students and teachers went off to fight in the war, the Confederate Army took over the main buildings, but Therese and her mother were allowed to remain in the cottage on the edge of the grounds.

Mother had never complained about the little house while Father was alive—at least not in front of Therese, although there were times her parents argued into the night about money and their station in life. Overall, though, Mother never compared their home to the grand house she'd grown up in or the homes of her childhood friends. Even though she seemed disappointed in Father's income, Therese knew Mother truly loved him.

And she couldn't blame the woman now for growing weary. These were hard times. But it was her mother's fear that concerned her most. Father always said fear made people irrational, and Mother was beginning to show signs of just that. Only the day before, she had said, "He never would have asked us to make such foolish pledges if he'd known we'd be on the verge of starvation."

Neither of them was close to starving, but Therese knew that was Mother's fear. Yet nothing had changed at Grandfather's plantation. In fact, it had only grown worse. Before the war, he'd talked about freeing his "servants" but then did no such thing. His tone shifted when the war started, and then by the time the fighting reached Virginian soil, he adamantly refused to even consider it. Instead, he raised less and less tobacco and sold off, over the last three years, a number of his slaves to help pay his bills.

Mother was still packing when Therese stepped into the small dining room, so she unwrapped the food—ham along with cornbread and two apple turnovers. God bless Auntie Vera. Therese had just finished arranging the food on plates when Mother appeared in her black silk dress, carpetbag in hand.

She set the bag beside Therese's near the door, and then they both sat and bowed their heads. Mother started the blessing.

Therese felt conflicted about eating the food that had come from River Pines, but the savory scent of the ham was irresistible. She half listened to her mother's flowery words as she added her own silent prayer of gratitude.

After Mother's "Amen," Therese waited for her to take the first bite, but she seemed to hesitate.

"God provides," Mother said finally, and then she met Therese's eyes. "Doesn't He?"

Therese certainly couldn't disagree. Food *and* money for the ferry. If only she could know what awaited them at Grandfather's. She gave her mother a nod before turning her attention to the plate in front of her and cutting the ham.

If her father hadn't fallen ill, Therese's life would be so different now. She would have taken a job as a governess, teaching in the home of a wealthy family in Richmond and contributing to her family's finances. When she was sixteen, she had attended the Women's Institute for a year, boarding there along with her best friend, Polly, and studying to be a teacher. It was a lovely four-story building surrounded by a brick wall with gardens and stables, located downtown on Tenth Street between Marshall and Clay. But then the war began, and Mother had insisted she come home. The school closed shortly after. But even just one year of teacher training had more than qualified her to work as a governess.

That's what Polly was doing now, living with a family in Richmond and teaching their two children. But both of Polly's parents were alive and could care for one another, not to mention Polly was the most daring person Therese had ever known. She was always up for an adventure and never hesitated to speak her mind. Therese didn't have the courage her friend did, but if life had turned out differently, she thought she would have been fine working as a governess too.

Therese slowly savored a bite of ham. Then she ate another and another. But she couldn't make it last forever—they needed to leave soon, and honestly, she looked forward to a ride in Grandfather's buggy. Mother and Therese's only horse and their old, rickety wagon had both been confiscated by soldiers three months before and taken off to the Shenandoah Valley. They had no hope of ever seeing either again.

When she finished the last bite of food, she rose and cleared their plates and then quickly wiped the dishes while Mother remained at the table. After Therese put everything away, wondering how long it would be until they returned, she stepped toward the window. Badan had seen to Grandfather's horses and was waiting at the fence.

Therese walked to the door and grabbed their bags and her worn parasol. "Ready?"

Mother stood. "Yes, I am. I've never been so ready for anything in my entire life."

Therese winced. This seemed to be the opportunity Mother had been looking for to escape their lowly existence.

As they left the cottage, Mother didn't look back. But Therese did. She thought of all the happy years her family had spent living here. Then the war had started, her brother Warner left to join the Confederate Army, and Father fell ill. They'd moved a bed into the parlor to be able to care for him better until he died. She imagined him there now, watching them go. If only she could run back and hug him one last time. If only she could assure him, and herself, that she'd continue to stand up for the ideals he taught her, no matter what.

By the time they reached the ferry, Mother was limp from the heat. But then a hint of breeze rose up from the river, and Therese moved closer, breathing in deeply, while her mother paid their fare.

"He said it will be a while before we go if we'd rather wait here." Mother gestured to a nearby bench resting in the shade of an oak tree. They were heading there when Therese heard someone call her name. She turned and spied her friend Polly, already on the ferry and waving her over.

"Well, look who it is. You go ahead." Mother lowered herself to the bench with a weary sigh. "I'll be there in a bit. I'm staying in the shade as long as I can."

"Yes, ma'am."

Therese felt revived as she hurried toward her friend. It had been nearly a year since they'd seen each other.

After a long embrace, they chatted and laughed and caught up as best they could. Finally, Therese asked Polly what she was doing there. "Shouldn't you be in Richmond?"

Polly grinned. "I came home for a few days. Michael is back from France."

Therese's heart raced. "Oh?"

"He sailed into New York a few weeks ago and then made his way south by land. He thought that would be safer than trying to run the blockade at sea."

"How is he?"

"You know my brother. He seems fine even though so many things happened while he was there. Would you believe he rescued a priceless heirloom from the *Alabama*?"

"He what?"

Polly grinned. "Sorry. I'm being a little dramatic. Here's what happened. A priceless heirloom was stolen from a Richmond rabbi, and it ended up getting confiscated at sea. When the *Alabama* was in Cherbourg, just before the big battle, the heirloom was unloaded from the ship along with lots of other valuables. After the sinking, Michael asked around and was able to locate the heirloom, buy it, and bring it back with him to give to its rightful owner. Isn't that amazing?"

Polly continued with her tale, but Therese slowly tuned her out. All she could think was, *Michael is home.*

Two years older than Therese and Polly, Michael was the same age as Therese's brother Warner. He'd attended Box Tree Male Academy, the boarding school where her father taught, and although Father never said it, Therese was sure Michael had been his favorite student. He was much more scholarly than Warner had ever been. The two classmates weren't especially close, probably due to Warner being a bit of a rascal, but they'd always been amiable.

Because Therese and her family lived on the grounds of the school, she and Michael saw each other fairly often. She had always been smitten with him, though she'd done her best to keep that particular secret to herself, not even telling Polly. Only Father seemed to have guessed at her true feelings. And although he greatly admired Michael, he didn't want Therese to make any rash decisions at such a young age. So he'd asked, the only time in his life, for Grandfather's help, requesting he pay the tuition to send Therese off to school in Richmond with Polly.

Not that it mattered in the long run, because just a few months after Therese left for school, Michael's parents sent him away to France on behalf of the family business. Therese had hoped he'd write, but in the four years he'd been gone, she'd never received a single letter. Granted, she'd never been sure whether her romantic feelings were reciprocated or not, but she'd at least thought they were friends. Apparently, he'd meant far more to her than she ever had to him.

Still, as much as she tried, she couldn't forget their walks around the pond behind the academy or the afternoons they'd shared a bench in the commons behind the enchanting Tudor-style building, discussing a sonnet or passage from Scripture. She treasured the time they'd spent together. Life seemed so peaceful then. So safe. They shared the same passionate ideals and hopes for the future. She felt understood by him and cherished in a way she hadn't experienced before. She'd felt as if there were an invisible thread between them, connecting them. He'd look for her in the dining hall and smile when he spotted her. She'd seek him out by the pond and join him there. If they found themselves in the same room, no matter how crowded, somehow they would eventually end up side by side.

The last time she'd seen him was in the courtyard of the academy. She was wearing a new frock and had taken extra care to look her best for her trip into Richmond. As they drew near to each other for their final farewell, she thought she could see in his eyes the same emotions she was feeling. Love. Sadness. Hope. They said goodbye, and though she yearned to throw her arms around him, in such a public place she had to settle for a simple curtsy instead, their eyes lingering even as their touch could not. But it seemed she'd imagined all of that.

When the war first started, Michael had been criticized severely in the community for not returning to Virginia to join in the fight, but after his two younger brothers, twins Gerald and Victor, died on the same day in the same battle, those who once spoke badly about Michael held their tongues—except for Mother, who never changed her opinion on his "terrible cowardice." Therese, however, was secretly grateful that he stayed away no matter how much she missed him. Not only did she want him far from the dangers of war, but she couldn't bear the thought of him fighting for the system that enabled slavery to exist.

Though she'd never told anyone, Therese had always felt intensely conflicted about the war. She wanted Virginia and all the southern states to retain their independence, which meant the South winning. But she wanted the slaves to be freed, which meant the North winning. Most of all, she just wanted the fighting to stop. She couldn't bear the thought of more men dying, especially those she knew and cared for.

"How is he?" she asked Polly now, trying hard to keep her tone light.

"Just fine. His time in France was productive. And he really enjoyed living with our French cousins, though hearing all the bad news of the war was tough, especially when..." Polly's eyes filled with sudden tears.

Therese nodded, patting her friend's hand. "I can imagine," she said softly.

She politely looked away so Polly could pull herself together. Directing her eyes toward shore, she saw that Mother was still resting in the shade, though several other passengers had joined her there.

When Polly spoke again, her tone was almost conspiratorial. "I think Michael has a French sweetheart."

Therese's head whipped around. "He told you that?"

"No, but I figured it out anyway. To begin with, he brought home the most exquisite trinket box. It's small and round, with tiny pink porcelain roses on top. At first I thought it might be for me or Mother, but it wasn't. He brought us each one of these."

Polly twirled the handle of the parasol she was holding, and Therese looked up to see that it was a lovely pink satin with delicate lace trim.

"It's beautiful."

"It is," Polly said. "But I wanted to know more about that box."

"Did you ask him?"

"Yes. I waited until later, when we were alone, so he could speak freely. But he just tucked it into his trunk and told me to mind my own business. He acted real funny about it."

"Still, that doesn't mean—"

"I went back later and took a closer look."

"Polly!"

She grinned. "Hey, I'm his sister. I have a right to know if he's in love with some *mademoiselle*."

Therese hated herself for asking. "And?"

"And there was nothing inside the little container, nothing engraved on it or anything like that."

"So what makes you think he has a sweetheart?"

"Because when I went to put it back in his trunk, I discovered a couple of photographs." She smiled triumphantly. "They were of Michael posed with a beautiful young woman, looking very much like a couple."

Therese's stomach dropped.

"They were *cartes de visite*," Polly added, referring to the popular prints that were the size and thickness of visiting cards. *Cartes de visite* had become hugely popular of late, partly because they were made from paper, which meant they were less expensive and far less fragile than previous kinds of photographs, such as ambrotypes, which were made from glass plates. If Michael had posed with a woman for some *cartes de visite*, then Polly had to be right. He'd found himself a French sweetheart indeed.

"So he plans to return to France, then?" Therese asked, trying to sound nonchalant despite the sudden ache in her heart.

"Or bring her here. I don't know. Either way, nothing can happen until the war is over."

"I suppose not."

"In the meantime, he's going into the army as a second lieutenant. He'll be working as a field hospital quartermaster with the 1st Virginia Infantry."

Therese's eyes widened. "That's Warner's unit." Her pulse surged with fear even as she told herself that at least Michael would be safer procuring supplies for the hospital than fighting.

They were interrupted by the activity of a wagon being rolled onto the ferry. They shifted over to the railing, and then Therese turned her attention back to Polly. "So where are you going now? Shouldn't you be headed to Richmond?"

"I am, just in a roundabout fashion. I have to go to the church to pick up some books from a member of the parish. I'll spend the night at my aunt and uncle's." Polly's parents lived on an old family property here on the north side of the river, while her uncle's family lived on the south side, about five miles from River Pines. "Then tomorrow they'll drop me at the station, and I'll be able to loop back around to the city by train."

"That's a pretty big detour. Hope the books are worth it."

She shrugged. "They're not for me. I'm just doing a favor for one of the priests over at St. Paul's. I'll drop them off to him tomorrow before I go back to the Baxters'. How about you two?"

"We're headed to Grandfather's place."

Polly gave her a questioning look, and Therese was about to elaborate when she heard shuffling behind her and realized that the rest of the passengers, including Mother, had boarded. So instead Therese simply added that he'd been injured in a fall. Mother wouldn't want her to go into too many details, especially when they knew so little.

"Sorry to hear that," Polly replied. "I'll keep him in prayer."

The three women sat down on the bench along the far side as two more wagons rolled onto the flat-bottomed vessel. Finally, Badan drove the buggy aboard.

The ferry set off, the captain navigating with his pole. Therese welcomed the coolness of the river water lapping against the boat. She gazed across at the opposite landing, framed by trees. Not too far beyond was the church where they were members, Manakin Episcopal. Though it had been founded by French Huguenots in 1701, the church, according to the laws of the Commonwealth of Virginia, had to be under the Church of England and therefore Anglican. At least the congregants had been able to worship in French for several decades before embracing the language of their new country in their services.

As they slowly made their way across the river, Mother asked after Polly's family. She replied that her parents were fine and that they'd had a letter recently from Lance, her youngest brother, who was now serving in Georgia.

"Oh, dear," Therese said. Sherman's current campaign involved a number of horrid battles throughout northwest Georgia and around Atlanta. For years the Union kept making tactical mistakes, but now it seemed that perhaps the Northern Army's decision making and fortune had both improved due to the new leadership of Grant and Sherman.

Polly asked what they'd heard from Warner.

"He's still near Petersburg," Mother answered. "Not that far away, although he has never come to visit."

No doubt Warner would come home if he could. Petersburg had been under siege for a couple of months. When Father died, the fighting had been so bad that Warner had simply sent a note saying he was sorry to have missed the funeral, that he was fine, and that he hoped Mother and Therese were doing as well as could be expected. "It's hard to get passes," Therese said to Mother.

"Yes," Polly interjected. "That's what I've heard too."

Warner's regiment had been in battle after battle. Bull Run. Antietam. Fredericksburg. Chancellorsville. Gettysburg. And now Petersburg. So many had died or been wounded, but not her brother—not yet, anyway. She prayed his good fortune would hold.

Therese asked how things were in Richmond. "All right," Polly said. "More crowded by the day."

The city had grown enormously since the war started, partly because it had become the Confederate capital and partly because it had been forced to absorb a huge number of refugees who'd fled their homes ahead of Union forces. Therese heard Richmond had grown from a population of thirty-eight thousand at the beginning of the war to currently well over a hundred thousand—and was still expanding.

"All those people." Mother clicked her tongue. "It must be dangerous."

"Not really. There are a lot of soldiers around. And we are still under martial law."

"Which must be incredibly unnerving."

"Not at all. It's been three years, and everyone's used to it by now."

Mother frowned. "What about the food shortages?"

"Yes, that's a problem. But it sounds as if it's a problem everywhere, and we have farmers who are able to bring in produce."

"Not meat?" Now Mother seemed almost angry.

As if sensing her escalating mood, Polly gave in on that one. "Well, yes, meat can be difficult to come by at times."

With a satisfied half smile, Mother settled back in her seat. "So have you made new friends there?" she asked in a more pleasant tone.

Polly shrugged. "Not especially. I teach the Baxter children during the week and attend church on Sundays. That's really the extent of my interactions with anyone in Richmond. Well, other than volunteering in a hospital." Her eyes twinkling, she turned toward Therese and added, "The one that's in our old school. What used to be the Women's Institute is now the Institute Hospital. I can't tell you how odd it is to be bathing soldiers in our former classrooms."

Before Therese could respond, Mother cried out, "You work in a hospital? That's men's work!"

"Not anymore, Miss Helene," Polly said. "The men are all off fighting."

Mother crossed her arms. "It's not respectable."

Polly's eyes lit up in alarm. "It wouldn't be very respectable to let our soldiers die either, would it?"

Therese had to interject. Given the circumstances, working in a hospital was a generous act, not a scandalous one. "Times have changed, Mother," she said softly. "We all have to do our part, from knitting to farming to, yes, even hospital work."

"Absolutely," Polly said. "There are close to fifty hospitals throughout the city and not nearly enough people to staff them. Nurses are desperately needed."

Mother sniffed. "Nuns, certainly. Or older women. Matronly women. But not young women. Not girls your age. You have your reputations to think of."

Polly laughed. "Matron Webb would agree with you on that. She'd much prefer women in their thirties and forties or older, but she has no choice now." Polly lowered her voice a little. "I feel privileged to help. The suffering is nearly unbearable, but it's the most meaningful work I've ever done. Let me assure you, Miss Helene. Nursing hasn't ruined me."

Mother shook her head. "Why aren't soldiers sent home so their families can care for them? Hospitals are only for the destitute."

"Not anymore. There are too many specialized procedures that can't be done at home. Cleaning wounds. Treatments that aren't readily available. Surgeries that country doctors aren't trained to do. And there are so many dire illnesses—dysentery, influenza, typhoid, tuberculosis. The list goes on and on. And most soldiers are far away from home and don't have the option to be cared for by family, no matter what."

Mother harrumphed, probably feeling Polly was being insolent to challenge her. "I wouldn't allow Warner to be cared for by others, I can tell you that."

"I understand," Polly said. "I truly do. But times *have* changed."

Therese had always appreciated Polly's forthrightness and couldn't help but enjoy hearing her challenge Mother this way.

"Well, in my opinion," Mother said, "which is universally shared, for a young woman, teaching is a much more respectable vocation than nursing."

Polly's dark eyes lit up, and she turned to Therese. "Speaking of teaching, a clerk in the secretary of state's office is looking for a governess."

Therese's eyes widened.

"The family's name is Galloway," Polly continued. "Their last governess left a few weeks ago. They've been trying to find a replacement since."

"Oh?" Therese tried to keep her voice casual. She would love nothing more, but she knew her mother wouldn't agree to it.

"If you're interested, I could put in a good word for you." Polly gave her a wink. "They live just around the corner from the Baxters."

"I'd never allow Therese to go to Richmond," Mother declared. "It's much too dangerous."

Polly shrugged. "Those living in the countryside are vulnerable too."

With one dismissive grunt in response, Mother closed the subject.

"Thank you just the same," Therese told Polly softly, giving her a meaningful look. Her friend nodded, seeming to understand.

Oblivious to the awkwardness of the moment, Mother brought the conversation back around to Polly's family, asking about her mother, who was a close friend. As the two of them talked, Therese only half listened. Her mind was stuck on the idea of living and working in Richmond as a governess. She would give anything to do that, but it was useless to yearn for what she could never have.

They reached the far shore and disembarked, and though Polly had intended to walk to the church, they offered her a ride instead. Badan helped all three women into the buggy, and they set off. Therese asked Polly more about their old school, which she missed terribly, and for details on how it could possibly be functioning as a hospital.

"It's actually one of the better ones in the city," Polly replied. "It's clean, ventilated, and well lit, thanks to the gaslights. The staff has room to board when needed. The gardens are tended, so there's fresh produce. And we have an outstanding doctor, if I do say so myself." With a proud smile, she added, "He's a distant cousin all the way from Maine."

"Maine?" Therese asked.

"Yes, by way of Boston, where he's been working for the last few years. But he plans to return to Maine after this and take over his father's practice."

"What's he doing down here?" Mother asked. "Is he a sympathizer?"

Polly shook her head. "He's a Quaker, although he doesn't speak Plain. At least not around us."

Therese nodded. Using *thee* and *thou* would bring a lot of attention to him in Richmond, she felt sure.

Polly continued. "As a Quaker, he's a pacifist, of course. The Union allowed him to come for a few months. Considering the North has three times the number of surgeons we do, they weren't really in a position to turn him down."

"I suppose not," Therese said.

"I didn't realize you had Quakers in your family tree," Mother said, using the same tone for *Quaker* as she might for *coward.*

Polly didn't seem offended. "Like I said, he's a very distant cousin. And as far as I know, his is the only Quaker branch of our family tree."

Therese didn't know much about Quakers, but she did know her father respected both their beliefs and their actions.

Badan turned toward the church, and when he stopped the horses, Therese hugged her friend.

Polly hugged her back. "Remember what I said about the governess position."

Therese wanted to cry into her friend's shoulder over the unfairness of life. Oh, how she yearned to take that job! Instead, she gathered her courage and simply replied, "I wish it were possible."

Polly hugged Therese one last time, and then after Badan helped her down, she slipped into the church. Therese swallowed hard, willing herself not to cry. If only Grandfather would free his slaves, then Mother could stay with a clear conscience at River Pines, well taken care of, and Therese would be free to go. If only Father hadn't died. If only this horrible war didn't keep dragging on and on and on.

By the time they reached Grandfather's ornate iron gate, Mother dozed with her head leaning back against the high seat. Brush and trees crowded Grandfather's fields that had once grown tobacco. Before the land had been cultivated, it was forested—and it seemed it would be again.

As the lane turned, the house came into view. Therese couldn't ever remember a time when it had appeared so shabby. Paint peeled from the siding, the trees encroached on the house and needed to be trimmed, and the grass was dry and brown from the summer heat. Once exporting tobacco became difficult due to the Union blockades, Grandfather had sold off so many of his slaves that there was no longer the manpower, the money, or the supplies to keep the place in repair. Still, the three-story structure was grand, with double columns on the front porch and a veranda on the side.

As they neared the house, Therese sighed in relief at the sight of the verdant garden and healthy orchard. There was no concern for the dry lawn—the vegetables and fruit were what mattered. Perhaps the estate was far enough off the road that soldiers hadn't looted the food. Granted, they gave what was required to the Confederate Army, but oftentimes soldiers helped themselves too. No matter. What counted was that Grandfather didn't seem to be lacking.

Badan drove the buggy around to the back entrance, where he helped Mother down and then Therese. Her feet landed on the hard ground as Aggie came out of the kitchen house. She wore a blue scarf around her head and a white apron over her dress and carried a pitcher. She was thin and tall and held herself as straight as an arrow. She broke into a smile at the sight of Therese.

Therese grinned back at her friend. As a child, she would have rushed into the young woman's arms, just as she had Polly's. But Grandfather had broken her of that when she was thirteen with a harsh scolding, telling her it was time to accept that she and Aggie had very different roles in life.

"I'm headed up to Master LeFevre," Aggie said. "Mother's with him for the moment. Come along."

"So he's injured badly," Therese said.

"That's right," Aggie answered. "He's been asking for the two of you."

Mother was already headed toward the door.

"I'm sorry," Aggie said.

Therese nodded and followed her mother. Grandfather had always favored Warner, his only male descendant, over Therese. Father had cautioned Warner not to take Grandfather's blessing to heart and not to think better of himself because of it, but Warner had long ago stopped listening to Father—if he ever had. He much preferred Grandfather's grandiosity compared to Father's humble warnings.

A time or two, Father had confronted Grandfather about his favoritism, which was probably why the old man had agreed to pay for Therese's school tuition.

Father and Grandfather had other disagreements, some louder than others. By the time the war started, the two barely spoke to each other. But when Father died, Grandfather and Badan arrived with a wagon full of supplies and a pine box. Mother requested that Father be buried at River Pines against Father's wishes, but Grandfather refused. He attended Father's burial in the churchyard, keeping his distance.

Prior to that, the last time they'd visited River Pines, not long after the war first started, Father and Grandfather argued once again. Father quoted, "He that stealeth a man, and selleth him, or if he be found in his hand, he shall surely be put to death." The old man quickly shot back, "Servants, obey in all things *your* masters according to the flesh; not with eyeservice, as menpleasers; but in singleness of heart, fearing God."

"Servants," Father had said. "Yes, please. Make them servants. Free them. Pay them."

"Out of my house!" Grandfather had bellowed.

Therese shivered at the memory. Father had rounded her and Mother up and escorted them out the door while Grandfather yelled profanities at the "Yankee" who'd stolen his daughter, adding that at least Warner had brought honor to the family by fighting for the South.

Now, by the time Therese reached Grandfather's room on the second floor, Mother was kneeling at his side, holding his hand. The sight made Therese's eyes fill with tears. She well remembered how she'd felt just over a month ago, kneeling next to her own father's bed.

Grandfather's long white hair was fanned out around his head, and his eyes were closed.

Auntie Vera stood against the wall, a rag and a basin in her hands. She gave Therese a welcoming nod, and they shared a fond glance. Aggie approached with the pitcher, filled the basin, and then took it from her mother.

Mother looked up at Aggie. "What does the doctor say?"

"That time will tell. He'll be back in the morning."

"What happened?" Mother leaned closer to her father.

"He rode the gelding down by the river yesterday evening," Aggie said. "When it grew dark and he wasn't back yet, Badan went after him. He found Master on his stomach, his head against a rock. Badan's pretty sure his foot got caught in the stirrup and he was dragged." Aggie stepped to Grandfather's side, put the basin on the table, and mopped his face with the cool cloth. When she finished, she said she needed to check on the bread baking in the kitchen house, but she would return. Auntie Vera stayed, her back still against the wall.

Grandfather began to stir, and Mother rose and sat on the edge of the bed, taking his hand. "I'm here, Father."

"Helene?"

"Yes, Father."

He turned his head toward her, and his eyes fluttered a little. "You came."

"Yes, and Therese too."

"Warner?"

"No. He's off fighting."

"That's right." He managed to open his eyes. "I changed the will."

Therese's pulse surged. He changed his will? Did that mean he had decided to free Aggie and Auntie Vera and Badan and the others after all?

"Don't speak of that," Mother told him. "You'll be fine. We'll stay until you're on your feet again."

Grandfather shook his head. "Everything is written down with my solicitor, but I need to know you understand."

Somehow he found the strength to keep talking, but Therese's heart soon fell. The new terms of the will had nothing to do with the slaves at all but instead were mere technicalities about how Warner would receive his inheritance. Apparently, upon Grandfather's death everything was to go into a trust to be administered by Mother until Warner turned thirty. If Warner didn't survive the war, Grandfather said, then everything would go to Therese instead.

"Except Therese wouldn't inherit at thirty," he added, his eyes on Mother. "You would remain beneficiary of the trust for the rest of your life, with the trust not to be dissolved until your death. Do you understand?"

Mother nodded. "Yes. Of course. Now stop talking and try to rest."

"All right." Grandfather's eyes fluttered and then closed. Therese wasn't sure if he tried to shake his head or had a spasm. She stood and stared for a long time before she slipped from the room.

When she reached the back door, she stopped for a moment, her eyes adjusting to the late afternoon sun. Two figures stood on the side of the kitchen house, their arms wrapped around each other.

For a moment, Therese felt overcome by her losses. She squinted through the glass in the door. Aggie pulled away, a sassy grin on her face. Badan laughed and headed for the barn. Aggie had with Badan what Therese wished she could have, but never would, with Michael. She chided herself for the self-pity. There was no comparison. She didn't have Michael, but she did have her freedom.

Therese stepped back into the hallway. She couldn't just traipse out to the kitchen house as she had as a child. Everything in her life had changed through the years a thousand times over. And unless Grandfather recovered and she and mother returned to their cottage, even more would change. If it came to that, she felt confident her mother would do the right thing and free Aggie and Badan and the others too. God had a plan for all of them—she was sure.

CHAPTER SIX

Therese

*T*herese spent the night taking turns with her mother and Aggie watching over Grandfather. At dawn she relieved Mother, who asked that she wake her when the doctor arrived or if Grandfather worsened. Therese assured her she would.

"Aggie will be in soon," Mother said. "Stay out of her way."

Nodding, Therese settled on a chair that had been pushed close to the bed. She reached for her grandfather. His skin had a papery feel to it, and age spots speckled the back of his hand. He turned toward her, his mouth open a little. Early in the night, she'd read to him from the Scriptures by the light of the lamp, but she didn't have the energy for that now.

She'd been wary of him as a child, aware of the tension between him and her father, and of how gruff he could be. Now he seemed so harmless. So vulnerable. And so alone at River Pines except for the overseer, Alden Porter, whom Therese loathed, and the five slaves that Grandfather had kept.

Her grandmother had died long before Therese was born, back when Mother was a girl. Grandfather said once that he'd spoiled his only child, and that was why Mother had done such a foolish thing as fall in love with Father, a Northerner, and then marry him. "Falling in love can't always be helped," Grandfather had said to Therese in one of the rare conversations they'd had. "But marrying is a choice. Your mother was determined to get what she wanted."

Therese's father had first arrived in Virginia at the age of twenty-two, straight from the College of New Jersey. He was from a wealthy family who owned textile mills, but he was also an abolitionist. He rejected his family's business and money, saying they were making a fortune off the cotton picked by slaves, lining the pockets of Southern slave-holders as well as their own. Determined to make his livelihood as a teacher and believing he could somehow influence the young men of the South with lessons about justice and liberty, he took a teaching job at a boys' school west of Richmond. He met Mother at a dance in the city when she was seventeen and a new graduate of finishing school. She was to return home the next day, but after she met Willis Jennings, she sent a message to her father saying she wished to remain in Richmond another week. And then another. By the time Grandfather ventured into the city to collect her, she was deeply in love. She insisted, if Father wanted to marry her, that he stay in Virginia, and Father, who had fallen head over heels for her, had agreed.

"Nothing makes a person more foolish than love," Grandfather had said to Therese.

There was no doubt her parents had loved each other, although she doubted her mother had been aware when she agreed to marry Father just how poor they would be. After all, he was from a wealthy family, but Father never relented on his stance of refusing their help. And once he saw just how dependent his new wife's family was on their slaves for their livelihood, he refused all help from them as well.

If the young couple lived modestly, his teaching job at Box Tree Male Academy meant they didn't have to take money from either family. Their housing and food were included, and as long as he didn't outright criticize the livelihoods of most of the fathers who sent their sons to be educated at the school, he could get by with presenting Christ's teachings and the basic tenets of liberty, equality, and justice. Upper-class Southerners valued education in general and Box Tree in particular. The academy had been a peaceful place for Therese to grow up, and it was her favorite spot in the world.

She even loved the name, Box Tree, which had been taken from a passage in Isaiah about God bringing a desert to life, how He would grow "the fir tree, and the pine, and the box tree together" in that once-arid place. Father, who delighted in any sort of poetic writing, felt the passage in the book of Isaiah was a promise that someday the desert of slavery would come to an end and, just like the trees named by the prophet, the people of the South would grow together.

A year ago, the closure of Box Tree had devastated Therese. A few months later, when the main building had been turned into a munitions warehouse, she'd been ill with sorrow.

Father was an outright Yankee, and although his students and their parents respected him as a teacher, most never embraced him. Warner and Therese were accepted, to a certain degree, but there was no doubt they were viewed as Southern Yankees. Therese would certainly accept the title for herself, although she was too timid to speak out about her views. Warner, on the other hand, resented Father's stance and did all he could to prove himself a true Southern man. He challenged Father every chance he could, and as soon as the war broke out, he joined the Confederate Army.

Mother, as a former Southern belle, was simply pitied for having married a Yankee. Therese heard one woman whisper to another, just before the war started and behind Mother's back, "I wonder how she likes the bed she made now?"

The stress between Father and Grandfather never lessened, and that weighed heavily on Mother. As much as Therese loved living at the academy, throughout her growing-up years she couldn't help but wonder what their lives would have been like if Mother had been willing to let them live in the North. Now she wondered that more than ever. Warner wouldn't be fighting for the South. They wouldn't have the issue of slavery to deal with in their own family. She sighed. Clearly, it had been the Creator's will for her to grow up where she did, but she couldn't help but hope God had a different plan for her future. She longed to live where she could be absolutely honest about her beliefs.

Her gaze fell back on her grandfather, on his pallid skin and gray whiskers. The wrinkled skin around his eyes drooped downward, and his still-thick white hair fell over his forehead.

He opened his eyes, sputtering a little. Therese grabbed the glass of water from the bedside table and offered him a drink, but he shook his head. A wisp of white hair shifted over his eyes, and Therese brushed it away.

"I'm sorry. I should have freed them." He took a raggedy breath. "Forgive me."

"You can now." Therese shifted forward. "It's not too late."

He nodded. "I'll speak with your mother."

He closed his eyes then, and Therese leaned back in the chair, nearly overwhelmed with relief. God was at work. The slaves would be free and Mr. Porter soon fired.

She dozed, but not for long. When she awoke, Aggie and Dr. Landers were in the room, and the morning sun wasn't much higher. She stood, ready to take her leave, when the doctor leaned over Grandfather. "His breathing has slowed."

Aggie stepped closer.

The doctor placed his hand on Grandfather's chest, and then he looked at Therese. "Go get your mother. I fear he hasn't much time left."

"Yes, sir." She hurried out of the room and down the hall. Mother was already at her door as if she'd sensed something.

Therese reached for her hand. "Come quickly."

Mother didn't speak, not even when they reached the room. The doctor looked up and simply nodded. Mother fell on the bed next to her father, wrapping her arms around his neck. "Don't go," she begged.

A sense of peace settled over her, something Therese was sure wouldn't have happened if it hadn't been for Grandfather's final declaration. He'd confessed his wrongdoing at last. Father's goodness had won in the end.

The doctor suggested Mother move to the chair so he could examine Grandfather's body one more time. Therese knew she needed to bring to light what her grandfather had said—and soon. There would be decisions to make. Papers to draw up. Financial concerns to address.

Therese knelt beside her mother and took her hand. "His last words to me were about his slaves. He said he regretted not freeing them. He intended to talk with you about doing so."

Mother gasped.

"Yes, it's wonderful, isn't it?"

Mother shook her head. "I can't think about that now."

"You can't run this place without help, Helene," Doctor Landers said.

Therese bristled. She'd been foolish to bring it up in front of him.

The doctor pulled the covers back. "There's hardly enough help here as it is."

Therese stole a look at Aggie. She stood at the end of the bed, her face expressionless. Therese turned her attention back to her mother. "Don't you see? This is what we wanted all along. What Father wanted. Grandfather was very direct with me."

The doctor cleared his throat and directed his gaze at Therese.

She met it.

He cleared his throat again. "Sounds more like the wishful thinking of a fanciful girl, one with an abolitionist for a father. Mr. LeFevre never mentioned such a thing to me." He shifted his gaze to Mother. "Helene, don't give this another thought. It won't leave this room."

He didn't look at Aggie, but his message was straightforward. Therese pursed her lips. She'd talk to Mother in private after they'd all gotten some sleep. She would choose her words carefully and do her best not to upset Mother. She wouldn't confront her. Instead, she'd try to gently persuade her. Surely Grandfather's final wish would be honored in the end.

Mother didn't rest that day. Instead, she met with the Anglican priest about the funeral. It would be a simple service the next day at the LeFevre burial plot on the far side of the property.

Word spread quickly, and neighbors began bringing what food they could spare. A ham. A pecan pie. A pan of johnnycake. A pot of greens. Some didn't stay long, most likely feeling uncomfortable with Therese and her mother. But others stepped into the parlor and took a seat, behaving as if nothing untoward had happened in the past, as if they hadn't criticized and then demonized Father for the articles he wrote about abolition. He never spoke about his convictions in public, not in the South anyway, but his articles were published widely. Many felt he was a traitor living among them, as if he belonged, all the while judging them and writing about their beliefs in an exploitative way. When Therese talked with her father about what people were saying, he replied he genuinely cared about the community in which they lived—but on the issue of slavery they were wrong, and although he held his tongue in person, he couldn't not voice his opinions in print.

The truth was that Father had been an exceptional teacher at Box Tree Male Academy. And although he'd chosen not to speak publicly about the issue of abolition in Virginia, he made occasional trips up to Philadelphia to speak to groups there on the topic.

Even though Therese agreed with her father's position, the many comments made behind their backs had stung. The remarks continued even after he fell ill. The most hurtful was that the tumor in his abdomen was God's judgment for his beliefs.

"Daughter?" Mother stood over her. "I was asking if you could take Mrs. Johnson's rhubarb pie."

Therese stood quickly and grabbed the dessert with both hands. When she started toward the dining room, the woman, who'd been ancient when Therese was a girl and now seemed practically mummified, followed her and flapped her black fan as she walked. Her gown was black also, as were most women's nowadays. She'd lost a nephew, two grandsons, and a great-grandson in the last year. Therese's heart ached for the old woman.

"My goodness, you look like your mother." Mrs. Johnson spoke loudly. "You've grown into a beauty since the last time I saw you."

"Thank you," Therese murmured, sure she'd never be the beauty her mother was.

"I'm guessing the two of you will be staying here now."

"For a time..."

"There's no reason for you to go back across the river," Mrs. Johnson said as they entered the dining room.

Therese ignored the woman's comment.

"Your mother has been in exile long enough." Mrs. Johnson wagged her finger as she spoke. "It's time she came home, that you both came home. And time for you to put your father's foolishness behind you and embrace the life that was meant to be yours."

Therese smiled slightly. The cottage across the river would be much more manageable than Grandfather's estate. The doctor was right. There wasn't any way she and Mother could live here on their own. They would have to close this place up for now and deal with it after the war.

Therese gazed kindly at the old woman. She set down the pie and said, "I'll walk you back into the parlor." Mrs. Johnson meant well.

A few minutes later, Therese slipped out and into the dining room again and then to the back door, hoping to catch sight of Aggie or Auntie Vera. The yard was empty except for several chickens pecking around and Grandfather's hound dogs sleeping under the willow tree.

The kitchen house door opened and Aggie stepped out, followed by Auntie Vera. Both carried pitchers of lemonade, and both had serious expressions on their faces. Aggie appeared to have been crying, but perhaps her eyes were red from lack of sleep due to caring for Grandfather.

Therese stayed in the shadows along the house, moving toward the front. She bunched the skirt of her mourning dress in her hands, careful not to break a hoop. She didn't want the two women to see her. She expected Aggie had shared what Grandfather said with Auntie Vera, but she knew neither woman would bring it up with her. Therese hoped that by tomorrow the matter would be sorted out. She had been foolish to bring up Grandfather's wish with Mother in front of the doctor. Of course Mother didn't want to talk about it in that setting, but no doubt she would soon. Once she could catch her breath.

As Therese rounded the house, she spotted a young man walking up the stairs to the front porch. She stopped at the corner. He had long dark hair under a wide-brimmed hat. He wore boots much nicer and newer than most people in the area could obtain, and an expensive leather haversack hung over his shoulder. He stopped on the top step and then turned toward her as if sensing her presence.

Her heart began to pound so strongly it took a moment to find her voice. "Michael?" she managed to choke out. "Michael Talbot?"

He took off his hat. "Therese, is that you?" He hurried back down the steps.

"Yes." She moved out of the shadows, feeling the tug of the invisible thread between them.

He bowed and then took her hand and kissed it. Her heart raced even faster.

As he let go, his brown eyes filled with compassion. "Please accept my condolences. I was so sorry to hear about your grandfather."

Therese swallowed the lump growing in her throat. The old man had been harsh and unkind, but he was the only grandparent she'd ever known. "Thank you."

"And I was devastated to hear about your father's passing too."

Therese thanked him again, blinking back her tears. She struggled to control her grief and the unwelcomed excitement she felt in seeing Michael. He hadn't written. He hadn't communicated in any way— and yet she still felt joy.

Her stomach lurched but then fell as she reminded herself what Polly had told her about his having a sweetheart back in France.

"Is your mother inside?"

"Yes," Therese answered, but before she could invite him in, the front door swung open.

Mother stepped out, fanning herself in the heat. "Who's there with you, Therese?"

"Michael Talbot."

Mother was quiet for a moment, and when she spoke, her voice was tight. "So you're back from France. Finally willing to fight for your country and give up your 'French leave.'"

It was a term meaning a soldier was absent without permission— hardly Michael's case at all.

"Mother." Therese started up the steps. Michael followed her.

"You should be ashamed of yourself," Mother hissed. "Leaving your younger brothers and brave men like Warner to do the fighting—and the dying."

"Mother! Please don't."

Michael bowed. "I'm so sorry for your losses, Miss Helene." He completely ignored what Mother had said. "Of both your father and your husband."

Mother crossed her arms. "It means little coming from you."

Therese stepped to her mother's side and took her arm. "Please stop. Michael doesn't deserve this. Not at all."

Mother stiffened and pulled away, fanning herself frantically as she went back inside, leaving the door ajar behind her.

Mortified, Therese turned toward Michael. "I'm so sorry. I don't know what's come over her."

He smiled wearily. "It's all right. I know many feel that way about me."

"No, I don't think people do. And you're back now."

"Yes," he said, though his eyes broke from hers as he added, "Ready to do my duty. We need to fight for our rights, don't we? Protect our economy. Battle to retain our property."

A wave of despair swept over Therese. By property, did he mean slaves? Was that what Michael Talbot really believed now? That four million humans, as Father's magazines proposed, should continue to be owned by others? Perhaps she'd misjudged him before. Or maybe his thinking had changed over the past four years.

It was as if someone had cut the invisible thread between them. She reminded herself that it had only been imagined anyway, by her. She took a step backward, her stomach falling.

Michael looked past her to the door. "Hello, Dr. Landers."

The doctor stepped onto the porch, saying that Therese's mother wanted her inside. With a wink at Michael, he added, "But I see you're in good hands. I'll tell her you'll be along in a bit."

"Thank you, sir." Michael returned his attention to Therese and lowered his voice. "So you and your mother will live at River Pines now? And manage the plantation?"

"I-I don't know," she stammered. Perhaps it had been a plantation at one time, but she hardly thought of it as that now. It was barely a working farm.

"Well," he said, taking a step back and again avoiding her eyes. "I'll see you tomorrow at your grandfather's service. My parents and Polly will be there too."

"I thought Polly went back to Richmond."

"Her train wasn't leaving until this afternoon. Once she heard about your grandfather, she decided not to take it."

"What about her job?"

Michael shrugged. "I'm sure she'll work things out. She can head back to Richmond on Thursday, God willing." He gave a nod, returned his hat to his head, and walked briskly down the steps.

But then he stopped and turned, his voice softening as he spoke. "Is there any chance Warner will be coming home for the funeral?"

"Mother sent a message." Therese shrugged. "But I doubt he'll be able to come."

"I can deliver a letter if you wish when I reach the 1st by early next week."

"That would be appreciated. Thank you."

He told her goodbye again and continued on his way. She sighed as she turned to go into the house. Yes, she was disappointed in Michael. Extremely. But maybe it was just as well. Maybe now she'd finally be able, after all these years, to put her feelings for him to rest.

Chapter Seven

Therese

Grandfather's pine box sat next to the hole Badan had dug the night before. Therese stared at the pile of clay dirt. Even under the trees, the sun shone hot as the priest began speaking about Grandfather. "He was a good man who cared for his family, even through troubling times." Therese held her breath, hoping the priest would stop there. He didn't. "He cared for his servants too."

Therese glanced at Aggie, Auntie Vera, and Badan, standing on the far edge of the group, along with Old Joe and the youngest of the lot, sixteen-year-old Sonny, whose mother had been sold the year before. The thought of it still broke Therese's heart.

Mr. Porter, wearing a vest over his stained and wrinkled shirt, stood off by himself. Therese suspected he had a drinking problem. He seemed unsteady on his feet—and she'd seen him ogling Aggie earlier.

He hadn't been conscripted into the army before because of the Twenty-Slave Law, which stated that overseers in charge of twenty or more slaves were exempt from service, though the total number could be from a single farm or a combined total among neighboring farms. Grandfather used to have that many, but once he started selling off his slaves, Mr. Porter had been forced to start working elsewhere as well so that he continued to meet the requirement. He also did some handy-man work for the Talbot family on the side, an arrangement that gave him some extra pocket money and that served as a big help to the Talbots. Mr. Stephen, who as a papermaker was exempt from military service, spent so much time at the mill that it was hard for Miss Amanda to keep up with everything on their property, especially with her sons and all the available hired hands having gone off to war. It had brought Therese's mother comfort to know that her friend, who didn't have any slaves, had some help now and then.

Even before Mother freed the slaves, she should fire Mr. Porter. There was no reason for him to remain. Relief swept through Therese. Tragically, Grandfather had allowed this man to harshly discipline the male slaves, but at least he'd forbidden Mr. Porter from touching the female slaves in any way. Though Therese feared that now, without Grandfather around, the man would feel free to do as he pleased. He was perhaps forty, not all that old. Thank goodness he'd soon be gone. She couldn't wait to say good riddance.

All five slaves kept their heads down. Grandfather had owned them. Owned their bodies. Owned their souls as much as he could. Therese shivered at the offense. They were treated as *chattel*, a concept Therese found as abhorrent as anything in the entire world. Yes, she and Mother needed to talk the issue through as soon as possible. She'd even tried to bring it up early that morning, before breakfast, but again Mother said she was in no shape to discuss it.

"Frederic LeFevre was also a man who loved his country," the priest continued. "He didn't inherit this land. No, he worked hard and bought it. And then built the house, barns, and stables. And then made a good living from the raising and selling of tobacco." Therese shifted her feet. Yes, he'd done all that—with the help of people he'd owned.

She'd heard the story of the LeFevre family her whole life, how they'd fled France in the late 1600s along with so many other Huguenots and made their way to South Africa. A hundred years later, hoping for a better life, they had immigrated to the New World. But once here they had continued to struggle for decades, barely eking out a living—until Grandfather came along. Smart and industrious, as a young man he'd worked three jobs so that he could invest nearly every cent he made in the Midlothian coal mines, closer to Richmond. When that investment paid off, he sold his shares and used the money to buy what would become River Pines—along with enough slaves to successfully cultivate and harvest the land.

"He's an example of a man who worked hard, made a good life for himself, and then did the right thing for those for whom he was responsible."

Therese lowered her head as the priest continued praising her grandfather, fixing her gaze on her tattered boots. She'd shined them with a mix of lard and ashes that morning, hoping that would help. The hem of her dress had frayed in the last year, but she doubted anyone would notice. They were all doing the best they could.

Except for Michael, who stood next to Polly, more handsome than ever in what looked like a new suit. What a shock it must have been for him to return to such impoverished conditions. Now having him near, compared to yesterday, generated no feelings of fondness in her— only intense disappointment.

Her eyes moved to his parents, lovely people both, and she thought of their family history as well. From what she could recall, the Talbots had come to Virginia long before the LeFevres, emigrating from England in the early 1700s to establish an inn and a lumber mill. Their real interest had been in printing and paper, however, and eventually they'd been able to convert their inn to a print shop and the lumber mill into a paper mill. Now, a hundred fifty years later, Talbot Paper and Printing was a solid business with an outstanding reputation.

Best of all, according to Father, the Talbots had done it without ever owning a single slave. These days, the war had taken its toll on the business, of course, as it had with companies throughout the South, but they were managing as well as could be expected. To Therese, they were living proof that it could be done, that a company could succeed without the need for forced labor.

Finally, the priest said, "Yes, Frederic LeFevre was a man who embraced all that had made this country what it is: God's sovereignty, hard work, and love of family."

Therese glanced down at her mother, who sat in a chair Badan had carried out from the house. As expected, Warner hadn't shown up. Mother had said that morning, "He wasn't able to. It's as simple as that." He was thirty miles away, under siege, but it seemed others managed to come and go with passes. Everyone they knew had seen their soldier, if he was fighting nearby, at some point during the war. Everyone except for them.

Therese had never been particularly close to Warner, not the way Polly was with her brothers. But she hadn't thought he would abandon them the way he had. She had to hope he had a good reason.

After the casket had been lowered and Mother and Therese each dropped a handful of dirt into the hole, they followed the others back to the house. Mother looped her arm through Therese's and leaned heavily against her. Therese breathed in deeply, taking in the warm scent of pine and pitch, willing herself to be strong for her mother. Thunderclouds gathered on the horizon, and the day had grown even muggier. By the time they reached the house, it was just starting to sprinkle.

The men gathered in the parlor, and the women helped spread the food on the dining room table, with Aggie bringing bowls and baskets back and forth in the rain from the kitchen house. Therese met her at the back door each time to take the items from her and hand them off to someone else to add to the growing spread.

As they worked, Therese saw Miss Amanda, Polly's mother, lead Mother over to a pair of chairs in the corner where they could sit and talk. Outside, thunder cracked, and a few times lightning flashed, yet Aggie just kept going back and forth between buildings without even seeming to flinch.

Therese was hovering at the door, waiting for Aggie to bring another load, when she heard Miss Amanda ask Mother what their plans were now.

"Therese and I will stay at River Pines," Mother replied. "There's no reason for us to live at the cottage anymore—except to be closer to you and your family, but y'all can always come visit us here. Plus, we'll still see you at church on Sundays, right?"

"Of course." Physically, Miss Amanda was a tiny woman, but emotionally she was strong and trustworthy. "How will you run things, though, just the two of you? This place is so big."

"We'll have the help..." her voice trailed off and Therese froze, waiting for clarification. Surely Mother meant *hired* help. *Paid* help. Not owned help.

"Oh." Miss Amanda sounded startled too. "I just thought, considering your late husband's views, that you'd free—"

Mother interrupted her. "In time, yes, but for now that wouldn't be what's best for them, would it? Where would they go? What would they do? Surely they would starve. No, we'll all remain here together. That's what's best."

Therese felt as if she might be sick. She turned her gaze on her mother, but the woman patently ignored her.

"I see," Miss Amanda said.

Mother took her friend's hand. "I'm afraid I owe Michael an apology."

"Oh?"

"Yes, I was rude to him last night. I...overreacted."

Therese almost laughed out loud at her mother's attempt to change the subject and curry favor in one fell swoop. She hadn't changed her opinion of Michael. She was just throwing Miss Amanda—and her own daughter—a bone.

"Don't give it another thought," Miss Amanda said. "You've been under duress. I know he understands."

Therese simply glared until Mother finally met her eyes, but her face was void of expression. Therese's heart broke. Was there no one she could trust any longer? No one left who shared Father's ideals?

What was she going to do?

It wasn't until most of the mourners had left that Therese finally found the chance to speak with her mother in the corner of the parlor by the piano.

"Why won't you free them?" she demanded. "That's what Grand-father wanted. What Father wanted. What *we* wanted all along."

"It's not what Warner wants, and it's up to him now. I'm merely the administrator of the trust."

Tears flooded Therese's eyes.

"Stop," Mother said. "It's not that simple." Her voice was grow-ing hoarse. "I don't expect you to understand. You're too idealistic—and sensitive. But I have a responsibility to protect them and Warner's future too."

Therese blinked hard. "At least let Mr. Porter go so he can't hurt any of them again."

"Oh, he's harmless." Mother kept her head down.

"Mother, he's not. Don't you remember when he beat Badan? And haven't you seen him leering at Aggie?"

Mother lifted her red, weary eyes. "Please don't talk coarsely."

Therese shook her head in disgust but did her best to keep her voice calm. "Perhaps you need more time to think about this."

Mother shook her head. "I have no husband, no father. Someday Warner will care for me, and you too if you never marry. We're just doing what we must."

"No. We'd be fine at the cottage."

"That's enough. I don't know how we'll survive here, let alone back there, without any income." Tears filled Mother's eyes. "We were ide-alistic far too long. My love for your father clouded my judgment. This is what's best—for all of us. Auntie Vera and Aggie too. And Badan and the rest. None of them would be safe if we turned them out."

Her mother knew that wasn't true. There were ways to get them to the North. But before Therese could say as much, Mother dropped her voice to a whisper and added, "We'll all take care of one another. I promise."

Therese stepped away, aghast that she would be willing to leave such a legacy. That was one of the things Father often talked about. He said it was one sin for a person to purposefully do the wrong thing, but it was a far greater sin to purposefully do wrong and leave an unworthy legacy for one's offspring.

Miss Amanda started toward them but then must have decided she shouldn't interrupt. "It's all right," Therese said. "We're done."

"We just wanted to say goodbye. We need to catch the ferry back."

"Of course," Therese said.

Mother stood and hugged her friend. Mr. Stephen, Michael, and Polly all offered their condolences again and then their goodbyes. Therese walked them to the door and gave Michael a letter for her brother, avoiding eye contact with him. She'd only written a short note, asking Warner to come when he could. As the Talbots headed down the front steps, she could feel anger at her mother building inside her, like a roaring furnace freshly loaded with coal.

The rain had finally stopped, but in her mind she kept seeing Aggie from earlier, arms loaded down with food for the master's funeral, sloshing through the muck back and forth, back and forth, her dress heavy with water, her face impassive, her world so dictated by others that even lightning had to be ignored. Poor, sweet Aggie, who had always been Therese's friend. Who was one of God's beloved children. Who was no different from anyone else here, save for the circumstances of her birth.

Suddenly, heart pounding, Therese knew what she had to do. She flung open the door and raced down the steps. Badan had hitched the Talbots' horse to their buggy and now held out his hand to help Miss Amanda into it.

"Wait!" Therese called out. Both Polly and Michael turned toward her.

"Polly," she said, nearly breathless.

Her friend started toward her. "What is it?"

Therese stopped and waited until her friend drew near, and then she spoke in a voice low but urgent. "I'm interested in the governess position in Richmond after all."

Polly glanced at the house. "But what about your mother?"

Therese felt her hands ball into fists. "Mother can stay here with her...choices. But I won't be a part of it. I can't."

Polly's brow furrowed with concern.

"Could you speak with the family and tell them of my credentials?"

"Yes. Of course I'll do that." In a softer voice, Polly added, "You're sure this isn't too much too soon?"

Therese shook her head, feeling a resolve as solid as the pines for which the plantation had been named. She stood up straight, deeply grateful for this trusted friend and the lifeline she had thrown without even realizing it.

"Quite the opposite, actually," Therese said. "It's not enough, not nearly enough. But it's all I can do for now. And I've never been more certain of anything in my life."

There was no reason to tell Mother of her plan until Therese heard back from Polly. But it was all she could think about, her anger eventually giving way to sadness and then to a deep sense of longing. Maybe for what could have been had Mother not allowed herself to be ruled by her own anxieties. Maybe for the dream of Michael that she'd finally let go. Maybe for something more.

Therese had wanted to return to Richmond ever since she left. She'd loved her time there—walking along the James River past the flour, cotton, and iron mills and the tobacco factories and warehouses. Watching the water tumble over the falls, the fish jumping in the pools, and the birds swooping down over the river. Exploring the different neighborhoods. Learning everything she possibly could in school. Now, God willing, that dream would actually come true. If only it could happen under different circumstances.

They spent the next few days at River Pines, Therese distracting herself with a book she'd found near her grandfather's chair. It was the recent memoir of the famous spy, Rose O'Neal Greenhow, and the story of how she used her charms and social connections to gather and convey important military information to the Confederacy during the first two years of the war.

Therese had heard of the book, which was all the rage in England, and of Mrs. Greenhow, who had become an international celebrity. Therese found herself fascinated by the story, especially its account of the five months that Rose and her daughter, Little Rose, spent locked in prison. Apparently, the woman continued to pass along messages even from there. Though Therese couldn't imagine such audacity, she was impressed by it. Misguided as Rose's loyalties were, she was still a brave and daring woman, and she'd acted on her beliefs without thought for her own safety or well-being. Once released from prison, she spent time in Richmond, where she was hailed as a heroine. Then, a year ago, she ran the blockade and had been in Europe ever since.

Early the following Monday, Therese finished the book and then Badan drove her and Mother back to the cottage to collect what they needed and to close it up. As Therese knelt at the bookcase in the tiny parlor, boxing up books—her schoolbooks and also Father's much larger collection—she decided to give her mother one more chance to change her mind. Surely here, among Father's most important abolitionist materials, Mother would finally admit the wrongness of keeping Aggie and the others enslaved.

But when she brought it up, Mother snapped at her sharply, telling her the subject was closed. Therese's eyes began to sting, and she returned her attention to the books. She felt as if they, along with the articles Father had written, were all she had left of him. After she closed the box, she retreated to the back room for her clothes and personal items. When she returned, she saw that Mother had opened up the box and removed a stack of books, magazines, and papers from inside.

"What are you doing?" Therese knelt. "I already packed those."

"We're only taking what's appropriate."

"Appropriate," Therese echoed, not believing her ears as she looked at the stack of rejects. *Uncle Tom's Cabin. Twelve Years a Slave.* All of Longfellow's poems, as well as Thoreau's essays and Dickens's work too. Mother certainly remembered which authors were abolitionists. Therese could feel the knot of rage solidifying again inside her.

Copies of magazines—the *National Anti-Slavery Standard* and *The Liberty Bell*—were there too, issues in which Father had articles published. The papers were those he'd been working on at the time he fell ill. "We can't dispose of these." Therese held up Father's last article, appalled at the very thought.

"We'll leave them here and collect them after the war."

Therese knew they wouldn't survive. Someone would soon realize the cottage was empty and set up housekeeping—and she wouldn't blame them. They'd most likely be displaced by the war, looking for a safe place to squat, or soldiers who oversaw the stash of munitions in the academy building. The cottage would be occupied in no time.

For a moment, she almost stood up to her mother and insisted they bring these things to River Pines. But then she thought of what lay ahead, the larger stand she would take as soon as she got confirmation about the job from Polly, and decided to hold her tongue. Mother could have this battle.

Therese would win the war.

She hid the books and papers in the attic as best she could. As she did, her father's *carte de visite* of the escaped slave fell from between the papers. She quickly picked it up and slipped it into the pocket of her apron.

Next she turned her attention to Warner's things, packing up a couple of books, a compass, a watch Grandfather had given him, and his clothes. He'd need these items when the war was over.

With Badan's help, they loaded the wagon with everything, including a few boxes of household items and the rest of their threadbare clothing. Then, while Mother waited in the shade of the porch, Therese and Badan dug up the potatoes and harvested the beans, okra, and greens. The corn wasn't ripe enough for them to eat, but they took it anyway to feed to the hogs.

Badan helped Mother into the wagon while Therese stared back at the cottage, thinking of Father. "I'm sorry," she whispered.

Perhaps Mother overheard her because she said, "Hurry along."

Badan extended his hand. The breeze picked up as Therese stepped high. She thought she heard Badan say, "Things will work out." Then again, maybe she imagined it, or perhaps it was the wind. Either way it was good advice.

～

On Wednesday, Therese was practicing scales at Grandfather's piano and Mother was on the settee, taking her turn reading the spy memoir, when Aggie brought a letter into the parlor.

"For you." She handed it to Therese.

"Who's it from?" Mother asked.

"Polly." Therese opened the letter and read quickly. The Galloways were delighted she wanted to work as a governess, and they desired her to come to Richmond as soon as possible.

She pulled in a breath, her heart suddenly pounding. This was what she'd been waiting for, the logistical solution to her moral and ideological problem. It was time to reveal her decision to her mother.

"Well?" Mother demanded, setting her book aside.

Therese had expected to feel anxious in this moment, but instead her heart filled with a sense of rightness, of purpose. A person either lived by their beliefs or they didn't. She was going to live by hers, even if Mother would not. She lowered the letter to her lap and then slid around on the piano bench to meet her mother's eyes.

"Are you absolutely certain you won't free Grandfather's slaves?" she asked, intentionally using the term her mother always tried to avoid.

Anger flashed in the woman's eyes. "What did I tell you? The matter is closed for discussion! Do *not* bring it up again." With an exasperated sigh, she returned her attention to her book.

"Yes or no, Mother. Are you going to free them?"

The woman froze, her features growing hard and cold. "Not at this time, no."

Therese nodded. She took in a deep breath, held it, and then slowly blew it out. When she spoke, she could hear the sadness within her resolve. "Then I'm leaving. I'm sorry, but I simply cannot go against Father's wishes or my own beliefs. I won't stay here."

Mother leaped up, the book tumbling to the ground. "What? You're not going back to the cottage. I absolutely forbid it!"

"I'm not going to the cottage," Therese replied calmly. She stood as well, still clutching the letter, her hands at her sides. "I'm taking a job as a governess. I'm going to Richmond to work and live."

Chapter Eight
Therese

Over the next several days, letters passed between Mr. Galloway and Therese that secured the position. Then, as Therese organized her few teaching materials and packed to go to Richmond, she slipped Father's *carte de visite* into one of her books. She couldn't help but admit to herself that Mother was becoming more and more helpless as Aggie and Vera began to see to her needs. Disgusted by her mother's behavior, Therese began avoiding her as much as possible.

However, there was one good moment that mother and daughter shared as they looked through the family tintypes and daguerreotypes. There was the image of Mother and Father taken in a studio, one of Warner when he finished his studies, one of Therese taken in front of the main building at Box Tree Male Academy. In it, she was wearing her favorite dress at the time, yellow with white lace cuffs and pink flowers appliqued at the waist.

Saturday morning, Mother insisted that Badan drive Therese into Richmond instead of her taking the train. Therese hoped Mother would ride along, but she said she had a headache and needed to rest. The day had dawned extra warm for mid-September. Mother wrote Badan a pass, while Therese marveled at how quickly she'd resumed her role as mistress, even though it had been twenty-three years. By the time Therese descended the stairs, Mother had retreated back into the house. Badan took Therese's book bag and her clothes bag, while Auntie Vera told her she'd look after Mother. Aggie stood by the buggy, and without Mother watching, Therese gave her a hug.

"Go on," Aggie said. "I know how much you like Richmond. You're going to have a fine time."

Therese let go of her friend. "You take care of yourself."

"Oh, we'll be just fine." Aggie smiled. "We have the chickens, a couple of hogs left to butcher, and a garden full of vegetables, not to mention all the apples to put up. You let us know if you need any food, and Badan will bring some in."

Therese hesitated to say anything, but because Mother refused to fire Mr. Porter, she asked, "Do you feel safe here? Has anyone tried to hurt you?"

Her friend shook her head, but Therese wasn't convinced. "Aggie?"

Auntie Vera stepped forward and patted Therese's back. "No need to worry about anything except those little girls waiting for you. Now get going."

Therese told the two women goodbye. As the buggy drove away from River Pines, Therese glanced back over her shoulder. Aggie and Auntie Vera stood side by side in the driveway, watching her leave. Mother stood on the front porch, all alone. Therese was surprised she was waving goodbye at all. As Badan directed the horses onto the road, Mother stepped back into the house.

A couple of leaves fluttered down to the ground, but it would be a few weeks before any changed color. Thankfully, it hadn't rained, and the road was dry and passable, although a cloud of dust swirled behind them.

By the time they reached the outskirts of Richmond and the rolling hills ahead, it was nearly noon. Soon they passed through a checkpoint manned by Confederate soldiers. Badan showed his pass from Mother, and Therese explained why she was headed into the city, holding out the letter from Mr. Galloway. A soldier waved them on, and in a cloud of dust along the dirt street, they continued forward. Soon they passed houses and shops and tenement buildings.

The row house the Galloways lived in was on Grace Street, not far from downtown. Therese was familiar with the neighborhood. She and her classmates had often walked along the tree-lined street.

When Badan found the address and stopped, Therese leaned back against the seat for a moment and took in the view. There were linden trees growing in front of the brick building. A wrought iron fence surrounded the property. No children were visible, but perhaps they were inside for their dinner.

Badan helped Therese down and then retrieved her bags for her. She led the way to the door and knocked. When no one answered, she knocked again. Finally, it swung open, and a girl of about nine stood before her.

"I'm Miss Therese Jennings. Is your father home?"

The girl shook her head.

"Your mother?"

"She's resting."

"Would you please tell her that I'm here?"

The girl nodded and shut the door. A few minutes later she returned with a woman who appeared to be around thirty. Therese towered over her. "Oh, dear," the woman said. "Charles told me you'd be coming, but I completely forgot. Please come in." She wore a housedress, and strands of hair had fallen from the bun at the nape of her neck.

Therese curtsied and introduced herself.

"I figured," the woman said.

Therese took her bags from Badan and thanked him. "Be careful," she said. He had his pass and all should be well, but there was always the chance that someone would try to steal the horses or make some other sort of mischief.

Badan dipped his head toward her and headed back to the buggy.

The house was dimly lit and fairly cool. "Cook is just finishing up our dinner," the woman said. "One of our maids recently ran away, so we're scrambling to get everything done."

Because Therese couldn't respond in sympathy, she didn't respond at all. She hoped the slave made it to safety.

Her new employer didn't seem to notice. "However, the remaining maid is very competent—with both the house and helping me care for the children too, plus the girls are finally of an age where they're quite reasonable and helpful themselves." She stopped and faced Therese. "Oh, where are my manners? I'm Delpha Galloway. I'm glad you're here."

Therese smiled. She liked the woman.

"Our last governess missed home and up and left." She continued on down the hall, past the door to a parlor. "I don't blame her. I miss home too. I didn't think I would as much as I do. It's cooler here than in Louisiana, and this is the heart of everything that's happening, but I haven't felt myself at all. Home is a good place to be."

Therese didn't contradict the woman, but right now she was happy not to be at the cottage or at River Pines.

"The girls are Eleanor, Lydia, and Florence. Eleanor is who answered the door. Charles keeps hoping for a boy, but I keep telling him not to."

Therese's face grew warm. It appeared as if the woman could be expecting, but Therese wasn't sure. Again, she didn't respond.

"Cook came from Louisiana with us, and so did our maids, both the one who ran and the one who stayed. We were renting out our stable boy to Tredegar Iron Works. He ran too." She stopped, took a breath, and then continued. "Your room is ready. It's in the attic." She turned into the dining room, which had a large oak table—functional but not fancy. It was set with plain white dishes. All three girls sat on the far side of it.

"Girls," Mrs. Galloway said, "this is Miss Jennings, your new governess."

Eleanor nodded and smiled just a little. Lydia pursed her lips. Florence stared straight ahead. They were stair steps of one another with their big brown eyes and dark braided hair.

"I'm afraid we're having porridge for our dinner today," Mrs. Galloway said. "And for supper too. Isn't that right, girls?"

They all nodded.

"It's been hard to get meat and produce, but Cook has managed to get us some for tomorrow. We'll have a Sunday dinner. But some days it's just porridge."

Therese said that was fine. She'd had plenty of meals like that while living in the cottage.

"As far as your duties, your primary one will be teaching the girls, of course. On occasion we may need your help during the evenings or on Saturdays, but otherwise that time will be your own, as will Sundays after church. "

"Thank you," Therese said, curtsying. "I'll do my best to serve your family well."

"No doubt," Mrs. Galloway said, and then she smiled. She turned toward her oldest daughter. "Eleanor, show Miss Jennings to her room." Mrs. Galloway turned toward Therese. "I hope it will be all right."

"It'll be fine."

She followed Eleanor up the stairs to the second floor and then on up to the attic. There was a narrow cot, a bureau, a washstand with a pitcher and basin, and a small desk. It was warm now, though Therese imagined it would be cold in the winter, but it was more than adequate. She thanked Eleanor and sent her back downstairs, washed up quickly, and then joined the girls in the dining room. They ate their porridge slowly. As Therese ate hers, she decided she'd ask Mother in the letter she would write tonight if Badan could bring a box of apples and other produce in for the Galloways sometime soon. She knew, after the harvest, that Mother would be required to give a substantial amount of food to the army to help feed the troops, but she hoped there would be enough left over to be generous in other ways.

The rest of the day went well, with Therese settling into her room and then spending time with the girls in the parlor, evaluating their reading skills with her McGuffey's primer. Eight-year-old Eleanor did quite well, but six-year-old Lydia barely knew how to read at all, and five-year-old Florence could only identify some of her letters. Mr. Galloway came home late, after the girls were in bed. He introduced himself to Therese, thanked her for coming to Richmond, and then slipped down the hall toward the kitchen, probably to get a bowl of porridge.

The next day she walked to St. Paul's Church with the family. The two older girls skipped ahead, but Florence stayed back and took Therese's hand. Mr. and Mrs. Galloway walked slowly, a few steps behind. Mr. Galloway was short like his wife, but quieter. He seemed like a gentle soul, although preoccupied.

Therese had attended St. Paul's as a student. The congregation, of course, was much bigger than back home, and the Greek Revival–style building was much more ornate with its columns, stained glass windows, and balconies than the simple church where she'd grown up.

The sermon was more ornate as well, flowery in speech if eloquent and intelligent. Therese spotted Polly a few pews ahead of her and wondered if this was the priest she was friends with, the one she'd gone to Manakin Episcopal to pick up some books for.

After the service, Therese found Polly. The first thing her friend said was that she'd had a letter from her younger brother, Lance. "He's in a prisoner of war camp. He said they're being treated well, though."

Therese squeezed Polly's hand. At least he was alive.

She then introduced the Galloways to Polly. After she greeted each one, she asked Therese if she wanted to go to the hospital with her that afternoon.

Therese was startled at the suggestion, but then she realized that she did want to go, that she would like very much to help in any way she could. She turned toward Mr. Galloway and asked him if that would be all right. Before he could answer, Mrs. Galloway said, "Of course. By all means, please do. I tried to volunteer a few times, but I don't have the stamina for it right now. Your volunteering would be a boon to all of us."

Mr. Galloway nodded in agreement.

"I'll come by for you at two," Polly said. "It will only take us a short time to walk there. You'll be home by a little after eight this evening."

It would be dark by then, but Therese trusted Polly. She couldn't say that she looked forward to working in the hospital, but she did feel it was her duty. Caring for Father had been hard, and she was known for her sensitivity. She hoped she'd be strong enough to do the job that needed to be done for the soldiers.

"Nurses are to wear dark colors and dress modestly, of course. Make sure to wear something old."

Therese nodded.

"And no hoops," Polly said.

Therese hadn't thought of that, but it made sense.

"And make sure you can push the sleeves of your dress up," Polly added. "Things can get messy. We used to have sleeve covers to put on, but they all wore out. Now we just have aprons that protect our dresses, somewhat."

Therese winced a little, realizing tending wounded soldiers could be quite a bit different than caring for Father.

Later that afternoon, Polly led the way along the Virginia Capitol building and up Ninth Street and then to Tenth. Therese relished being in Richmond again, even though it had obviously changed since her school days. Many of the homes and buildings she passed appeared shabbier and needed to be painted and spruced up. And she'd heard there was more public drunkenness, bar brawls, and violence. But there was also an air of excitement. Soldiers marched by on the other side of the street. Important-looking men dashed into buildings. And women, doing their best to dress fashionably with the resources they had, bustled about. Therese could easily imagine the intrigue that could be going on, even now.

"Have you read Rose O'Neal Greenhow's memoir?" Therese asked her friend.

"Oh, goodness," Polly answered. "I haven't had time to read since I started volunteering at the hospital. Besides, isn't that all...well, rather sensationalized?"

Therese nodded and then grinned. "But terribly interesting, nevertheless." Taking her friend's arm, she said, "She did her spying up in

Washington, but," she lowered her voice, "it's so easy to imagine what might be going on here in Richmond as well, as far as spies and secret messages and that sort of thing. Don't you think?"

"I don't know. Things seem pretty boring here to me." She smiled. "I don't hear of anything exciting, at least not as exciting as the injuries and diseases we take care of at the hospital."

Therese was a little disappointed. She imagined tunnels under businesses and houses that led down to the river, where spies could easily escape. And their old school, now a hospital, would be perfect for some sort of clandestine activity, she was sure, considering the number of people who came and went.

Polly pointed ahead. "Here we are." Halfway up the block was the former Women's Institute, four-stories high with two towers on either side of the front entrance and two on either side of the back exit too, which led to the loading docks, kitchen, gardens, and stable. A brick wall surrounded the property. It still looked like the school she and Polly had attended except for the wagon that pulled around to the back, filled with injured soldiers, perhaps from the Petersburg area. Therese shivered, even though the afternoon was warm.

They hurried up the stairs and through the heavy wooden doors into the foyer. The smell was the first thing Therese noticed. The iron odor of blood. Less noticeable was a hint of lye soap and what she guessed was chloroform. It was much different than the scent of polished floors that she remembered from her school days in the building.

Therese's eyes took a moment to adjust to the dim light as Polly directed her to hang the light shawl she'd brought for the walk home in the closet to the right. Beyond it were two offices.

"We'll be giving sponge baths first and then serving supper," Polly said.

Therese nodded. That sounded manageable.

A woman walked by with a hamper filled with linens.

"The laundry is out back, just as it always was, along with the kitchen," Polly explained. "And, of course, the baking room is in the basement."

Therese could imagine all the people and jobs it took to keep a hospital working. Much like a school—but even more so.

"As far as the patients, most are enlisted soldiers from North Carolina or officers from Virginia, but of course there's a sampling of soldiers from all over who have ended up here for one reason or another. Many of them have lost arms or legs, and lots of them have suppurating wounds. Healing often takes much longer than expected and sometimes doesn't happen at all. Some have been here for months and months, while others expire the day they arrive. We can't always predict who will make it and who won't. The injured are mostly on the second floor, while the sick—typhoid, diphtheria, measles, chicken pox, all of that—are on the third floor. Some of the high-ranking officers are in smaller rooms scattered throughout the building. We'll be working exclusively on the second floor. If the wounds bother you at first, know you're not alone. Just do your best, and in time you'll adjust."

"All right." Therese offered up a prayer for strength. She'd be mortified to embarrass a soldier due to her own weakness.

Polly led the way to the first office, where a woman, who was probably nearing fifty, sat behind a desk. Her gray hair was pulled back into an austere bun, and she wore a plain brown dress. Polly introduced Therese and then said, "This is Matron Webb." Polly smiled. "She's in charge."

The woman stood. "Don't tell Dr. Talbot that." Smiling at Therese, she lowered her voice and added, "He may be Polly's cousin, but he couldn't be more different if he tried."

"Isn't that the truth?" Polly smiled in return.

"Don't get me wrong," the matron added. "He's a good man with a good heart."

Therese nodded, remembering Polly mentioning him when they'd met on the ferry.

Matron Webb wrinkled her nose. "He just has very different ideas about some things than we do—both as a Yankee and a Quaker."

"Different?" Therese asked.

"Abrupt. Arrogant. A bit of a bully. But he's a good doctor and a good man." She smiled. "So we'll keep him."

Therese didn't respond. Again she thought of how much her father admired the Quakers he'd known, and some had accused him of being arrogant too. She'd take what Matron Webb said with a grain of salt.

"Regardless of his beliefs, he is the best surgeon we've ever had." Matron Webb tightened her apron as she spoke. "But he makes the water boys pump and carry boatloads of water, and he's forever opening all the windows in the place. Still, we're thankful he's here."

Polly nodded in agreement.

"Did you tell Therese the rules?" Matron asked.

"No," Polly answered. "I thought they should come straight from you."

The woman looked pleased. "No fraternizing with the patients. Care for them quickly and efficiently. Don't encourage feelings toward you in any way. Appear as matronly as possible." She looked Therese up and down, frowning as she did. "Do your best to look frumpy. No hoop skirts, which it appears you already know about. You'll be given one meal per shift if there's adequate food available. And you'll do as you're told and follow orders without complaint. Do you agree to follow these rules?"

"Yes, of course." Therese hoped she'd be able to complete the tasks they assigned her. Being new, she had expected them to start her out doing something like laundry, but that clearly wasn't the case. She knew she could sponge bathe and feed the patients, and administer medicine. She wasn't as sure if she'd have the stomach to clean wounds and change dressings. She'd soon find out.

The woman opened a desk drawer and took out a piece of paper. "Here's a pass for you to be out after curfew. The streets are well patrolled by soldiers, and none of our nurses have had a problem, but always travel in pairs after dark."

She took the pass and thanked the woman.

As Polly and Therese started up the stairs, Polly said, "Even though Alec is my cousin, I only refer to him here as Dr. Talbot."

"Of course," Therese said, understanding the need to be as professional as possible.

Polly led the way to a large, deep closet halfway down the hall that had shelves on two sides that were filled with basins, sponges, cloths, and dressing material. A cistern sat on the third side. They each filled a basin, grabbed a sponge, and headed to a large room at the end of a long hall. Soldiers on cots filled the room. The smells were much stronger now.

The first soldier Therese bathed barely said anything, and she guessed he was on morphine. He'd lost his left arm at his elbow, and that side of his body was peppered with wounds that were thankfully all covered by bandages. He said he'd been in the hospital for more than a month.

Therese prayed silently as she washed his right side—for his healing, for his family, for his soul.

When she finished, he muttered, "Thank you."

The next soldier chatted away. He had a wound on the side of the head, but it seemed to be healing. "I should be back in the battle in no time," he said. "I just need a doc to release me." The soldier was from North Carolina but had been fighting with the 1st Virginia Infantry.

"Do you know Warner Jennings?"

"Captain Jennings?"

"Yes," Therese said. "He's my brother."

"I'm acquainted with him. He seems like a good man. His men respect him."

A pang of longing settled in Therese's chest. All she had were Mother and Warner. No aunts and uncles or cousins. There was just the three of them now. She hoped she and Warner would grow closer once the war was over.

She continued on with her work until the soldier from the 1st Infantry called out to a person standing in the doorway. "Doc!" he yelled. "Come take a look at me. I want out of here."

A tall, lean man with a trim beard started across the room. He wore an apron over a white shirt, brown vest, and black pants. "Bucky, isn't it?"

"That's right." The soldier pointed to the side of his head. "I need you to release me."

The doctor stepped closer. "Let me take a look." He placed one hand on the soldier's chin and tilted his head, peering at the wound on the right side. "How have your headaches been?"

"I haven't had any for the last two days. I'm telling you, I'm fit as a fiddle."

The doctor pointed at a sign on the far wall. "How's your vision?"

The sign read: *Men Wanted, No Boys Need Apply, to Be Mustered Immediately.*

The soldier read it with ease.

The doctor chuckled. "I'm afraid you may have that memorized."

The young man grinned.

"Let him go." Matron Webb stood in the doorway. "He wants to leave, and his fellow soldiers need him. There's no rational reason to hold him back."

The doctor ignored the woman and asked the soldier how his appetite had been.

"Great!" Obviously, the soldier was going to answer all of the questions in a positive light.

"How will you get back to the front line?" The doctor asked.

He shrugged. "I'll find a way. Probably the train."

"You'll need someone to keep an eye on this," the doctor said.

Polly stepped toward the two. She'd been listening also. "Michael's working in the field hospital there," she reminded him.

"Oh, yes." The doctor turned toward her. "Lieutenant Michael Talbot."

The soldier put his hand to the back of his neck. "I don't know him."

"He joined a couple of weeks ago."

The soldier asked, a hint of sarcasm in his voice, "Where was he before that?"

"France," Polly answered. "Studying."

"La-di-da," the soldier said, but then he smiled.

"How was Michael's time there?" Dr. Talbot asked, his familiar tone reminding Therese that this man was Polly's cousin. "He was working on some new papermaking techniques, yes?"

"Yes," Polly replied, "from sources other than rags. He also helped create a new kind of photography paper."

"Interesting. He was in Lyon?"

"Yes. And Le Chambon, up on the Vivarais-Lignon Plateau."

The doctor's hazel eyes shone so vividly at the thought that the words popped out of Therese's mouth before she could stop them. "Have you been to France?"

He turned toward her. "Yes, several years ago." He reached out his hand. "I'm Dr. Alec Talbot, by the way."

Therese shook his hand quickly. "Therese Jennings. I'm a friend of Polly's."

"Jennings. Any relation to Willis Jennings, the writer? I believe he's from this area."

Willis Jennings was her father's name, but it took a moment for Therese to answer the question. She'd always thought of him as a teacher, but of course he had been a writer too. "Yes. He was my father."

"Was?"

She nodded. "He passed in July."

"My condolences." Dr. Talbot's expression fell, and he lowered his voice as he turned away from the soldier. "I met him a few years ago in Philadelphia, and I so enjoyed making his acquaintance. I was already familiar with his articles. What a blessing for you to have had a father of such high morals and intellect."

Therese nodded again and struggled to find her voice. "It was."

Polly began chatting with the soldier.

Dr. Talbot continued to speak in a subdued voice. "His thinking matched mine in many ways—right and wrong. Black and white."

Therese believed her father saw life in a much more nuanced way than that, but she didn't feel comfortable contradicting the doctor.

"Not only was he an ardent abolitionist, but I remember he also supported women's suffrage." Dr. Talbot smiled, and it seemed he did too. "I recall him mentioning a daughter, one who excelled at academics."

Therese's face grew warm.

He whispered, "Do you have a sister?"

She shook her head.

"Well, then," he said. "How delightful to meet the subject of a most enjoyable and memorable conversation. I'm honored." He smiled. "We'll talk more when we can. In the meantime, it's good to have you here, Miss Jennings. Thank you for your help."

"Of course," she said, raising her voice a little. "Thank you for coming all this way. Your work is greatly appreciated."

He dipped his head. "I'm grateful for your appreciation."

He retreated from the room, passing Matron at the doorway without saying a word. Therese and Polly continued with their work until they heard a commotion from the bottom of the stairs and someone called up, "We need help down here!"

Polly said, "Let's go." They both dropped their sponges into the basins and headed for the stairs.

Dr. Talbot was in the foyer. A wounded soldier was on a stretcher on the floor, and two soldiers were bringing in another on a stretcher. The afternoon sun shone through the open back door, making it hard to see the soldiers' faces. The one walking backwards turned around, and when he spoke she realized it was Michael.

Her heart started to race involuntarily, but then it lurched, remembering his newfound stance.

She wondered why he was here, as it seemed a long distance for him to bring the wounded, all the way from the vicinity of Petersburg. But then she noticed they were lieutenants. Polly had said this hospital was primarily for officers.

Michael's eyes lit up at the sight of her, but then he cast them down and began to speak to Dr. Talbot. "This one took shrapnel in the chest. He may have a collapsed lung."

"Michael!" Polly called out as she realized it was him.

"Michael?" Dr. Talbot echoed, looking surprised. "It's been so long, I didn't recognize you. I hear you've been off in France, working and learning with the Gillets?"

"That's right."

"Good to see you again. Though not under these circumstances. Let's catch up later." Dr. Talbot gestured toward the larger room to the left. "Get them in there. Nurses, go get more supplies—clean cloths, a basin of water, gauze, and bandages."

"We have three more wounded." Michael's uniform was covered with blood, though he didn't seem injured, so Therese assumed it wasn't his own. Thank goodness.

"Get them in here quickly," Dr. Talbot answered. As Therese and Polly hurried up the stairs, he called for orderlies to move the patients.

"Will we help with the wounded?" Therese felt light headed as she spoke.

"Probably," Polly said. "You can watch to see what's done so you can help next time."

"All right." Yes, all of this was far more intense than what she'd experienced nursing Father.

They worked on the wounded for the next three hours. Michael helped too, cutting off uniforms, cleaning out wounds, and dressing them. Polly seemed fascinated by the work and continually asked Dr. Talbot questions. He obliged her willingly, explaining what he was doing.

He and an orderly propped up the man with the collapsed lung so he could breathe. "Hopefully, the other lung isn't compromised," Dr. Talbot said.

Then he moved on to the next soldier. "This one will need surgery as soon as possible." The man's leg dangled at an odd angle. "Matron will need to assist me." He glanced at Polly. "Next time I'll have you do it. You'll soon be ready."

Polly nodded and seemed eager to take on more responsibility. Therese shivered, knowing she could never do anything like that.

As the time passed, Therese mostly just watched. She felt useless, and yet she knew she was learning through Dr. Talbot's explanations and what she observed. She hoped, in time, she'd make a good nurse.

Eventually, Michael helped move the men who didn't need surgery to the second floor, and Polly and Therese followed. Polly introduced him to Bucky, saying that Michael could give him a ride back.

"We're not taking the train?" Bucky asked.

"No," Michael said. "One of the tracks was bombed night before last." Therese couldn't imagine the railroad repair work that was constantly needed in war. "I came in a wagon."

Bucky whooped. "I'm fit as a fiddle and looking forward to the ride. Let's go."

"Not yet," Polly said. "Both of you need some supper."

The girls served bowls of bean soup and thin slices of bread without butter. After they finished, Therese helped clean up and carry the dishes out to the kitchen on trays. An hour later, exhausted and ready to go, she couldn't locate Polly. Finally, she found her on the loading dock of the building, in conversation with Michael and Dr. Talbot. They stopped in mid-sentence when she approached.

"I'm sorry to interrupt," she said, taking a step back.

"No, it's fine," Dr. Talbot replied. "Would you believe Michael and I were still in short breeches the last time we saw each other?"

Michael nodded. "A family reunion, up near Fredericksburg. The two of us stole a cake out of the kitchen house and made ourselves sick eating the entire thing behind the barn."

They all laughed, and then Dr. Talbot excused himself to get back to work.

"How's Warner?" Therese asked, turning to Michael.

"He's all right. I'll tell him I saw you."

"Thanks. Would you ask him to write Mother? As often as possible."

Michael frowned a little. "He's probably doing the best he can as it is, Therese. Paper is hard to come by. And energy…"

She nodded, realizing how she must have sounded. "Never mind. Just tell him hello and that I'm praying for him."

"I'll do that." Michael stepped toward the door. "Next time I come, I'm using this loading dock."

"Hopefully, there won't be a next time," Polly said.

"Unfortunately, there will," Michael answered.

Polly lowered her voice. "Do you wish you would have stayed, you know, over there?"

"No. I'm exactly where I should be. Doing my part for the cause of our country, to save our way of life. I should've come home a lot sooner than this."

Therese shuddered inside, again alarmed by Michael's shift in ideology. Surprisingly, Polly didn't seem bothered by it. Therese knew from numerous private conversations that her friend was against slavery, but, of course, under the circumstances, she wouldn't contradict Michael in public.

Polly led the way back into the building, followed by Therese and then Michael. Dr. Talbot stood in the foyer, speaking with Matron Webb. When he saw them, he ended their conversation and then stepped toward Therese.

"It was so good to meet you, Miss Jennings. I look forward to seeing you again soon." He smiled warmly, and Therese responded in kind. In just one afternoon and evening, she'd come to respect him immensely.

The girls took off their bloody aprons and deposited them in the hamper in the closet, collected their wraps, and headed to the door. "Do you have an escort?" the doctor called out.

Polly answered, "We'll be fine."

"I'll give you a lift," Michael said. Therese would have rather walked but didn't say so.

When they reached his wagon, Bucky sat on the bench.

"In the back, soldier," Michael told him, his voice light. "We're giving the ladies a ride home."

Bucky tipped his hat. "Yes, sir. Gladly." He scampered into the back.

Michael helped Polly up into the wagon and then Therese. By the light of the streetlamp she could see into his kind brown eyes, and he smiled slightly. Therese wondered if he had any idea how disappointed she was in him.

Michael stopped at the Galloways' townhouse first and helped Therese down. She said goodbye, but then he fell in step beside her as she started toward the row house.

"You have a long journey ahead of you, Michael. There's no need to walk me to the door."

"Of course there is." Again his voice was light and easy. "My mother would be mortified if I didn't treat you like the lady you are, the way she taught me to treat all women."

Therese couldn't help but wish he'd honor what her father had taught him too. Once they reached the porch, she quickly told him goodbye.

"Stay safe," he said to her.

She nodded, but it was a funny thing for him to say, considering he was the one going off to the front line and she was simply teaching three little girls—and learning to take care of the wounded.

The truth was she didn't feel very safe, though her new life didn't feel scary either. It felt exhilarating, and so did the idea of getting to know Dr. Talbot better.

Chapter Nine

Nicole

We sat at Nana's table in the sunroom going through the old family photos and having such a good time that when Aunt Cissy said she needed to leave, I realized I'd nearly forgotten what I'd come there for.

"Just one last thing," she told us, reaching into the bottom of the box and pulling out a small stack of papers. "I stuck copies of these in here too. They're little love notes that Therese's husband wrote to her over the course of their life together."

"Love letters?" I asked.

"Not letters. Just little notes. He would leave them for her to find." Sliding her glasses up her nose, she read the top one aloud. "'On the coldest of winter days, 'tis your smile that keeps me warm.'"

"Oh, how sweet," Nana said.

"They really are. You'll enjoy reading through them." Aunt Cissy returned the pile to the box, added in the rest of the pictures, and then said she really, really had to get going. "Don't worry about returning anything. As I said, these are extra copies."

We rose, and I gave her a goodbye peck on the cheek.

"Okay if I stick around a little longer?" I asked Nana.

"Of course. Be right back."

Grateful for a few minutes to clear my head, I practiced how I was going to say what I'd come here to say. By the time Nana returned from seeing Aunt Cissy to the door, I had it all worked out.

"Something to drink, dear?" she asked, but before I could reply, she called out to the cook to bring us two coffees.

"After that," I said in a low voice, "maybe you could tell her to take off for a while? We need to talk. In private."

Looking curious, Nana nodded and gestured toward the sitting area, so we resettled there and made small talk until we had our cups and the woman had been sent out on some errand.

"Is everything all right?" Nana asked once we were alone. "You haven't crashed the new car, have you?"

I was so surprised by the question I actually laughed. "No, of course not."

"Good. Well, then. What is it? By the look on your face, it's no small matter."

I set down my coffee, took a deep breath, and forced myself to begin. I started by saying how, over the past year and a half, I'd learned a lot of important things about myself, including the fact that I was a habitual liar. "I used to lie sometimes even when the truth would've done just as well. It's a habit I got into when I was using, but I've been working really hard to change."

"That's wonderful, dear. So is this one of those step things?"

"Step things?"

"You know, the twelve steps? Isn't one of them about making amends or something?"

I sat back, running a hand through my hair. "Yes, but this isn't a step thing. It's a...family thing. Specifically, a Granddad thing." Swallowing hard, I met Nana's eyes as I continued. "I have a secret I've been keeping for most of my life. But if I want to keep healing and growing, I can't keep this secret any longer. The time has come for me to share it—with you first, but then with others too."

"I agree. The truth is always best, even when it's difficult."

"Exactly."

"So what is it that you need to confess, dear? I'm sure there's nothing you could've done to your grandfather that would've made him love you any less."

My eyes widened. "No, Nana, it's not something I did to him. It's something I saw him do. In June of 1995 when I was six years old."

Pulse surging, I trained my eyes on the plush Turkish rug and kept going.

"The Thursday of that year's family reunion, a few hours before it started, you sent Granddad on some errands in town, and he let me ride along. While we were out, we ran into someone who seemed to know him." I swallowed hard, remembering the scene as if it had happened yesterday. "It was a man, and he was angry. The two of us were just coming out of the florist's, and Granddad was carrying a big flower arrangement, so his hands were full. I think if they hadn't been, the guy might even have punched him. He was that mad."

"Who was it?"

"I didn't know. I'd never seen him before. But he started yelling at Granddad, right there in the parking lot, saying things like, 'You're lying to me!' and 'You're trying to trick me!' and 'You're in cahoots together!' Granddad told him to calm down, and then he put the flowers in the car, pulled out some money, and handed it to me. We were in that strip mall with the ice cream parlor, and he told me to go get myself whatever I wanted and he'd be there in a minute. So I did. But the guy started yelling again before I even got inside."

I glanced at Nana, but she was simply sitting there, her hands clasped in her lap as she waited for me to get to the point. She probably thought it had been one of Granddad's golfing buddies, mad about a game, or a business acquaintance, angry for having been bested in some deal. I continued.

"I sat inside the ice cream parlor and ate my cone—a double scoop—and I was nearly finished with it by the time Granddad finally showed up. I remember thinking he seemed really upset, and he didn't even want any ice cream for himself. On the drive home, I asked him what that man was so angry about. I don't remember his answer, but it wasn't any sort of explanation. I think he just said the guy was confused but not to worry because he was leaving town and wouldn't bother us any-more. I didn't think about it again the rest of the day."

Feeling antsy, I stood and moved over to the wall of windows and looked out at the rolling landscape of the estate. It was so beautiful here, so peaceful, but it had also been a place of tremendous shock and pain.

"The reunion started that evening with dinner, and I was happy to be with the cousins. I think the four of us played for hours. We played all the next day too, running around at the reunion and enjoying the activities. Then on Saturday, we decided to take a hike in the woods next door to our favorite place, the old cabin where we liked to play house." Two squirrels scampered from a tree and chased each other for a moment before disappearing up another. "But that was the year of the incident. The dead body and the police and everything. It was all so traumatic, such a shock, I could barely process it. And I was only six."

"Yes, so young," Nana murmured.

"The aftermath is such a blur. There was a lot of confusion, but I do remember realizing that no one believed us. I was so surprised that I went over to Granddad to tell him an important part so that at least he would know we were telling the truth. Instead, as soon as I said it, he got really mad. He picked me up and carried me into the house and set me down in the office and shut the door. Then he made me prom-ise I would never repeat it again to anyone else, ever. Not my sister, not our parents, not the police. No one. 'This will be our little secret,' he told me. 'You have to take this to the grave, Nicole. Promise me you'll never tell a soul what you just told me.' And so I promised. And I kept that promise...until now."

Turning, I looked at my grandmother's face, not sure what to expect. Skepticism? Anger? Dismay? But she might as well have been a statue for all the emotion she was exhibiting.

"And what exactly did you promise not to share?" she asked stiffly.

"That the man in the cabin, the one who'd been murdered? He was the same man Granddad had argued with in town two days before."

That night, when I shared the secret with Maddee, she was furious—not at me but at our grandfather. She ranted around her little apartment for ten minutes, saying things like, "You were only six years old! How dare a grown man ask a little girl to keep a secret like that, especially after what we'd been through?"

I let her rant, taking delight in her reaction. The things she was saying were true, but I'd never let myself think them before, much less utter them aloud. With every exclamation, I could feel little pieces of myself healing inside. I don't think she had any idea how much her righteous indignation on my behalf was helping me.

"And then there's Nana!" she cried, returning to the couch and plopping down across from me. "What did she say again when you told her?"

I tilted my head back against the cushion and closed my eyes. "She said, 'All right, then. I only ask one favor, that you don't report this to Detective Ortiz until after I've had a chance to speak with my lawyer.'"

"That was it? No, 'You poor thing,' no 'I'm so sorry he did that to you.' None of that?"

"Nope. She got up from the couch, told me to take the box of pictures, and walked me to the door. 'I'll speak with him in the morning, and then you can do whatever you feel compelled to do. I won't stop you.'"

"'I won't stop you?' Who says that?"

I opened my eyes and peered at my sister. "Do you think she thinks..." Unable to say the words, my voice trailed off.

"Thinks what? That Granddad had something to do with..." She couldn't quite get them out either.

We grew silent for a long moment.

"There's no way Granddad killed Taavi Koenig," I said finally, refuting the fear that had plagued me for years. "No way."

"Not even in self-defense? You said the man was really mad when y'all saw him in town on Thursday afternoon. What if Granddad arranged to meet at the cabin on Saturday morning so they could talk, and the guy attacked him?"

"Well, first of all, why would he choose to have a conversation there? The place was totally ramshackle even then, not to mention way out in the woods. If Granddad needed to speak with the guy in private, he would've just brought him to his office."

"Maybe he didn't want anyone to see them together."

"Oh, right. Like he and Granddad could've slipped into the woods unnoticed during a Talbot reunion? Are you kidding? With two hundred and something people milling around on the lawn? No. I don't buy it."

"Well, there are other ways to get to the cabin, you know."

"There are?"

"Sure. There's a path in from the other side. And another one that comes up from the river. How do you think the body got removed without anyone seeing? They took it out some other way."

Of course they did. I felt dumb for never having realized that before.

"So what do you think any of this means?" Maddee asked. "Do you have a theory? I know you must've thought a lot about it over the years."

I sat up and leaned forward, elbows on knees, and shook my head. "Um, I spent years specifically not thinking about it. I buried it however I could, using whatever I could."

Maddee didn't respond, and when I glanced at her a minute later, I was surprised to see tears running down her cheeks.

"I'm so sorry," she whispered, wiping at her face with one sleeve. "So, so sorry he did this to you."

I wanted to wave it off, to say it was no big deal. Instead, I swallowed back tears of my own and simply reached out, whispered a gruff thanks, and took my sister's hand.

The next morning, I awoke feeling about a hundred pounds lighter than I had in years. After Maddee and I talked the night before, we'd called Renee and Danielle and told them everything. I guess the truth really does set you free.

My first day on the job went well, even though the equine therapy department was closed on Tuesdays. There was still plenty to get done, and it felt good to work hard. School was so brain-centric and sedentary, I'd forgotten how nice it was just to focus on physical tasks. Better yet, a summer of this much lugging and lifting and walking would totally keep me in shape for volleyball and then some.

Fortunately, my coworkers all seemed real friendly, and I had some nice moments with the horses as I tended to them. One, a chestnut Arabian named Hutch, nickered every time he saw me. I decided I could live with working here.

I never ran into Tattoo Cowboy even once, thank goodness, though I found myself looking around for him now and then. Maybe we really would make it through the summer without much interaction—which was a good thing, I reminded myself sternly.

That theory was blown by noon of the next day, however, as I'd already encountered the guy about ten times. Not only was he even hotter than I remembered—looking especially buff in black hat, black T-shirt, and jeans—he was also apparently the boss. Though I didn't work directly under him, it seemed to me that he was pretty much in charge of everyone here. People weren't exactly chummy with him, but they did seem to respect him.

He was friendly enough in return—to everyone except me. First thing that morning, he'd come through and introduced himself to all the newbies as Nate Harrison, but when I responded, "Nicole Talbot, nice to meet you," he hesitated.

"Nicole Talbot. You're the intern?"

"Yep. That's me."

For some reason, his smile faded. After an awkward moment's hesitation, he simply moved on to the next person. Odd. Did he have something against interns or equine therapy?

I thought I might find out when I headed over to the therapy area after lunch to observe my first session and then assist with several others. But between the work and all the people who were around, I never had a chance to chat with the therapist one-on-one. As before, she was a woman of few words, though I could tell she really knew what she was doing with the clients. Over the course of the afternoon, we saw a nice variety—a little girl with anxiety issues, a teenager who struggled with anger management, two different veterans with PTSD, and even an older woman with dementia. In almost every case, I was surprised to find that these people never actually *rode* the horses as part of their therapy. Instead, they worked with them from the ground.

My favorite was the teen boy, who was given a lead rope and told to go get one of the horses and bring it back. He headed out into the field with attitude to spare, his movements aggressive, his demeanor the very opposite of what a horse might respond to. For fifteen minutes the kid tried everything from yelling at the animals to chasing them to standing still and then pouncing as they drew closer. Nothing worked. I thought the therapist might intervene at some point, but instead she just kept watching until he finally seemed to get that no animal was going to respond favorably to that kind of behavior. Not a horse—and not a person either. As the boy finally calmed down, he changed his technique and eventually managed to lure one of the animals over with sweet words and a gentle touch. Success at last. As he clipped the rope to his equine buddy's halter and easily led him back toward us, the kid was beaming from ear to ear.

At the end of the day, once I'd showered and changed, I headed straight to the police station, where I was to meet up with Maddee and go to the appointment she'd arranged for us. On the way, I found myself growing terribly nervous about the fact that I'd withheld this information for so long. I even wondered if I might be hit with some sort of obstruction charge. I hoped not, considering that I'd only been six years old when it happened.

As it turned out, I needn't have worried. Once we were settled in with the detective, the first thing she said to us was that she already knew the big news, thanks to a visit from our grandmother and her lawyer.

Maddee and I looked at each other, astounded.

"She told you about what happened?" I asked. "About Taavi Koenig arguing with my grandfather two days before the guy ended up getting murdered?"

"Yes. Your grandmother said she knew I would need to speak with you directly, but that she wanted to tell me about it herself, in person, beforehand."

"Why?"

Ortiz shrugged. "I think she was worried about how it might come across and wanted to vouch for your grandfather's character before I drew...certain conclusions."

Wow. My grandmother was nothing if not surprising. Between the new car and this shocker, the woman had thrown me two massive curveballs in one week. The first one was good of course, but the second one...well, I wasn't sure. I didn't know what to think, and from the expression on my sister's face, neither did she.

Despite having heard it from Nana, Detective Ortiz had me go through the whole story myself several times. The first time through, she just listened, but as we went over it again, and then again, she would stop to ask me questions, weird ones about various details, some of which I could remember, but most of which I could not. By the time I was finished, it almost felt as though I'd relived it all.

After that, Ortiz put away her notes in what I assumed was the case file, though it was lot fatter than it had been the last time I saw it a year and a half ago.

"I've been in touch with the Koenigs," she said, shifting gears, "because this news begets new questions. Unfortunately, neither the victim's wife nor his kids could shed any light on the encounter between the two men."

"Big surprise there," Maddee said, and then she turned to me to explain. "By the time Taavi disappeared, his family had completely divorced themselves from his obsession with the illuminated manuscript. If he told them anything about what he was doing or where he was going, they don't remember it. The more anxious he became, the less they wanted anything to do with it."

"Well, they're certainly interested now," Ortiz said, "and they have been ever since they learned of his fate."

I nodded, remembering how Maddee had gotten Miss Vida to track down the name and identity of the victim based on the DNA report of the blood found in the cabin. That had all happened when I was living with Maddee the last time, between my accident and rehab.

"In fact," Ortiz continued, "it sounds like Gabe might be coming here again."

"Gabe?" I asked.

Maddee nodded "Whenever there's been a new development in the case, Taavi's son Gabe has dropped everything and come running."

"All the way from Cleveland? Why? What does he want?"

"He's just frustrated at the lack of progress," Ortiz answered. "I think it helps him to feel more involved if he's able to see things firsthand. If he does come this time, he'll probably want to speak with you directly, Nicole, to hear the story of what happened from your point of view. May I put him in touch with you if he does?"

"I don't know. Is that a good idea?" I looked from her to my sister.

"He's kind of a hothead, but he's all right," Maddee offered. "You can't help but feel sorry for him. He spent twenty years wondering where his father went and why he never came back. Once he learned that the man's life ended shortly after he disappeared—and that he was murdered no less, not to mention his body subsequently vanished—he's been desperate for more answers. You can't blame him."

"It's up to you whether you'd want to meet with Gabe or not," Ortiz said. "There's no pressure if you feel uncomfortable with it. And he may not come. You never know."

"If he shows up, you can give him my number," I said. "I'll talk to him if it'll help him feel better."

"All right." Ortiz placed both hands atop the thick stack of papers and announced that she was now going to share some information with us, information that had previously been withheld.

"If I give you some additional facts," she explained, looking at me, "there's always a chance you might remember more from that time."

Swallowing hard, I glanced at Maddee and then gave the detective a nod. "Okay. Let's hear it."

The woman extracted several official-looking documents from the file, reports of some kind but with a lot of words crossed out in thick black marker. After glancing through them for a moment, she flipped them around and placed them on the desk in front of us.

Leaning forward, I started to read but was stopped by the header across the top. It featured a logo, a gold badge with an eagle on it, followed by the words *United States Secret Service*.

Chapter Ten
Nicole

"Wait, what?" My head jerked up in surprise. "Secret Service? What is this?"

Suddenly, I understood why Nana's knee-jerk response was usually to call a lawyer. Things could come out of the blue and just smack you upside the head without any warning!

"The United States Secret Service?" Maddee repeated. "The guys who protect the president?"

Ortiz nodded. "They do protection, yes, but they're also the ones in charge of financial crimes, such as fraud, securities, and counterfeiting. They came into the picture once we tracked down Taavi's car to a chop shop owned by a known syndicate. That changed the parameters of the investigation and led us to a federal case that was being worked at that time. We were able to obtain some information, though much of it has been so redacted that it's not all that helpful for our purposes."

Maddee and I looked down at the pages and saw immediately what she was talking about. On some, the thick black lines covered so much text that there was barely a full sentence. Other pages had been left alone, however, including the one on top, which was a summary of the contents. It identified the subject of the documents as "Operation

Paper Trail," the dates of investigation as March 1992 to September 2004, and the primary crime as counterfeiting.

Counterfeiting?

Next came a summary of the case that ran for a good fifteen pages, followed by a variety of memos, emails, letters, reports, and more. The summary was dry and detailed, so I started skimming through, searching for the words "Talbot" and "Koenig" but spotting neither. I assumed if the names were there, they were probably among the parts that had been blacked out.

"Was Taavi a Secret Service agent killed in the line of duty?" Maddee asked, ever the innocent optimist. I'd been wondering the opposite. Considering he was in such dire financial straits, my thought was that he'd become involved with the counterfeiters somehow and ended up getting killed for it.

"No, Taavi wasn't with the Secret Service," Ortiz replied. Then, as if reading my mind, she added, "Nor was he involved with the counterfeiters as far as we can tell."

"What about our grandfather?" I asked. Was it possible that he had been a Secret Service agent?

"His situation is a little more...complicated."

Maddee and I shared a concerned glance as Ortiz continued.

"I'll try and explain the information we were able to glean from all of this, but it needs a bit of explanation first. Do you have any money on you? Just a paper bill, any denomination."

Maddee took a ten from her wallet and held it out.

"No, you keep it. Touch it. Run your fingers over it and rub it and pinch it and tell me what it feels like."

My sister and I did as instructed, feeling a little silly.

"I don't know," Maddee said finally. "It just feels like money to me."

"Me too."

"Exactly," Ortiz said. "It feels like money because the paper that money is printed on is unlike any other paper in the world. Only money feels like money, if that makes any sense."

We both nodded as Maddee returned the bill to her wallet.

"Money has become a lot more high tech, starting as far back as

1996," Ortiz continued, "but prior to that, the biggest hurdle facing any aspiring counterfeiter was simply how to replicate the paper money is printed on."

She went on to say how, unlike other paper, which was made of cellulose from trees, the paper for money, called rag paper, was made from a blend of cotton and linen fibers. "The formula is well known among papermakers and law enforcement officials. In fact, the fastest way to get busted for counterfeiting is to try and place an order for rag paper that's seventy-five percent cotton and twenty-five percent linen. Most papermakers won't even produce it because they know how it could be used."

She explained that making matters more complicated for counterfeiters were two additional features. The paper for money contained a unique mix of tiny blue and red fibers, and that during the printing process the paper would get squeezed with thousands of pounds of pressure. "That's what makes new bills so thin and crisp."

Ortiz took a deep breath and then dove into more of an explanation. In 1992, she said, a certain type of counterfeit bill began turning up in various places around the country, so the Secret Service began looking into it. "What they would ultimately find by the end of what would become a nine-year investigation was a global operation that involved a papermaker in Switzerland, a printer in Virginia, and distributors in five states plus Peru, Russia, and China. The investigation was considered a success, numerous arrests were made, and millions in fake bills were seized."

I shot Maddee another look. Was this for real?

"The syndicate was also deeply impacted," Ortiz continued, "with a number of its chief players coming under indictment for a wide variety of related crimes."

"So what part of all this ties in with our situation?" I asked. The story seemed over the top, and I couldn't help but wonder when Ortiz would get to the point.

She took back the documents, flipped to one in particular, and read a section aloud, my pulse surging when I realized what it said, that surveillance was being conducted at Talbot Paper and Printing as well as at the Talbot home on Willow Lane, for a period in June and July 1995, including the date that Taavi was murdered.

Maddee gasped. "Why would they have been surveilling our grandfather's home and business?"

Ortiz said, "That's the problem. There's so much redacted that we can't be sure. My assumption is that your grandfather was under suspicion for some sort of involvement with the counterfeiters, though he was never arrested or charged, so either he got away with it or he was exonerated in the end."

"It has to be the latter," Maddee said.

"Unfortunately, I tend to think it was the former," Ortiz replied. "Take a look at this."

She flipped through the pages until she came to a receipt for a "plate presser" purchased by Talbot Paper and Printing from the manufacturer, and a second receipt for the same piece of equipment sold to a company called Greenaway Manufacturing just a week later.

"As it turned out, Greenaway Manufacturing was a shell corporation." She pointed to the details on the first receipt, where it referred to "twenty-ton capacity." "Twenty tons is the exact amount of pressure applied to money during the printing process."

"What exactly are you saying?" Maddee asked.

"I think your grandfather bought this machine through his company and then sold it to the counterfeiters."

"Why?" Maddee asked.

"Because a purchase like that would raise red flags if just anybody tried it. But a longstanding customer and international paper and printing company could order such a thing as a matter of course."

Maddee sounded as dumbfounded as I felt. "So you think our grandfather supplied machinery to counterfeiters so they could print fake money?"

"Purely a guess." Ortiz closed the file. "I'm sorry, girls. I'd like to give the man the benefit of the doubt, but between the evidence we already had and the new information given to me by your grandmother yesterday, it's not looking good."

I finally found my voice. "It was just an argument in a parking lot. Why would that implicate him in any of this?"

Ortiz shook her head. "No, I'm talking about the other thing your grandmother told me. The phone call."

I squeaked. "The phone call?"

"Yes." She glanced from me to Maddee and sighed. "Looks like you haven't heard about this." She shifted uncomfortably. "After your grandmother told me about your revelation, Nicole, she made an admission of her own."

Ortiz explained that on the day of the murder, when the four of us girls came out of the woods screaming about a dead body, Granddad was the one who went to call the police. Nana followed after him, but he must not have realized she was there because when he got to the phone, he made another call first to someone else before he called the cops.

"W-what?" I stuttered. "To whom? Why?"

Ortiz shook her head. "All we know is what he said."

"Which was?"

Ortiz leaned forward. "'We have a big problem here. You need to take care of it. Fast.'"

I was still in a daze by the time we got home. Maddee and I found parking places just a few cars apart and then headed to the carriage house together. We were starting up the walkway when we heard odd, muffled sounds coming from the direction of Miss Vida's backyard. Pausing to look, I noticed that there seemed to be an odd glow emanating from there as well. Not wanting to snoop but needing to make sure the woman was all right, we stepped to the fence and called out to her.

"Girls? Is that you?" she responded excitedly. "Come on in. Come see!"

We swung open the gate and stepped into her yard to find, in the dim glow of twinkle lights strung along the fence, Miss Vida and her new beau, Lev, sitting in a steaming hot tub.

"What?" we both cried in unison, moving closer.

"Isn't it wonderful? It was Lev's idea. They just installed it today."

We were both speechless. For a few moments, the only sounds were the gurgle of bubbles from the tub and the slurp of Lev eating a spoonful of ice cream Miss Vida was feeding him. Good grief.

"Would you like to join us?" she asked.

"No," we both said, a little too quickly.

"Thanks, though," Maddee added.

"Yeah, maybe next time." I had to stifle a laugh.

"Well, feel free to use it whenever you'd like. You may as well take advantage of it."

"Thanks," we said in unison.

"And don't be concerned if you hear loud noises coming from back here," she told us. Maddee's cheeks were already bright red when, oblivious, the older woman added, "I made sure to get one big enough for my women's group, and when we're together we really cause a ruckus."

I laughed, both at my sister's misconception and at the thought of a babbling pool of *bubbes*.

Miss Vida went on about the group for a bit, saying how they'd finally picked the date for their summer getaway, to which Maddee replied that that was the same weekend as this year's Talbot family reunion.

"Speaking of," Lev said, "how's the investigation going?"

"About the same," I said quickly before Maddee could respond. For some reason, I didn't want this guy to know our business even if he would probably hear about it some other way sooner or later.

"No new developments?" he asked. Miss Vida put down the ice cream and leaned forward against the edge of the hot tub, interested to hear as well. Maddee and I glanced at each other.

"You know how these things work. Even new developments don't necessarily lead to answers," Maddee said, deftly evading the question. "We still don't know what happened out in that cabin."

"Aw, don't lose hope, girls," Miss Vida said. "That detective is a sharp cookie. She'll figure it all out one of these days."

We thanked her and made a quick exit, not speaking again until we were safely inside the carriage house.

"Is it just me," I asked in a low voice, "or does something about that guy bother you?"

Maddee shrugged, though I could tell she was trying to be nice.

"Why is he so intrusive?" I pressed.

"Probably because he knew Granddad. Maybe he feels bad for our family and wants to keep tabs on things."

I thought about that as I moved into the living room to put down my stuff. Maddee headed to the spiral staircase but paused before going up. "To be honest, I have had one concern."

"Yeah?"

"I just...well, I hope he's not after Miss Vida for her money."

"Ah," I replied, nodding. "That crossed my mind too the day I first met him."

"I don't know anything about his financial situation, and it's not as if Miss Vida's a multimillionaire, but she's comfortable. And she has that beautiful home too. Now here he is, talking her into buying a hot tub...I just hope she's being careful."

Maddee continued up the stairs, but as she went I had a feeling we were both thinking the same thing. If our sweet grandfather could've been a bad guy, then anyone could.

CHAPTER ELEVEN
Nicole

*W*e ambushed Nana the very next night, showing up at her house unannounced at a time we knew she would have just finished her dinner. Sure enough, we found her in the living room, sipping tea, but then we saw that she had a visitor, a rather short, stout, balding man I didn't recognize but whom Maddee greeted warmly.

"Nicole, this is Dr. Harold Underwood," she said, turning toward me.

I knew the name. This was the expert in diasporas who had authenticated Granddad's priceless Huguenot pamphlet before it was donated to the Smithsonian. I stepped forward and shook the guy's hand. He told me to call him Harold.

Nana seemed nervous that we were there, which had been the point. We'd wanted to hear the full story straight from her and had known there would be a greater chance of that happening if we caught her off guard. Now that we saw she wasn't alone, however, I feared this visit would be a bust.

Instead, much to my relief, as soon as Maddee and I were plied with steaming cups of tea and a plate of sweet little treats, Nana got right to the point despite the presence of a guest.

"I assume you've spoken with Detective Ortiz?" she asked, glancing from me to Maddee.

We nodded.

"So now you have questions for me." Suddenly, she looked very tired. With a heavy sigh, she set down her teacup and seemed to sink into her chair.

"Don't judge your grandmother too harshly, girls," Harold said. "Sounds like she wasn't the only one withholding information from that time."

"Oh, yeah?" I snapped, unable to stop myself. "I was a traumatized six-year-old child who had just witnessed a horrific crime scene. Nana was a grown woman who protected her husband at the cost of her four granddaughters!"

"Nicole," Maddee scolded softly.

"I understand why you're angry, and I am sorry," Nana said. "But bear in mind that I had no idea you had seen that man with your grandfather two days before. Still, I assure you, the secret I've kept all these years weighed as heavily on me as yours did on you."

I gave a sarcastic laugh and was about to lash out again when I felt Maddee's hand on my knee, giving it a squeeze.

"Tell us everything," Maddee said to Nana instead. "From the very beginning."

And so, as I held my tongue, Nana launched into her story, describing the same sequence of events we'd learned from Ortiz except with additional details such as how quickly Granddad was walking as he strode across the lawn toward the house and how, when she finally caught up with him, she was surprised to see he'd taken the time to go all the way to his office rather than make the call from the phone in the mudroom. At the office, she opened the door without knocking and stepped inside. He was standing at the front of the desk with his back to her, leaning forward and dialing the first of his two phone calls.

She overheard that one, and then once he was on with the police, she left the room and went to get some blankets for the children, who couldn't stop shivering.

"We weren't cold, Nana. We were shaking from *terror*," I said, unable to keep the anger from my voice.

"Well, dear, I didn't know what else to do. They always have blankets on TV shows. They talk about not allowing the person to go into shock and all that. It was the only thing I could think of."

"Here's something you could've done," I said. "You could've confronted Granddad about what you overheard."

"Frankly, I didn't realize the implications of it until later, when the police went out there and came back, and then everything took such an odd turn. First, the police said there was nothing there. Then you girls insisted on going back with your fathers. Then you all returned looking even more shocked than before."

Turning to Harold, Maddee explained. "Whoever cleaned up the crime scene and took the body had staged things inside the cabin to look like it had all been a figment of our imaginations. Instead of a dead body and a knife and blood, they'd left behind a pile of blankets with a stick poking out of them and a puddle of rainwater on the floor."

"Yes, I'd heard that part before." His brows furrowed in concern.

"When the police finally left and your fathers all agreed you girls hadn't seen what you thought you had," Nana continued, "only then did I remember that first phone call. I asked Douglas about it, but he acted as if it were nothing unusual. He said he'd called law enforcement and that was that. I let it go, thinking—I guess *hoping* would be more like it—that he was telling me the truth. As the years passed and nothing ever came of it, I rarely thought of it again—until two years ago, when you girls showed up the morning after that year's reunion announcing that you'd spent the night testing the cabin for blood and then giving statements at the police station."

"I remember your face when we told you that," I interjected. "You looked dumbfounded."

"I was."

"You accused us of 'blindsiding' you, and then you excused yourself and went upstairs to call your lawyer." To Maddee, I added, "We should've known then there was something Nana wasn't telling us."

"Nicole." Maddee gave me a warning look, so I didn't say any more. I knew I was pushing things, but I was just so angry I couldn't help it.

The four of us shared an awkward moment of silence, which was broken by my phone ringing from my pocket. Excusing myself, I moved into the hall, pulled it out, and checked the screen, but it wasn't a number I knew. I decided to answer anyway.

To my surprise, it was Gabe Koenig, the son of the murder victim and the man Ortiz had said might show up wanting to talk with us. Sure enough, he was in town asking if I would be willing to meet with him now. He suggested a coffeehouse off of I-195, but I invited him to come here instead, without even checking with Nana first. I gave him the address, and he said he could be here in "twenty minutes at the most."

When I returned to the room, I saw that the conversation had moved to far less contentious ground and was now focused on Harold's interest in diasporas.

"Do you have a collection of your own," Maddee asked, "or do you just evaluate items for other collectors?"

He smiled shyly. "Oh, I'm a collector too. I have been for years. In fact, I'd have given anything to buy that Huguenot pamphlet from your grandfather—not that I could've afforded it, but even if I could have, his answer would've been no. Douglas was dead set on giving it to the Smithsonian."

"What sorts of things are in your collection?" Maddee asked.

Harold's eyes sparkled as he listed all sorts of documents as well as the odd item, such as a Beothuk hide scraper from Newfoundland and a brick thrown by passengers of the refugee ship *Komagata Maru* when it was turned away from Canada.

Back in my seat on the couch, I only half listened, reserving my other ear for the sound of Gabe's arrival.

Still, Harold was an interesting guy, and I was starting to feel guilty for how I'd jumped down his throat earlier—especially once he shared with us the sad tale of his own experience with diaspora. He said his parents had been missionaries to Rhodesia back in the '60s and '70s, but that during the Rhodesian Bush War, when he was just eight years old, he saw them gunned down by ZANLA guerrillas, leaving him and his little brother all alone. The two boys managed to escape to Mozambique and were eventually taken in by relatives in Baltimore.

"I suppose that's how I ended up specializing in documents relating to diaspora," he concluded, "because of what I'd been through in my own life."

"That's so sad," I blurted out, the first words I'd said since returning from my phone call.

He nodded. "Sadder for my younger brother, who didn't fare so well. He's a truly gifted artist, but he went through so much at such a young age that I can't really blame him for how he turned out."

"Turned out?" I asked.

He shrugged. "At some point in his life, he headed down the wrong track, and things deteriorated from there, as you know."

Maddee glanced at Nana then back at him. "Did we miss something? Who is your brother?"

Harold's eyes widened. "I'm sorry. I thought the detective would have told you that part. She told your grandmother."

"That's why I asked Harold here tonight," Nana added, "to see if he could shed any light on your grandfather's involvement with the counterfeiting operation back then."

Maddee and I both sat there stunned, listening as Harold explained further, saying that his brother was currently serving time in prison for his part as a counterfeiter.

"His job was to engrave the plates from which they printed the money," Harold added. "When all was said and done, he was one of the ones who ended up getting arrested, tried, and convicted."

I was so confused. "Wait. I don't understand. I thought your connection to this case had to do with Taavi Koenig. Didn't Granddad refer him to you, and then he contacted you to help him find the old illuminated manuscript?"

"He did."

"So it's just a coincidence that your own brother was involved in the counterfeiting operation being investigated by the Secret Service at that same time?"

Harold shook his head. "No. As I was about to explain to your grandmother when you two arrived, back in 1996, my brother came to me and asked for a favor. He was in need of a certain piece of equipment that could only be bought through a printing company, but he didn't know where to start." Harold explained that because he dealt with documents and papers all the time, his brother thought he might have some contacts in the industry, someone he could recommend. "I told him yes, that I'd just recently been speaking with Douglas Talbot of Talbot Paper and Printing about a lost illuminated manuscript. I said Talbot was a good man and that he should start there."

Folding his hands, Harold continued. "Once he heard that, he asked if I'd be willing to request the machinery on his behalf because Douglas might sell it to me at a lower price given our prior dealings. Not realizing the significance of the machine in question, I agreed to try. I came down and met with Douglas and made the request. Though he seemed rather nervous about it, he complied. Maybe he suspected what the machine would be used for, maybe not, I don't know. But I sure didn't."

Harold told us he arranged for the purchase and saw that it was paid for and delivered within a few weeks, but then he thought nothing more about it until 2004 when federal agents showed up at his door.

"They arrested you?" Maddee cried.

He leaned forward. "Not exactly. They brought me in for questioning." He added that they were rounding up everyone connected with the counterfeiting ring. That was the first he'd heard of it, but it didn't take long for him to figure out what was going on. His little brother had been mixed up with the wrong people for a long time, and he'd tricked Harold into doing something illegal on his behalf.

"Well, buying the machine wasn't illegal, per se," he said. "It's just that the enterprise in general was illegal, and he dragged me into it without my even realizing it."

"Were you charged?" I asked, dismayed at the thought of this help-less little man in prison.

Harold shook his head. "It was obvious to the authorities that I'd been duped. I was an ignorant fool who had allowed myself to be tricked by my own brother. At least they understood the situation for what it really was and let me go in the end."

We were all quiet for a moment.

"So, Nana," Maddee said, "was Granddad taken in for question-ing too?"

"Not that I know of," she replied, seeming startled at the thought. "Then again, there were obviously a lot of things about your grand-father I didn't know. Whether he was or not, he was never charged with any crime. Even the detective will tell you that."

The ring of the doorbell interrupted us. I admitted to all of them that would be Gabe Koenig, son of the murder victim, who had called a while ago.

"You asked him here?" Nana whispered, obviously not very happy about it.

"Why not? Seems like this is the week to lay everything out on the table. It can't hurt to answer his questions—or to ask him a few of our own."

Our visit with Gabe Koenig ended up being fairly uneventful, espe-cially compared to the time we'd spent thus far with Harold Under-wood. A tall, slim fellow who looked to be in his early forties, Gabe had an intense, curious sort of demeanor that reminded me of a ferret or a meerkat. He seemed uncomfortable to be in Nana's home, but to his credit he settled in and accepted an offer of tea and got to the point rather quickly.

"I'm here for answers—or at least as many as you can give. I'm sorry for barging in like this, but as you can imagine, every time there's a new development in my father's case, I get my hopes up again. If you don't mind, I'd just like to hear straight from the two of you the new information you told the detective this week about what happened back then." He looked first at Nana and then at me.

There wasn't much to say beyond the basics, though I was glad to see that the more times I went through this with someone, the easier it was to talk about it. Nana seemed far less comfortable, but at least she did as asked, running through the same detailed version she'd given us earlier. When we were both finished, he simply nodded and thanked us, though I could see the disappointment in his eyes, and I knew he'd been yearning for more than what we'd been able to give.

Nana seemed a bit overcome by the discussion and excused herself to make a fresh pot of tea. As she headed for the kitchen, I wondered if she even knew how. Most of the time, she had people to do that sort of thing for her.

"I'd like to hear the story from your side, if you don't mind," I said, returning my attention to Gabe. I added that I'd been off at school and was coming in a little late to the game.

"Sure," he replied, seeming relieved to be asked. He began his own tale, and it was interesting to hear it from the point of view of a troubled nineteen-year-old whose father simply disappeared off the face of the earth. Gabe talked about how he'd pleaded with his mother back then to file a missing persons report, but she wasn't having any of it. "'Your father chose to leave us high and dry, and I'm not about to send any cops chasing after him. He wants out of here? Fine. Good riddance.' She was bitter and angry and maybe even a little relieved he was gone."

According to Gabe, their marriage was a mess by then, torn apart by arguments over money and by "my father's obsession with that *stupid* illuminated manuscript."

Bristling at the words, Harold seemed to go on the defensive. "At least some good came out of it," he blurted out. "Like your scholarship."

Gabe looked at Harold as if to say, *Do you really think a scholarship could make up for the loss of a father?*

"Scholarship?" I asked lightly, trying to diffuse the situation.

Gabe shrugged. "Uh-huh. My siblings and I all went to Ohio State on full rides."

"Really?"

"Yeah, the Door of Freedom scholarship. It was a government thing for children who have been abandoned by one or both parents." As an afterthought, he added, "I guess there is a certain irony there. If we'd known the truth back then, that Dad hadn't abandoned us at all but instead had been murdered, we wouldn't have qualified for the money in the first place."

We were all quiet for a moment until Maddee said softly, "This must be so hard for you."

He nodded, and I thought I could see tears in his eyes. "It's almost harder now that we know. For the past two years, ever since we learned what happened to him, I can't seem to stop going through scenarios in my mind. I've pictured my father's final moments a thousand different ways. Was he just strolling in the woods that morning when it started to rain and so he ran for the nearest shelter, which happened to be the cabin? Maybe the sudden chill sent him over to the cot, where he wrapped himself in a blanket, and as he waited out the storm he accidently drifted off to sleep? Did he even see the beautiful double rainbow in the sky that morning, or was he already dead by then?"

Gabe went on with several completely different scenarios, each of which sent his dad to the cabin for a different reason. "Sadly, with no body to examine for evidence, we may never know why he was in that cabin, much less who killed him."

Later, in the car, I took a different way home, zigzagging along back roads south of the James toward Richmond proper. Maddee was so lost in thought she didn't even seem to notice or care. I think we both needed the quiet of the longer but far less congested drive, the lull of the dark, empty streets, to process all we'd been through.

Eventually, I pulled onto Lee Bridge, heading north, and as we crossed over the water, Richmond's beautiful nighttime skyline loomed in front of us. How different this would've looked, I thought, back in 1864, back when Great-Great-Great-Grandma Therese lived and worked in this city.

One of the pictures in Aunt Cissy's box came to mind, an image taken from a bluff overlooking this river. Back then, there had been no interstates or highways here, much less miles of suburbia filled with houses and stores and people and more. In that old photo, the land-scape had seemed bucolic. Rural. Nearly devoid of development.

Yet that had been deceptive, I thought as I reached the other side of the bridge and continued onto Belvidere. Whether the photographer had done it on purpose or not, according to Aunt Cissy, just outside the range of that picture had been an encampment of refugees and two Yankee prisons. The signs of war.

As we neared the turn that would bring us the rest of the way home, I decided that perhaps life was never as simple as it could appear for anyone—not now and not back then either.

Things could be deceptive, whether you were working to unravel a seemingly unsolvable puzzle in the here and now or watching the whole world crumble around you in 1864.

Chapter Twelve

Therese

*I*t rained over the next three days. At night, Therese dreamed about caring for the wounded and woke up in a panic several times. During the day, she thought about the hospital in every quiet moment she had. She aimed to concentrate on schooling the girls, and she did, working on reading, writing, and arithmetic. But still her mind returned often to the tragedies she'd witnessed.

Florence mostly observed her older sisters, while Eleanor worked diligently and Lydia longed to spend her time outside, whether it was pouring rain or not. She stared out the window as much as she could. On Thursday, when the rain stopped, Therese took the girls on a long walk. Eleanor and Florence did their best to stay out of the mud puddles, but Lydia splashed through each one she could find.

They went as far as Harvie's Woods, a place Therese had walked to as a schoolgirl—though now an encampment of tents lined the edge of the trees, most likely the temporary homes of displaced people who'd fled the nearby battlefields for safety.

Therese and the girls stood at the edge of the bluff, overlooking the James River and the Falls. All sorts of people—black and white, children and adults, female and male—were fishing along the banks. She pointed out Belle Isle to the girls, which had been turned into a prison for Union soldiers.

Factories—including Tredegar Iron Works, where artillery for the war was produced—spewed puffs of black smoke above and across the river, which were carried by the breeze.

Therese directed the girls' attention to the Virginia capitol and reminded them that Thomas Jefferson had designed it.

"That's where Papa works," Lydia said.

Therese thought perhaps he worked in a nearby building but agreed with the little girl anyway. She knew it had been an effort to squeeze the Confederate government in alongside the government of the Commonwealth of Virginia. Considering their father was a clerk for the secretary of state, his office would definitely be somewhere in the vicinity.

Below she could make out the slave auction off Wall Street, several blocks southeast of the capitol, but she didn't mention that to the girls either. Instead, she gestured toward the seven hills, covered with trees that were just beginning to change color, flashing hints of gold and red among the evergreens. It was such a beautiful city.

As they walked along the bluff, they came across a young photographer taking an image of the water. They paused and observed for a while before they moved on, Therese feeling appreciative for all the recent advances in photography. The beauty that photo would convey was needed now, more than ever.

As they walked farther down a bluff, a muffled explosion startled Therese, and she looked behind her.

"That's just artillery going off," Eleanor explained.

"Yes," Therese answered. "But from where?"

"Petersburg."

"You can hear it all the way from there?"

Eleanor nodded. "You'll get used to it."

Therese guessed she would. The girls certainly had.

When they returned home, Mrs. Galloway met them at the door. As Therese apologized for the state of Lydia's boots, the woman quickly dismissed any worry. "We've been invited to the Davises' for a singing tonight after supper. We'd like you to come along."

Therese tried not to show her reaction. This was *President* Davis the woman was talking about. Mrs. Galloway didn't specify that Therese was being included for childcare purposes, but she knew her role and didn't mind. At least she would get to see the president and first lady in person, not to mention the inside of their beautiful home.

Far less impressed, Eleanor groaned, which wasn't like her. Of the three girls, she was usually the most compliant.

Mrs. Galloway sighed. "Mind your manners, Eleanor, and set a good example for your sisters."

Lydia crossed her arms and stuck out her lip.

"And you, young lady. Go get cleaned up," her mother commanded.

"I'll see to her boots," Therese said.

"Bless you."

Therese headed to the pump in the backyard with Lydia's boots, Eleanor trailing along behind her.

"Mother thinks I don't like the Davises," she said. "But that's not it. It makes me sad to think about going there."

"Why is that?" Therese asked as she grabbed the brush for the boots, but she could guess. The middle Davis boy, Joseph, had died in April after falling off the porch of their mansion. It had been in all of the papers.

When Eleanor didn't answer, Therese asked, "Does it have to do with their little boy?"

The girl nodded. "We played with them outside last time we visited, before the accident."

Therese placed her hand on the little girl's shoulder.

"And now they have the new baby, and I worry something will happen to her. And I know I'm not supposed to know this, but I worry about Mama's baby too."

"Oh, dear." Therese wasn't sure how to respond. The truth was, lots of babies died. Her mother had lost three that Therese knew about. All of the families she knew had lost at least one baby. It was a part of life, but now with the war on and a lack of food and other supplies, a pregnancy was even more dangerous. "How about if we pray for the Davises' baby? And for your mother's little one too?"

Eleanor nodded and Therese bowed her head, saying a quick prayer. After she said, "Amen," she got to work on the boots.

"Do you get along well with Margaret Davis?" she asked, referring to the president's oldest daughter.

Eleanor's eyes lit up. "I like her a lot." Then her face fell. "But I'm not sure what to say to her now."

"Tell her you're sorry for her loss. And that you've been thinking about her."

Eleanor's eyes grew shiny with tears. "It's nice she has a baby sister, isn't it?"

"Yes, Eleanor. That's wonderful."

The young girl took a deep breath. "I think you'll like their house. It has gaslights."

"Really?" The school—now the hospital—had gaslights, but Therese hadn't been in a home with them.

Eleanor dropped her voice. "And a water closet." She giggled.

"Oh, my. It all sounds very modern."

After supper the family walked to the Davises' home in the Court End neighborhood, which was about a mile away. Therese appreciated the warm evening after several days of rain, but a hint of autumn was in the air. Soon the weather would change for good.

When they neared the Confederate White House, Lydia ran ahead and bolted up the steps.

"Wait!" her father called out.

A couple approached from behind. Mr. Galloway called out a hello, and Mrs. Galloway whispered, "Another clerk from the secretary of state's office." The woman carried a baby.

As the Galloways and the other family started up the marble steps,

Lydia knocked on the door. A butler opened it. He greeted Lydia and then the rest of the group, welcoming them into the home. As the butler announced the Galloway family, President Jefferson Davis and First Lady Varina Davis stepped forward to greet them. Therese tried not to seem rattled. Who would have ever thought she'd be in the presence of the couple she'd heard so much about? She didn't agree with everything they stood for, but still she found it fascinating to be in their home.

She thought of Rose O'Neal Greenhow's memoir and how she used her access to important men in Washington to spy on them. Could Therese ever do the same, should the opportunity present itself? Standing in the Confederate White House, it didn't seem to be that outlandish of an idea. There certainly had to be spies in Richmond.

Several months before, Therese had heard that a couple of Davis household slaves had escaped with help from the Union after spying on them for years. The thought made her spine tingle, and she guessed that many of the slaves throughout the South had been spies their entire lives in one way or another. Their owners considered them practically invisible. It wouldn't have been hard to gather information simply by listening as they went about their duties.

When no one introduced or acknowledged Therese directly, she busied herself by gazing around the foyer and taking everything in. But when President Davis pulled Mr. Galloway aside and handed him a document that quickly disappeared into a pocket of her employer's suit jacket, she found herself staring. Her heart raced at the realization of what sort of information Mr. Galloway must deal with every day. She quickly averted her eyes to two statues just as a young girl—most likely Margaret—skipped into the middle of the room. She greeted Eleanor and invited her up to the nursery with the other children.

Mrs. Galloway nodded at Therese. "Go along with them," she whispered. "Follow Margaret."

"Of course." Therese would have liked to be included with the other adults, but such was the life of a governess.

She directed Lydia and Florence to follow Margaret and Eleanor, bringing up the rear as they ascended the back staircase. On the third floor, as Therese walked down the hall toward the nursery, she glanced into a room that appeared to be an office, presumably President Davis's. She'd heard that he conducted his business up here on the family floor, where he could have privacy from the hustle and bustle of the household downstairs. She shivered a little, imagining the decisions that took place behind his desk.

The nursery was large, with rows of windows on the two outside walls. The carpet was bright and busy. The room held two small beds and a cradle as well as a larger bed, most likely for the children's nurse. Margaret led the girls over to two small rocking chairs with porcelain dolls sitting in them. Therese simply observed, wondering where the other Davis children and nannies were. A few minutes later, a middle-aged black woman and two boys joined them. Therese guessed the woman was the nursemaid and the boys were Jefferson Jr., who would have been around seven, and William, who was two. The family certainly had a lot to keep track of between children, the war, and their politics.

"Oh, good! You're here already!"

Therese turned to find Polly coming into the room with the two Baxter boys she taught. They were ten and eleven and didn't look happy with being sent to the nursery. Therese greeted her friend, who then turned toward the other woman and said, "Beth, I'd like you to meet Therese. She's the new governess for the Galloway family. Beth is the governess for the Davis family."

They greeted each other, and Therese asked Beth how long she'd been working for the Davises. "For a few years now. I came with them from Mississippi."

Therese knew Varina Davis had a bit of Yankee in her background. Her grandfather had been the governor of New Jersey, and though she was raised in the South, she was educated in Philadelphia and still had relatives in the North. Even so, Therese was surprised that they had a black woman teaching their children. So many things in life weren't what she expected.

Beth arranged a game of Daisy in the Dell, and all of the children joined in the fun. Another woman—a white one—holding an infant and wearing a large apron, came into the nursery and grabbed a blanket from the cradle. When William nearly crashed into her, she patted his head. "Careful, wee one," she said, and then she left the room.

As the children played, piano music and voices carried up through the floors. The adults sang a couple of hymns and then "Dixie" and "Bonnie Blue Flag." As they began to sing "The Yellow Rose of Texas," Beth changed the game to Simon Says.

Polly and Therese stood against the wall and watched the children, talking about the work in the hospital. "Did you dream about it afterward?" Polly asked. "I did at first."

"Yes." It had been disturbing, but she'd found it gratifying to care for the soldiers. She enjoyed the staff too. She told Polly that.

"My handsome cousin in particular?" Polly nudged Therese with her elbow.

Therese smiled. "Time will tell." Had she been that obvious about her admiration of the man?

"Just don't tell anyone else you're interested in him," Polly whispered. "Lots of people aren't happy with a Northern doctor coming to Richmond."

Therese could guess why not. "Is he generally vocal about his views? He was with me."

"No, not at all. He's usually quite discreet. And, honestly, the two of you were speaking so quietly I couldn't hear what was being said. I'm sure the patient couldn't either—he most likely thought the whispering was about medical concerns." She gave a reassuring smile. "Most importantly, I've never seen Alec *not* do his *very* best to save a patient, so in that way he's neutral. But he is from Maine, and he is a Quaker. Everyone knows what his beliefs are."

"Why is he here?"

Polly shrugged. "To save lives. He and Father stay in touch, so he knew the South didn't have enough trained doctors. I guess the thought kept weighing on him until he decided to do what he could to assist. He had just finished working in Boston and was about to return to his father's practice in Maine, but he had been feeling called to help somehow, so he took advantage of the situation and came down here first. It has worked out well for everyone concerned."

Therese lowered her voice even more. "How exactly are the two of you related?"

"Emmanuel Talbot emigrated to Virginia from England in 1704. His youngest son ended up going to Maine, and Dr. Talbot is his descendant."

"It's amazing the two families kept in touch all of these years."

"Yes, well..." Polly grinned. "The Talbots seem to do that well. So do the Gillets, another branch of the family, the one back in France that Michael stayed with. It's pretty amazing."

One of the "maids" brought up a tray of cookies for the children, and they all sat around in a circle to have their snack as she lit the gaslights and then closed the curtains. Watching the woman work, Therese decided that this euphemism for slaves was as equally offensive as Mother's favorite, "servants."

Eleanor spoke quietly to Margaret as they ate, and then the two girls sat and held hands.

Therese put her arm around Polly. "I'm so thankful for you and that we can be in Richmond together."

Polly hugged her back. "It's a dream to have you here."

After a while the music downstairs stopped. Therese guessed the adults were having refreshments too.

"I volunteered at the hospital last night," Polly said. "I'm going to try to go every Wednesday evening. Do you think Mr. Galloway would allow you to add Wednesdays to your schedule?"

"I'll ask." Therese liked the idea. She loved teaching the three Galloway girls, but after just one day of volunteering, she longed to do more of it—and to get better at nursing the wounded as soon as she could.

Polly nudged her again. "And you'd get to see more of Alec."

Therese couldn't help but smile. Polly knew what Therese's father's views had been about slavery, although life was a lot more complicated now than it had been when her parents fell in love twenty-three years ago. Sadly, Michael hadn't turned out to be the man she thought he was.

On the other hand, his cousin Alec seemed kind, intelligent, and quite interesting. Perhaps she'd finally met the right Talbot for her.

When Therese and the girls returned to the others in the foyer, Mrs. Galloway and Varina Davis were deep in conversation. Mr. Galloway ushered the girls outside and Therese followed, feeling awkward standing next to him as they waited. He was cordial enough, but she had no idea what to talk with him about. Polly left with her family, and all of the other guests did too. Mrs. Galloway slipped out the front door and came down the steps.

Eleanor took Therese's hand as they walked, and then Florence took her other one. Lydia skipped ahead.

"Stay close," Mrs. Galloway called out.

After a few minutes of silence, Eleanor whispered, "It was good to see Margaret."

Therese squeezed the girl's hand, happy to have witnessed the young friendship. It had been fascinating to catch a glimpse of the Confederate first family. She'd heard rumors that Varina Davis was a harsh woman who treated others badly. She hadn't seen that tonight, not in person. She seemed to genuinely care about Mrs. Galloway.

Everyone, Therese included, was capable of doing good or bad. She'd like to think that it simply came down to one's choices, but she feared, as with Mother, that perhaps it became more complicated than that as one aged. She sincerely hoped she'd take the moral high road, and she guessed that marrying a man of principle would help her do so. Sadly, Michael no longer fit that description.

The next morning, Therese sat in the dining room and read in the *Richmond Daily Dispatch* that the Union Army had crossed the James River to attack the Richmond defenses, but the Confederates rallied, contained the breakthrough, and counterattacked.

As she read, Mr. and Mrs. Galloway stood in the hall, most likely unaware she was within hearing distance. "Lee will reinforce the lines north of the James," Mr. Galloway said. "Unfortunately, that means weakening the lines at Petersburg."

"Now, now," Mrs. Galloway said. "Try not to fret too much."

Their voices trailed on down the hall, and a moment later the patter of the girls' feet coming down the stairs distracted Therese.

She tried not to worry about Warner, but she couldn't help but wonder what the change in positioning would mean for him. Perhaps he'd be moved north. Either way, it sounded as if he would be more at risk. It sounded as if they all were.

She put on a smile for the girls, doing her best to ignore her concerns. That afternoon she went on a walk again with the children after dinner. When they were nearly back around to the row house, they could see up ahead that a buggy was parked out front—Grandfather's buggy, with Badan in the driver's seat.

Therese's heart raced, worried that he'd come with bad news, perhaps about Warner, but she didn't say so to the girls. When they neared the buggy, Therese called out a hello. Shading her eyes, she asked, "Is everything all right?"

"I think so, Miss Therese," Badan said. "Your mother's inside."

The girls led the way. When Therese entered the house, Mrs. Galloway called out to her from the parlor. The girls hurried in first, followed by Therese. Mrs. Galloway introduced them to her guest and then told them to go to their rooms for a rest. Mother seemed calm and collected.

"Hello." Therese stepped forward to give her mother a hug. "What are you doing here?"

"I brought some fresh produce. I received your letter yesterday. We brought a box of apples and a few things from the garden."

"They've been delivered to the kitchen," Mrs. Galloway said. "And we are ever so grateful." She beamed at Mother. Then she stood and said she was going to go rest too and leave them to visit. She curtsied to Mother. "It's been a delight to meet you, Mrs. Jennings. Therese has blessed our family. Both of your children are now serving their country."

Mother nodded vaguely, and then she told the woman goodbye. After Mrs. Galloway left, Mother wiped a tear from her eye. "I've been missing you terribly. Much worse than I anticipated."

"It hasn't even been a week." Therese hated seeing Mother this way. On the other hand, at least neediness was better than anger.

Mother's blond hair was pulled back in a bun, but a strand had come loose. Therese noticed a thin streak of gray.

"What have you been doing to stay busy?" Therese asked.

Mother shrugged. "Missing you and Warner. Thinking about your father."

"Maybe you could help Auntie Vera with the house chores." Mother had cleaned and done the wash when they lived at the academy.

She shook her head. "I'm too tired for that." She inhaled sharply. "I want you to come home."

Therese narrowed her eyes. "Have you...has anything changed?"

To her credit, Mother almost looked ashamed as she lowered her eyes to the floor and replied in a whisper. "I can't free them."

"Then I can't come home." Therese was pleased at how easily the words rolled off her tongue. But then Mother looked so miserable that for a moment she almost felt sorry for her.

"Remember," she added in a low voice, "this family is depending on me, just as Father's students depended on him. Not to mention that I'm actually making money here—most of which I'll be sending on to you."

Mother nodded, seeming mollified. They both knew how badly they needed that.

"We went to the home of the Davis family last night," Therese offered with a smile.

Mother looked up. "President Davis's?"

"Yes."

She leaned forward. "What was it like?"

"I only saw the foyer and the nursery, but it seemed very nice." She told Mother all the details she could think of, but then she said it was time to get back to the girls' lessons.

"Yes. Of course." They both stood.

"Come see me again when you can," Therese told her. "Thank you so much for bringing the apples and produce." She knew the entire family would appreciate it.

"I had a letter from Warner this morning," Mother said.

"Oh?"

"Michael Talbot is in his unit, remember?"

With a nod, Therese told her mother about seeing Michael at the hospital on Sunday night.

"Therese! I don't want you working at a hospital. No matter what Polly says, it's not proper for a lady."

She sighed. "They need help, Mother. You know that. Caring for the wounded is the Christian thing to do. I'm going to start volunteering on Wednesdays too with Polly." Mr. Galloway had given her his blessing the evening before.

Mother huffed, but she let it go for now. "I can see you haven't had much time to miss me," she said instead, her tone betraying her hurt.

"No, I do miss you." Therese had written to her every night, just as she'd promised. "You should have a letter each day."

"It's not enough. I want you home. It's not safe here. There are too many people, too much commotion." Lowering her voice to an anxious whisper, she added, "From what I hear, there are spy networks everywhere."

Therese had to stifle a smile, remembering thoughts from the night before. "Spy networks?"

Mother nodded gravely. "Who knows what dangers lurk in the shadows?"

Therese could no longer contain her smile. "You're thinking of that memoir we both read at Grandfather's about the spy. Isn't that right?"

Mother smiled a little. "Well, yes."

"There you go. You just have spies on the mind. It's fine. *I'm* fine." Therese was sure she had absolutely no chance of encountering any spy networks herself.

She walked her mother out to the buggy and then waited as Badan helped her get settled. She waved as they started off, but Mother didn't look back.

She turned at a shuffling noise behind her to see Mrs. Galloway standing in the open doorway.

"She misses you very much," she said.

"She shouldn't have come," Therese replied, watching the buggy disappear in the distance. "I'm sorry about that."

The woman brushed off her apology. "She just wanted to see where you're working and meet the people you're living with. I know I would."

Therese shrugged. "She's lonely."

Mrs. Galloway stared out the open door. "A lot of us are..."

Though Therese nodded in response, she couldn't say the same for herself. She wasn't lonely, not at all. Yes, she missed Father and Warner and the home they had shared at the academy, but that was gone. Honestly, it was a relief to be away from Mother and her gloominess. Therese enjoyed teaching the Galloway girls and volunteering at the hospital. Even in the horror of the war around them, this new chapter felt like a fresh beginning.

But she wouldn't say any of that to Mrs. Galloway. "What do you miss the most about home?" Therese asked as they stepped into the row house.

"Family," Mrs. Galloway answered. "My parents have passed on, but Patrick's folks and brother live on the Galloway estate outside New Orleans, where we have a home too. Patrick would travel into the city to practice law, and the girls and I would spend our days on the estate with his family. Neither Patrick nor I wanted to come to Virginia, but his father told him it was the opportunity of a lifetime." Mrs. Galloway lowered her voice as she rested her hand on her belly. "Oh, I long for this war to be over."

Therese agreed. They were all weary of it. She patted the woman's shoulder. "I'll go collect the girls. You should rest more."

"Thank you." She took a step away, but then she turned her head. "Thank you, too, for being here instead of at home with your mother. I feel selfish saying it, but I'm grateful we get to have you."

Mrs. Galloway knew nothing of Therese's stand against slavery and how that had been the impetus for her coming here, and she had no intention of telling her. Instead, she just nodded humbly and then turned to go. As she moved toward the stairs, she said a prayer for her mother, asking the Lord to give her strength.

Chapter Thirteen
Therese

On Sunday, after church, Therese again walked to the hospital with Polly. They both wore wool cloaks and hoods, trying to stay dry against the pounding rain. Therese stepped in a puddle by accident, and water filled her boots. She needed a new pair, but of course there was no money for such a thing. Aggie and Auntie Vera needed footwear far more than she did. She'd have to try to repair hers.

"Did you hear Rose O'Neal Greenhow drowned?" Polly asked.

Therese stopped in shock. It had seemed the woman was invincible—until now. "When? And how?"

"Yesterday. Off the coast of North Carolina, near Wilmington. The *Condor* ran aground. She made it into a lifeboat, but it capsized."

Therese gasped. "Oh, goodness."

"She had more than two thousand dollars in gold sewn into her underclothes and around her neck, royalty money from her book. At least that's what Mr. Baxter heard."

Therese shook her head at the irony of it. Perhaps Mrs. Greenhow would have survived without the weight of the gold. She didn't admire the woman's loyalties, but she'd been inspired by her courage and spunk and was now saddened by her tragic passing.

When they reached the hospital, Matron Webb met them in the foyer and instructed them to hang their cloaks and go to the kitchen for a cup of tea before they started. "Do your best to dry off," she said. "We can't have you getting ill."

Polly led the way toward the kitchen but then stopped, whispering, "Oh, bother. We don't want to waste time on getting a cup of tea when soldiers need to be cared for."

Therese agreed. The rain hadn't been particularly cold, and she wasn't chilled. They put aprons over their plain black dresses and headed up the stairs to the supply closet. They filled basins with water and grabbed cloths from the shelves. When they reached the east ward, Dr. Talbot was making his rounds.

"Polly," he called out from one bedside. "Would you come here a moment?"

Polly put her basin and cloth on a table, stepped closer, and peered down at the soldier lying on his side in front of them.

"He just came in on the train," Dr. Talbot said. "What do you think of this wound?"

Polly studied the patient for a moment. "It looks as if the bullet went through his bladder and out his back."

"Correct."

"Will you operate?"

"Yes. I'll repair the wounds, and hopefully the bladder will heal."

Therese couldn't imagine what life would be like for the soldier if it didn't. Not wanting to stare, she turned her attention to her own duties, cloth and basin in hand, and went over to the first bed along the wall. As she began bathing the soldier there, she heard Dr. Talbot instruct Polly to give the soldier with the bladder wound some whiskey, saying that would help him until they could put him under for surgery.

He moved on to the next man after that, the three of them each tending to their own duties. Soon, however, Polly started telling him all about another patient, one she'd cared for on Wednesday. Dr. Talbot was in the middle of another examination by then, but he didn't seem to mind her chatter.

"He'd been hit with shrapnel in the throat," Polly was saying as she poured some whiskey into an invalid feeder, a little cup with a long spout. "He nearly fell into the James River."

"So, north of here?" the doctor asked.

"Just a bit to the north."

Right about where General Lee split his troops, Therese thought, recalling the story in the newspaper.

"He was hit in the chest too, and that wound seemed to be worse," Polly continued. She trickled the whiskey into the soldier's mouth, causing him to sputter a little, but then he swallowed.

"Someone else already told me about that patient," Dr. Talbot said. "I'm not sure what the outcome was, though. Keep your eye out for him."

"Will do."

When Dr. Talbot reached a man with a wounded arm, he asked Therese to help him change the dressing. She put down her basin.

"Wash your hands first with soap," he added, nodding toward the station by the door. "Then grab some gauze and a clean cloth." He motioned toward the cupboard. "And scissors."

"Yes, sir."

Dr. Talbot gave her an amused glance, and she curtsied. When she returned, he was stripping the dressing, revealing a weeping wound. The smell caught Therese off guard, and she gasped.

Without looking up, the doctor asked, "Are you all right?"

"Yes." The soldier had his eyes on the doctor and didn't seem to notice her reaction. The gaping wound oozed pus and blood.

"There was nothing to stitch here." Dr. Talbot studied the wound. "We have to hope this will eventually heal on its own."

The soldier, who had a babyish face, winced. "Them Yankees must be using poisoned bullets."

Dr. Talbot shook his head. "They're not poisoned, but the bullets are designed to tear through tissue and do as much harm as possible."

He dropped the dressing into a bucket, saying under his breath, "One of the many atrocities of war."

Therese cut a strip of gauze the same length as the previous one.

"Another problem," he continued, "is that there's not enough water and soap in the field hospitals. Even if all of the surgeons on the front lines understood that good hygiene can help prevent infection, they wouldn't have the needed resources. Granted, some infections originate here, but most of the injured are infected by the time they arrive."

Therese concentrated on the doctor's words, not the wound, as she avoided taking a deep breath. She couldn't imagine why better hygiene would prevent infection, but he seemed so intelligent, she had a feeling he was right.

The doctor pulled a pair of tweezers from his kit. Therese turned her head toward the soldier, whose eyes were wild with pain.

"Where are you from?" she asked.

"North Carolina, up in the highlands. My parents have a little farm." He gritted his teeth as the doctor tugged at the wound. "I'm the oldest of eleven. I got conscripted last year and ain't been home since." He lowered his voice. "Worst mistake I ever made, not running the other way. I been so homesick. When I got shot, I called out for my ma like I was a baby." He seemed to find comfort in talking. "Now I'm gonna be maimed and not much use to my pa. I just hope I can keep my arm..." He looked around. "It's not right how men who have twenty slaves or more don't have to fight while those of us who have none do."

Therese gave him a sympathetic nod and took another shallow breath.

"I'm finished." Dr. Talbot put the tweezers down.

The young man exhaled. "I 'preciate your care, Doc. And I don't mean to complain. So many are worse off than me."

"That may be true." Dr. Talbot took the gauze from Therese. "But you can't help but be in pain." He looked up at Therese. "Give him more morphine when we're done."

She nodded.

"How does it look?" The soldier raised his head, trying to see.

"It's still infected."

"No better?"

Dr. Talbot shook his head, a sad expression on his face, as he applied the gauze.

"Am I going to lose it?"

"I don't know yet. We'll give it more time—and prayer."

"Thank you, sir." The young man tried to smile. "I'll gladly take both."

From Therese's very limited experience, it didn't seem gangrene had set in. That was the biggest concern. But the wound didn't look good, that was for sure. She hoped God would answer Dr. Talbot's prayers, but she also hoped the soldier could handle the possibility of life without his arm.

Her eyes filled with tears at the thought, and Dr. Talbot patted her shoulder.

"I'm sorry. I'll do a better job trying to control my emotions."

"No, don't. We can use some tenderness around here. I admire that in you." He smiled and then retreated to the washbasin beside the door. Dr. Talbot was the steadiest person she'd ever met. Nothing seemed to faze him.

The afternoon turned into evening, and Polly and Therese fed the soldiers bowls of soup for their supper. Therese declined one herself because her stomach hadn't settled since helping Dr. Talbot, but Polly stopped to eat.

Nothing seemed to bother Polly either. Several times she assisted the doctor, asking to be involved in the hardest cases. She changed the dressings on several wounds herself. Therese hadn't realized Polly knew so much about medical matters. She used a lot of unfamiliar terminology and seemed to understand whatever Dr. Talbot explained. Therese couldn't help but be impressed by her friend.

When it was time to leave, Polly said she planned to stay another hour or so. "You go on home," she told Therese. "We'll find someone to walk with you."

Dr. Talbot was a few beds away. "I'm leaving in a few minutes," he said. "I'd be happy to escort you, Miss Jennings."

Therese thanked him and then asked Polly how she would get home. "One of the orderlies will be leaving around then."

"All right." Therese wished Polly were leaving now. Therese admired Dr. Talbot, but she wasn't sure if she could carry on a conversation with him for half a mile. Next to her father, she was sure he was the smartest person she'd ever met. Polly would have no trouble thinking of what to say, but Therese feared she wouldn't be able to contribute much to a conversation with him. She admired him, yes, but she didn't feel she was his equal—not at all.

Therese waited on the front steps for Dr. Talbot. It was completely dark except for the light from the streetlamps and a few stars peeking through the clouds. She took a deep breath and exhaled slowly. The rain had stopped, leaving a fresh, hopeful scent.

The wards were fairly well ventilated, with windows left open even in the chill, but still the odor of blood, lye, and chloroform lingered, plus the ever-present stench of decay. She took in another big breath. At least she could leave, unlike the majority of the people in the building. Her eyes filled with tears at the injustice of it all. The young farm boy from North Carolina hadn't wanted to get caught up in a war that had little to do with him. All he wanted was to be with his family, working on his father's farm. She blinked as the front door opened and Dr. Talbot came down the steps, holding his hat in his hands. "Sorry to keep you waiting."

"It's fine. I needed to catch my breath."

"Yes." He put his wide-brimmed hat on top of his head. "That's important."

"Well, I have no reason, based on the little I'm doing, to compare my needs to yours, especially when you seem to be able to work nonstop."

"That's not true." He placed his hand on her elbow to steady her and led their way down East Broad Street. "I have to catch my breath too."

"Which can't be easy, considering you live and work at the hospital."

He smiled. "Once a week, I force myself to leave for the night. A

Quaker couple lives not too far away, and they let me stay in a guest room. One good night of sleep away from the hospital each week can do wonders."

"A Quaker couple? Is there a meeting place in Richmond, then?"

"There was, down on Cary Street." He kept his hand on her elbow. "But it's been occupied by Confederate soldiers for the last two years. The congregation is quite small, so they take turns meeting in homes now."

"What brought you to Richmond?"

"Mostly I was inspired by a Quaker nurse from Boston who has been working in the South. I felt led to help out as well, so I wrote to the Confederate surgeon general to see if I could be of assistance."

"To Dr. Moore," Therese said, nodding.

"Yes. Do you know him?"

"No, but I've heard of him." In fact, Mr. Galloway had mentioned him at supper the other night.

"I met him in Washington, DC, several years ago. He impressed me. He doesn't have the resources that the North does, with the blockade and everything."

"But why would you come here? You're a Northerner."

"I'm a Quaker first. A pacifist. I find war reprehensible and have empathy for the victims of both sides. Yes, I'm a Yankee, and I've taken care of Northern soldiers too, but it doesn't matter to me what side they're on. If they need medical help, I want to provide it."

Therese remembered Father mentioning a Quaker woman who spied for the Patriots during the Revolutionary War, but usually it seemed Friends remained neutral. "How can someone be both an abolitionist and a pacifist?" she asked, her voice rising. She quickly lowered it. "People are being traded like chattel. Is that not worth fighting against?"

He glanced at her, and she realized she'd just hinted strongly at her own stance as an abolitionist. He seemed to appraise her anew, a slight smile on his lips, and she could feel her cheeks grow warm.

"Well," he finally answered, "I don't believe war is the best way to achieve freedom for our enslaved brothers and sisters. I would rather slaveholders had a change of heart or that our government legislated an end to slavery, as was done in England."

She sighed. "But the South didn't agree to that," she responded sadly, admitting to herself once and for all the truth, that she wanted the North to win this war. Yes, she would regret the loss of independence for Virginia and the other southern states, but her time for old loyalties was over. The South had its chance to renounce slavery and had rejected it. Now it needed to lose, even at the cost of states' rights, and despite all that had been sacrificed.

"The South is the enemy," she said softly in wonder, as much to herself as to him. To be against slavery was to be against the South.

"Not really the enemy," he responded, interrupting her thoughts. "More like a prodigal brother. Though yes, I clearly felt God calling me to 'love my enemy' by coming here to help."

They grew quiet for a long moment, but it was a comfortable silence.

"You know," he said, "there's an odd confidence in Richmond, as if there's still a chance the Confederacy might win. But looking at the big picture, I can tell you the war won't last much longer. The Union will be victorious by spring."

Therese, encouraged by his words, wasn't sure what to say in return, and when she didn't reply at all, Dr. Talbot spoke again, loosening his hold on her elbow. "I apologize. I fear I've said too much, regardless of who your father was."

"Oh, no." Therese patted his hand. "I appreciate your honesty—and your approach." He'd found a balance between being helpful and not being harsh, even though it was warranted. "I try to be sensitive in public, but those who know me know I'm in complete agreement with all of my father's views. It's how I was raised." She took a deep breath, realizing she needed to reveal the other side of her family's story, though. She didn't want to mislead Dr. Talbot.

She went on to explain that her brother was fighting for the Confederacy and then provided details about her father's illness and death, about her grandfather's passing, and about how quickly her mother fell back into the role she'd grown up with at River Pines, a plantation that still held five slaves.

"I couldn't bear staying. I'm grateful to be needed in Richmond, both as a governess and a nurse."

"Well, Richmond is grateful you're here," he replied, his tone light. "As am I."

Therese's heart swelled. Conversing with Dr. Talbot had turned out to be surprisingly easy, and she realized she was actually enjoying herself.

They turned right, alongside the capitol, and passed several Confederate soldiers coming from the opposite direction.

"Tell me about growing up in Maine," she said, smiling up at him as she steered the conversation to safer ground.

"Well, my father is a doctor too. He raises cattle on the side. I have a cousin, Ruth, my paternal uncle's child, who was raised by my parents. She's quite a bit older than I am and took on the role of big sister." He laughed. "Let's just say she's been my protector all these years. In fact, she plans to visit in a month or so."

"How lovely." Therese looked forward to meeting her.

"She'll come as a nurse. But mostly she wants to check on me to make sure I'm taking care of myself."

"That's nice of her."

"I'm sure she'll try and talk me into going home. But I'll be leaving soon anyway, by Christmas at the latest."

Therese felt a pang of sadness. Of course he wouldn't stay for long. He was a Northerner. There was no reason for him to remain in Virginia forever, even if his ancestors had originally come from here, even if there were plenty of Talbot cousins around.

They continued chatting as they turned down Grace Street, and for the last few blocks talked about infection. The doctor said how hard it was to get the staff at the hospital to follow basic hygiene. Then he complained about the lack of supplies, not to mention the lack of knowledge regarding dressing wounds. "Medical science hasn't kept up with the weaponry," he explained. "Today's guns are devastating. More soldiers are dying in this war than ever before."

Therese couldn't help but be touched by his concern for all soldiers.

When they reached the row house, she asked how much farther he had to walk.

"Oh, we passed the Corbetts' street a long time ago."

Flabbergasted, she asked, "Why did you walk all this way with me, then?"

He chuckled. "I needed to stretch my legs." He stepped back. "More so, I needed the company. Thank you, Miss Jennings."

Therese curtsied. "Thank you, Dr. Talbot," she replied. "For everything."

As she stepped into the house, Mr. Galloway stood in the hall. "Who walked you home?" he asked.

"Dr. Talbot," she answered, slipping out of her cloak. "From the hospital."

"Well, then. That seems harmless enough."

Therese nodded. She wouldn't tell him Dr. Talbot was a Yankee and a Quaker. What mattered was that he was a perfect gentleman—and a very interesting one besides.

Later, in bed, she thought about their conversation and the realizations she'd come to as they'd spoken. She had always believed that leaving the Union was a terrible mistake and that the issues coming between the North and the South were things that should've been negotiated and debated. Instead, secession had led to this bloody and devastating war, one that she could only hope the South would not win.

Were such thoughts treasonous? She couldn't imagine that standing up for the freedoms guaranteed in the US Constitution could ever be a treasonous act, but then again, technically speaking, the very existence of the government of the Confederacy was treasonous. All she knew was that these issues should be settled in Washington and not on the battlefield. Reasonable men could find a solution if given enough time. But the war had to end first if that process was going to happen.

On Wednesday, when Therese and Polly reached the ward, Dr. Talbot greeted them, telling them that a photographer with the *Daily Richmond Dispatch* had spent the afternoon at the hospital, taking photographs of the soldiers, and now he wanted to get some of the staff.

Dr. Talbot met Therese's gaze and then glanced toward Polly. "I'm hoping you two will accommodate him. The light is fading, so we need to hurry. He's up in my office."

As he led the way up the first flight of stairs, Polly asked if Matron Webb was in agreement.

"Dr. Moore's orders. Matron Webb doesn't have a say in it. The photographer has been taking images around the Richmond area—of soldiers in their camps, of civilians, of all sorts of people. The newspaper wants some pictures of patients and hospital staff too."

They hurried up the remaining flights of stairs and into Dr. Talbot's office. The place was sparsely furnished with a desk, a table, and a washstand. Papers and books were stacked on every surface, and a poster of a skeleton hung on one wall. Against the far wall, which was brick, a soldier leaned against his crutches. Ten feet from him stood a tall young man with a camera on a tripod. All of the gaslights were on and the shades were up, letting in the afternoon sun.

When the photographer finished with the soldier, he thanked the man and helped him out, and then Dr. Talbot introduced him to the ladies as Mr. Jay Lewis, explaining that a lot of the etchings in the newspapers were done from his images.

"I've seen you working," Therese said with a smile. "Out on the bluff, at Harvie's Woods. You were photographing the river."

"Ah, yes. That I was." He smiled broadly and shook her hand, thanking her for her work in the hospital. "I seem to recall you with several children in tow, stopping to watch for a while."

"Thank you for your documentation of...events," Polly said as they shook hands. "It's important work."

Therese agreed. Just as her family's tintypes and daguerreotypes helped to preserve memories, the images of the war that the photographer took would help all of them remember these times—and be evidence for future generations of what had happened.

Mr. Lewis instructed Polly and Therese to stand against the brick wall. "Dr. Talbot," he said, "would you join them?"

"You don't want me in the photo. I'll ruin it."

"Nonsense," Polly said, scooting over to make room.

"Come on," Therese said, pleased to have her image taken with him.

He stepped between the two women and faced the camera. All three of them wore clean aprons, but the photographer glanced around and said, "We need some props."

He then collected the empty basin and pitcher from the washstand and a medical book from Dr. Talbot's desk. Once he had them positioned as he wanted, he instructed them not to smile or move a muscle until he said they could. It was harder than Therese had expected, but somehow they managed to stand like statues until he told them time was up.

When he'd finished, Polly asked if the photograph would be etched for the paper.

"Perhaps, but more likely we'll keep it on file. If a reporter writes a story about a hospital in town, it may be used then."

"May we have copies?" Dr. Talbot asked.

"I don't see why not. This camera makes negative images, so copies can be generated." Mr. Lewis went on to explain when and where they could be retrieved, and they all thanked him.

As they started down the stairs, Dr. Talbot whispered to Therese that he hoped they'd have time to talk later. Then he turned to Polly and invited her to examine a patient with him. It truly seemed the doctor was mentoring Polly in medicine. Therese admired him for it. It wasn't every surgeon who would share his knowledge so freely with a woman, even if she was his cousin.

They all entered the east ward. As Therese checked on the soldiers, Polly and Dr. Talbot hovered over a patient near the windows, talking quietly between them.

"It appears the bullet entered the left lobe of the lung," Polly said.

"Left?" The doctor laughed. "Clearly it's the right."

Polly groaned. "You're correct. I'm so sorry."

"Do better. That sort of mistake could be deadly."

An hour later, Dr. Talbot again asked Polly to join him, this time to assist in surgery. Tears welled in Therese's eyes when she realized it was the young soldier from North Carolina. His arm was to be amputated just above the elbow.

Two orderlies arrived to transport the soldier. Therese prayed for him as they carried him out, and for Dr. Talbot and Polly too. Her friend pushed up her sleeves, replaced her soiled apron with a fresh one, and then washed at the basin on the table.

Therese put her hands together to let Polly know she was praying. In response, her friend mouthed, "Thank you," and hurried out the door.

Therese continued feeding a soldier who had lost both of his arms, forgetting to talk as she did. Finally, she noticed the fear and pain in his eyes, and she asked where he was from.

He swallowed and replied with a deep twang, "Alabama. I hope I'll be back there soon."

Therese nodded. "Do you live in the country?"

"No, a town—"

"Don't encourage them to talk." Matron Webb had slipped into the room. "Or you'll never get everyone fed."

Therese felt her face grow warm, even with the cool air blowing through the east ward.

"And who opened all the windows again?" Matron Webb headed toward the nearest one and closed it. "The soldiers will all catch colds. Dr. Talbot can't seem to understand that a draft is bad for the health."

"Fresh air is good for the injured and ill," Therese said.

"Not if they end up with pneumonia." Matron Webb closed another window. "He's supposed to be well trained, but sometimes I wonder. Although it's true that he's good with a saw."

Therese winced.

"But all this fresh air and the endless hand washing. The man doesn't have any common sense."

Therese continued to feed the soldier as Matron Webb closed every window in the ward. The wounded man didn't say another word except for thanking her after he swallowed the last bite.

When their shift came to an end, Dr. Talbot thanked Therese for her efforts. "Will I see you on Sunday?"

"Yes, of course."

"Perhaps you'd allow me to walk you home again."

Her face grew warm, but she managed to say, "I'd like that."

A few minutes later, as she and Polly hurried down the front steps into the crisp evening, her friend asked, "What's going on between you and my cousin?"

Therese stepped around a pile of fallen leaves. "What do you mean?"

"He asked about you during the surgery, once the patient was out."

"What did he ask?"

"How long I'd known you and your family."

"Oh. Anything else?"

"No." Polly nudged Therese. "But I can tell he's smitten with you."

"Don't say that. He won't be around much longer." A pair of orange leaves fell from a tree ahead, dancing in circles as they swirled slowly to the ground. "I do enjoy watching him teach you, though, asking you to describe different wounds and help him in surgery. You're amazing."

Polly groaned. "No I'm not. And I'm not impressing him at all. Did you hear me say left lobe instead of right? I'm surprised he wants me anywhere near the patients."

"Don't be silly. It's incredible how much you know. I love listening to the two of you talk."

She glanced at Polly and saw an odd look cross her features for just a moment.

"What?" Therese asked.

"Nothing. Just…I hope no one else feels that way. I don't like people listening to me."

"Oh, right." Therese grinned. "Says the girl who has not an ounce of self-consciousness in her body."

She expected her friend to laugh, but instead Polly just changed the subject, updating her about the young soldier from North Carolina.

"It breaks my heart," Polly said. "He's such a trooper. He said he'll do fine with just one arm. His family will take care of him." She swiped at her eyes. "I hope we got all of the infection. I'm praying he'll live, and we'll be thankful for that, but his whole life has changed now."

Therese nodded. No one was sacrificing more than the soldiers. Body and limb. Their very lives. She wondered if anyone in either government foresaw the horrible losses. A generation of young men— dying, maimed, or forever changed by war.

They continued on, crunching through the dried leaves. Therese knew that soon enough the rains would turn the streets to mud. Polly asked after the Galloway girls, and they began sharing endearing stories about their charges.

But the truth was that working in the hospital made the rest of life seem downright boring. On Saturday afternoon, Therese sat on the stoop, reading the morning paper about a Union attack near Petersburg on Thursday night. Remarkably, no one had been injured. Relieved, she folded the paper and raised her head to watch the girls play under the linden tree as a buggy stopped in front of the row house.

Therese stood and shaded her eyes. Someone jumped down from the buggy and came running toward her. It was Polly, breathless as she called out, "Michael just brought Warner to the hospital. He's badly injured! Dr. Talbot said for you to come right now!"

CHAPTER FOURTEEN
Therese

Matron Webb stood in the middle of the foyer when Therese flew through the door of the hospital, with Polly right behind her. "He's in surgery," the woman told her. "Dr. Talbot said to wait in the hall."

Polly grabbed Therese's hand, and as she led her up the stairs, she said, "I'll see if I can help."

After washing her hands in a basin of water outside surgery, Polly eased the door open, and Therese peered into the room over her shoulder. She could see Warner's body on the table, flanked by Michael on one side and Dr. Talbot on the other.

"May I help?" Polly asked from the doorway.

"Please." Dr. Talbot turned toward them, a saw in his hand. "It's his right leg. We may need you to administer more chloroform..."

Therese stepped back, overcome with a wave of nausea, relieved to find Matron Webb at her elbow. Polly continued on into the room, the door closing behind her as the matron took Therese's arm and led her to a chair across the hall.

Therese stammered, "I-I wish I could help."

"No, you don't." Matron Webb forced Therese to sit. "It's hard enough when you're taking care of strangers, but nearly impossible when it's kin."

"I nursed my father when he was dying."

"This is different." The matron stayed quiet after that, but she didn't leave Therese's side. She leaned up against the wall as Therese stayed put on the chair.

A scream erupted in the room, and then they heard muffled voices. Therese put her head in her hands and started praying fervently. For Warner. For Polly. For Dr. Talbot. For even Michael. And for Mother, once she received the news.

Warner was alive. She thanked God for that. One of the best surgeons available was caring for him. Michael, despite his moral shortcomings, had gotten Warner to the hospital. There was much to be grateful for.

A half hour later, the door opened and Polly appeared. Her apron was spotted with blood and her complexion pale.

Therese stood. "How is he?"

"Alive." Tears welled in her eyes. "I'm going after orderlies to move him to the ward. The doctor will talk with you soon." Matron Webb patted Therese's shoulder and followed Polly down the hall.

Therese paced the hallway. She would need to get word to Mother immediately. Badan would bring her into Richmond, but where would she stay? The hotels were expensive, and she couldn't impose on the Galloways. Perhaps Polly might have an idea.

She continued her pacing until the orderlies came. She held the door for them, once again taking a look inside. The room smelled strongly of blood, and soaked rags covered the table and floor. Dr. Talbot's back was to her, but Michael glanced up and met Therese's eyes, his expression full of sympathy. Again, she felt the threat of tears.

The men transferred Warner from the operating table to a litter and then carried him out of the room. Therese reached out and touched his forehead as they passed, brushing a lock of dark hair to the side. His eyes were closed, but his nearly white face, the parts not covered by a scraggly beard, was twisted in pain. She couldn't bear to look where his right leg had been even though it was now covered with a sheet. Michael followed, stopping for a moment. "After you talk with the doctor, come find me. I can get word to your mother."

"Thank you," Therese whispered.

A moment later Dr. Talbot was at her side. "I'm sorry."

For a moment, Therese thought he didn't believe Warner would live.

But then the doctor continued. "There was nothing I could do to save his leg. It was too badly mangled."

"What about infection?"

"Michael put a tourniquet around his leg and brought him straight here instead of taking him to the field hospital, which was smart thinking." Dr. Talbot sounded matter-of-fact, but she knew he was simply being professional. "I couldn't detect any infection, but we'll have to see what the next few days bring. He also has a wound that went through to his stomach. I did my best to stitch it up. That could be problematic too."

Therese nodded. She knew enough to understand the odds of Warner recovering weren't good. "Thank you for everything you've done. I'm going to go find Michael and figure out how to get word to my mother."

"Does she have a place to stay here in Richmond?"

Therese shook her head.

"I can ask Mr. and Mrs. Corbett."

"Pardon?"

"The Quaker couple I stay with. They're very hospitable and have several extra rooms."

Therese's face grew warm with shame. "My mother will most likely be accompanied by one of her...slaves." It was one thing to tell Dr. Talbot about the sins of her family and quite another to have him witness them firsthand.

"I see." Dr. Talbot frowned. "I'll check with the Corbetts and let you know what they say."

⁓

Michael was kneeling beside Warner and sponging his face with a wet cloth when Therese stepped into the ward. Polly stood at the end of the cot. As Therese approached, Polly repositioned the sheet.

Warner stirred, and Michael said, "Therese is here."

She knelt on the other side of the cot and reached for her brother's hand. He had dirt under his fingernails, and blood streaked his arm. She took his hand and squeezed. "I'm here," she said. "Everything's going to be all right."

Warner squeezed back, his eyelids fluttering.

"I gave him morphine," Polly said, "so he might not fully wake up for a while."

"That's good," Therese said. The more he rested, the better. He'd have a horrible shock when he awoke.

His abdomen was bandaged, along with his right arm, and there was also a small wound on the right side of his head.

"What happened?" Therese asked Michael.

"From what I heard, a grenade landed in front of him." Therese knew that was a new weapon, like a small bomb. "He must have had his right leg extended. Fortunately, it didn't take both legs. Shrapnel from the grenade also hit him in the belly and up his right side." Michael met Therese's eyes. "It's incredible he survived."

Therese clasped her hands together. "Now we'll need to do everything we can to make sure he lives."

Michael took a deep breath. "Yes." His uniform was covered in dirt and dried blood, and he looked as if he hadn't slept in a week. He stood. "I need to get going. I'm headed home. My father has been collecting supplies for the unit, and I've been ordered to pick them up. I'll stop by River Pines and tell your mother what happened."

"Thank you," Therese said. "It will be so much better coming from someone she knows."

"Yes," Michael said. "I thought so too."

"Tell her to come as quickly as she can. Dr. Talbot is going to ask friends of his if she can stay with them, although they're Quaker, and I'm sure she'll have Badan with her."

Michael cocked his head. "And you're afraid they won't approve."

"Oh, I know they won't approve."

Michael smiled a little. "It's amazing how accommodating people can be at times, even if they don't agree."

Therese wasn't sure what he meant, exactly. But maybe she did. Dr. Talbot probably fell into that category.

"I could give you a ride back to the Galloways so you can rest," Michael said. "Warner will need you once he wakes up."

Therese glanced at Polly.

"I'll be here until eight o'clock tonight."

"I'll come back then." Therese gazed down at her sleeping brother.

"Dr. Talbot sent the buggy to get you earlier," Polly said. "I'll ask him to arrange for the driver to take me home and then pick you up."

A wave of relief washed over her. God was seeing to Warner's needs—and hers too.

Michael told Warner goodbye, even though he wasn't conscious, and then Therese did the same. She numbly followed Michael to his wagon, which was already hitched, and let him help her up to the bench. The stable boy handed him the reins, and Michael pulled the team of horses, four in all, onto the street.

Therese wrapped her arms around herself against the late afternoon chill. "You must be exhausted."

"I'll get some sleep once I reach home."

"How is it—on the front?"

He sighed. "Usually it's pretty boring, but then we'll have bursts of chaos, like in the middle of last night. Then everything gets crazy and falls apart."

"Were others injured?"

He exhaled. "Two others were killed."

Therese put her hand over her mouth. "Oh, no."

He nodded and turned toward her. "And for what? What's the point of all this?"

Tears welled in her eyes. Perhaps Michael hadn't changed as much as she thought.

"I'm sorry," he said. "Forget I said that."

"No, you're right."

He shook his head. "Don't get me wrong. I'm committed to the cause. To states' rights. To the Confederacy. To saving our economy. To all of that…" His voice trailed off. He really had changed for the worse. "I'm tired. I just need a good sleep, is all."

They rode along in silence past the capitol. She wanted to ask him what could possibly have happened to change his ideals this way, but she held her tongue. When he turned on Grace Street, she said, simply, "I appreciate what you did for Warner. Driving him so far to get good care."

"It was fortunate they were already sending me to get supplies. I had a good excuse to take him straight to your hospital, which from what I've seen is currently the best around." He smiled a little. "Besides, I'd do anything I could for your family."

Again her eyes welled with tears at the inconsistency of what he was saying. If he admired her family so, why didn't he remember her father's lessons?

When they arrived at the row house, Michael walked her to the door and then helped explain to Mr. Galloway, who'd just gotten home from his office, what had happened.

"Oh, dear," he said. "Sounds as if your brother may have a rough time of it these next few weeks."

Therese nodded. "I'll go back to the hospital tonight. Michael is on his way to tell my mother. I'm sure she'll be here soon, and then I can attend to my teaching again."

"Let's see how things go," he said. "Delpha seems to be feeling a little better. You should concentrate on your brother for now."

"Thank you," Therese said. "I'm going to get some rest, and then Dr. Talbot will send a buggy for me later this evening. I'll spend the night looking after Warner."

Mr. Galloway nodded and then invited Michael inside.

"No, thank you," he answered. "I need to be on my way."

"Have you eaten?" Therese asked.

He nodded. "Polly sent me to the kitchen when I first arrived at the hospital, before Warner's..." His voice trailed off.

"Ask Auntie Vera for a box of apples and a bag of potatoes when you stop by River Pines," Therese said. "They should have plenty to share. That would be good for the troops."

Michael thanked her, said goodbye to Mr. Galloway, and then as he turned to go smiled wearily at Therese. "We'll all get through this," he said gruffly.

She nodded, hoping he was right. He was the one whose change of heart was so troubling. She truly hoped he'd make it through and see the error of his thinking.

Therese tried to rest on her cot in the attic, but the image of Warner helpless on the table flashed over and over in her mind. This war had to end soon. If Dr. Talbot was right, the Confederacy didn't have much of a chance. If the Union won, Auntie Vera and Aggie and Badan and the others would be free. Warner would end up with River Pines. They would be poor as church mice, but they would be alive and together—as long as Warner survived his wounds.

Her mind turned it all around, over and over, as tears trickled down the sides of her face. If only she could help somehow, but what could any one person do? She wondered if her mother was right about the spy networks, that they were all around her in the city. There was an older woman who roamed the streets that Eleanor told her was rumored to be a spy. If even children knew about such things, they were most likely true. The Union Army was both to the north of Richmond and to the south. Surely information was dispatched that helped with their planning. With so many in the city working for cabinet members and for Jefferson Davis himself, surely secrets were leaked.

Therese knew Mr. Galloway dealt with the kind of information the Union could use if they had access to it. He did work for the secretary of state. There would be lots of important secrets in that department.

Therese had never been a brave soul, but she realized that if she could do something to help end the war sooner—even spying—she believed she should do it. *Lord,* she prayed, *if You can use me, please do. Show me how I can help stop this terrible suffering.* The prayer didn't stop her mind from racing, and finally she admitted she wasn't going to be able to sleep. She headed downstairs and joined the family in the parlor. The candlelight cast shadows around the room as the girls turned toward Therese. Eleanor said how sorry she was about Warner.

"But he'll be all right, won't he?" Lydia interjected.

"I hope so," Therese answered. "I'll go sit with him tonight and take care of him. I'm thankful I at least have a little experience helping the wounded."

"That is fortuitous, isn't it?" Mrs. Galloway said over her knitting needles. She was most likely making socks for the soldiers. "Your volunteering at the hospital now puts you in the position to take better care of your brother."

Therese nodded, though she knew Dr. Talbot and Polly would be the ones who would truly take good care of Warner.

The lamp burned dimly in the room, most likely to cut down on the use of fuel. Therese couldn't help but notice that Mr. Galloway had a stack of papers in his lap. She couldn't see what any of the writing was, though. A shiver ran through her. The family had been so good to her—could she really consider spying on them? Even if she did, she wouldn't know what to do with that sort of information anyway. She couldn't exactly employ the techniques of Rose O'Neal Greenhow, such as smuggle it in her hair or use candles in the window to signal passersby, if there was no one to deliver the information to.

Therese gazed around the room, trying to put such thoughts from her head. Eleanor was reading a book, and Lydia was using a stub of a pencil to write on a piece of paper. Florence was curled up next to her mother, her eyes nearly closed. Therese enjoyed working for this family. They'd been nothing but kind to her. But technically they were the enemy. Would she really consider spying on Mr. Galloway in his own home?

Just as the clock in the parlor struck eight, they heard a knock on the door. A moment later the maid appeared, saying that a Polly Talbot was here for Therese.

"Oh, dear." Therese hurried to the door, afraid Polly might have bad news.

But before she could say anything, Polly blurted out, "He's no worse. I came because I'm going to work the night shift. I'll go back with you."

"Oh," Therese said. "Are you up to that?"

Polly nodded. "Two nurses sent messages that they aren't feeling well, so I volunteered to stay."

After telling the family a quick goodbye, Therese grabbed her cloak. The night air was cold, and she and Polly sat side by side in the buggy for warmth. Polly said Warner was awake. "He's still groggy, but I told him you'd be back soon."

As they rolled down the dark streets, Therese longed to ask Polly if she knew of any Union spy networks in Richmond or of any other way to help bring the war to a close. But it would be foolish to ask, even in a whisper, with the buggy driver so close. Maybe she'd find the opportunity—and the nerve—to mention it later.

When they reached the hospital, Therese led the way up the stairs to the east ward with Polly following her. Polly seemed tired but determined to do all she could. Therese would help with the other patients too and not just Warner.

After she'd hung up her cloak and put on her apron, she went straight to her brother's ward. A few of the hanging gaslights were lit around the room, casting long shadows and a little light. Therese knelt beside her brother's head and whispered, "Warner, I'm here."

His eyes opened slowly. "Mother?"

"No, it's me. Therese."

"Where's Mother?"

"She'll be here in a day or two. Michael's on his way to tell her."

Warner reached for Therese's hand. "Thank you, sister." He smiled a little and then closed his eyes again.

"Rest," she said. "I'm going to help with the other patients, but I'll check often to see if you need anything."

"Do you work here?" He kept his eyes shut.

"I volunteer. I started a couple of weeks ago."

"Does the surgeon know what he's doing?" Warner murmured.

"More than you can imagine."

"But did he really have to take my leg?"

"He wouldn't have done so if it wasn't absolutely necessary."

"All right. I'll trust you." A tear slipped down the side of Warner's face, and he clenched his eyes closed. "Go on now." His voice faltered a little. "Others need your care."

Therese patted his shoulder and then helped Polly distribute the nighttime medication. She didn't see Dr. Talbot until they were nearly finished with their rounds. He was in the west ward, leaning over a young-looking soldier and tending to a throat wound.

Polly walked toward him as soon as she saw him, saying, "I heard of an interesting case today from my employer. He mentioned it when I stopped by his office earlier to tell him I was working another shift tonight."

"Oh?" Dr. Talbot didn't look up from the wound he was cleaning, but once again he seemed capable of listening to her talk as he worked.

"It was about an injury that happened near Vicksburg. Mr. Baxter was sharing an old war story." She stepped closer and lowered her voice. "A soldier had his femoral artery shot straight through."

"Left or right?" Dr. Talbot asked.

"Right," Polly answered.

"That would certainly put an end to things, wouldn't it?"

"Yes," Polly said. "He died on the battlefield."

"Too bad someone didn't know to do a tourniquet."

"Someone tried—another soldier. But he was too late."

Therese tried not to listen—or at least not to look as though she were listening. Something was so strange about their conversation, as if they weren't just talking about injuries. Her brow furrowed, she busied herself tending to a nearby patient.

"Goodness, that's fascinating," Dr. Talbot said. "I hope next time that happens the outcome is better." When he finished the wound he was working on, he stood and stretched, only then noticing that Therese was there too.

He gave her a smile and announced that this would be a good time to take a break and walk over to Mr. and Mrs. Corbetts' house to ask if they would be able to accommodate Therese's mother. "The fresh air will do me good," he said. Then he excused himself and left the room.

Therese and Polly kept working, finally collapsing halfway through the night on cots in the crowded dormitory room for the nurses. But by dawn they were up again, administering medication to the soldiers, including the farm boy from North Carolina who was running a fever. Therese comforted him as best she could and then gave him a shot of medicinal whiskey.

When she ran into Dr. Talbot later, he told her that he'd spoken to the Corbetts, and they would like to host her mother. "They're ready for her whenever she arrives. And they have a cot off the kitchen where her driver can sleep."

Therese thanked him even as Polly began chiding him about not getting any sleep the night before. "You won't do anyone any good if you keep working around the clock like this," she said, and Therese realized he did look exhausted, his usually neat hair tousled and circles dark under his eyes. "Go take a nap."

He relented without any struggle, dragging himself wearily to the stairs and heading up to his quarters on the fourth floor.

When Therese next checked on Warner, he was sleeping, although not peacefully. She felt his forehead and found it warm. She filled a basin with water and grabbed a cloth from the closet, pulling a chair to the side of his cot. She mopped his forehead with the cool cloth, hoping to bring down the fever. A few minutes later, Polly came by and lifted the sheet that covered his stump.

"How does it look?" Therese asked.

"Inflamed. We'll need Dr. Talbot to look at it as soon as he wakes." They worked through the morning, feeding the invalid soldiers, many who had been in the hospital for months and months. After that they began bathing patients.

When Warner awoke, he wasn't himself. Therese tried to get him to eat, but he spit out the porridge.

"Don't take it personally." Polly sat a few rows away, feeding another soldier. "Warner's not acting that way on purpose."

"He has to eat so he can have more morphine," Therese said.

"Give him the medicine anyway," Polly answered. "He needs it more than the food."

Therese did as her friend instructed. Warner didn't spit out the morphine, and in no time he had fallen asleep again.

Chapter Fifteen
Therese

Therese and Polly continued to work throughout the day. Therese wasn't sure how her friend did it, but even though Polly had to be near exhaustion, she continued to lead the way, redressing wounds, administering medicine, and tending to the needs of the patients.

In the late afternoon, Dr. Talbot appeared at the door. Polly motioned him over to Warner, saying, "He's been running a fever."

The doctor stepped to the cot, first feeling Warner's forehead and then lifting the sheet to look at the stump. "Get me a pan of hot water," he said to Therese. "And soap and clean rags." Therese stepped to the door as he asked Polly when Warner's last dose of morphine was.

When Therese returned a few minutes later, Warner had his eyes open, and the doctor was explaining that he intended to wash out the wound again. "We'll wait a few minutes until the morphine begins to work," he said.

Someone had pulled a small table to the end of the cot, and Therese set the basin of water down and then the other things. The sheet was pulled back, but she avoided looking at Warner's wound. She'd stayed up by his head.

Polly approached Warner with a glass of water. Therese helped him raise his head enough to drink, and he quickly drained the glass.

"Thanks, Polly," he said, handing the glass back and then turning his attention to his sister.

"Are you ready?" Dr. Talbot asked. "We should get on with this."

"As ready as I can be." Warner searched Therese's eyes. "What is he doing, exactly?"

"Like he said, cleaning the wound. It's infected. Polly is assisting."

"Is it going to hurt?"

Before Therese could respond, Warner let out a scream. Then he stammered, "I-I'm sorry. I didn't mean to do that."

"It can't be helped." She slipped her hand into his. "Squeeze tightly." She felt as if he might break all of the bones in her hand, but he didn't scream again. Not until Dr. Talbot took a sponge to the wound, and this time Warner sounded as if he were being murdered. Mother appeared in the doorway mid-scream.

"What in the world is going on?" she cried, and then she darted forward, her hoop skirt swinging against the cots and smacking the soldiers lying on them.

"Stop!" Dr. Talbot ordered, but she just kept coming.

"Miss Helene, stop!" Polly yelled. "Get back to the door. Your hoops are hitting the patients!"

Finally, Mother seemed to hear. She froze, her face a mix of agony and confusion.

"Miss Helene, you could hurt someone," Polly explained. "Or knock something over."

Therese's face grew warm. Mother could be so impossible. She started to retreat, slowly.

Dr. Talbot returned to his work. "I'm almost done," he muttered.

Warner writhed in pain. "Thank goodness."

"Are you all right?" Mother called out. "I'll get you home as soon as possible and have Dr. Landers take care of you. Badan and I can drive you back tomorrow."

Warner groaned. "Is she crazy?"

"No," Therese said. "Just obtuse." She didn't add that their mother's anxiety, which had begun when Father fell ill and grown even worse with Grandfather's death, would likely reach new heights now, thanks to Warner's injury. Therese couldn't fault their mother for being fearful. It was understandable during such times. She just wished the woman had enough fortitude to toughen up and rely on her faith instead of her emotions.

Warner gritted his teeth again. "How did you ever convince her to let you come to Richmond?"

Therese hesitated, not wanting to go into it at the moment. "I didn't," she said finally, a hint of defiance in her voice. Warner seemed to understand.

A quick smile crossed his lips, and he squeezed her hand again, though this time more from affection—perhaps even respect—than pain. Her heart warmed at his kindness, something she hadn't seen much in him before.

"I doubt Dr. Landers can give me any better care than I'm getting here," he said.

"I know he can't," Therese replied. "Michael brought you to the best surgeon in the South—even if he is a Northerner."

Warner groaned again and lifted his head. "A Yank's working on me?"

Dr. Talbot barked, "Don't move."

Therese put her other hand on Warner's shoulder to keep him still. "He really is the best. And at least he's a Talbot," she added. "A cousin of Michael and Polly's, descended from good ol' Emmanuel himself."

Once Dr. Talbot was finished, Polly offered to stay with Warner so Therese and the doctor could speak with Mother. Therese looked over at the doorway, where her mother was standing a step inside the room, her skirt blocking the way. Matron Webb was behind her, trying to get past. The matron finally asked her to move.

Dr. Talbot washed his hands, dried them on a towel, and motioned for Therese to lead the way. When they reached the door, she took her mother by the elbow and led her farther down the hall and then gave her a quick hug and introduced her to the doctor.

At the name Talbot, Mother's face softened with relief. "A relation of Stephen and Amanda's?" she asked.

"Yes. Not a close relation, but we both trace back to the same Huguenot ancestors."

"Remember, Mother?" Therese added. "That day on the ferry? Polly told us how her cousin had come down to help at the hospital?"

Mother's smile disappeared. "Oh, yes. From somewhere...up north."

"Maine," he offered.

Mother's lips pursed in distaste, as if he'd uttered a profanity. "And why are *you* caring for my son?"

Therese's cheeks grew warm. "Dr. Talbot is an excellent surgeon, Mother."

Before she could reply, the doctor simply launched into an explanation of the injury, the surgery, and now the treatment. "Only time will tell what the outcome will be."

"Yes," Mother replied. "Back home. We're better equipped to care for him there than here."

Dr. Talbot didn't respond. Therese rolled her eyes and then hooked her arm through Mother's. "Let's get these hoops off you so that you can see Warner."

"Can't you move the cots?" Mother asked.

"No, we can't." Therese pulled her mother down the hall and directed her into the nurses' quarters. She then helped her take her skirt off, removed the hoops, and helped her dress again.

"I feel practically naked." Mother straightened her skirt.

"We went without hoops all the time back at the cottage." Therese opened the door. "You didn't mind then."

"Well, it's been a while since I had to weed a garden or cook over a hot stove. I've grown accustomed to wearing them again."

Therese didn't respond. "How is Aggie?"

"Fine."

"Who's in charge back at River Pines?"

"Mr. Porter, of course."

Therese stepped into the hall. "Why don't you let him go?"

Mother shrugged. "He's only working for room and board."

"But there aren't any crops, Mother. What's the point?"

"He does handyman-type work around the place—and over at the Talbots' too. Most importantly, though, he oversees the servants. Otherwise they might run off." Now that Mother was a single white woman living alone, the Twenty-Slave Law allowed for her to keep an overseer even though she had less than twenty slaves, with no need for him to work at other plantations anymore.

Therese decided to change the subject. "I have good news. Dr. Talbot has arranged for you to stay with friends of his. They have space for Badan too."

"Oh?"

"Unless you have another plan," Therese said.

"Taking Warner home is my plan."

"Mother, you can't. He may need more surgery." She'd seen several soldiers who'd had to have more of their stumps amputated. "Plus, Dr. Talbot has the best rate of curing infections of any doctor in Richmond."

"Goodness, you sound as if this man is some sort of savior."

"No," Therese answered. "But he is a good doctor. You'd be foolish to take Warner away from here."

Mother made a noise of disagreement but didn't say anything more. When they reached the ward, Therese told her to wash her hands. Mother protested, saying they were clean, but Therese insisted.

Soon they were making their way between the cots to Warner. Polly sat at the end of the bed, redoing the dressing. Mother gave her a distracted nod and then sat on the stool beside her son.

"Warner?" she asked softly. "It's Mother. I'm here now."

His eyes fluttered, but he didn't open them.

"He just had a dose of morphine," Polly told her. "He'll probably sleep for a while."

Mother sighed heavily. "You can't imagine how I felt when Michael told me. Auntie Vera brought him into the parlor, and right away I knew something had happened to Warner. Michael sat beside me and held my hand while I cried." She swiped at her eyes, and Therese put an arm around her.

"He couldn't stay long, even though I begged him to. Once he was gone, I had to sit there all by myself while Auntie Vera finished pulling my things together."

"Mother." Therese couldn't help it. "You're perfectly capable of packing a bag."

"But it's so nice to have help. I'd forgotten how comforting it is."

Therese caught Polly's gaze but refrained from rolling her eyes again. She turned back to her mother. "Did you send food with Michael for the troops? A box of apples? A bag of potatoes?"

"Oh, I meant to," Mother said. "Perhaps he asked Auntie Vera or Aggie."

"Did he leave before you did?" Polly asked.

"Yes. He said he needed to get back."

Polly sighed. "He must have been tired."

"He didn't seem so. Not particularly anyway." Mother waved her hand, as if dismissing Polly's concern. "He's young." She directed her attention back toward Warner, saying his name and then, "Son, please wake up."

Therese pursed her lips. Mother's lack of empathy concerned her. She seemed to be becoming more and more centered on herself and less concerned about others. Even so, didn't she realize the kind of pain Warner was in?

Mother stood and turned toward the end of the cot. For a moment Therese thought she was going to go look at Warner's wound, but instead she said, "Polly."

"Yes?" Polly kept working.

"Don't you think I should take Warner home and have Dr. Landers look after him?"

Polly's head jerked up, her eyes wide. "Absolutely not! In fact, Miss Helene, you would have to do it over my dead body."

Mother scoffed. "Don't be ridiculous."

"I'm not," Polly said. "If you want to lose your boy, by all means put him in a buggy and bounce him over miles of rough roads. Then trust him to a doctor who's never treated a shrapnel wound in his life, let alone an amputation." Her eyes narrowed as she stared Mother down. "On the other hand, if you want Warner to have the best chance he can, you'll keep him here."

Mother didn't respond. Instead, she sat back down in the chair and took Warner's hand in hers. Finally, she said, "I guess I'll take Dr. Talbot up on staying with his friends—at least for tonight."

After supper, Therese found Badan on the loading dock, helping with a wagonful of supplies, and told him that he'd be staying at the Corbett home with Mother.

"Yes'm."

"She'll be ready to go in a few minutes," Therese added. "Dr. Talbot will ride along and make the introductions."

He tipped his hat. "I'll go get the buggy, then."

Therese and Polly told Mother goodbye in the foyer, and then Therese thanked Dr. Talbot for his care and kindness.

"I'm happy to help your family." He stepped closer to her. "How long will you stay tonight?"

"Polly and I will leave within the hour. I'll come back late tomorrow afternoon." She didn't think the Galloways would object.

"Very good. I'll see you then." His eyes were filled with concern. "In the meantime, our prayers for Warner will not go unheard."

"Thank you." Her heart raced. She knew the situation was dire, but Dr. Talbot's care for Warner—and for her—gave her strength.

As Therese started toward the stairs, she saw Polly step closer to Dr. Talbot and then brush against his hand. Surprised, Therese hesitated for a moment—she was sure Polly had slipped the doctor a piece of paper—and then continued on to the second floor.

She thought about that for the next hour as she and Polly finished administering the medications. Something odd had transpired in that hallway between the two cousins, something suspicious, almost covert. Almost…like two spies, passing a message between them.

Startled at the thought, Therese looked across the room at her best friend, who was helping a soldier swallow his medicine. Polly, who was always so brave, so self-assured. Who had always believed slavery was wrong, and that the strong should stand up for the weak. Who had strange conversations with Dr. Talbot about left lobes and right arteries and tourniquets and more. Was it possible that the two of them had been speaking in some sort of code? Right there in the midst of injured soldiers and hospital workers, could they have been using medical terms in place of logistical ones?

Therese's heart pounded at the thought.

She was able to bring it up a short while later, once she made a final check on Warner and she and Polly started out for home. The evening was dry and cool, but not cold, and the streets mostly quiet as usual.

Therese waited until they'd gotten past the capitol grounds and turned onto Grace Street before she linked her arm through her friend's and spoke softly into her ear.

"What's going on?"

"About?"

"That piece of paper you slipped Dr. Talbot tonight."

No reaction.

"The odd accounts you give him about wounded soldiers," Therese added. Then she simply stayed quiet, waiting for her friend to respond as they walked.

"Do you think anyone else saw?" Polly asked, her voice low, stride unaltered, expression casual.

"I don't think so. People were busy. A lot was going on. I just happened to be in the right spot at the right moment."

"Good."

Therese waited, but when Polly didn't go on, she prodded her again. "So what was it? What are you up to, my friend?"

"Nothing."

"Uh-huh. Are you saying you can't tell me?"

Polly hesitated. "It's for your own good."

"What if I said I'd like to...help? Mr. Galloway is a clerk in the secretary of state's office, after all. I know for a fact that puts me in a somewhat...accessible position."

Polly drew Therese closer and then put her other arm around her. "I'll think about it."

"Think about what?" a voice asked from behind them.

Both women startled and clung to each other as they turned their heads. A soldier had snuck up on them.

"Whether I can work at the hospital again tomorrow evening," Polly said quickly as she pulled out her pass and held it up. "I worked yesterday, last night, and today. As you can imagine, I'm exhausted and am wondering if I can manage to return tomorrow."

The soldier stared at her for a moment and then said, "I see." He tightened his grip on his rifle. "Nurses or not, you two should hurry on home and keep your conversations to a minimum. You don't want to raise suspicions."

"Of course not," Therese stammered, showing her pass too. "We're nearly home now." She pulled Polly along, slipped her pass back into her pocket, and called out over her shoulder, "Good night!"

"Oh, goodness," Polly said, putting her pass away too. "What a fright."

"I didn't think anything scared you." Therese willed her heart to stop galloping.

"You'd be surprised." Polly walked even faster. "You know what scares me the most? How our soldiers can be alive one day and dead the next. I didn't want to tell you, but you'll find out soon enough. The farm boy from North Carolina passed Saturday morning."

"Oh, no." Therese felt as if she'd been kicked in the stomach. "Poor thing." She couldn't help but think of her brother.

"I know," Polly said. "Death happens in the hospital a lot, but it's still an injured soldier's best chance for survival. Warner's so fortunate to have you as an advocate. To have all of us. Don't let your mother take him home."

"I'll do my best," Therese said.

When they reached the row house, Polly gave Therese a quick hug. "I'll come by for you at four thirty tomorrow."

Therese tried to lighten the moment by teasing her friend. "Are you sure you feel up to going back?"

"You couldn't keep me away from there. I used to like teaching until I started nursing. It's all I want to do now."

"Get some sleep," Therese said. "And I'll see you tomorrow."

She stood and watched Polly hurry to the corner and disappear, confident she'd cover the last block in no time. Therese let herself into the row house and stopped in the hall for a moment. A dim light burned in the parlor, but no one was in the room. She stepped through the door. Mr. Galloway's papers from the evening before were still on the table. She glanced down at Eleanor's book on the floor, taking a closer look at the stack on the table as she did. The first page read, TOP SECRET.

A rustling down the hall caused her to bend down and pick up the book.

"You're back." Mr. Galloway stood in the doorway.

"Yes," she said, standing, book in hand, heart pounding wildly in her chest.

"How is your brother?"

Tears stung her eyes. "His wound is infected."

"Did your mother arrive?"

"Yes, this afternoon. She's staying with a couple who lives near the hospital." She hadn't told her mother the Corbetts were Quaker—and she guessed she'd get a piece of Mother's mind about it later. "I'd like to go back to the hospital tomorrow evening, if that's all right."

"Of course." Mr. Galloway stepped into the room.

Therese put the book on the table, quickly told him good night, and headed for the hall as he gathered up his stack of documents. Therese had a feeling that was how Polly garnered information—by snooping through Mr. Baxter's papers. The man worked for the War Department, which meant he was even more likely to have sensitive materials around than Mr. Galloway.

So how did it work from there? Therese wondered as she slowly climbed to her room in the attic. Did Polly take the information about troop movements or ammunition stores or vulnerabilities and translate them into stories about head wounds and stomach punctures and severed arteries? Stories that Dr. Talbot would decode and then convey, perhaps to the Corbetts?

Therese could only guess at the details, but still she yearned to help, to contribute to their efforts. She didn't want any more soldiers, Northern or Southern, to be wounded as Warner had been. And she certainly didn't want any more to die, not like the sweet farm boy from North Carolina had. If Polly's little spy network was helping to bring the Confederacy down, then Therese wanted in.

If they would have her, she was ready.

Chapter Sixteen

Therese

The next afternoon Mother sent Badan in the buggy to collect Therese and Polly. Instead of inquiring more about Polly's secret work, Therese asked Badan how Aggie was doing. He hesitated a moment and then answered, "Just fine."

Therese wanted to pry for more information, but not with Polly in the buggy. "And Auntie Vera? How is she?"

"She's fine too."

"How about Mr. Porter?"

Badan hesitated again but then said, "I guess he's fine too. He mostly keeps to himself."

Therese wondered if that meant the man spent most of his time drinking.

"Who is seeing to the property?" Therese asked.

"Old Joe, Sonny, and me, with Aggie and Auntie Vera's help. We've been pruning the trees in the orchard."

"I see." Therese hoped Mr. Porter would actually do some of the work for his room and board. She felt compelled to talk with Mother again about freeing the slaves, but it sounded as though the woman was becoming more and more dependent on their labor. Therese wondered why they didn't just leave—but of course they had nowhere to go, and heading North without help or a plan would be too risky. Even if Mr. Porter was too drunk to go after them, the slave patrols would. President Lincoln had signed the final Emancipation Proclamation nearly two years ago, but of course it carried no authority in the South.

When they reached the hospital, Badan stopped on the street and helped both of the women down. Again, Therese led the way to Warner's ward, finding Mother sitting beside him and Dr. Talbot standing behind her.

"How is he?" Therese was a little breathless from rushing up the stairs.

"No better or worse," Dr. Talbot answered.

Warner turned his head toward Therese and gave her a vague smile but didn't speak. Perhaps he'd just had his morphine.

She turned toward her mother. "How are you?"

"Exhausted." Mother rubbed the back of her neck. "But not from lack of sleep or help." She glanced toward Dr. Talbot. "I have to say, the Corbetts are very gracious and have a comfortable home, especially considering they're Quakers." She straightened her skirt and without looking at Dr. Talbot added, "I'm grateful for your assistance in making the arrangements."

"I'm pleased it's working out so well."

Apparently, Mother had decided to at least be cordial to the doctor, or perhaps his good manners—and good looks—had won her over.

Polly stepped to the other side of the cot, and Dr. Talbot asked her if she'd assist him in surgery.

"Not on Warner, I hope," she said.

Dr. Talbot shook his head. "No, he's holding his own. It's a soldier in the west ward, across the hall. He has a bullet embedded in his shoulder that needs to come out."

Polly stood straight. "Is he up in surgery already?"

"Yes," Dr. Talbot answered. "I was just headed there now."

"Of course I'll assist." She turned toward Therese. "Serve supper. Then start administering the medications if I'm not done."

Therese assured Polly she would take care of it. "Would you like to help, Mother?"

"Oh, goodness no. I'm going back to the Corbetts' so I can return here early in the morning. I figure we can take turns with Warner until he can go home, hopefully by the end of the week."

"Mother, you know that's not a good idea."

"But he's doing better, right?"

"Wait until Dr. Talbot says it would be safe."

She exhaled. "I don't want to stay in Richmond any longer than I have to."

"You can go home and then return. There's no reason to stay here continually."

"Warner needs me," Mother said.

He needs Dr. Talbot and this hospital more, Therese wanted to say but didn't, knowing it would only make matters worse. "Of course he does," she said instead. "That's why you should pace yourself. There are soldiers here who have been recovering for months. There's no set timetable to any of this. There's no way to know how long it will take Warner to heal. If you go home and rest up and then come back, you'll be better equipped to care for him."

Mother seemed to ponder that for a moment. Then she asked, "Did Badan come in with you?"

Therese shook her head. "He dropped us off. I'm guessing he parked the buggy back by the stables."

"He was helping Dr. Talbot earlier with lifting some of the patients." Mother stood. "I'll offer his services tomorrow."

"Thank you, Mother." It was helpful work. There were never enough orderlies to do all the lifting, and it was hard on the nurses' backs. It seemed Mother at least planned to stay the next day. "I'll get your cloak."

Mother leaned over Warner and patted his head. "My boy, I'll be back tomorrow."

He stirred but didn't speak. His body had to be in horrible shock, not to mention who knew what the years of war and the last attack in particular had done to his mind and soul. Therese felt overcome with compassion for her brother. Perhaps he'd be awake enough later to speak with her some more.

When she reached the closet, Badan was coming up the stairs. "My mother is about ready to leave," Therese said.

"All right." He glanced toward the ward across the hall. "Do you think I have time to check on a soldier? He was having a hard time before I left to get you."

"Yes, but first I need to ask you something." She stepped closer and lowered her voice. "How are things, really, at River Pines? Is Mr. Porter treating all of you well?"

"Well as can be expected," Badan answered, lowering his eyes.

"What is it?"

"I can't say."

Therese exhaled. "Does Mother know of your concerns?"

Badan shook his head.

"Is he violent?" Therese asked.

"I can't say."

"If you could, would you—" She looked around. No one was in sight. She dropped her voice to a whisper. "Would you leave?"

He shook his head.

"If Aggie could go too?"

This time he looked around but even though no one was near, he still didn't answer but his eyes grew large.

Therese sighed. "Go along to the ward. I'll come get you when Mother's ready." But when Therese reached Warner's ward, Mother stood in the doorway.

"What were you talking to Badan about?"

Therese felt her face grow warm. "About the soldier he had helped earlier today. He's back there now. He'll be done in just a minute."

Mother shook her head. "I need to go now."

"Wait just a moment. He'll be right out."

Mother shook her head again. "I don't think you understand..."

"Please stop," Therese said.

Mother pouted for a moment, but then she said, "I'll send Badan to take you home tonight. I'll write another pass."

"That won't be necessary. The weather's good. Polly and I will walk." Therese wanted to have a chance to talk with her friend again.

"It's not safe," Mother said.

Therese helped her mother with her cloak. "We'll be fine, Mother. We have our passes. Soldiers patrol the streets. Please don't worry."

The night sky had grown cloudy, but the rain held off as Therese and Polly started home. They were quiet at first, and Therese became lost in her own thoughts about Badan and the conversation she'd had with him earlier. For a long time, she had assumed there were only two options for the slaves of River Pines. Either Grandfather—or, later, Mother—had to legally free them, or the South had to lose the war. Today, however, it had struck her that there might be a third option, for Badan and Aggie at least. To flee north.

That thought filled her with guilt for two very different reasons. On the one hand, she knew that by aiding their escape, she would essentially be stealing them out from under her own family. On the other hand, Badan and Aggie were *people*, not property, no matter what anyone said. That was why Therese's guilt was far greater for the second reason, that this option had never occurred to her before.

She simply had to do whatever she could to facilitate their escape. Of course, she would keep working on Mother to free them. That would be the safest for all involved. Certainly for Badan and Aggie, but also for whoever assisted them. God willing, Mother would change her mind. But if not, there needed to be an alternative plan. These things could take a while, so the sooner she began inquiring about escape, the better.

Summoning her nerve, she began by sharing with Polly her concerns about Mr. Porter in as tactful a method as possible. "He's been violent before." She'd always worried about Mr. Porter beating the men, but these days she worried even more about the women—Aggie, of course, but the thought of him accosting Auntie Vera wasn't out of the question either. Still, Badan and Aggie were the two who were the most at risk. Old Joe and Sonny wouldn't be as much of a threat.

"I was wondering if you would know of any way to send a couple of slaves north, like on the Underground Railroad," Therese whispered. "If perhaps you've...done anything...in that capacity."

Polly gave a sympathetic murmur but didn't reply.

"Polly?"

Her friend skipped a step and twirled around, looking behind her. Then she whispered to Therese, "I'm not certain what the treatment for a lacerated liver is, but I'll find out."

Therese allowed herself a small smile, pleased that her theory had been correct.

"And yes," Polly added, "I've helped in a number of capacities."

"And Dr. Talbot is involved."

"The less you know the better."

Therese thought of Rose O'Neal Greenhow and her work as a spy. To do the opposite of what Rose wanted, to help bring slavery to an end, would be an honor for Therese. "I understand there are things I shouldn't know," she said, "but if you need more helpers...if there's anything I can do to help speed—"

Steps fell behind them.

Polly, using a normal voice, said, "The success of the Confederacy."

"Yes," Therese answered.

The voice behind them was deep but wavered. "Where are you two ladies headed?"

"Home," Polly answered without turning around. Both women kept walking, close enough that their shoulders touched. Therese took comfort—and courage—from her friend.

"Stop," the man said.

Polly linked her arm through Therese's and pulled her even closer. The man stepped quickly and grabbed Therese's other arm. She could smell whiskey on his breath as she struggled away from him.

"Are you a guard?" Polly asked, yanking on Therese. "Or a soldier? Because you don't look like one."

"No. I'm a concerned citizen," he sneered.

"Then leave us alone." Polly let go of Therese. She reached her hand into her cloak and seemed to aim something at the man, under the cloth.

"I'll shoot," Polly said.

"You wouldn't," the man said.

"Of course I would." Polly held the object higher.

He froze.

"One, two—"

"I'm going." The man turned and hustled away from them.

Therese's hand flew to her mouth as she turned toward Polly. "Why didn't you tell me you have a gun?"

Her friend smiled and held up her hand, her index finger extended. "Because I don't."

Therese couldn't help but laugh, but then she fell serious. "I thought we were safe."

"We are."

Therese shook her head. This war had to stop. "Tell me what I can do. Please."

"About?"

"Helping."

"Right now, you can help best by keeping quiet about it. I'll let you know if an opportunity arises." Polly grabbed Therese's hand. "And please don't say anything to my family about what I'm doing, especially not Michael. He wouldn't understand. Not at all."

Therese bristled. Even his own sister knew he couldn't be trusted.

When they arrived at the hospital the next day, Matron Webb was in the foyer, consulting with Dr. Moore. Seeing the young women, she excused herself. "I have a proposition for the two of you," she said.

"What about?" Polly asked.

"Two more nurses resigned, and we were understaffed as it was." Matron Webb folded her hands together. "You're coming in every day anyway, so I wondered if we could hire the two of you for weeknights and Saturdays. That would give you Sundays off. Not to mention you would be paid employees rather than volunteers."

Therese and Polly said "Yes" in unison.

"Do you want to know what the pay rate is?"

The girls shook their heads.

"Well, that's good," she said. "It's not much, but it will help your families a bit more."

As they climbed the stairs, Therese asked Polly if she thought they could keep up with their teaching duties too.

"We'll just have to get more efficient at planning our days. I'm certain we'll manage."

Polly headed straight to the west ward and began assisting Dr. Talbot, while Therese went to check on Warner.

He was propped up on his cot. Mother sat beside him, sipping a cup of tea. Warner gave Therese a half smile as she approached.

"Finally," Mother said. "I thought perhaps you weren't going to make it."

Therese didn't answer. Instead, she kissed her mother's cheek and then bent down and kissed her brother's forehead. "How are you today?" she asked.

"Better. I ate some lunch, and Dr. Talbot said my wound is improving."

"My boy will be going home soon," Mother said.

"Really?" Therese stood. "Is that what Dr. Talbot told you?"

"No." Warner's voice was as forceful as it had been since he'd arrived at the hospital.

"That man doesn't know what he's talking about," Mother retorted. "I'm going to consult with Dr. Landers tomorrow."

"Mother. The issue is best left to Warner, based on Dr. Talbot's advice. After all, Warner is a grown man and the head of our family now."

That stopped Mother for a moment, but then she patted Warner's shoulder and said, "Of course Warner is the head of our family. But he's hardly in any condition to make such a decision at this time. He needs me now more than ever."

A pained expression passed over Warner's face, but then it turned into a bit of a smile. Perhaps he understood that Mother needed him to need her now more than ever.

Mother continued. "I'll have Auntie Vera and Aggie get the parlor ready, and then I'll return to collect Warner."

"Mother, you *can't*. Please follow Dr. Talbot's instructions."

"That Yankee from Maine doesn't know anything."

"You were married to a Yankee from New Jersey."

"That was different." Mother finished her tea and then handed Therese the cup. "Would you take this down to the kitchen? And tell Badan I'm ready to go. I'll meet him out front."

"He's waiting for you now." Therese handed her back the cup. "And you can take this to the kitchen yourself."

Mother looked startled. "Don't be impertinent. It's ugly on you."

Therese crossed her arms, feeling even less timid than she had the day she announced she was moving to Richmond.

"That's not a pretty look either." Mother tossed her head as she spoke, but then her expression softened as she patted Warner's shoulder. "I'll be back by Thursday or Friday. You'll be home in no time." Mother turned toward Therese. "Tell Dr. Talbot what my plan is, please. I'll let Mr. and Mrs. Corbett know."

Therese shook her head. She wouldn't tell Dr. Talbot a thing. It was a ludicrous plan.

Mother shrugged. "Goodbye." She held her head high as she left the ward, empty cup in hand.

Therese sat down on the stool. "Do you want to go home?"

"No. Don't let her take me unless the doctor thinks it's what is best."

"I won't, but you're the one with the most say. I'll back you up, of course."

"Sister, you've changed. You aren't as meek and mild as you were as a girl." He smiled again, just a little. "Regardless, I think Dr. Talbot will listen to you. Rumor has it he's quite fond of you."

Therese wrinkled her nose. "Polly doesn't know what she's talking about."

Warner shook his head. "I didn't hear it from Polly. Matron Webb told me."

"Oh, my." Therese felt her face grow warm—and her heart too.

"You could leave all of this." Warner made a sweeping motion with his left arm. "Head to Maine. Have a bunch of little Talbots."

Therese shook her head. "I'm not interested in leaving."

"You should be. I would if I were you. It's going to get worse, and even after the war ends, it will be a long time before anything gets better."

Therese was shocked by his assessment. "What are you saying?"

He sighed. "I should have listened to Father. I'm afraid he was right. Remember how he used to say sin separated people? Slavery did that. It's separated our nation. And now families. There's no reason for you to stay and live through the consequences if you don't have to."

"But you and Mother are here."

Warner lowered his voice. "I know I haven't always been the best big brother, and maybe you don't care to hear my advice now, but you should definitely leave if you can."

Therese studied his face. "Not long ago you were upset because your doctor was a Yankee. Now you want me to run off with the man?"

His eyes watered as he spoke. "Perhaps I brought a little battlefield bravado with me, but I can't let that be my compass when it comes to my sister's future."

Her heart swelled. He was the big brother she'd always longed for after all. "We'll talk about it later," she said. "Right now I need to serve supper. I'll bring yours soon."

He closed his eyes. "I'm not hungry."

"That doesn't matter. I'll bring it to you anyway."

The evening sped by quickly. Dr. Talbot approached her several times, but each time, before they could have a conversation, they were interrupted. Toward the end of her shift, she spotted him in the empty hallway and walked over to him, needing to ask about a wound.

"Dr. Talbot."

His face lit up when he saw her. "Please, call me Alec."

"Pardon?"

"Call me Alec," he whispered, "when it's just the two of us."

She shook her head, making him smile.

"Well," he added, eyes twinkling, "at least think of me as Alec."

"I'll try," she replied, her heart fluttering a little.

She asked him about a patient, and he followed her to the soldier's bedside to take a look. He was a drummer boy, not more than thirteen, with just the beginning of peach fuzz on his chin. His company had fallen under mortar attack, and a wound in his back was of particular concern.

Dr. Talbot prodded the patient's abdomen for a moment. Therese watched as he did, realizing how much she'd grown as a nurse. She no longer felt sick to her stomach or at a loss in caring for the patients. She spoke to the boy softly, but he didn't answer. His eyes were glazed with fear. She patted his hand. "You'll be all right."

Dr. Talbot concurred, adding, "Miss Jennings will give you something to help you sleep."

The boy nodded.

"Give him another dose of morphine." Dr. Talbot suddenly appeared tired. "Keep him comfortable."

Therese gave him a knowing look and tears welled in her eyes, but she quickly blinked them away.

He nodded. "I've arranged for a driver to take you and Polly home after your shift. She told me what happened last night. I'm so grateful it was nothing more than a scare. From now on, the wagon master will take you home."

As he passed by her, Therese answered softly, "Thank you, Alec."

He smiled and then brushed against her arm. For a moment, she thought she'd imagined it, but then he glanced over his shoulder at her, a playful expression on his face. She smiled, longing to spend more time with him.

When she turned back toward the drummer boy, however, her moment of joy immediately vanished.

He moaned. She patted his shoulder and went to get the medicine. When she returned, she quickly gave him his dose and then sat and held his hand until he fell asleep. She doubted he'd live for long.

⟿

The next day, because Badan had left with Mother for River Pines, Therese and Polly walked to the hospital. When they arrived, Warner was asleep. Matron Webb said he'd had a good day and eaten more than before. "I think he's on the mend," she said.

Relief rushed through Therese. She knew not to get her hopes up, but perhaps he would make it after all.

She checked on the drummer boy, but as she expected, he had died that morning. She took a deep breath and said a prayer for his family.

As she collected more supplies, Dr. Talbot greeted her.

"Hello, Dr. Talbot," she answered.

He stepped into the large closet with her and to the left, out of sight from anyone passing by in the hall. "Alec," he whispered.

She smiled and then asked about the boy who had died. "We kept him out of pain," Dr. Talbot answered. "It was inevitable."

Therese nodded. She understood.

Dr. Talbot echoed what Matron Webb had said about Warner. She thanked him, knowing he took good care of all of the patients, but that he was especially looking after her brother.

"I'm wondering if you'd want to join me for church on Sunday morning," he said. "I'd like to know what you think of our services."

She cocked her head at him, intrigued. "What are they like?"

He leaned against the doorframe. "Members take turns with the teaching each week, except when we have silent meetings."

"Oh?"

"For those, we sit and listen to God, especially seeking His 'still small voice.' Individuals share what He's teaching them. It's all very contemplative and reflective."

"It sounds lovely." Her father would have appreciated such a service.

Alec glanced behind him and lowered his voice. "We also focus on equal rights between the races and men and women. We take seriously the verse in Galatians that says we are all one in Christ Jesus."

Yes, Father would have definitely appreciated the doctrine of the Quakers. Galatians 3:28 was one of his favorite verses.

"Here in Richmond, as I've said, we meet in members' homes. This Sunday's service will be at the Corbetts'."

Therese sighed. "I would love to join you. I have no issues with the Quaker faith." She hoped she was communicating her thoughts as to what the future might hold. "But I can't go while I'm staying at the Galloways. I couldn't explain it to them."

"I'm sure you could."

She shook her head. True, her father believed in equality of all people, but that didn't mean the rest of the South did. Attending a Quaker meeting would be seen as being disrespectful to her employers and subversive to her community, plus it would bring attention to her. Sure, she could make up an excuse. Or lie and say she was working at the hospital. But she didn't feel comfortable doing that. "I hope I can go to a Quaker meeting with you sometime soon though," she added.

He frowned. "I'd feel better if you went with me now. It's a big part of my life."

She understood that. No doubt, his beliefs truly made him the man he was. "In time," she said, and then she smiled as sweetly as she could.

"Why does it feel as if I've known you for years?"

Therese felt the same. His way of life appealed to her, as did his goodness and commitment to others.

"Perhaps it's because I met your father and enjoyed his writings so much that you seem so familiar," he added. "But I think it's more than that."

A shiver shot down Therese's spine. She'd always dreamed of Michael until she realized how much she'd misjudged him. There was no misjudging Alec. He was exactly who he seemed to be.

"Dr. Talbot!" It was Matron Webb.

Alec smiled at her again and then slowly turned around. Therese resumed collecting supplies.

"Here I am." He stepped out into the hall.

"I've been looking all over for you," the matron said. Therese sighed in relief. The woman hadn't seen her. She'd been positive about Therese's growing relationship with Dr. Talbot—but Therese didn't want to be found alone in a closet with him nonetheless.

Later, as Therese fed a soldier too weak to feed himself, she thought more about Alec. If he truly cared for her as he seemed and she returned his affections, she would have to move to Maine. She was surprised to find that the thought encouraged her. She would put all of the worries of her family behind, along with the horrible injustices around her. In Maine she wouldn't have any financial concerns. She could focus on being a wife and, God willing, someday a mother. Have a bunch of little Talbots running around, as Warner put it.

She shivered a little and then chastised herself for thinking of such things. Perhaps that wasn't what Alec had in mind at all. On the other hand, it seemed possible that was exactly what he intended. Why else would he be so eager for her to visit a Quaker service? The thought of sharing her life with a kind, intelligent, and caring man warmed her soul.

Later, not too long before she and Polly needed to start home, Alec stopped her in the hall. "Do you remember me mentioning my cousin Ruth?"

Therese nodded.

"I just received word that she'll arrive in a couple of weeks. I don't have the time to tell you now, but I have a story concerning her and a lacerated liver. Remind me to tell you before she arrives."

"All right." Therese's pulse surged.

"Good." He smiled, his brown eyes shining. "I look forward to seeing you tomorrow."

She spent the last minutes of her shift by Warner's bed, overcome with exhaustion—and gratitude that Alec had arranged a ride home for her and Polly.

The next day sped by as she taught the girls, trying not to yawn too much as she helped them with lessons she'd hastily planned before breakfast. That afternoon, when she and Polly arrived at the hospital, Alec was in surgery. Polly immediately went upstairs to assist him while Matron Webb, an anxious expression on her face, cornered Therese in the hallway.

"There are rumors of the hospital closing down," she said.

"I see." Therese's heart nearly stopped at the thought of it. She knew Alec would be leaving not long after Ruth arrived, but she'd still been hoping he'd change his mind. If the hospital closed, he wouldn't have a reason to stay.

And where would Warner go? To Chimborazo Hospital, where many of the Virginia soldiers ended up? Polly had told Therese it had three thousand wounded, compared to three hundred at their own hospital. Mother would be more determined than ever to take him home if the Institute Hospital closed.

She stood frozen in the middle of the hallway as Matron Webb continued on down the staircase. A moment later, she realized Michael stood in the doorway to the east ward, holding his cap in his hands with his haversack across his shoulder.

Therese stepped into the supply closet, wondering about the hospital closing and what it meant for her family.

When she came out with a basin filled with water and a sponge, Michael stood in the hallway as if waiting for her.

He swept his hair, which now fell to his shoulders and across his forehead, away from his eyes and gave her a questioning look. "What was Matron Webb saying?"

Therese explained there were rumors the hospital might be closing down soon.

As Michael rubbed the dark stubble on his chin, a concerned expression settled on his face. "Does Polly know?"

Therese shook her head. "Although Dr. Talbot may be telling her as we speak. She just went to assist him."

He rubbed his chin again. "How's your brother?"

"Better."

"Has your mother arrived?"

"Yes, and thank you again for telling her about Warner."

"She was pretty upset, and justifiably so."

"She's already gone back to River Pines. She's getting it ready for Warner."

Michael raised his eyebrows. "So soon?"

Therese shrugged. "She's determined to move him." She changed the subject before he could say anything more. "What are you doing here?" It didn't seem he'd brought any patients.

"I'm after supplies for the field hospital. We're out of ether and bandages. Linens. Pretty much everything." He grimaced. "I thought I'd start here first and then go begging, from hospital to hospital, asking for a little at each."

That sounded like an arduous task. The blockade at sea had stopped the shipment of supplies and medications from Europe, although a limited amount was still smuggled in.

He took a step toward the stairs and then stopped, turning back around. "Therese?"

"Yes?"

"I've enjoyed getting to know you again. The circumstances are horrible, but seeing you every once in a while is the one bright spot in all of this."

Therese's face grew warm. "Thank you," she answered. She couldn't honestly say she'd enjoyed getting reacquainted with him in light of how troubling his new way of thinking was, so she didn't respond in kind.

"As far as the rumors about the hospital closing—perhaps there's no truth to them."

She nodded in agreement, and he continued on up the stairs. She followed, ready to get back to her duties, knowing it wouldn't do any good for her to confront Michael about his flawed ideas. She had another Talbot to consider. One who shared her hopes and—God willing—her dreams.

Chapter Seventeen
Nicole

On Friday, I felt grateful for all the mundane elements of my job, including stalls to muck, water buckets to scrub, hay bales to stack, and more. That's because the harder I worked, the less my mind wandered back to everything Maddee and I had learned the night before at Nana's with Harold and Gabe. There was just so much to process that my brain needed a break. For the time being, I would set all that aside and focus on my tasks and on these beautiful four-legged creatures, who were grace and strength personified.

Speaking of grace and strength, Nate was around all morning. He spent a lot of time working with a horse out in the exercise ring, and there was something about the way he moved that was almost mesmerizing. After sneaking more than a few glances, I realized what it was. He had the kind of fluidity that came with a lifetime spent around horses. For such big and intimidating animals, they could spook so easily that one had to learn not to make sudden movements or broad gestures. Everything this guy did was like one long, smooth motion.

I could've watched him all day.

Fortunately, I had to spend the afternoon in a mandatory equine first aid class, which took me into the main building and far from the ring. Unfortunately, as it turned out, Nate was to be our instructor. I couldn't get away from this guy.

"Hey, boss, wouldn't you rather be at the racetrack right now?" one of my coworkers asked as Nate entered the room.

"Yeah," he replied, setting one of the bright-red equine first aid kits on the table up front. "But I'm stuck here teaching you dummies instead."

"We won't tell if you won't," the guy said, looking around with a grin for others to back him up.

"Uh-huh. And what happens when your horse goes lame or develops a fever and you miss the symptoms?" Nate asked.

That earned a few whoops from the class and an embarrassed shrug from the guy.

Frowning, I leaned toward the girl next to me and whispered, "The racetrack?"

She nodded. "Powhatan Downs. Nate's over there like twice a week."

I thought about that as the class commenced. Powhatan Downs was a thoroughbred horse racing track about half an hour away. Was he going there in some professional capacity? Or did he just play the horses?

I didn't have much time to ponder the question because the class started then. Nate unzipped the large red bag and then began walking along the rows, getting each person to reach inside and pull out two items. When he came to me, I stuck my hands in and came out with a rubber tube and a disposable baby diaper. Great. If this was some sort of contest, I'd just won the booby prize—or maybe the poopy prize would be more like it.

Next, he went around the room and had each person stand up and show their items one at a time and explain its use and purpose in first aid—even though he'd had yet to teach us a thing. That was fine for those who'd pulled stuff like thermometers and rubber gloves, but for the ones with more specialized items, it was a bit of a guessing game. Still, as students did their best, giggling self-consciously, Nate used the moment to explain and elaborate. It turned out to be a fun way to learn—at least until it was my turn, and I stood up to find all eyes on me. Luckily, I knew the first one, only because I'd once seen a horse run into a hornet's nest.

"This is a rubber tube," I said, holding it up and modeling it as if I were on a TV game show, "which can be inserted through a horse's nose to aid breathing."

Nate nodded. "And why would a horse ever need you to do that?"

"If he had an allergic reaction, like to a bee sting or maybe a snake-bite, and his airway started constricting?"

"Good," my teacher said brusquely. "And?"

"And..." I said, setting down the tube and picking up the diaper with a flourish, which caused a chuckle to ripple through the room.

"Well?" Nate urged impatiently. What was this guy's problem? He'd been a lot nicer to the others.

"Well," I said slowly, thinking, "this diaper can be used in a variety of ways. First, if you have an extremely tiny foal and you don't want it to make a mess, you might be able to put it—"

One of the students made a buzzer sound, cutting me off.

"Try that one again," Nate said, not smiling.

"Well, uh, you can..." I was about to make another joke but, see-ing the glare on Nate's face, I refrained. "I suppose it might be useful for packing hooves."

"Good. What else?"

What else? "Maybe if a horse is bleeding, you could—"

"Correct," Nate said, cutting me off. "Diapers are highly absorbent and can be used to staunch blood flow from wounds. Okay. Gabby?"

And that fast, he was done with me and on to the next person. I sat, feeling heat rush to my cheeks. If this guy wasn't ignoring me entirely, he was being rude to me. What was up with that?

At the end of the day, I had just reached my car in the parking lot when I saw him ahead of me and decided to find out. I put my things in the car and then kept going, catching up with my boss just as he reached a big black truck.

"Talbot?" he asked when he saw me, his expression a mix of irritation and confusion. "Do you need something?"

"What is your problem with me? I know you're the boss and all, but I can't deal with this attitude of yours."

He studied me for a long moment before replying that he had no problem.

I wasn't buying it. "Look, I'm a hard worker. I'm good with the horses. I'm more than earning my pay."

"For now."

He tossed his duffel into the bed of the truck and stepped to the car door, as if we were done.

"For now," I repeated. "What does that mean?"

He gave a frustrated sigh. "It means I don't like wasting my time or the farm's resources training employees who are only going to end up ditching the job after a couple of weeks."

I blinked. "Excuse me?"

"You heard me."

"Ditching the job?" I asked, incredulous. "Why would I do that? I happen to love it here—well, except for this really mean guy who has it out for me. But I'm not going anywhere."

He shrugged. "We'll see. I've heard that plenty of times before, from other..." His voice trailed off.

"Other *what*?"

He blew out a breath. "Other...friends of Bill W?"

My mouth dropped open. "Friends of Bill W" was a euphemism for alcoholics and, by extension, drug addicts. "First of all," I managed to say, "my past isn't any of your business. In fact, I think you just violated some law by even bringing it up."

He shrugged and then surprised me by jingling his car keys in front of me so I could see the key tag. It was a familiar rounded triangle, with the letters *NA* on the front.

Oh great, so this guy was an addict too.

"Takes one to know one," he said. "And if I had my way, I'd be the only one here."

I was astounded at his words. "Look, buddy, I've been sober for a year and a half."

"Yeah?" He flipped the tag around so I could see the words on the back, *Clean and Serene for Fifteen*. "That's years, Talbot. Fifteen *years*."

I shook my head, trying to understand this exchange. Nate looked to be in his early thirties, which meant he'd become an addict at a young age but then sobered up in his teens and stayed that way. Good for him, though what that had to do with me, I hadn't a clue.

"Just say what you're trying to say," I insisted.

He hit the button to unlock the truck and then slid the keys into his pocket. "I don't hire addicts when I can help it, no matter how long they've been sober. You know the stats. The relapse rate is forty to sixty percent. I'm sorry, but those aren't odds I'm willing to play."

Odds I'm willing to play? At least that answered one question. His frequent trips to the racetrack *were* to gamble, which meant that, fifteen years drug-free or not, all he'd done was trade one addiction for another. Sure enough, I'd known this guy was bad news the moment I met him.

"So if that's your policy," I said, my tone even, "why did I get this job?"

"Because interns are hired by the therapist, not by me."

And that was it, the reason he'd grown hostile when he first realized I was the new intern. He didn't have anything against equine therapy. He just had something against me.

That also explained how he knew about my past, because I'd gotten this job primarily on the recommendation of a therapist from my former drug rehab facility. As I neared the end of the program, she'd been enthusiastic about my plan to major in psychology and had helped me narrow down several local options for an internship this summer. I'd given her permission to ask around on my behalf and even share some of the details of my story if need be. Apparently, not only had she told the therapist here, but for some reason the therapist had then felt compelled to share that information with Nate.

"Regardless," he said, swinging open the door and climbing into the truck's cab, "you got the job. There's nothing I can do about it now, so whatever. You say you'll stick around? Good. I hope you do."

"But you don't expect me to."

He met my eyes and shook his head. "Sorry," he said, almost sounding like he meant it. "I'd love to give you the benefit of the doubt, but I've been burned more times than you can imagine. After a while, you learn to expect the worst of people. It's just easier that way."

That night, Maddee had a date with Greg, so for the first time since moving in, I had the house to myself for an entire evening. I'd picked up Chinese takeout and a tub of Cherry Garcia in preparation, and ordinarily, I would've enjoyed the peace and quiet. But as I sat on the sofa in the glow of the television, ice cream in hand, I was suddenly overwhelmed with sadness.

Was Nate right? Was I going to fall in with the statistics? After all my hard work, everything I'd been through, was I destined to fail in the end? I certainly hoped not, but how could I know for sure?

I hadn't been this uncertain of my sobriety in a long time, and it unnerved me.

"You know the routine," I said aloud, reaching for my phone and dialing my sponsor, Riley, just as I'd been taught to do. My call went straight to voice mail, however, so I hung up without leaving a message.

I tried to go back to my show, but that didn't work. I just sat there growing more and more upset and agitated until finally, with a loud groan, I grabbed my phone and did a quick Google check to verify what I already knew. Then I flipped off the TV, put away my food, and headed to the Episcopal Church on Monument Avenue. I hadn't been to an NA meeting in ages, but I knew enough to admit that I needed one tonight.

Otherwise, the weekend passed uneventfully, and on Monday I enjoyed a real change of pace at work when one of the year-round staff members called in sick and I was assigned to take her place. Despite spending all day, every day with horses, I didn't really get to ride them much, so I jumped at the chance. One of this other staff member's main duties was to exercise the animals when their owners were out of town or otherwise unavailable to do it themselves.

Today there were three such horses, and I had the option of riding them in the exercise ring, in one of the pastures, or along the trail. I chose the trail, eager to take the long, meandering path that looped for more than a mile around some of the prettiest parts of the farm.

First up was Queenie, a stunning palomino mare with beautiful brown eyes and a sassy attitude. Once I had her saddled and ready to go, I led her to the trailhead, climbed on, and started her out at a walk, moving down the path under a thick canopy of trees. After a long straightaway, we found ourselves curving around to the right, where the path began to run alongside Dover Creek. As I moved Queenie into a trot, I found myself relaxing with her, allowing her movements to become mine, and I felt a surge of pure joy.

I thought of Friday night's NA meeting and how glad I was that I'd gone. I never understood why something so simple could make such a difference, but it did. By the time we'd gathered in a circle for the closing prayer, my head was totally back in a good space.

I'd decided that Nate Harrison was not going to derail my sobriety no matter what he thought or said or did. He may be, physically speaking, the man of my dreams, but otherwise he was my worst nightmare. I didn't need his kind of pessimism, and from here on out, my plan was to steer clear as much as possible.

Today I felt doubly confident because it just happened to be my six-hundredth day of sobriety. I was past the point of counting, really, but when one of the speakers had dragged on a little too long the other night and I found myself getting bored, I had decided to calculate where I stood and was startled to realize I was nearing this milestone.

Smiling now, I thought of the surprise party Maddee had thrown for me when I was staying with her the last time and had managed to make it to "thirty meetings in thirty days." Now I was at six hundred days, a far greater accomplishment, but there would be no big party. I probably wouldn't even mention it to her. This was different, almost private, an accomplishment I would mark with humility and silent prayers of gratitude.

Or so I thought, until my workday was over and I saw I had a message from Riley. She'd seen my missed call the other night and got back to me first thing the next morning, fearing I'd needed her and she hadn't been there for me. We'd chatted for a while, and I had mentioned the six hundred days thing. Now she had texted to say that big plans were in the making.

> Okay, Miss Sober-for-600! To celebrate, I reserved a court at the Petersburg YMCA for 7 tonight, put the word out to the girls, and it looks like 4 can make it. With you and me that's 6, so we can play 3 on 3. Let me know if that works for you!

Grinning, I texted her back right away and told her I would absolutely be there. With school out, the team felt so scattered, but I had to remind myself that most of us were from Virginia. And if anybody could pull together those who lived in this general region of the state, it was Riley.

The night ended up being a blast and the highlight of my week—at least until that Friday, when something even bigger and better came along.

It started on Thursday, actually, when I got a text from Greg. He wanted to know if I was free on Friday evening and could I help him out with something at the carriage house around six. I told him that was fine, but according to the whiteboard, Maddee had a late appointment and wouldn't be home till seven that night.

> I know. See you at 6. Mum's the word.

When Friday arrived, I could hardly contain my curiosity—or my excitement once Greg showed up and explained the plan. I helped him fill the downstairs with a huge load of flowers and candles we carried in from his car, and then, at his request, I tinkered with my sister's whiteboard, emulating her handwriting as best I could.

At 6:50 I got ready to leave so they could be alone, but Greg wouldn't hear of it.

"Please stay. She'll want you here for this, and so do I. Besides, if it weren't for you, Nicole, Maddee and I might never even have met."

Blinking back tears, I busied myself with adjusting some of the flowers. My accident had brought them together, literally. A verse from the Bible came to mind: *In all things God works for the good of those who love him.* He sure did.

By the time I saw Maddee coming up the walk, Greg and I had managed to light every single candle, and the place was aglow. I was on window duty, and as soon as I whispered, "There she is," he went and stood in the middle of the room, facing the door.

"What is this?" she cried as she stepped inside. Once she'd taken everything in, her face broke into a radiant smile. "Aww. You remembered our year-and-a-half anniversary!"

She put down her things and threw her arms around her boyfriend to give him a long hug. Over her shoulder, Greg shot me a wink, and it was all I could do to sit there quietly as I watched his plan unfold.

"I think there might be more going on tonight than just our anniversary," Greg said as they pulled apart. "You'd better check your whiteboard."

Maddee's smile faded. "Oh, no. I didn't forget an appointment of some kind, did I?"

She crossed the room to where it hung on the wall, and as her back was to Greg, he stepped closer and then lowered himself to one knee.

Maddee read aloud, quickly, matter-of-factly, "Friday, May 19, 9:00 to 6:45 work, 7:00 p.m. home, proposal from Greg, 8:00 p.m. reservations for dinner date—" She stopped. "Wait. What?" She hesitated, went back, and read more slowly this time, "7:00 p.m. home, proposal from Greg..."

With a gasp, she spun around, and there he was, still on his knee, open ring box in hand, asking her to be his wife. Her reaction was so precious, so wholehearted, so over-the-top emphatically *yes* that I don't know who was laughing and crying more, her or him or me.

By the time he slipped that ring onto her finger, I was scrambling for tissues and thinking to myself that even if their union was the only good thing to come out of all of the pain and suffering of my accident, it still would have been totally worth it.

CHAPTER EIGHTEEN
Nicole

"There's one thing you need to fit in this weekend," I told Maddee the next morning when I saw her at the kitchen table, scribbling out a new to-do list, "assuming you can find time between bouts of staring at the ring on your finger, scrolling through bridal Pinterest boards, and calling everyone you know to tell them your big news."

She grinned. "Better watch the sarcasm, little sis. Remember, I have the final say on bridesmaids' dresses."

"Meaning..." I crossed to the fridge to grab some juice.

"Meaning the more you tease me, the more I'm willing to consider fuchsia-and-lime-green taffeta with a giant matching bow for your hair."

I pulled out the carton and reached for a glass. "An empty threat," I scoffed. "You have such fashion sense, you couldn't make me look ugly if you tried."

"Good thing I don't have to try."

I laughed.

"So what is it I need to fit in?" she asked, returning her attention to her list.

"A visit with Nana."

Maddee looked up again, her smile fading. We hadn't seen or talked to our grandmother for a good ten days, not since the night when we were there with Harold and Gabe. That evening had ended awkwardly, without any sort of answers or resolution and not even a goodbye hug. Instead, Nana had simply returned empty handed from her trip to the kitchen for tea, announced that she wasn't feeling well and needed to get on to bed, and then saw the four of us to the door. She hadn't contacted either Maddee or me since, not by phone or text or even email. For a woman who was usually part of the near-daily chatter of our lives, her silence had created a weird void.

"I guess you're right," Maddee said, accepting the inevitable. "We're going to have to make peace with her eventually, or at least form a truce."

"Hopefully the news of your engagement will make it a little easier. At least it'll give us something to focus on."

"True." She thought for a moment. "Okay. Why don't I tell her I have a surprise to share with her and that I'm wondering if she might be free for lunch tomorrow after church? I'll suggest a restaurant, but knowing her, she'll insist on eating at her place."

"Sounds good," I said, not looking forward to it but glad at least that we had a plan. "Why don't you have Greg come too? He and Nana have always gotten along, but if he's really going to be a part of this family, you might as well throw him into the deep end now."

Just as I'd hoped, lunch with our grandmother on Sunday wasn't nearly as uncomfortable as it could've been, thanks to the distraction of my sister's engagement. Nana was over-the-moon excited when they told her, though we could tell she had guessed at what Maddee's big surprise was going to be. She'd had the household staff lay out a beautiful spread in the dining room, a celebratory brunch complete with almond-crusted caramel French toast and scrambled eggs topped with smoked salmon and crème fresh.

Greg looked totally dreamy—Maddee's term, but I agreed—in a

crisp dark suit, one I felt sure Maddee had picked out for him. She was all dressed up too, and the glow in her eyes made her even more gorgeous than usual. Though I didn't have a handsome man at my side or a big rock on my finger, I had taken the time to do my hair and makeup for the occasion. Considering the tremendous difference in height between my model-tall sister and short little me, we couldn't exactly share clothes, but she had spruced up one of my few dresses with some of her accessories.

Fortunately, Nana was on her best behavior, oohing and ahhing over the ring, sharing the story of her own engagement, and even offering the use of her estate for the wedding.

"There's no obligation," she added, "but I just want you two to know that it's an option. You're welcome to have it here if you'd like, inside or out. Or both."

"Thank you, Nana," Maddee said. "We haven't even thought about a date yet, much less a venue, but we'll definitely keep that in mind."

"Of course," Nana replied. With a wink to me, she added in a faux whisper, "I suppose this is the part where we pretend she also hasn't picked out a dress or a honeymoon destination or the names of their first three children."

We all burst out laughing, even Maddee, though her cheeks turned a vivid red. Anyone who knew my sister knew she'd been planning for this her whole life.

As our meal continued, conversation turned to my final grades for the semester, which I'd gotten the day before and forwarded along to my benefactress. I'd already known what they were going to be, but it had still been fun to see the row of A's and then a box down at the bottom listing my GPA as 4.0.

"I'm just so proud of you," Nana said now, beaming. "I always knew you could do it."

"It's not exactly Harvard, Nana," I said, feeling the heat in my cheeks as I ladled more syrup onto my French toast.

"Silver Lake University is a perfectly good school."

"True, but for reasons other than academics. Don't get me wrong. I love it there. But it wasn't all that hard to make the grade. Literally."

"Don't sell yourself short," Nana scolded. "Regardless of the academic rigors, or lack thereof, I would claim those grades with pride. What was that old quote your grandfather used to say? 'Education is the key to unlocking the golden door of freedom'?"

Maddee and I both nodded, remembering. Granddad had always been really big on education.

"Well, thanks, Nana," I said. "That means a lot coming from you."

Eager to change the subject, I was about to bring up the elephant in the room when Nana did it herself. Out of the blue, she dabbed at her mouth with a napkin, set it in her lap, and announced in an earnest voice that she was so, so sorry for keeping quiet about the mysterious phone call she overheard our grandfather make after we found the dead body in the cabin.

"It's so easy to lie to oneself," she added, staring into the distance. "For years, even. But now that the truth has finally come out, I'm realizing more and more the damage I did by keeping it in. I do hope you girls will find it in your hearts to forgive me someday."

Of course, after such a heartfelt apology, Maddee and I both rushed to our grandmother with open arms, where we became an instant jumble of tears and hugs. Nana wasn't totally off the hook for what she'd done, but at least the lines of communication were open again.

When I retook my seat, I glanced over at Greg, who'd been watching the scene with a wry smile on his lips.

"You sure you want to be a part of this family?" I teased with a grin.

He looked from me to Nana to Maddee and replied, "You better believe it. I've never wanted anything more in my life."

After that, talk turned to the much lighter subject of next month's family reunion, and I was pleased and surprised when Nana mentioned, in a nod to me, that this year she'd added a volleyball court to the rental setup. In turn, we told her that we'd been trying to talk Renee and Danielle into coming early so we could have a little extra "cousin time" together before the festivities kicked in.

"Oh, and I've already arranged to have Thursday and Friday of that week off from work," Maddee added.

"Me too," I said.

"Speaking of work." Nana turned my way. "I keep meaning to ask how you like working for Nate Harrison."

"Excuse me?"

"Nate Harrison. Isn't he the one in charge over there at Dover Creek Farms?"

"Yes, he is. You've met him?"

Nana took a sip of her coffee, swallowed, and then slowly set her cup down again. "Oh yes, such a lovely young man. We've known each other for years."

Had she told me she'd known a gangsta rapper for years, I couldn't have been more surprised than I was in that moment. I glanced at Maddee, who seemed bemused. She'd heard me griping about Nate since day one.

"How do you know him, Nana?" she asked on my behalf, as I'd been rendered speechless. I reached for my water glass.

"Through the Richmond Ecumenical Association. He does presentations there. All the ladies think he's so handsome, in that Marlon-Brando-Rebel-Without-a-Cause sort of way."

"He...does what?" I asked before taking a big gulp.

"He speaks. About his racetrack ministry."

I nearly did a spit take. "Racetrack ministry?"

She sighed. "Yes, dear. He's the chaplain over at Powhatan Downs. He comes and gives a talk every year so we can learn where the needs are and how we can help. It's a wonderful cause. You can't imagine the lives of those poor people on the backside." Turning to Maddee and Greg, she added, "That's what they call the part of the racetrack you don't see, the area where all the support folks live and work. Such a difficult existence, such poverty, and the population can be rough—not to mention there's always the risk of injury with the horses."

Looking at all of us now, she continued to explain, saying that the jobs there were seasonal and that the workers lived on-site. "They put in so many hours that they can't get to church, so Nate brings church to them. He also facilitates twelve-step meetings, runs a men's group, holds youth events, and tends to the sick and the needy. Through the

REA, he has ties with all the local ministries, so he's able to connect the people of the backside with the groups that can help them."

She went on and on, and as I listened to her talk, my worldview began spinning around.

I kept thinking, Nate wasn't going to the racetrack as an addict, to gamble. He was going there as a minister, to serve.

I was so thrown by the Nate thing that every other conversation from the day got pushed to the back of my mind. It wasn't until I was lying in bed that night that I thought of what my grandmother had said about how proud she was of my accomplishments at school.

Her words had been so kind, and yet something bugged me about them. What had she said that gave me such a weird feeling in the pit of my stomach now? Shifting to my other side and punching my pillow, I tried to think back over the entire exchange.

And then it hit me. It wasn't Nana's words that were bugging me—it was *Granddad's*. The quote he used to say, that "education is the key to unlocking the golden door of freedom." The golden door of freedom. *Door of freedom.*

That was the name of the scholarship Gabe Koenig and his siblings received when they were young, their "free ride" through Ohio State. What an odd coincidence.

Or was it?

I opened my eyes, knowing I'd never get to sleep until I thought this through. On a hunch, I retrieved my laptop and returned to the bed, sitting up now as I started poking around on the web.

First, I typed in the full quote just to see where it was from. My results attributed it to George Washington Carver, the famous botanist and inventor who'd lived around the turn of the century. Googling some more, I found that there was more than one scholarship named from that quote, things like "Golden Door" and "Key to the Golden Door." But even after a lot of digging, I could only find one called the

Door of Freedom. According to the listing, it had been created in Virginia in 1995 with a private endowment of $100,000, and it was no longer in existence. Though Gabe had said his scholarship was "government administrated," I could find no signs of that. I did find the name of a private company that was connected with it somehow, "River City Investments," along with an address here in Richmond, so I wrote it down.

Except for the investment firm, which was unfamiliar to me, this stuff had Granddad's name written all over it. His favorite quote. The year it was created. The amount of the endowment, which was probably just about exactly what it would have taken to fund the educations of Gabe and his siblings.

If my hunch was right and Granddad really had created an anonymously funded scholarship for Taavi's kids, what did that mean? Had this been his way of paying penance for something he'd done? Was Granddad Taavi's killer? Certainly not in any sort of premeditated way, but perhaps, as Maddee had suggested, in self-defense?

I hated to give the police yet another piece of evidence that implicated our grandfather in Taavi's murder, but I knew I had no choice.

The next morning, I told Maddee what I'd discovered, and she agreed I had to tell Ortiz. I saved that conversation for my lunch break. I slipped out to my car so I could call her from there in private.

The detective's reaction was surprisingly nonchalant, though I wasn't sure why. She promised to look into it, though in a way it felt as if she was just humoring me. I supposed my theory sounded like a bit of a stretch, but not if you knew Granddad the way I did.

Once our call was over, I just sat there for a bit, wondering what would happen if it turned out that my grandfather was a killer. He was dead now, after all. It wasn't as if they could prosecute him. But it would still be a tragedy for our family, and especially for Nana. In a way, I could almost—almost—understand why she'd kept her own secret all these years.

Putting such thoughts from my mind for now, I finished my sandwich, got out of the car, and went back to work—where I was facing a new and disturbing problem.

Ever since my confrontation with Nate in the parking lot a week and half ago, things had gotten better between us. He hadn't exactly been warm and fuzzy with me, but at least he hadn't glared at me or picked on me or dismissed me. Now that I knew the truth about him thanks to Nana, however, I was suddenly almost shy whenever he came around, which made me furious with myself.

I wasn't the shy type. I'd never been shy a single moment in my entire life. Yet here I was, tongue tied and red faced whenever Mr. Rebel Without a Cause even glanced my way. Good grief.

Somehow I managed to make it through the day, and the situation slowly improved as the week progressed.

On Wednesday night, I finally got around to sharing the old family photos with Maddee. She had a lot of questions I hadn't learned the answers to, so we got in touch with Aunt Cissy and invited her over.

She came the next night for coffee and dessert, tickled to death that Maddee had also taken an interest in the pictures. As they went through them together and she answered Maddee's questions, I focused on reading the little love notes that Therese's husband had written to her. Though each one had been penned separately on its own small strip of paper, Aunt Cissy had made copies in batches of four or five per page.

Even so, there were a lot of pages—and the notes were all just so sweet. The language of that era was a bit different, so there were some I didn't really understand. But the overall impression was of a man who deeply loved his wife.

Maddee and I were both fascinated to learn that one of our distant cousins, Henry Fox Talbot, had been the inventor of paper photography. According to Aunt Cissy, not long after the glass-based daguerreotype process was introduced, Henry came out with a paper-based method—which he continued to develop and improve for decades to come.

"Some of his early works are so delicate and ephemeral," Aunt Cissy told us, "that even though they still exist, they can no longer be exhibited or even exposed to light because doing so would destroy them. They're kept in storage that's completely light proof."

"So why bother?" I asked.

"What do you mean?"

"I mean, what's the point of keeping something around if you can't even look at it?"

Aunt Cissy thought about that for a moment. "I suppose for some people, there's just something about owning a piece of history whether you can share it with others or not. Reminds me of that song..." Not surprisingly, she burst into a rendition of an old classic, "Fragile Hearts and Faded Memories," and though we let her get through one verse without stopping, I couldn't even glance at Maddee lest I start laughing.

By the time she finished, however, I felt guilty for my reaction. Shame on me. If it made her happy to belt out the occasional tune, who was I to make fun? There were worse habits. At least she didn't belch them out like a guy who used to hang at one of my favorite bars.

When it was time for Aunt Cissy to go and she hugged me goodbye, I whispered a quick "Love you," surprised to realize it was true. Pulling back, I could see genuine delight in her features as she replied, "I love you too, sweetie pie. I'm so proud of how far you've come."

Once she was gone, I settled back at the table, where Maddee and I slowly returned all of the pictures to the box. One caught my eye, and I hesitated, studying it.

Again, it featured the beautiful face of Therese, only this time she was standing with two other people. The wall behind them was brick, though it was clearly an interior, with a washstand nearby. The man was between the two women, sporting an apron and holding a thick book in the crook of one arm.

Flipping the picture over, I read the label on the back, which said it had been taken at a Civil War hospital and featured "Dr. Alec Talbot, Polly Talbot, and Therese Jennings." Dr. Alec Talbot? Was this Therese's future husband?

Flipping it back over, I looked closer. He certainly was a handsome guy, with a neat beard and, under his apron, a white shirt and dark pants. In a way, he could almost pass for a modern-day hipster, which wasn't all that surprising considering the cyclical nature of fashion.

My eyes went again to Therese's face and to the bravery that shone through in her expression. Aunt Cissy had said Therese worked in a hospital during the Civil War. With a shudder, I couldn't help but wonder where she'd found the courage to survive in such a tragic and heartbreaking world.

Chapter Nineteen
Therese

Warner wasn't happy to see Michael, not the way Therese thought he would be. He kept his head turned away from his friend.

"Your boys send their prayers," Michael said.

Warner's voice wavered as he spoke. "They don't blame me?"

"Of course not. Nor should you blame yourself. You were ordered into those woods."

Therese stepped away to give the two men privacy, busying herself by distributing medications to other nearby patients. Michael's voice was low and comforting. After a few minutes, he picked up the Bible she'd left on the stool and began reading to Warner from the Psalms.

A half hour later, Michael approached her and said he was going to talk to Alec to see if he would go to the quartermaster with him to ask for supplies. "I'm a chicken," he said and then made a clucking noise.

Therese's heart lurched. "No, you're being prudent, that's all." She doubted anyone with the last name of Talbot could be a coward. Wrong, yes, but not a coward.

Michael smiled. "It was Warner's idea."

"It's a good one." The quartermaster was more likely to meet Michael's request if Alec was with him.

"Warner is fond of my cousin," Michael said, his still voice light, "as it seems everyone around here is."

Therese hoped her face wasn't growing red again. She couldn't tell if Michael was teasing her or not. She nodded toward the hall, though, not wanting anyone to overhear their conversation. Michael followed, saying, "He has to be a good man, right? Being that he's a Talbot." He smiled again.

Therese stopped in the middle of the hall and smiled back, certain now that he was teasing. "Of course."

Michael's grin faded. "Look." He lowered his voice. "It's none of my business, but if you care for Alec as much as it seems he does for you, I have to agree with Warner that you should consider leaving with him."

Therese took a step backward, deeply hurt. Clearly, this confirmed once and for all what she'd long suspected, that Michael had no lingering feelings for her himself—and perhaps he never had.

Oblivious to her dismay, he glanced around and then continued. "I know you're concerned about Warner and your mother, but I promise, as long as I'm able, I'll look after them as best I can."

She took in a breath, forcing away the pain and telling herself it didn't matter now anyway. "I appreciate your commitment to my family," she managed to say, "but there really isn't anything to discuss as far as Dr. Talbot." Her relationship with Alec was none of Michael's business.

He gave her a questioning look and then said, "All right. Just remember this conversation if the time comes."

As Therese gave him a curt nod, Alec approached.

Michael waved him over and explained his need, and Alec agreed. "We don't have much to spare, but if the boys can't be cared for on the front line, most of them will never make it to us. It's the right thing to do to share what we have. I'll be down in a minute. Wait for me in the foyer."

"Thank you." Michael took a step toward the stairs, but then he turned and asked, "How does it feel to miss the election?"

The Union citizens would vote the next day in the presidential election between Lincoln and McClellan. For months it seemed Lincoln didn't have a chance, but the latest polls had shown him winning.

Alec shrugged. "I know God's plan will come about whether I have a part in voting or not."

"I wanted to share a quote I heard recently, attributed to Jefferson Davis. Maybe not your favorite politician," Michael added, speaking to his cousin.

Alec laughed. "Oh, I can assure you, I'm not fond of any politicians. But I am interested in what Davis said."

Michael cleared his throat. "He told it to a nurse. It made me think of all of you here." Slowly he recited, "'Remember, if you save the lives of a hundred men, you will have done more for your country than if you had fought a hundred battles.'"

"That quote applies to you too, Michael." Therese's eyes welled with tears, proud of his efforts regardless of his politics. If only everyone aimed to save lives—not destroy them.

"Hear, hear," Alec added. "Davis may be wiser than I've given him credit for."

Michael didn't seem offended by the comment. Instead, he pointed toward the staircase again and, over his shoulder, said, "I'll head on down. Come find me when you have a moment." Turning toward Therese, he added, "I'll see you later, little lady." He grinned again.

She watched him go, remembering all those years she'd pined for him.

"Little lady, huh? Was he more than a childhood friend?"

"No," Therese said, wondering for half a moment if she'd just lied. She hadn't. Obviously, Michael had only considered her a friend. "He used to tease me."

"It appears he still does," Alec said.

Therese shook her head. "Not really." Then she smiled. "Well, maybe just a little."

Michael's attention felt comforting, actually. As if the world really wasn't upside down, even though it was. As if she could pretend that he hadn't abandoned all the ideals they used to share.

"Well, as long as it's only teasing—and not flirting." Alec smiled down at her, and she understood that now he was teasing her too.

Michael had never been a flirt. Looking back, he'd never given her any reason to care for him as deeply as she had all those years either. She would get over that eventually, she was sure, even if her heart still raced at the sight of him.

She met Alec's eyes. "I'm waiting to hear the story about the lacerated liver." If Mother moved Warner home, Therese would never be able to help Badan and Aggie escape from there. "Time may be running out."

"Oh?" he asked.

"In fact, I'm hoping for two stories."

"I may be gaining more of an understanding of your interest." He cleared his throat. "I can't walk you home tonight, but perhaps tomorrow?"

"I'd like that."

The next afternoon, after finishing their teaching duties, Therese and Polly hurried to the hospital. When they arrived, Mother sat at Warner's bedside while Alec stood at the end of the cot.

Therese stepped to her mother's side and kissed her cheek. "How was your trip?"

"Fine." Mother didn't appear to be fine. She looked exhausted, with dark circles under her eyes. "We readied the parlor for Warner."

Alec turned toward Therese. "Warner's been running a fever today. I want to make sure it comes down and that he doesn't have an infection, although your mother doesn't seem to understand the importance of waiting to move him."

Mother threw up her hands. "This seems to be an endless proposition."

"You can wait here," Alec said. "Or you can return home, and I'll send a message once Warner is better."

Mother sighed. "I'll retire to the Corbetts, God bless them." She patted Warner's cheek. "And hope my boy is well by morning."

Therese wondered if Mother comprehended the gravity of the situation. She stepped closer and placed her hand on Mother's shoulder, trying to comfort her.

Mother reached up and gave her a pat. "You'll have to come home, of course," she said. "We'll need your help."

"Pardon?"

Mother turned toward Therese. Her eyes were rimmed with red. "I understand now. God brought you to Richmond so you could learn to care for your brother back home. It was the Lord's will. We'll all be together at River Pines soon."

Not unless you free the slaves first, Therese wanted to reply but didn't. It was one thing to take a stand against Mother, yet another when that stand involved her brother's health—and possibly his very life.

Therese held her tongue for now, knowing she would need to think this through, and pray about it, later.

That evening, Alec escaped the hospital to walk Therese home. Polly stayed behind, saying she'd get a ride in an hour or two.

Therese couldn't stop thinking about the conversation with her mother, even with Alec at her side. Mother was wrong. Aggie was perfectly capable of caring for Warner by herself—there was no reason for Therese to return to River Pines.

Unfortunately, one big catch loomed: If Aggie escaped, then Mother was right. Therese would have to move back home to care for her brother in Aggie's stead. And while she knew that a person's freedom was worth almost any cost, the thought of giving up all she'd gained by coming to Richmond simply broke her heart. She would make the sacrifice for Aggie's sake, but it would be the hardest thing she'd ever done.

"Are you all right?" Alec held an umbrella over her head as they walked.

"I'm fine. Just thinking..." Therese clutched her skirts tighter, pulling them up as they crossed the street. Her feet felt each of the cobblestones through the thin soles of her boots as she hurried along, matching Alec's stride.

"What are you thinking about?"

Therese answered, "Warner. Mother. Other things."

"The lacerated livers?"

"Yes."

Alec whispered, "I see. Well, I already told you my cousin is a nurse, but did I mention that she's had quite a bit of experience with lacerated livers?"

Therese's hope grew. "Really?" She needed someone who had done this sort of thing before. "When is she arriving?"

"I'm not sure exactly, but soon."

Therese nodded. "Good. In the meantime, I'll keep working on Mother, trying to talk her into...handling the matter in a different way, if you know what I mean."

"Yes, I do." Alec's walking slowed as he added, "But perhaps there's something else you need to speak to your mother about."

"Oh? What is that?"

"We haven't known each other long, but it truly seems as if we have. I can't bear the thought of leaving—in fact, I'm hoping you'll go back to Maine with me."

Therese stopped and looked up into his eyes. "Are you asking me to?"

"Yes." He gently cupped her cheek in his hand. "Will you return with me, Therese? Will you marry me?"

She barely noticed the rain beating against the top of the umbrella, or the water soaking through the bottom of her boots. She opened her mouth to speak, but no words came out.

He smiled, just a little. "I know it's sudden. Perhaps that's the way it is in times of war." He dipped his face closer to hers. "You don't have to tell me now. Think about it. Talk with your mother. If your answer is yes, I'll ask Warner for his permission."

He shifted the umbrella and reached for her hand. She let go of her skirt and took his. His skin was warm even in the cold. His hand held hers firmly. "We'll pray for a solution to all of this," he said. "For us. For the slaves at River Pines. For Warner. For the hospital."

She looked into his eyes. "Yes," she answered.

His expression grew even more serious. "Yes to praying? Or yes to my proposal?"

"Both," she answered, smiling up at him. He hugged her until a group of soldiers with a drummer and a flutist marched by to the tune of "Dixie." As Therese and Alec started walking again, she promised to talk with Mother soon, though she dreaded the conversation.

"Good," Alec said. "But I doubt we should tell anyone else, not yet, except perhaps Polly. I don't want Ruth finding out from someone in the hospital before she finds out from me."

"I agree." Therese was happy to hold the news close to her heart. And it would make things less complicated, in the long run, not to tell even Polly—at least not just yet.

Besides, she wasn't ready for Michael to find out either. And not because she was afraid of his teasing. It was absurd, she knew, but she felt as if she were betraying him, which was absolutely ludicrous. Those days were behind her.

The next morning, Therese read the *Daily Dispatch* after Mr. Galloway was finished with it, searching for the news from Petersburg. She found it on the third page.

> There was considerable firing Monday night on our left centre. There was a heavy fog at the time, and doubtless there was an attempt made by one picket line to capture the other. Nothing definite is known, but the cannonading was very heavy, and so was the musketry.

She thought of Michael and hoped he was all right, but then the three girls thundered down the stairs. Therese folded the paper and put it away. He hadn't been to the hospital since he came to procure the supplies. She hoped that, between all of the hospitals he'd visited, he found what he needed.

As the rain continued to fall outside, Therese spent the day teaching Florence to read and working with Eleanor on her times tables. Lydia was engrossed in drawing a picture of soldiers marching through town, and although Therese didn't think it was the right use of the child's time, it was a relief to have her sitting in a chair on a rainy day when they couldn't be outside.

Throughout the morning, Therese's mind kept going back to last night's proposal and what it could mean for her future. Then, with a start, she realized that this could affect Badan and Aggie's future as well. If Therese headed north, she could take the two of them with her, as long as Mother freed them first.

That still left one problem, however, because if both Therese and Aggie left, there'd be no one to care for Warner at River Pines. She puzzled on that for a while until it struck her that perhaps Polly was the answer. If the hospital closed down, Polly's work there would be done, and if Alec left town, the spy network would likely close. Given all of that, maybe Polly would be willing to take a leave from her governess job in Richmond, move back home for a month or two, and spend her days taking care of Warner. It was certainly something to think about.

As Therese and the girls were walking out of the parlor after the lessons were done, she noticed a document Mr. Galloway had left on the table beside his chair. She peered closer. It was a memorandum with the title: "Grant Headed to North Carolina." She didn't dare read more.

At four p.m., before Polly arrived, Therese stood on the stoop of the row house. The afternoon sun was low in the sky, and the rain had stopped, but the weather had turned icy cold. As she waited, she debated if she should tell Polly about the memorandum. If she really did want the North to win so that the slaves could be freed, then she needed to tell her friend what she'd seen—even if it felt as if she were betraying the kindness of her employers. In this case, it wasn't that the North wouldn't know what General Grant had planned—but they might not know that the Confederate Army knew. There were spies on both sides, and obviously someone from the North had leaked the information to the South.

Polly came around the corner, her head high and her stride long. Therese's heart warmed at the sight of her. She hurried down the walkway and through the gate, greeted Polly, and then linked arms with her.

"I read about a medical case today," she said, "one that you might want to share with Dr. Talbot—although I'm not sure of the correct terminology."

"Tell me," Polly said. "I'll translate it for him."

They began to walk, and Therese waited till they were well away from the row house. Then she lowered her voice, explained where she'd seen it, and gave the title of the memorandum.

"Sounds as if there's a possible bleed to the brain," Polly replied. "And a clot in the left hip. I'll tell Dr. Talbot about it today."

When they arrived at the hospital, Alec stood in the foyer, with his back to the door, conversing with Matron Webb. "No," he said. "She won't try to displace you. She'll assist you."

The matron scowled at Alec but then looked past him and greeted Therese and Polly. Alec turned, but instead of his usual warmth, he appeared downcast.

"Is everything all right?" Therese feared Warner's fever had grown worse.

"Mostly," Alec said. "My cousin Ruth arrived this morning."

"She's early."

"Yes," Alec said, "and she's already stirred up trouble, criticizing things about the hospital, I'm afraid. To say the least, it doesn't meet her standards."

"Oh, dear." Now Therese understood the scowl on Matron Webb's face.

Alec's eyes brightened. "At least she brought word that Lincoln has in fact been reelected." He nodded toward the stairs. "Come up and I'll introduce you to her. She's working in the east ward today."

Therese glanced at Polly, wishing she'd thought to ask her about Ruth when they were alone. The woman was a Talbot, after all. Surely Polly knew a bit about her, whether or not she'd ever met her in person.

Both women hung their cloaks and then followed Alec up the stairs, but when they reached the top, he fell back and let Polly lead the way. As she did, Alec slipped Therese a piece of folded paper. "It's for you to read later," he whispered, eyes twinkling. "Just some words of endearment from me to you."

When they all reached the ward, Ruth—a woman who appeared to be at least a decade older than Alec—was bending over a soldier with a chest wound. She wore an austere gray dress, and her dark hair was pulled back in a tight bun.

"Ruth," Alec said, "I'd like you to meet two of our nurses."

The woman looked up.

"This is Polly, one of the Talbot cousins I told you about, who assists me in surgery, and this is Therese, who demonstrates her tender heart toward our patients on a daily basis."

"Pleased to meet you both." Ruth smiled at Polly and added, "Cousin." Then she looked directly at Therese and said, "I need more gauze and a sponge."

"Yes, ma'am," Therese quickly replied. Alec certainly had never minced words, but it appeared his cousin was even more abrupt. Therese stepped to the cupboard and, as she retrieved the supplies, noticed there were only a few more pieces of gauze left. At least there was more morphine than there had been the day before, behind the locked door on the left.

When she returned to the gathering around the cot, she excused herself, explaining that she needed to restock the cupboard with gauze.

"That's all there is," Alec replied. "Our quartermaster hasn't been able to procure any more."

"How about the morphine?" Therese asked. "There's more today. Funny he could get that but not gauze."

Ruth pursed her lips.

"What?" Therese glanced from Ruth to Alec.

"I brought it," Ruth said. "Wrapped in cloth and tied to my hoops."

"Oh." Therese smiled, filled with admiration for the woman. The Northern Talbots, or at least these two, weren't just resourceful but brave as well. They really did want to help soldiers—no matter what side they fought on.

"What will we do about the lack of gauze?" Polly asked.

"Start washing dressings," Alec answered. "And reusing them."

Ruth looked up from the wound. "That's ridiculous."

"It's the South," Alec retorted.

"Speak to Dr. Moore," she snapped back. "Surely, as surgeon general, he can help you."

Alec sighed. "It's not that simple." They all turned to look at him as he added, "Besides, the surgeon general plans to shut the hospital down by December."

"Already?" Polly's voice was heartsick.

Therese tried not to react. She'd liked it better when it was just a rumor. With the closing of the hospital imminent, Alec would be leaving soon. And she with him.

"I'm not happy about it closing either," he said. "I'm holding out hope that he'll change his mind."

At the most, it seemed Therese had a month to convince Mother to free Aggie and Badan so that they could go with her and Alec.

If only the war would end by then and set them all free.

A few minutes later, Therese ducked into the supply closet and pulled Alec's note from her apron pocket. *Therese, my love,* it read. *You've made me so happy. I look forward to being your husband. Alec*

A smile crept onto her face as she refolded it and slipped it back into her pocket. She was blessed indeed.

—❧—

Friday after dinner, while the girls sat quietly in the parlor working on their lessons, Therese scanned the *Daily Dispatch* until she found what she was looking for, an article confirming the reelection of Abraham Lincoln to the presidency of the United States.

Next she scanned the runaway slave notices, something she did occasionally even though it left her feeling ill. Today, she prayed for the people by name. *Nat. Margaret. Pete.* Even though they weren't on the list and hadn't run, she added *Aggie* and *Badan* to her prayers. Then *Auntie Vera. Old Joe.* And *Sonny. God, help them.*

Help us all.

CHAPTER TWENTY

Therese

On Saturday morning, Therese slipped the *carte de visite* of the escaped slave into her bag before she left the Galloway home. She needed to speak with Mother one last time, and she planned to use the image to make her point.

As Therese and Polly arrived at the hospital, three army wagons pulled away. The photographer they'd met before, Mr. Jay Lewis, stood on the sidewalk with his camera equipment beside him. He slipped a glass plate into a bag.

"What's going on?" Polly asked.

"They've started transferring patients," he said. "Dr. Moore asked me to document the event."

Alarmed, Therese headed up the stairs. Surely, no one would have allowed Warner to be moved, but she needed to know for sure. Polly called out a goodbye to the photographer and followed her friend.

When they entered the building, Ruth stood in the middle of the foyer, berating an orderly for not having finished a job she'd given him. Apparently, Matron Webb had pulled him away to perform some other duty.

"Now go up and do what I asked you to do half an hour ago." Ruth ended her scold, and then she turned and headed up the stairs, not even bothering to tell Therese and Polly hello.

"Was Captain Jennings transferred?" Therese asked the orderly.

"I don't know, ma'am." He hurried after Ruth.

Polly grabbed Therese's hand. "Let's go check."

They hung their cloaks in the closet and tore up the stairs. As they stepped into the east ward, the bright morning sun shone through the windows. Therese's eyes adjusted to the light, and she began searching for Warner. There were fewer soldiers in the room, and the cots had been rearranged.

Finally, she spotted her brother in the far corner. He was still here, thank goodness.

Therese hurried to Warner's side and felt his forehead. It was hotter than she expected.

Polly lifted the blanket and studied his stump. "It doesn't look good."

"Could you examine his stomach too?" Therese couldn't bear to do it herself.

Polly stepped to his side and spoke softly, "Warner, I'm going to check your other wound."

He didn't open his eyes, but his mouth twitched a little.

"Are you in pain?"

He nodded.

Polly lifted the blanket and then removed the dressing. Therese glanced away, back to her brother's face.

"It doesn't look good either," Polly said. "I'll go find Dr. Talbot."

As soon as Polly stepped into the hall, litter bearers came into the ward carrying another lieutenant. Therese stood. How odd that some soldiers were being transferred while others were still arriving. As she stood, two more litter bearers brought in another wounded officer. Behind them was Michael, covered in mud and limping.

Polly called out. "Are you hurt?"

"No," he answered. "But our unit took a big hit. Most of the soldiers went to Chimborazo, but I brought the officers here."

Warner stirred and opened his eyes.

"Michael's here," Therese said. "He brought in two injured officers."

Michael stepped close, looking down at Warner. "How are you?"

Warner shrugged. "What happened out there?"

"A mortar," Michael said. "It hit the field hospital."

"How many killed?"

"Three. An orderly and two who were already wounded. Eight others were injured—worse than they already were."

"Anyone I'd know?"

Michael replied, "Maybe..." But Therese didn't hear any more of the conversation. Alec had returned to the ward, Ruth and Matron Webb right behind him. They headed to the new officers, who the litter bearers were transferring to cots. Therese hoped Alec would be able to take a closer look at Warner soon.

"Nurse Jennings." Therese turned to face Matron Webb. "The Confederacy is not paying you to stand around chatting."

"I wasn't, ma'am."

The matron crossed her arms. "See to your duties, please."

"Yes, ma'am." Therese got busy with her morning chores, keeping an eye on all that was going on around the ward.

Michael stayed by Warner's side while Polly and Ruth helped Alec tend to the two officers. Therese washed the faces and hands of patients. She thought through the girls' lessons for the coming week as she worked, mentally making notes so it would be easier to jot everything down that night. When she finished, it was time for breakfast. First, she delivered bowls to all of the soldiers who could feed themselves, including Warner. He said he wasn't hungry, but she insisted. Michael took the bowl from her and said he'd make sure Warner ate.

Therese began feeding soldiers who couldn't feed themselves, and after a while Polly came to help. As she retrieved a bowl from the tray, she said, "Dr. Talbot is looking at Warner's wounds now."

Therese glanced toward her brother. Alec and Ruth examined Warner's stump with serious expressions on their faces. Therese started toward them as Michael stood and drifted away from the group.

"How is Warner?" Therese asked, not sure she wanted to hear the answer.

"We may need to operate on his leg again," Alec said, "and his stomach wound is definitely infected."

"Mother still wants to take him home," Therese said.

"Well, she can't," Ruth snapped. "Unless she wants to kill him."

Therese's eyes began to sting with tears, both because of the sharpness of Ruth's words and because of the threat to her brother. She turned, accidentally catching Michael's eye, and he gave her a sympathetic smile.

Therese lowered her eyes and quickly retreated back to the tray of porridge. She retrieved another bowl and then sat next to the double-arm amputee and asked how he was doing.

"As well as can be expected," he answered. "Could you write a letter for me later?"

"Of course."

"I'm afraid I'll never get home."

Tears filled her eyes. "I think you will. I'll pray you do."

"Thank you, ma'am."

She fed him several bites, and then he said, "That's enough. I think I'll nap for a while."

He scooted back down on the cot as best he could, and she pulled up his sheets for him. Then she returned to the table and put the bowl on the tray of dirty dishes. Someone touched her elbow as she did. She turned to find Michael motioning her toward the hall. She walked beside him.

"Your mother will have to leave Warner."

Therese nodded. "She won't be happy. She doesn't trust Dr. Talbot."

"Because?"

"He's a Yankee."

"He's also a Talbot. Besides, what about your father? Has she forgotten her devotion to a certain other Yankee so soon?"

"She's fearful," Therese said. "She seems to be ignoring everything Father stood for." She shot him a sharp glance. "Like others I know."

Michael narrowed his eyes and pointed to his chest.

She nodded.

He grimaced. "I suppose that's fair." He ran his hand through his long hair. "You have to understand, Therese, things...change, especially when you're living far enough away to gain some perspective."

Their gazes locked, and though she wanted to understand, all she could feel was disappointment. And sorrow.

Surely sensing her thoughts, he said, "I'll be on my way just as soon as I get something to eat. I'll look for a bowl of porridge in the kitchen." As he walked off, a trickle of blood seeped from his boot.

"Michael, stop," Therese said. "You're hurt. Go back and tell Polly to look at your leg while I get the food for you."

When Therese came out of the kitchen building with Michael's porridge, Badan stood in the backyard of the hospital, his hat in his hands.

"Where's Mother?"

"Upstairs."

Therese explained that Warner was now fighting infection.

"Mrs. Jennings isn't going to be pleased. She's bound and determined to head back today." He wrung his hat. "And I hate to be away any longer."

"From Aggie."

He nodded. "We jumped the broom last week, but that doesn't stop..." He pinched his lips together and shook his head.

Therese lowered her voice. "Perhaps Mother would let Aggie come back here and nurse Warner. That would keep her away from River Pines."

"And from me," Badan said, clearly not liking that idea.

"It would be temporary."

"I doubt Mrs. Jennings would agree to any of it. Mr. Porter seems to have convinced her that nothing's going to change after the war ends." He dropped his eyes to the floor. "Do you think that's true?"

"No, Badan, I don't. I think a lot of people are trying to make everything change." She held up the bowl. "I need to get this to Michael."

She headed up to the ward, where she found Michael sitting on an examination table with his pants leg rolled up while Polly washed out a shrapnel wound in his calf. Therese handed him the bowl and then continued on to Warner's cot. Mother stood talking to Ruth and Alec, but just then an orderly interrupted them and said, "Dr. Talbot, Dr. Moore is downstairs. He needs to speak with you."

Alec excused himself and followed the orderly, nodding at Therese as he passed her.

Ruth and Mother continued speaking, and then Mother said, loudly, "I don't believe you."

"I'll show you." Ruth pulled back the blanket covering Warner's stump. "Most likely more will need to be amputated." Ruth's gruff demeanor had been growing so tiresome to Therese, but suddenly she couldn't have been more grateful for it. If ever Mother was going to meet her match, it was Ruth Talbot.

"No," Mother said. "That won't do."

"You, madam," Ruth replied, "are an idiot."

Therese stepped closer, stifling a laugh despite the seriousness of the situation. "He has to stay here, Mother. If it's his leg or—" she dropped her voice, "—his life, then there's no room for discussion."

"But everything's ready back at River Pines. And Aggie is such a good nurse."

"Why don't you send her here?" Therese suggested. "Warner can have Aggie's individual care, and I'll check on him during the evenings. So will Polly. It's the next best thing to the care he'd receive at home, plus here he'd have Dr. Talbot's surgical skills."

"That's not what I planned," Mother said.

"None of this is what any of us planned."

"Besides, Aggie and Badan just got married," Mother said. "He won't want her to come here."

"You should ask him," Therese said. "You might be surprised."

Mother crossed her arms. "Do you expect me to go home and leave Warner here and not see him at all?"

"No," Therese said. "I'm sure you can stay at the Corbetts whenever you need to, like before." That would keep Badan in Richmond too. "But please consider sending Aggie. It's what would be best for Warner."

Mother's voice wavered. "I've lost too much already this year. My husband. My father. My daughter. I have no intention of losing my son too."

Therese wasn't surprised at being included on Mother's list, though she resisted the urge to remind the woman that she hadn't been "lost" at all but rather had been forced away by Mother's decision not to free the slaves.

She turned to where she could see her brother's face. His eyes were open and his mouth was pinched. He blinked, and then very quietly he said, "I'm staying here, Mother. I'll come home when I can, but now is not the time."

Mother wrinkled her nose and then asked Warner, "Should I bring in Aggie to care for you?"

Therese didn't realize that Michael had been listening, but he must have because he limped toward them, looking to Therese for permission. She gave him a slight nod, and then he joined in the discussion.

"Don't you think that's a good idea, Warner?" Michael asked. "To have your own personal nurse here full-time? Therese and Polly can only come on weeknights and Saturdays. The nurses are overworked, as are the orderlies." He turned to Mother. "Doesn't Aggie have a knack for nursing?"

Mother nodded.

"Then I'd definitely send her. Have Badan bring her tomorrow. And I'll check on Warner as often as I can as well. If there's any change, you'll be notified immediately."

After a long pause, Mother gave a heavy sigh. "I guess I'll go home and send Aggie—for a week."

Ruth huffed. "Finally, a bit of progress."

Mother glared at the woman. "Who are you, anyway?"

"Dr. Talbot's cousin."

"Oh, heaven help us," Mother said. "I should have known. If you're done with my son, I'd like a few minutes alone with him."

Ruth stared Mother down. "I'm not done with your son. I'm scrubbing out his wound, hoping to save him from gangrene. Give me a half hour or so." Ruth returned to her work.

Warner let out a gasp. "Mother, please leave. I'll do better if you're not hovering over me."

Tears filled Mother's eyes, but she retreated to the door without saying another word. Therese returned to the dirty dishes, deciding she would take them out to the kitchen. Mother still stood in the doorway. "Come down with me," Therese said, hoping to have a moment to talk with her about Aggie and Badan.

"I'll meet you in the foyer," Mother answered, her eyes still on Warner.

Therese felt relief as she headed to the kitchen. Warner could stay, and he'd have his own personal nurse. Surely he would start to get better soon.

After she returned from the kitchen, she found her mother waiting for her in the foyer. Therese pulled her into the cloakroom, leaving the door open to allow some light to shine in.

"Mother," Therese said, "I'm concerned about the way Mr. Porter treats Aggie and Badan."

"Please don't worry yourself," Mother said.

"I can't help it. If we'd followed Father's wishes, not to mention Grandfather's, they'd be free by now."

Mother crossed her arms. Therese stepped to her bag hanging from a hook and took out the image of the escaped slave. "Remember this? Remember what we discussed with Father when we first saw the etching in the magazine and then the *carte de visite*?"

Mother turned her head away.

"Remember when Mr. Porter whipped Badan?"

Finally, Mother met Therese's gaze and then pointed at the image. "It wasn't as bad as that."

Therese shook her head. "He was fourteen. He'd done nothing wrong."

When Mother didn't answer, Therese pressed forward. "Please free them."

Mother shook her head. "You don't comprehend the seriousness of our situation." She stepped out of the cloakroom. "And you need to mind your own business."

Therese gasped as Mother fled the hospital. She didn't go after her to tell her goodbye. Instead she stayed in the cloak room, clutching the *carte de visite,* feeling as if she'd failed her father and, even worse, as if she'd failed Badan and Aggie.

Chapter Twenty-One
Therese

Mother left the next day while Therese was at church with the Galloways. Though Therese no longer worked Sundays at the hospital, she should have gone in anyway to check on Warner. But for some reason, she couldn't manage to do it. Instead, she spent the afternoon reading with the girls.

Later Alec came by and invited Therese for a walk. The sun would set in a half hour, and the day had grown cold. She bundled up as best she could, borrowing Mrs. Galloway's muffler, and headed out.

They walked in silence for the first block, and then he took her arm and pulled her closer.

"How's Ruth settling in?" she asked, an attempt at conversation even though she didn't really feel like talking.

Alec shrugged. "Fine. Her needs are simple. As you've seen, she's pretty much all business, all the time."

Therese smiled. And all bossiness and crankiness too.

"I spoke with her about the lacerated livers," he added.

Therese held her breath, waiting for him to go on.

"She's willing to take over the treatment of your cases."

"Wonderful." Therese exhaled slowly, reminding herself that angels came in all sorts of packages—even frumpy, perpetually angry, self-righteous ones.

"What's the general timing?" he asked.

"Hopefully, both cases will arrive at the hospital tomorrow, or the next day at the latest—though one may not be able to stay for long. I'm not sure..."

"All right. I'll keep Ruth updated."

They walked along in silence for a minute, and then Alec said, "I'm sorry about Warner. That his wounds have become infected."

"I didn't go see him today."

"I noticed."

Her face warmed.

He quickly added, "It's all right. Polly sat with him and read to him."

Therese knew that Polly often went in on Sundays, even though it was their day off. "How is he doing?"

"About the same," Alec answered. "I'll most likely need to operate again tomorrow. I just couldn't bear to do it today."

She reached for his hand. None of this was easy for him either. In fact, she didn't often think about just how hard it was for Alec. They continued to walk. The changing leaves were now a riot of bright orange and red, crowning the city and offering a distraction from the artillery that could be heard from the fighting around Petersburg. Each time a burst of shells exploded, Therese thought of Michael. *God, keep him safe.*

Alec brought her mind back to the streets of Richmond, pointing out houses he liked, mostly stately brick Georgian homes. Therese imagined sharing a similar house with him in Maine.

Strolling through the neighborhood with him and admiring homes seemed like the most normal thing they'd done together. For a moment the hospital and Warner and Mother and the need to get Aggie and Badan to the North all seemed far away.

As they stood gazing at a three-story mansion, Alec asked, "Did you have a chance to tell your mother that..." He paused. "That I've made my intentions known?"

"No," Therese answered. "I didn't see her outside of the hospital. I'll speak to her when she returns."

He nodded. "And then I'll speak to her after that."

Yes, it would do no good for Mother to be broadsided. She was feeling defensive enough as it was. Therese was no longer timid when it came to caring for others or working out her future, but she still needed to approach her mother with care—especially when the topic at hand would be that of the Yankee Quaker doctor wanting to take her daughter away with him to Maine forever.

Alec operated on Warner the next day, removing more of his leg. Therese waited late into the evening, but Mother, Aggie, and Badan didn't arrive. Nor did they the next day after, nor by a week after. Therese sent letters to Mother every day, updating her about Warner and asking when Aggie would arrive, but Mother didn't write back. Therese had no way of knowing if the letters hadn't reached Mother— or if she simply chose not to respond. But she couldn't help but grow more concerned for Aggie and Badan.

The next Thursday was the day Abraham Lincoln designated as a national day of Thanksgiving, celebrated as a federal holiday for the first time since James Madison was in office. Of course, folks in Richmond—and throughout the South, for that matter—were not celebrating.

Once Warner's fever was finally down, Therese decided she should return to River Pines herself to see what was going on, fearing some catastrophe had befallen them. She asked Polly to keep an eye on her brother while she was gone, but her friend insisted on going with her. "Dr. Talbot and Ruth will see to Warner," she said. "But who will see to you?"

They decided to go on Saturday and return on Sunday after church. Polly knew of a farmer from her parents' area who would be coming into Richmond on Friday to deliver produce, and he could give them a ride back once he was done.

On Friday afternoon, as Therese sat in the dining room grading Eleanor and Lydia's mathematics, she heard Mr. and Mrs. Galloway talking in the parlor. She stood and stepped toward the doorway, trying not to appear as if she were listening.

Mr. Galloway said, "I can't fathom why he's agreed to it after all this time, but the secretary of state has decided that giving male slaves weapons to help fight the Union is the best course to take for now. At some point after the war, they'll then be freed." Footsteps came toward the hall, and Therese slipped back into the dining room.

"He had me draft a letter saying so and signed it. It's on its way to President Davis today."

The two stopped in the foyer, and Therese stepped out in the hall. Mrs. Galloway told her husband goodbye at the front door. Therese quickly slipped back to the table. A moment later the front door opened and closed.

Polly had gone on to the hospital early, and Therese planned to meet her there. She decided to finish correcting the girls' schoolwork later and be on her way.

By the time she reached the hospital, the day had grown frigid. Therese shivered as she hung her cloak and hurried up the stairs. Matron Webb was working in the west ward and informed Therese that Polly, Ruth, and Dr. Talbot were all in surgery—working on Warner.

Therese braced herself against a table. "On his leg again?"

"No, his stomach."

That didn't sound good.

"They'll be a while, I'm sure," Matron Webb added.

Therese filled the time delivering meals to the soldiers, and then she concentrated on feeding the ones who couldn't feed themselves. Finally, she spotted Polly coming toward her.

Therese rushed to her side. "How is Warner?"

"He came through it all right."

"What happened?"

"Part of his small intestine was infected. Dr. Talbot removed it."

"Oh, no." Therese's hand went to her abdomen. "Is he going to make it?"

Polly's eyes filled with tears. "It's possible."

"Should I not go home?"

"No, you should. Ruth promised she'd make Warner her top priority. If we can bring Aggie back, it will make things easier for all of us."

"All right." Therese glanced around and then whispered. "I have something else I need to tell you—or Dr. Talbot directly."

"Go up to the operating room. He's still there with your brother. Warner won't be conscious yet."

"Thank you." Therese hurried up to the third floor, knocking on the surgery door.

Alec seemed surprised to see her, but he assured her that Warner was stable as soon as she stepped in the door.

"Yes, Polly told me." She closed the door behind her. "I have information. Can I say it straight out?" She didn't know what the correct medical terms would be.

He nodded.

She stepped to the corner of the room by the windows overlooking Tenth Street and motioned for him to join her, not wanting Warner to awake to her words. Quickly, she told Alec what she'd heard about the plans to arm slaves as soldiers for the Confederacy. He thanked her and assured her he'd pass the information on.

"In the meantime," he added, "why don't you broach the subject with the other nurses and the orderlies tonight? Say you heard a rumor—of course don't give a hint as to where you actually got the information. The Confederacy has been batting this idea around for years, so it's not as if it could be traced back to you."

"All right, but why?"

"If we can turn public opinion against it, we might be able to put a stop to it. I can't imagine the citizens of Richmond being all that thrilled about the notion of slaves having rifles and ammunition."

"I see." She then added, "The last thing I want is for Badan to be conscripted, even if it would mean he'd earn his freedom. He could be killed first."

"Oh, I doubt they'd actually carry through with their promise of freedom. Or they might, but then they'd figure out a way to take it back." He shook his head. "The South can't compete with the North's endless supply of soldiers."

Therese agreed. Other than the slaves, all the South had left to recruit were boys who hadn't even started shaving yet.

The door flew open, and Ruth stepped into the room. Alec's back was to his cousin, but Therese had full view of her face, which held her usual sour expression.

Therese simply said hello and then slipped around Alec and moved to Warner's side. As she stood looking down at her still-sleeping brother, she couldn't help but wonder if the rest of Alec's family was like Ruth. Therese had grown up in the South, where people were warm and friendly and put a high value on manners. Could she really make her home where folks scowled and barked and insulted without provocation? Surely this wasn't what everyone in Maine was like. Ruth was one of a kind.

Wasn't she?

Just as Alec requested, Therese brought up the topic of conscripting slaves with several different orderlies and nurses, and by the time she and Polly left at nine, the hospital was abuzz with the rumor. Soldiers were riled up about it, as were the staff, visitors, and volunteers. The citizens' own prejudices were working against the goals of the Confederacy. Therese was surprised how easy it was to agree with their concerns. True, she didn't want enslaved males to fight for the Confederacy either, but for very different reasons than the others. They feared the slaves would turn against the South. She was afraid they would be slaughtered for the South—either that or turn the tide and allow the South to win. Chances were, as Alec had voiced, freedom wouldn't be granted to those who fought anyway. And for those who didn't fight, such as Auntie Vera and Aggie, they would definitely remain enslaved.

Despite being a Quaker, it seemed Alec could still do plenty to influence the war. She was impressed with his presence of mind, working as both a surgeon and a spy. Her admiration of him grew throughout the evening. No one would ever expect that he was doing more than doctoring patients.

As the wagon master drove them home, Polly and Therese made plans to meet the next day at the market, late in the morning when the farmer would be done selling his produce. Therese imagined him peddling squash and apples, and possibly potatoes, all in big demand. The Galloways hadn't been able to buy meat all week, and Mrs. Galloway spent most of her time, when she wasn't in bed, redoing the girls' dresses with the one needle she had left, trying to come up with warm enough and big enough clothing to get them through another winter. She'd also cut up a small rug in half and was trying to make shoes for Eleanor, who had completely outgrown her last pair. Therese decided she'd look in the trunks at River Pines to see if there were any old ones from when Mother was a girl. Therese would also patch the soles of her boots. She had income to give Mother, both from the Galloways and the hospital, but she wanted the money to go toward what was needed at River Pines, shoes for Aggie and Auntie Vera in particular, and not her own needs.

Polly went to the hospital for a few hours Saturday morning, but Therese had taken the whole day off so she could finish her grading for the girls and her lesson plans for the next week. As she worked in the parlor, she noticed Mr. Galloway had left a stack of papers next to his chair, but they didn't seem to be anything important—a few old memorandums about acquisitions and troop movements was all.

The girls sat in the parlor with her, reading their books, but at midmorning Therese took them for a walk in the crisp, cold air. By the time they arrived home, Mrs. Galloway was sipping a cup of tea in the dining room. Therese grabbed her bag from the chilly attic and told the family farewell, saying she'd be back the next evening or at least by Monday.

Mrs. Galloway insisted that Therese take her muffler again and a wool blanket. "It will be a cold ride," she said.

Therese thanked her and hurried out the door.

When she reached the market, Polly wasn't there, and Therese wasn't sure which farmer her friend had arranged the ride with. Therese asked around, but no one was headed west. Finally, she decided to wait at the entrance to the market, but she wondered if she should hurry to the hospital. Perhaps there had been some sort of catastrophe. Multiple admissions. An epidemic—they'd gotten several cases of influenza the week before. Or perhaps Warner had taken a turn for the worse.

She began to pace back and forth as vendor after vendor packed up and left. Finally, just as she'd decided to go to the hospital after all, Polly shouted her name. She was sitting on the bench of a wagon—but not a farmer's wagon. It was a covered army wagon, driven by Michael and pulled by a team of four horses.

Relief swept over Therese as she hurried toward her friend. Michael stopped the wagon, set the brake, and jumped down. By the time Therese reached them, he was ready to help, offering her his hand. Polly scooted over, and Therese settled beside her, spreading the blanket across the two of them.

"Michael has been ordered to procure more food, so he's giving us a ride," Polly said. "Hopefully, our parents and your mother will be able to help."

Therese nodded. She hoped Mother would allow it. "How was Warner when you left?" Therese asked.

"About the same. He said to tell you not to worry—to focus on sorting things out with your mother." Polly yawned, quickly covering her mouth. It looked as if her lack of sleep was finally catching up with her.

Michael turned onto Broad Street, passing shops and then houses, until the cobblestones gave way to gravel. Thankfully, it hadn't rained all week.

As they approached the edge of town and the checkpoint, Michael pulled his pass from his pocket. A guard studied it carefully and asked about Polly and Therese. "My sister and her friend," Michael said. "They work as governesses and nurses in Richmond but are going home to see family. They'll return with me tomorrow evening."

"All right," the guard said. "Be on your way."

Michael drove the team forward but before they picked up speed, Polly said, "Do you mind if I sleep in the back? I'm exhausted."

"Good idea," Michael said. "You'll find a couple of blankets—clean ones. I borrowed them from the hospital." He smiled.

"Quite resourceful, aren't you?" Polly teased.

"Aren't we all," he quipped.

It would be a rough ride in the army wagon, but as tired as Polly was, she could get a couple hours of sleep.

Once the wagon stopped, Polly scooted past Therese and jumped down before Michael could step around the wagon to help her. But he did help her into the back, under the cover. When he returned, he had blankets for both Therese and him to bundle up in. Therese thanked him. Another layer of warmth would help further protect her from the cold.

Soon they were back on the road, headed on the north side of the James to the Talbot estate. Then they would take the ferry across the water and continue on to River Pines.

Fog streamed along the top of the forested hills like a shroud, and an icy wind blew east. Therese wrapped one of the blankets over her head and held it up over the lower half of her face. She looked like a ragamuffin, she knew. Michael didn't seem to mind, and she wondered if Alec would if he were with her. And what would he think of River Pines? What would his opinion be of the obvious opulence that had existed just a few years ago, along with the current poverty, and the sad state of affairs of the five slaves left by Grandfather—whom Mother didn't have the bravery to free? With a shudder, she realized she was grateful Alec wouldn't see that part of her life.

Therese and Michael rode on in silence while Polly slept. After a while, he slowed the horses as another wagon passed them on the narrow road.

"Is this the first time you've been back to River Pines since you started working for the Galloways?" He encouraged his team to speed up again.

"Yes," Therese said. "But, of course, I've seen Mother at the hospital."

"I hope you can get a good rest and a few solid meals."

"Hopefully, you can too. You need both of those things more than I do."

"Oh, I don't know about that…" His voice trailed off.

Therese felt awkward that they were resorting to small talk, and she couldn't help but miss the rapport they'd shared years ago.

"How was your time in France? Polly was telling me about some big adventure you had rescuing a Jewish family heirloom or something?"

Michael flashed a humble smile. "Well, yes, it was pretty exciting, actually. How much did she tell you?"

"The basic story. How a con man tricked a rabbi so he could steal his valuable heirloom, and then the con man sold it to a merchant in New York City, who put it on a ship, and then the ship was captured by another ship, which ended up in France where you were, and so you bought it and brought it all the way back home and returned it to its rightful owner. Is that about it?"

Michael chuckled. "Well, except for the ending. Sadly, the rightful owner is currently off with the 25th Virginia in the Shenandoah Valley, so I haven't been able to give it to him yet."

"Oh no. Where is it now?"

Michael glanced around and spoke in a low voice. "My father put it in the safe, along with our family documents and a few other things."

"Well, at least the rabbi can be comforted by the knowledge that it'll be there waiting for him when he returns."

"True."

They rode along in companionable silence for a few minutes until Therese returned to the subject of France.

"Otherwise," she said, "your time over there went well?"

He glanced at her and smiled a little before returning his eyes to the road. "It was lovely in many ways. Meeting cousins I'd only heard of. Learning about the method of making paper from wood pulp instead of rags, helping to develop and sell a new kind of photography paper. Traveling between properties that the family owns in Lyon and then up to Le Chambon-sur-Lignon too, high up on the Plateau. It's a small village that some in our family have lived in for the last two hundred years, which is a relatively short time compared to how long the family has been in Lyon."

"What are your relatives like?"

"Hard workers, all of them. And faithful. They endured years of persecution…until the French Revolution, really. The ones on the Plateau live very humbly." He smiled. "It's funny. They have a printing press that still runs and an old paper mill they're dismantling because it's not profitable up there anymore. But a new one was opened in Lyon. Up on the Plateau, they have an old warehouse too and an old, beautiful house. The buildings all date back to the 1600s."

"Sounds like a wonderful experience for you."

"Actually, I missed home horribly. I worried about how everyone back here was doing. Getting the letter that the twins had been killed was devastating. Knowing the heartache my parents and Polly were going through after Gerald and Victor…I felt as if I'd been a despicable person not to have protected my brothers."

Therese couldn't help but wonder if perhaps that was what had made him change his mind about the issue of slavery. Perhaps he blamed the abolitionist crusade for their deaths. Perhaps he wanted revenge on the North.

"I was worried about Lance and wondered if he would survive…" Michael turned his head toward her. "And then hearing about your father's death—that was such a tragedy too. He was a good man who taught me so much."

Tears welled in Therese's eyes. "Why come back when you did?"

He shrugged. "I couldn't bear the thought of not helping in some way. I expected to be an infantryman, but I was commissioned as an officer because of my family's connections. I think I'm better at what I'm doing, procuring supplies rather than fighting. I know the area and have contacts that have helped with that. And transporting the wounded has fit in well with my duties."

Therese nodded. It seemed he was well suited for both of his jobs, along with delaying a resolution to the war. "I know many Virginian residents have been coerced out of food by the Confederate Army and resent that. How do you handle it?"

"I buy the food," Michael said. "And I always leave enough for the families, which means lots of trips and foraging to get what's needed. But I believe it's the right thing to do."

"How do you pay for it?"

Michael must not have heard her because he didn't answer. She asked again.

He evaded her question and instead asked, "What are you looking forward to the most when you get home?"

She couldn't help but frown. He was hiding something, but then, weren't they all?

"Looking forward to? At River Pines?"

He nodded.

"Nothing." She sighed. "Either Mother is sick and that's why she hasn't responded, or else she's miffed with me. I'm guessing the second. Either way, there will be some sort of conflict unless she's deathly ill, and then I'll regret what I just said."

Michael smiled. "I won't tell a soul."

"Thank you." Therese sighed again. "If she's miffed with me, we'll end up arguing about when Warner should come home. I'll ask again about her sending Aggie to Richmond, which she most likely opposes or she would have done so already." She wouldn't tell Michael what Mother thought of Alec. That would broach a topic she definitely didn't want to discuss with him, and thankfully he hadn't brought it up.

Michael glanced toward Therese. "So there's nothing you're looking forward to?"

"Well, yes. Seeing Aggie. And Badan. They married not too long ago, and I'm worried about them."

He glanced at her questioningly.

"It's Mr. Porter."

"The overseer?"

Therese nodded. "He's violent toward Badan." She paused. "And, um, too friendly toward Aggie."

Anger flared on Michael's face. Perhaps he hadn't totally lost his soul.

"I'm also afraid that the Confederacy might conscript Badan and Sonny and even Old Joe to fight."

"I heard about that at the hospital just this morning. It's a horrible idea."

Therese nodded again, knowing she and Michael agreed on the

topic for two different reasons. "And then I also worry—although I doubt Mother would actually do this—that she might sell one of them if things get too bad."

Michael kept his expression neutral. Yes, he truly did believe the economy of the Confederacy was at stake and that the slaves should not be set free. Michael Talbot was a son of the South as much as anyone she knew. He'd come all the way back from France to do his duty.

Thankfully, Alec was a man of honor. God willing, Therese would soon be on her way to Maine with him—and taking Aggie and Badan with her as free citizens. But to make that happen, Warner needed to survive so that Mother would have someone to take care of her.

CHAPTER TWENTY-TWO

Therese

By the time they reached the Talbots' place, Therese was stiff and sore. Polly stirred as the wagon stopped, sat up, and stretched. "Are we here already?"

Michael chuckled. His parents came out of the front door of their home, so he jumped down, helped Polly out of the back, and then hurried around to Therese. Every time he took her hand, she remembered how smitten she was by him all those years ago. A shiver shot up her spine. He let go of her quickly this time, though, and limped toward his parents, hugging his mother first and then his father. Polly hurried past and into her mother's arms. A wave of sadness swept over Therese. She missed both her father and the woman her mother had been before he fell ill.

Miss Amanda let go of Polly and stepped toward Therese, pulling her in for a hug. "It's so good to see you, dear," she said. "How are you? How is Warner doing? And your mother?"

Therese answered that her mother was doing as well as could be expected, and Warner was managing.

They ate vegetable stew at the Talbots', and then Michael and his father loaded boxes of potatoes, squash, and apples into the wagon.

When they were getting ready to leave, Therese realized Mr. Stephen was coming with them.

"Papa will help Michael find food around River Pines and then go to Richmond with him and on to Petersburg," Polly explained. "Tonight, we'll all stay at our cousins' house."

Mr. Stephen offered to drive so Michael could sleep in the back.

"You should rest," Michael said to Therese.

"Oh, no," she answered. "You need it more. I slept last night." She wasn't sure how long he'd been on the road. If he'd come from the Petersburg area, he hadn't slept in some time.

Michael said he would try to rest for a little while and settled between the crates of produce. When they reached the end of the Talbots' lane, Therese glanced back. It appeared he was already sound asleep.

They took the last ferry across the river, and by the time they reached River Pines, it was pitch-black. Badan came out to meet them and took the horses in hand, while Mr. Stephen jumped down.

Therese was cold, even with the layers of blankets. "You should all come in for something hot to drink before you continue," she said.

Mr. Stephen thanked her but said they needed to be on their way.

She turned toward Badan. "Do we have any food we can spare? Michael's collecting for the troops. Potatoes? Apples? Anything?"

"You'll have to ask your mother," Badan said.

Therese turned toward the house. "Is she doing all right?"

"I don't know," he answered. "Aggie's been looking after her."

"She's ill?"

"Seems so. She took to bed when we returned this last time."

Therese pursed her lips.

Badan dropped his voice. "I don't think it's serious."

Mr. Stephen held up an unlit lamp, and Badan said he'd take it to the kitchen and light it. Therese could see a soft glow through the window of the building and wondered if Aggie was in there or in the house with Mother. She'd soon find out. She told Mr. Stephen she'd have food ready tomorrow when they picked her up, and then she said farewell to everyone but Michael, who was still asleep in the back of the wagon.

Therese started up the back steps to the house just as Badan returned with the lantern. He was followed by Aggie, who called out a hello to Therese. The two young women hugged and then entered the house together.

"Is Mother in her room?"

"No. She's in the parlor. It's warmer in there." Aggie stopped in the dining room. "I'll wait here. Call if you need me."

Therese hurried toward the room but then stopped in the doorway, gaping. Mother was in a bed that had been moved down from upstairs. Auntie Vera sat at her side. Mother wore a nightgown and cap and had a stack of quilts piled on her.

"What's wrong?" Therese stepped to her mother's side. Perhaps Badan underestimated the situation.

"Oh, I had this bed moved in here for Warner, and then soon after I arrived home, I started feeling poorly."

"Did you get my letters?"

"Yes."

"Why didn't you reply?"

"I couldn't seem to manage it." Mother's eyes filled with tears. "I've felt so lost. Your father gone. My father. You. Warner wounded so badly. All I wanted to do was bring him home, but that doctor wouldn't let me."

"Now, now," Therese said. Auntie Vera stood and Therese, still wearing her cloak and the blanket from Mrs. Galloway, slid onto the seat by her mother. Auntie Vera nodded toward the dining room and made her escape.

"I felt so helpless," Mother said. "After you turned against me—"

"Mother—"

"You sided with that doctor, who seems completely smitten with you, by the way, and probably intends to take you back to Maine with him when he goes."

Therese felt a flush of guilt for not addressing that particular situation before. She was about to respond, but Mother kept going.

"My whole life is falling apart. All I have left is River Pines, and you want to take Aggie to Richmond—and I'm guessing on north." Mother glared at her. "Along with Badan, right?"

Therese felt shaky inside, but she took a deep breath and then her mother's hand in hers, knowing she needed to choose her words carefully. She couldn't deny that Alec wanted her to go to Maine—or that she hoped to take Badan and Aggie with her. Mother had guessed on the basis of rumors and her own speculation, both of which happened to be correct.

Therese sighed. Mother had been through hard times. She'd never been good in a crisis, and here she'd had to face a whole series of them. No wonder she felt so lost.

"I'm sorry you're not well," Therese said.

Mother nodded and swiped at a tear. "How did you get here?"

"The Talbots. Michael has an army wagon, and he gave Polly and me a ride. We picked up their father across the river."

"Oh." Mother struggled to sit up. "Did you ask them in?"

"I did, but they declined. They're spending the night at their cousins' and will come back to pick me up tomorrow afternoon." Therese stroked her mother's hand. "Do you feel up to going to church in the morning?"

Mother exhaled and then shivered. "Perhaps. I'll see how I'm doing."

Therese wouldn't ask her about taking Aggie back to Richmond until tomorrow. The less Therese said tonight about anything important the better, although there were a few matters they would need to discuss at some point.

First, she gave Mother her wages from the Galloways and the hospital. Mother thanked her and quickly took the money. "Will you use it for Aggie and Auntie Vera? For boots for them?"

Mother shook her head. "I found some that worked, old ones in a trunk. I'll save the money for an emergency."

Therese asked about possible shoes for Eleanor. "There might be a pair that would fit her," Mother said. "Look in the back bedroom. That's where the trunk is. And take any dresses you think the girls could wear too."

"Any chance you have an extra needle?"

"Ask Auntie Vera. I think we still have five."

Therese thanked her mother profusely. Because of the blockade, needles were hard to come by, but Auntie Vera must have had a good supply when the war started.

Next, Therese brought up the issue of food, quickly saying anything Mother could spare, above what she'd already given to the army once the harvest was completed, would go to the men Warner fought with. Mother pursed her lips, but then she said, "Talk to Badan about it. He has a better idea than I do. Perhaps there are still some hams from last year you could take. And some bacon."

Therese's mouth watered at the thought. People definitely ate better in the country than in the city. "Thank you." Therese couldn't help but take Mother's generosity as a good sign. She hoped she'd feel as giving in the morning when it came to their discussion about Aggie—and Badan too.

Her mother's eyes grew teary. "One of my brooches was missing when I returned."

"Goodness," Therese said.

"I asked Auntie Vera and Aggie about it, and of course they denied taking it. I had Mr. Porter search their cabin, but nothing turned up."

"They wouldn't take it," Therese said. Her mother had probably misplaced it. A few things had gone missing when her grandfather was alive, one time even some cash, but it had never been determined one of the slaves took anything. Sometimes Grandfather found his missing items and sometimes not.

Once her mother fell asleep, Therese took a candlestick from the mantel and started toward the stairs, realizing Mother hadn't asked about Warner and how he was doing. Not once.

Therese hurried up the stairs and into a cold back bedroom, where she found a pair of boots that would work for Eleanor, several old dresses that could be remade, and a bundle of her baby clothes, all in a cedar chest. If she were to go to Maine with Alec, there was no reason for her to save the garments for her own children someday. She'd be able to acquire new ones. She would give these clothes to Mrs. Galloway for her little one.

The next morning, Therese rose early, checked on Mother, who was still sleeping, and headed outside to the garden. The last of the pumpkins and squash still held to the vines as smoke from the kitchen house drifted above. Therese inhaled deeply. River Pines had once been a place of anxiety for her, and she hadn't been looking forward to coming back, but she couldn't help but take comfort from it now. It was the only home she had. She headed to the kitchen. Aggie stood at the stove, making a pot of porridge. Therese congratulated her on her marriage, and the young woman beamed. "I'm happier than I ever hoped to be."

But her face went slack as Mr. Porter entered the dimly lit kitchen. "Hurry up, girl," he barked. "I want my breakfast."

Therese stepped toward the middle of the room, out of the shadow. "Hello."

He grunted. "What are you doing here?"

"Looking in on Mother." Therese stepped to the cupboard and retrieved a stack of bowls.

Mr. Porter sat at the table. "How about some coffee?"

Therese knew it was made of chicory root. No one had had coffee for the last couple of years. But it was hot. That's what mattered.

Aggie poured the man a cup. The kitchen door opened, and Badan started to step inside, but then he retreated. A moment later, Auntie Vera entered.

"Miss Therese," she said. "Your mother's awake and saying she'd like to go to church with you."

"Wonderful." Therese handed Aggie two bowls. "I'll take her some breakfast."

"I'll send Aggie in shortly." Auntie Vera gave Mr. Porter a loathsome look, which he didn't seem to notice.

A half hour later, Aggie entered the parlor as Therese helped her mother dress. "Mrs. Jennings," she said. "You look good today."

Mother shook her head. "I don't, I'm sure, but I am determined to go to church." She patted Therese's arm. "Just having you here has done me good."

Badan drove them down the tree-lined Huguenot Trail Road to the church, where Therese and her mother quickly slipped up the steps of the white building, through the tiny foyer, and down the aisle to Grandfather's pew. The sermon was about hope. Therese listened closely to the passages the priest chose from the Psalms he read, "'I laid me down and slept; I awaked; for the LORD sustained me. I will not be afraid of ten thousands of people, that have set themselves against me round about.'" Next he read from Revelation, "'God shall wipe away all tears from their eyes; and there shall be no more death, neither sorrow, nor crying, neither shall there be any more pain: for the former things are passed away.'"

Therese took her mother's hand and squeezed it. God would sustain them. They needn't fear. Someday this would all pass. She held on to Mother's hand through the rest of the sermon.

At the end of the service, several friends welcomed Therese and then reached out to Mother, asking about Warner. Therese looked for Polly and found her speaking to the deacon as she took a book from him. The girl was a regular lending library.

Therese searched for Michael, finally finding him in the churchyard with his father, talking with a few men. He looked so much more at ease than he did when he came into the hospital. And rested.

Therese linked her arm through her mother's. "I have an idea. Why don't you come back to Richmond today and stay until Warner can come home? Bring Aggie—she can nurse Warner, like we talked about. And Auntie Vera too. I'm certain both of them can stay at the hospital."

"I can't do that," Mother said. "What about River Pines?"

"There's not much to be done, is there? Can't Mr. Porter see to it with Old Joe's and Sonny's help? I'm sure the Corbetts would be happy to have you stay again."

"I don't know..."

"You should be close to Warner and me at a time like this. Not isolated from us. Then, as soon as Warner is well enough, the two of you can return home."

"What about you?" Mother asked.

Therese quickly responded. "I'll visit when I can."

"What about that doctor?"

"Here comes Polly," Therese said. Michael and his father were right behind her. They greeted Mother warmly, and then Mr. Stephen asked how she was doing.

"All right. Although I'm reeling a little. Therese is proposing that I return to Richmond."

"That's a wonderful idea!" Polly said. "We've missed you since you left."

"Yes," Michael said. "I think that would be better for everyone, especially Warner."

Mother turned toward Mr. Stephen. "What do you think? Should I abandon River Pines?"

"Helene, you wouldn't be abandoning it. Mr. Porter can easily manage, and I'd be happy—once I return from helping Michael—to look in on things from time to time."

"Oh, goodness," Mother said. "That would make me worry less."

Surprisingly, perhaps under the cheerful influence of the Talbots, Mother decided to go to Richmond and take Auntie Vera and Aggie with her. But she also decided that Badan, after transporting them to Richmond, should return to River Pines.

"I trust him more than I do Mr. Porter," she whispered to the Talbots.

Therese balked. "Mother, you'll be left in Richmond without a buggy or a driver. Whatever will you do?" She hoped her protest sounded reasonable. Badan had to stay.

Mother pursed her lips but didn't answer Therese. She simply turned her attention back to Mr. Stephen and asked after Miss Amanda, who hadn't ventured alone across the river for church that day.

The change in plans meant rushing around once they reached River Pines, but by the time the Talbots arrived to pick up the food for Michael's unit, Mother and the others were packed.

As Badan loaded the buggy, Mr. Porter came out of his cabin without his hat, looking as if he'd been napping. "Where are you all off to in such a hurry?"

"Richmond," Mother said. "Hopefully, I'll return with Warner soon."

"Who's going with you?"

Mother answered as Auntie Vera motioned for Aggie to climb in the back of the buggy. Mr. Stephen jumped down from the wagon and began helping Badan load crates of cabbages and apples. Michael jumped down too and stood beside the team, his arms crossed.

"Goodness, woman, leave someone to cook for me. You don't expect me to do it myself, do you?"

"I'm sure you'll manage," Mother said. "The cellar is full, and the chickens are still laying."

He crossed his arms. "Leave me the young one or I'll quit."

That would present a problem. Mother couldn't leave Old Joe and Sonny at River Pines by themselves. On the other hand, Therese suspected Mr. Porter was bluffing. Chances were he'd end up in the army if he left. Badan hung his head, and Aggie slumped down in the front seat of the buggy.

Finally, Mother said, "If you feel that's what you must do, I won't stop you."

Therese wanted to applaud, but of course she stayed silent.

"Then at least leave the old one." Mr. Porter took a step forward.

Therese bit her tongue, glancing from Mother to Auntie Vera, who stood on the other side of the buggy.

"No," Mother said. "You can fend for yourself. You only have a handful of chores to do as it is."

"I'll have to think about it," he said.

"Send me a message at the Institute Hospital if you decide to go," Mother said. Therese doubted she worried about Old Joe leaving, but Sonny was still young, and without the overseer here, he could try and run off. Mother added, "If there's an emergency, send for Mr. Talbot. He's going to check on you now and then."

That didn't seem to make Mr. Porter any happier, but finally he slunk away. Therese asked Badan if Old Joe and Sonny would be all right with Mr. Porter.

"Yes, Miss Jennings. He's all bark and no bite to them."

Therese hoped so. Once the men loaded the food into the wagon, Michael and his father led the way, and the journey began. Mother, Therese, and Polly rode in the backseat of the buggy, while Auntie Vera sat up front with Aggie and Badan.

As they passed River Pines at the end of the lane, Therese felt a wave of compassion for her mother. Everything had changed. Mother had stood up to Mr. Porter.

Michael and his father stopped a couple of times at farms and purchased more food. By the time they reached the city, the sun was setting. All were exhausted, but mostly Therese was relieved that she'd managed to get both Aggie and Badan to Richmond. She wasn't sorry to have Mother along too, nor Auntie Vera. She hoped all of them would be better off in the city than at River Pines, despite the shortages in Richmond. Mother wouldn't be isolated. Aggie and Auntie Vera would be away from Mr. Porter. If only Mother would allow Badan to stay.

Badan stopped the buggy at the hospital and helped Therese, Polly, Auntie Vera, and Aggie down. He was going to take Mother on to the Corbetts', while Polly and Therese found accommodations for Auntie Vera and Aggie.

Michael and his father pulled the wagon into the driveway and around to the back. Therese and Polly hurried up the steps, followed by Auntie Vera and Aggie, and entered through the front doors. Alec stood in the foyer, speaking to Matron Webb, but he stopped when he saw Therese.

"You're back." He smiled as his eyes stayed on her.

"We've brought two more nurses," Polly said. "They'll need to board here."

Matron Webb's face lit up. "Perfect timing. We've been given an extension. At least another month."

Therese met Alec's gaze and smiled. He nodded. He seemed happy enough about it, but Ruth wouldn't be. That put them home well past Christmas.

"Show the women to the room down in the basement," the matron said. "Then you can give them a tour and basic training."

"Of course." Polly pointed toward the hallway.

"You managed to get Aggie to Richmond," Alec said once they were gone. "Well done."

Therese explained what had happened, and that Mother and Badan had gone on to the Corbetts', and Badan would be returning to River Pines in the morning. "I haven't spoken directly with Mother about sending Badan and Aggie north, but she's guessed what my intent is," she said. "I'm going to have one last conversation with her about it before it's time for you to go, I promise. And if she still refuses to grant their freedom, then I'll need to figure out a way to get Badan back to Richmond on my own."

Alec ran his hand through his hair. "I see." He inhaled deeply and then exhaled. "And how about the conversation about you and me?" he asked. "Did you manage to broach that topic with her?"

Even in the drafty foyer, Therese's face grew warm. "No," she said. "She brought it up, though. She guessed what we're planning. She was so out of sorts, so fragile. She'd taken to her bed when I got there." She turned her face up to his. "I didn't have the heart to force the discussion further. We have to take this step by step."

As they talked, Michael and his father came in through the back of the hospital. Mr. Stephen and Alec greeted each other warmly and spent a few minutes catching up on the doings of various relatives throughout the South and North.

Finally, Alec excused himself, saying rounds awaited him, and he headed up the stairs, taking the steps two at a time. Michael and Mr. Talbot followed at a slower pace. Therese paused for a moment in the foyer. Mr. Stephen glanced back at her and then continued on with Michael.

She followed them up the stairs and into the ward, where they had already gathered around Warner's cot. He was propped up on pillows but asleep.

"Warner." She took his hand. "I'm back. We're all here. Even Mr. Stephen has come to see you."

Her brother opened his eyes and then tried to scoot up in the bed a little higher. He said he was feeling about the same, which Therese knew meant poorly. She filled him in on Mother's return to Richmond and Auntie Vera and Aggie's new jobs at the hospital. After a few minutes of conversation, he and Michael started chatting about their days back at the academy.

"I miss our home there." Warner turned toward Therese. "Do you?"

"Yes," she answered, choking a little on the word. "River Pines will never feel like home the way Box Tree Male Academy did."

Warner nodded, and Michael stared at her for a long moment. Finally, he said, "But you've spent your entire life going to your Grandfather's place."

Therese shrugged. "It's hard to explain." Some of her fondest childhood memories were of playing with Aggie at River Pines, but there had been a constant tension when she was there—not only between Grandfather and Father, but between her parents as well. Plus, she was always on edge about what Mr. Porter might do to one of the slaves. At the academy, life was predictable. It was a safe, secure place.

She doubted Michael could understand. He'd never experienced that sort of conflict in his own family.

She would find a new home in Maine with Alec that would be a place of safety. Someday she wouldn't feel the loss of Box Tree Male Academy and all it represented so acutely.

CHAPTER TWENTY-THREE
Therese

The next morning, Therese stopped on the stairs on her way down from the attic. Though she'd never heard Mr. Galloway raise his voice before, he was now yelling from the dining room. Therese crept down the rest of the way and waited in the hall on the worn carpet.

"There, there," Mrs. Galloway said. "Maybe it didn't come from your office at all. The secretary has broached the idea before. Perhaps the rumor was simply referring to that."

"No," Mr. Galloway said. "I think there's a spy in our office. This was clearly a breach. Now the entire city is against the idea. Still, Secretary Benjamin plans to ask General Lee for his support."

Therese did her best not to react in any way as she tucked that bit of information away for later. She took a deep breath and headed to the foyer, where she'd left the clothes, boots, and produce. She decided to present the food first. She picked up the crate and headed into the dining room. "Good morning," she beamed. "I brought some things back with me."

Mrs. Galloway smiled at her, but Mr. Galloway had a sour expression on his face.

"Apples, cabbages, and squash." Therese dropped her voice to a whisper. "And a little bit of bacon." It felt odd to be both helping and spying on them, but perhaps that was part of the paradox of war. Anyone living in the South who was trying to help the Northern cause was doing the same thing.

"Oh, my." Mrs. Galloway clasped her hands together. "You're too good to us."

Therese placed the crate on the floor. "I have a few more things too." She retrieved the other box and placed it on the table, taking the boots out first. "These should fit Eleanor. And the dresses can be remade." She placed them on the table and then held up the needle.

Mrs. Galloway's hands went to her face. "Thank you."

"And I brought baby clothes too."

"Oh, goodness," Mrs. Galloway said. "I didn't know what we were going to do." She was on her feet, examining what Therese had brought. "Patrick, isn't this an answer to prayer?"

He nodded, and his face softened a little. "Thank you, Therese," he said. Then he turned back toward his wife. "I need to be on my way."

"All right." She took his hand. "Chin up. You've certainly done nothing wrong."

"I know." And then he was gone.

Therese spent the rest of the day, as she taught the girls, wondering if the information about Secretary Benjamin asking General Lee for support in conscripting slaves to fight was worth passing on to Alec. She expected it was.

Late that afternoon, once she arrived at the hospital, she found Alec in his office. Before she could speak, he held up a *carte de visite*. "I stopped by the newspaper office this morning," he said. "Mr. Lewis gave me copies of the photograph he made. Here's yours." He extended it to her.

"Thank you," she said, taking it from him. She looked from the image of the three of them back to Alec, standing in practically the same place it had been made, and smiled. "I'll treasure it always."

Then she quickly told him what she'd overheard that morning. He thanked her and said he'd pass the information on.

"Pass what on?" Ruth stood in the doorway.

"That we need more gauze," Alec responded quickly.

Ruth crossed her arms over her bosom. "What we need is to get on our way home." Turning to Therese, she added, "Alec said you may be coming with us."

Therese froze, not sure how to respond.

Alec cleared his throat. "I shared our plans with Ruth. I hope you don't mind."

"No, of course not," Therese replied, and then, mustering her courage, she addressed Ruth directly. "As long as you keep them to yourself for the time being. Neither my mother nor my brother are prepared for such information presently."

"I see," Ruth replied. Therese realized that wasn't an actual yes or no.

"Ruth?" Alec stepped forward. "This is a delicate situation." He took Therese's hand. "It stays just between the three of us for now. Yes?"

"Fine. I suppose that's one way to start a lifetime together, with secrets and half-truths." She abruptly spun around, and a moment later the soles of her new Northern boots were clicking down the worn tile of the hall.

"Has she always been so...angry?" Therese asked.

Alec laughed. "Only on the outside, I promise. On the inside, she's nothing but marshmallow."

Over the next three weeks, Therese was too busy to worry much about Ruth. Mother came to the hospital most days and sat with Warner. His infections continued, and Alec operated on his leg for a third time. Aggie cared for him first and then helped with other patients. Auntie Vera spent most of her time cooking in the kitchen. Matron

Webb paid a small amount for their services, and Therese persuaded Mother to hand half the money over to Auntie Vera and Aggie, citing the verse in Leviticus about not defrauding workers of their wages.

Mother sent Badan back, just as she said she would. Therese was sure Aggie missed him, but she didn't complain. Surely she was concerned about him too.

Therese wished she could have told Badan that she was doing her best to make plans for Aggie and his escape, but she didn't want to get his hopes up, nor did she want give him any information he might share with Aggie that could be overheard by others. All of their lives were at stake if any information was revealed.

A few days before Christmas, Mother accepted that she and Warner wouldn't be returning home before the holiday, and, reminiscent of her role at the academy, she vowed to make the day a celebration, even in the hospital. Therese encouraged her to send a message to Mr. Porter, asking him to have Badan return to Richmond with hams, potatoes, eggs, and apples. Mother agreed and then met with the cook and the baker, along with Auntie Vera, mapping out tasks to make a celebration possible. Next, she asked the quartermaster to find sugar. He balked, saying if there was any out there, he would have found it by now. She told him to keep looking.

Therese relished having her mother active and involved and wished Ruth would accept the inevitable too. She only seemed to grow more bitter with each day she was still stuck in the South. On the other hand, Alec was willing to wait for Therese—and, in doing so, for Aggie and Badan too.

Badan arrived on December 23 with the food, and Therese decided to talk to Mother one last time about freeing him and Aggie. By planning the Christmas dinner, Mother was thinking about others more than herself for the first time in a long while, and Therese hoped Mother might be willing to do the right thing at last. Therese made two cups of mint tea and then led Mother up to Alec's office.

Once they were settled, Therese started by saying, "Thank you for everything you're doing to make Christmas a special occasion."

Mother smiled but didn't respond.

"I have something important I need to discuss with you," Therese added.

"Is this about your going to Maine with Dr. Talbot? I put that rumor to rest. I hoped you'd done the right thing and expelled that thought from your mind."

Therese shook her head. "Mother, you are aware that I care about Alec."

"But you wouldn't leave me. And you certainly wouldn't leave Warner."

"You married for love," Therese said. "Would you have me not do so too?"

"Is he willing to stay in Virginia?"

Therese didn't answer for a long moment. "We haven't had that discussion," she said finally. She knew the answer, though. Why would he be willing to stay? The South had been decimated by the war. Even if the Confederacy won, which it surely would not, it would be years before this part of the nation was back on its feet. There'd been too much destruction, too much suffering, too much loss.

"Your father stayed."

Therese nodded. "But you didn't want to leave..."

"And you do?"

Therese hesitated. "I don't feel as strongly about staying as you did when you were in my position."

Mother clicked her tongue. "Well, all I can tell you is that your father loved me enough to remain here."

"Did you love him enough to go?"

Mother pursed her lips together and then said, "He loved me enough not to test me that way."

Therese said a quick prayer, asking God to help her be gracious toward her mother. And calm. "That actually wasn't what I needed to talk with you about, not right now." She would broach that topic later.

"Oh?"

Therese leaned against Alec's desk, trying to steady herself. "I want to discuss Aggie and Badan one more time."

Mother's face fell.

"I've found an opportunity to do what Father would have wanted—for them to go north."

Mother immediately shook her head.

"There's talk of forcing slaves to fight. Badan could be conscripted."

Mother put her teacup on the desk. "We'll have to wait and see what happens."

"It's not worth the risk."

Mother crossed her arms. "I need both Aggie and Badan. I can't run River Pines without them. I promise to care for them—clothe them and feed them."

"And then what? Will you pay them? Will they be able to make any decisions on their own? Will Badan forever have to bow his head to Mr. Porter? Will Mr. Porter ever stop leering at Aggie?"

Mother hissed. "I told you not to talk that way."

"I know you believe me about him because of what you did last time I was home. You stood firm against his ultimatum when he said, 'Leave me the young one or I'll quit.'"

Mother began fanning herself with her hand, even though the air was chilly. "Don't speak of such things," she said, her face pale.

"Please..." Therese swallowed the lump in her throat and lowered her voice. "You need to be realistic about this, Mother. Their lives depend on it."

"Everything will work out, Therese. Either way, I'll continue to care for them at River Pines with Warner's help. And yours too. We'll plant tobacco again."

"Who will harvest it?"

Mother wrinkled her nose. "Yes, we'll need more laborers."

"And what if Badan and Aggie don't want to stay at River Pines? What if they want a place of their own? Or to go north, where there are more opportunities?"

"River Pines is their home too. They won't want to leave."

Therese took a raggedy breath, afraid maybe she was saying too much, but she couldn't stop now. "They do want to leave."

Mother pursed her lips and shook her head. "I don't believe it. Your grandfather was good to them, and so am I."

"Have you forgotten what a sin slavery is? Have you forgotten everything Father stood for? Or were you only parroting his beliefs?"

"Things have changed, and River Pines is our only hope."

Therese tried not to sound as desperate as she felt. "That's not the legacy Father left for us. He would much rather that we live in poverty than off the backs of others."

Mother stood. "This isn't your concern, is it? Especially not if your plan really *is* to go to Maine with Dr. Talbot."

"Of course it's my concern. I'm part of this family. And I care about Aggie and Badan."

"But the property is under my supervision until Warner is thirty. It's my responsibility to see his home is maintained and to protect my own father's legacy."

Tears filled Therese's eyes. "You're living in fear, Mother. It's exactly what Father warned us about."

"That's enough, young lady. Your father would be appalled by the way you're speaking to me."

"He would be appalled by every step you've taken since the day Grandfather died. Examine what you believe, please. You know what's right."

"What's right? That a Northern doctor has come here to spy on us? That you endorse that? That perhaps others are assisting him?" Mother's eyes narrowed. "Is that what's right?"

Therese managed to stutter. "I-I fear those are simply more rumors."

Mother smiled wryly. "I fear *you* are lying." With that, she turned on her heel and, abandoning her teacup, left the room. Therese sank against the desk, fighting her own fear that her mother might turn on her and Alec and report the rumors to someone in authority. Therese was deeply alarmed because the penalty for spying could be death. She hoped Polly's name hadn't been mentioned as well. She couldn't imagine that her own had been—she hadn't played much of a role. But Alec would be in horrible trouble if he were found to be part of a spy network. She shivered, both because of the drafty room and the threat to them all.

Therese fought another wave of fear. Being forced to send Aggie and Badan off on the Underground Railroad was an unnecessary danger when Mother could simply free them. "God, please let this war end before things get even worse," she prayed out loud. "And, please, convince Mother to change her mind about freeing Aggie and Badan so they can go north with Alec and Ruth legally instead of having to resort to other, far more dangerous means."

Her hope was waning, but she wouldn't stop praying.

The anticipation of Christmas, even in such dire times, was a welcome respite from the tension at the Galloways', in the hospital, and throughout the city. On Christmas Eve, Therese attended church with the Galloways and then exchanged handmade cards with them after a light supper of potato soup sprinkled with some of the bacon she'd brought, and cider cake. In the morning, Badan picked up Therese and Polly and took them straight to the hospital, where they helped set up for dinner. Tables were pulled into the east ward for all of the soldiers who could sit, and for the staff too. Aggie helped Auntie Vera out in the kitchen, and Badan assisted by carrying trays of food into the hospital and up the stairs to the ward. Mother led the festivities, graciously asking Alec to say the blessing before the meal, and then the nurses and orderlies fed the patients who couldn't feed themselves while the others were served. Then the nurses and orderlies ate. By the time Therese and Polly approached the tables, most everyone else was done, but Mother and Warner lingered over their pie at one end, while Alec and Ruth sat at the other. Somehow, Mother had managed to procure enough flour and sugar—or at least honey—for thirty pies. Always a force to be reckoned with, Mother was at her best when using that particular character trait for the good of others.

Just as Therese was ready to join Alec, he stood and took his dirty plate to the table at the back of the room and headed out to the hall. Polly raised her eyebrows, but Therese didn't respond. He was done eating, that was all.

Therese barely saw him the rest of the day. In the evening, Aggie asked Therese if she could speak with her. They stepped out onto the loading dock. "Have you made any progress?" she asked.

"About?"

"Badan told me what you said to him."

Therese's face grew warm. Of course he had. She hoped no one had overheard. She shrugged, not wanting to say anything.

"So it's not going to happen?"

"I can't make any promises, but I'm doing everything I can." Therese shivered in the cold air.

The concerned expression on Aggie's face froze. "Badan is to be sent back tomorrow," Aggie said. "Mr. Porter has threatened him."

Therese's stomach twisted.

"And, just so you know, I'm carrying Badan's child." Aggie reached for Therese's hand. "I want this baby to be free, with my husband at my side. That's what I'm praying for."

"I'm doing everything I can," Therese repeated, her eyes filling with tears. She'd start with suggesting to Mother that she keep Badan in Richmond, explaining it was too cold for her to be walking back and forth from the Corbetts'.

The next day, because no lessons were scheduled for the girls, Therese arrived at the hospital in the morning and told Alec she needed to speak with him.

"I need to speak with you too." He put his hand on her shoulder and lowered his voice. "Have you made your decision?"

"I spoke to Mother about Aggie and Badan—and briefly about us, although we didn't really sort it out."

"And?"

"She's not in favor of it—any of it. Though I think she felt worse about losing Aggie and Badan than she did about losing me."

"Then you'll just have to decide for yourself, Therese, with or without her blessing."

Her heart ached at the thought. "But what sort of marriage would it be without my mother's blessing?"

"All that really matters is Warner's blessing. He's the man of the house, even if he is currently incapacitated. I feel sure he'll approve."

Therese looked away, for some reason reluctant to tell him that Warner had essentially done so already when he urged her to head north with Alec weeks ago. But could she really look to Warner rather than Mother for something like this? If only her brother weren't so weak right now—and Mother so overpowering.

"Therese, my time here is done. I'm ready to go home. I want you to come with me. I want you to be my wife."

She studied his face for a long moment, trying to see their future in his eyes. But then she remembered Mother's words and knew that if they weren't careful, he might not even have a future.

"We have a bigger problem." Therese took Alec's hand and pulled him into the alcove at the end of the hall. She whispered, "Mother says there are rumors about the...you know. Livers and lobes and arteries and such."

He nodded grimly. "I've heard. All the more reason for us to leave— and sooner rather than later."

"What about Polly?"

"She'll be fine. No one would suspect a young woman in her position."

Therese frowned. "What do you mean 'her position?'"

"Daughter of a prominent Southern family. Pro Confederacy. All of that. Women are much safer than men when it comes to this sort of thing."

She considered his words, hoping he was right. "But you know what the punishment is for..."

He nodded, a grim expression on his face as he drew a rectangle in the air with one finger. The gallows.

Therese shivered. "I guess that rules out marrying and staying here."

"Why would we ever do that?"

"So I don't have to go. So I don't have to leave my family."

"Oh, Therese. I can see why you feel that way, but you only have your mother, Warner, and an old plantation your family won't be able to sustain after the war. It would be ludicrous for us to stay and try to carve out a life here." He placed his hand on her shoulder. "Not to mention, it wouldn't be safe right now anyway. Do you understand?"

"Yes." A wave of embarrassment swept through her. "Of course." She'd been foolish to hope. But she had one more question. "If it weren't for the turmoil of the war, would you consider it? Would you be willing to return to Virginia someday?"

After a long pause, he said, "Honestly, I don't know. I've never had any desire to live in the South. But...yes. It's something I would consider." He remained as calm as ever. "For you."

Her heart warmed. He did care. "Thank you, Alec."

"For now, however, we need to get away from here. You know we do."

"Yes." She pointed toward the east ward. "I'll go check on Warner."

He nodded. "I'm going to make my rounds. I'll come find you later."

Therese gave his hand a squeeze and then slipped away into the ward. But before she reached Warner's cot, she could tell he was feverish by the look on his face. She placed a hand on his forehead—it was burning hot.

"How do you feel?"

"Worse," he answered. He'd been more despondent lately too. Nearly every day he'd say he wished the explosion had killed him.

Therese pulled back the dressing on his stomach wound. It didn't look any different. Then she lifted the dressing on his stump. The skin around the wound had darkened. "I'll get Dr. Talbot," she said.

She waited until he was finished with a patient who had a hip wound and then asked him to check on her brother.

Warner had fallen asleep and didn't wake as Alec examined his leg. "Gangrene," he pronounced.

"Oh, no. What can be done?"

"We'll scrub it out. I may have to operate again." He replaced the sheet. "Keep an eye on it and let me know if it changes."

That would be a fourth operation, which Therese knew wasn't unheard of, but she wondered how much more Warner could tolerate. His spirits grew lower with each day.

A few minutes later, Mother arrived, rubbing her hands together. "It's getting so cold, I've decided to keep Badan here in Richmond for now. We'll be going back to River Pines soon anyway."

Therese nodded, even though she knew it wasn't true. Now that Warner had taken another turn for the worse, Mother would probably want to stay. And Badan would never be going back to River Pines again.

Soon he and Aggie would be headed north for good, whether Mother gave her permission or not.

CHAPTER TWENTY-FOUR
Therese

Unfortunately, the gangrene did grow worse, and by the third week of January, Alec operated again. Mother paced outside the room, certain she should have taken Warner home weeks ago.

The surgery was successful, and after he'd finished, Alec pulled Therese aside and said he'd asked for Warner's blessing to marry her the day before and received it. Now he planned to go to the Corbetts the next day to speak with Mother, allaying her fears as needed.

Therese shook her head. "It won't do any good. She can't bear the thought of losing me."

Alec shrugged. "She's a mother. Surely when it comes down to it, she'll place the rescuing of her child above her own selfish needs."

Therese bristled a little. Was that how he saw her? As someone in need of rescue? But then his eyes warmed, and she softened.

The next evening Therese slipped away from the hospital with Alec after supper duty, saying a quick prayer that Mother would be in a gracious mood. Together they hurried to where Mother was staying. Mr. Corbett answered the door, happy to see Alec, who quickly introduced

Therese. He invited them into the parlor while he sent his wife to collect Mother.

"Is everything all right?" Mother wore a faded housedress, a worn shawl, and a cap on her head, and she froze in the doorway to the parlor at the sight of Therese standing beside Alec. "Is it Warner?"

"No," Alec answered, motioning to the parlor. Mother led the way. Once they'd all sat down, he said, "Warner is unchanged. This is about Therese and me. Warner gave his permission for us to marry, but I wanted to speak with you too."

Mother pursed her lips together and then said, "Have you decided to stay here in Virginia, then?"

"No. Therese will be returning to Maine with me."

Mother's face fell.

Alec spoke quickly. "I know this is hard for you, Mrs. Jennings, but Therese is a grown woman, and this is what she wants." His expression grew kinder. "You will always be welcome in our home. You will always have a place with us if needed."

Therese nodded in agreement.

Mother looked as if she might cry but didn't. Alec spoke more about his work in Maine, concluding with, "I assure you, I can take care of Therese as she deserves. She won't have a concern in the world, I promise."

"But she promised her father she'd care for me."

Therese nearly gasped, remembering the moment clearly. Mother was right, but would her father expect her to sacrifice in such a way now? Therese barely comprehended the rest of the conversation, except that Mother wouldn't change her mind. She'd never be in agreement with Therese and Alec.

That night in her attic room, Therese ignored the question of what she'd promised Father and thought more about the trip to Maine. Without Mother's permission, they'd be taking Badan and Aggie illegally, which would put all of them at risk. If they were caught, perhaps an investigation would reveal Alec's spying too. All of them could hang.

There had to be a safer way for Alec and Badan and Aggie. She stayed awake late into the night, weighing her options and trying to come up with a way to convince Mother to give Badan and Aggie their freedom.

The next afternoon, Therese arrived at the hospital to find Alec in the hallway on the second floor. After they greeted each other, she pulled him toward the supply closet. He smiled down at her.

"Is Mother with Warner?" she asked.

Alec nodded.

"Then I have a question to ask you."

"Go ahead," he said, smiling down at her and taking her hand.

"Will Badan and Aggie be treated well in Maine?"

He hesitated, and then he said, "For the most part. I'm not saying there's no prejudice, but it isn't like here."

"What is the difference?"

"There's no comparison. Here there is darkness, cruelty, and oppression. In Maine there is free discourse, social justice, and hope for all humanity."

"So even though they're black, they'd be accepted and cared for?"

"Yes. For the most part. At least I can say they'll be free."

"And you'd be willing to take them, no matter what?"

"Yes, Therese. No matter what. It's my Christian duty."

"All right." She let go of his hand and led the way toward the ward. Six months ago she wouldn't have stood up to Mother. But she would today.

Mother sat by Warner's side. Therese watched silently for a moment. Mother, with a weary expression on her face, had a hand on Warner's shoulder. Someone had propped him up with a pillow and combed his hair and trimmed his beard. His eyes were closed, but Therese knew he wasn't sleeping. The look of agony on his face gave it away.

Mother glanced up. "Therese." Her eyes narrowed. "And Dr. Talbot."

"Hello." Therese stepped closer as Warner opened his eyes and turned his head a little.

"I heard you told Mother what you were doing instead of asking." He smiled despite his pain.

Therese met her mother's eyes. "I'm sorry. I didn't mean to be disrespectful." She walked around the cot and knelt at her mother's side. "You're right. I did promise Father I'd take care of you." She glanced up at Alec. His expression was stoic, but she could see a glimmer of confusion in his eyes. Therese turned her attention back to her mother. "And you promised Father to do everything you could to seek justice for the oppressed. Do you remember that?"

Mother inhaled sharply.

"It was the day before he died. The two of you were talking about River Pines, of what would come of it. You told him you would do all you could to convince Grandfather to free his slaves."

"We've had this discussion—"

"I know, but now I have a proposal for you. I'll stay," Therese glanced again at Alec and then back at her mother, "if you'll free Badan and Aggie so they can go with Dr. Talbot and Ruth to Maine."

Alec crossed his arms.

Therese didn't make eye contact with him.

Mother whimpered. "You're manipulating me."

"Yes, I am." Therese stood. "But I'm only doing so to keep my promise to Father. That was the legacy he wanted for us."

"We'll starve, regardless of who wins the war." Mother turned her attention to Warner. "Your brother won't be able to farm. What will we eat without help?"

Warner shook his head. "Don't use me as an excuse."

"But you've always been in favor of the ways of the South. You love River Pines. I want nothing more than for you to live your life there, safe from worry."

Warner scooted himself up against the pillow. "Mother, none of us will ever be safe from worry. And my admiration for 'the ways of the South' had more to do with money than anything. Grandfather's money. But Father was right. Slavery is a sin that I don't want to benefit from. I realized that soon after I joined, realized what a fool I'd been. Send Badan and Aggie north—but don't make Therese sacrifice her future for theirs. She should be able to marry the man she loves."

Loves. The word stopped Therese. Did she truly love Alec? Did he truly love her?

A pout settled on Mother's face, but Therese could tell she was weighing Warner's words.

Therese glanced at Alec and said, "I'll stay for now, no matter what. I need to honor my vow."

Alec nodded curtly and then turned on his heel and headed for the door.

"Go after him," Warner said.

Therese hesitated.

"Please," Warner pleaded. "I don't want to be the cause of your unhappiness." He turned to Mother. "We'll allow Badan and Aggie to go—and Therese to decide her own fate and future."

Therese obeyed her brother before their mother could respond. By the time she reached the hall, Alec had started up the stairs to the third floor. "Alec, wait," she called out.

He stopped on the landing. She hurried up the stairs. "Can we give this time? And decide, once the war is over, whether you will return to Virginia or I'll join you in Maine?"

He looked down on her, his eyes heavy. "I will not return to Virginia. I know I said I'd be willing to consider it, but I've given it more thought since then and made my decision. The answer is no. I could never agree to raise children here."

"All right. I understand. Would you allow them to visit?" Would her mother never see her grandchildren?

He sighed. "It depends on how the war turns out—and what happens after. I'd hate to think of our children being exposed to—difficult situations."

"I see." She couldn't help but think of everything her father *hadn't* shielded her from. "That leaves me joining you in Maine then."

He nodded.

"I can't."

"What?"

She shook her head. "I've also changed my mind. I won't be joining you."

He crossed his arms. "I don't understand."

"It's not what I want." She met his eyes. "I'm sorry, Alec. Mother's right. I did promise Father I'd care for her, and with Warner doing so poorly, I can't leave her. They're all the family I have."

His eyes narrowed, but finally he acknowledged what she'd said with a quick nod.

"But you'll still take Badan and Aggie?"

"Of course." His shoulders sagged. "Ruth and I will sponsor them. Our community will help them find jobs and a home."

"Thank you." Her voice dropped to a whisper. "I appreciate it more than I can ever express." Badan and Aggie's freedom was much more important than her happiness.

He reached for her hand, in a tired, defeated sort of way. "I'm sorry things didn't work out, Therese, for both of us."

She swallowed hard. She couldn't blame him for not wanting to stay—or not wanting to return after the war. She thought of her father and all he'd sacrificed for her mother. If Alec couldn't do that, it was best to know now. Best to free him to the life he wanted to live, and free herself to the life God seemed to have for her back at River Pines.

But now, she needed to make sure Alec and Ruth left with Aggie and Badan before anything changed. However, she wouldn't say a word to Aggie until everything was set.

For the next week, Therese was sure Alec did his best to avoid her. She heard from others that he and Ruth were readying to leave. Mother wasn't very warm to Therese either, but she did say she had Aggie and Badan's papers with her and would give them their freedom when Dr. Talbot was ready to go. Therese still hadn't told Aggie and Badan, not wanting to get their hopes up in case the plan fell through.

The next day, as Therese taught the girls, Mrs. Galloway took to her bed. The maid had escaped two weeks ago, most likely taking her chances on heading north. Only the cook, who didn't seem to have any nursing skills, was left. Therese waited until Mr. Galloway returned home from work and told him she was willing to stay for the evening if needed. She could send word to the hospital that she was unable to come in tonight.

He insisted she go ahead. "Take care of our soldiers, Therese. I'll send for the midwife."

She left, hoping there would be a new baby in the house by morning. She said a prayer for Mrs. Galloway and the little one as she hurried toward the hospital.

When she arrived, Polly told her Michael was in the kitchen. "Go say hello to him," Polly urged. "They lost quite a few men last week. You might be able to cheer him up."

Therese doubted it, but she would give it a try. She found him in the back of the kitchen, deep in conversation with Auntie Vera. Neither saw her. Therese stepped closer.

"They're planning to escape with strangers. A man who was visiting a soldier here approached Badan. I'm afraid it could be a trap," Auntie Vera said, but then her face fell when she saw Therese.

Therese put a hand to her chest, guessing Badan felt he'd waited long enough and Therese didn't have a plan after all. But they couldn't do that—even if Mother didn't report that they were runaways, they might be pursued anyway. Or if they were captured without papers, they might be harmed. However, if Therese let Michael know that Alec planned to take them north, he might try to implicate the doctor as someone helping the slaves—and in doing so harm others in the spy network too.

Michael turned around slowly.

"It's too dangerous," Therese said. "Tell them not to follow through with that offer."

"That's right," Michael said. "Auntie Vera was telling me so that I would persuade Badan to wait until the war is over." He turned toward the old woman. "Isn't that right?"

She nodded.

Michael ran his hand through his hair. "This is a little awkward," he said to Therese. "I hope you'll take into consideration that Auntie Vera was doing the right thing."

Therese nodded, wishing she could explain her plan but knowing she didn't dare.

"You could have them punished, if you wish," he said.

She shook her head.

Auntie Vera muttered her gratitude and slipped by them.

Therese dropped her voice. "Tell Badan to be patient, please. Something will work out for them."

Michael stepped closer to her. "What are you talking about?"

"I can't say anymore...unless you let me know why Auntie Vera would be talking with you."

He shrugged. "She's concerned. Wouldn't your mother be if some man were trying to take you on a dangerous journey? One that might lead to death?"

Therese bristled. "Yes, but why was she telling *you*?"

He glanced over Therese's shoulder and then said, "Because she thinks I can talk some sense into Badan. That's all."

"Do you plan to threaten him? Turn him in?"

"What kind of person do you think I am?"

"I don't know, Michael. What kind of person are you?"

When he didn't answer, Therese left the kitchen, but later that evening, when he told Polly goodbye and that he was headed back toward Petersburg, Therese followed him down the stairs to the door of the loading dock. She waited until he would have had time to climb into his wagon to step out. Auntie Vera stood on the dock, her hands crossed over her chest as Michael tipped his hat to her.

"What's going on?" Therese called out.

Michael turned toward her.

The wagon master stepped out from the stables and asked, "Is there a problem, Miss Jennings?"

"Thank you, but no. I just have a question for Lieutenant Talbot."

For a moment, Michael appeared tense enough that she thought he might snap the reins and race the wagon out of the courtyard, but then he relaxed a little and remained.

Therese hurried down the steps of the dock and to the driver's side. "What's going on?" she hissed.

"Nothing."

She glanced at the back. There was a tarp spread over the bed of the wagon, but it was perfectly flat. Therese couldn't help but think of the Huguenots, so long ago in France, who had to escape persecution in such ways, lying hidden in the back of horse drawn carts for journeys of hundreds of miles. She returned to Michael's side, speaking quietly. "Is there a false bottom in this wagon?"

"Therese!" he hissed fiercely. "Stop asking questions."

"There is, isn't there?" she whispered. "And Badan and Aggie are inside."

Swallowing hard, Michael gave a slight nod.

Therese lowered her voice even more, despite the surge of anger in her veins. "What do you plan to do with them, Michael? Force them to serve the Confederacy? Coerce Badan to take up weapons and make Aggie to care for the wounded on the front lines? Or do you plan to sell them to raise money for food for soldiers? Have you done this with others in bondage? Do you trick them into trusting you, only to conscript them into service? Or sell them down south?"

"Please stop," Michael said wearily. "I can't explain, but trust me. Please."

Therese stared into his dark eyes. She didn't think she could trust him, not anymore. Not since he returned from France a different man, one whose ideals and beliefs had catapulted him to the opposite side.

Still, he was gazing at her with such intensity that for a moment she thought she could see a glimpse of the old Michael inside, the person who would have put himself in this position not to deliver his present cargo to the battlefield but to freedom.

Taking in a deep breath, she decided that she had no choice after all but to trust—just a little. Aggie and Badan's very lives might depend on it.

"A better plan is in the works," she whispered. "They're going north tomorrow. It's all been arranged. Mother has their papers ready to give to them. They'll be free."

"They're going north? How? With whom?"

"I can't tell you that."

His eyes narrowed. "Then the rumor is true. You're leaving."

She shook her head. "I was, yes, but my plans have changed." Glancing away, her cheeks growing warm, she added, "I made an arrangement with Mother. If I stay, then she will allow them to go."

Michael waited until she again met his eyes. "You traded your future for their freedom."

"I suppose it seems that way."

"Tell me. Is that the only reason you're staying?"

She tried to speak, but a lump formed in her throat. In that moment, she realized she didn't love Alec and never had, at least not in the way she'd thought. She loved *Michael*—the old Michael, the one she used to know.

"Please don't betray us," she managed to whisper, hoping he had once loved her too. Perhaps that past love would lead him to do the right thing now. If not, then she'd just sealed the fates of not only Aggie and Badan but also herself and probably Alec and Ruth as well.

Michael shook his head, and for a moment a wave of panic overtook Therese. What had she done?

"Our families have been friends for decades, Therese. I won't do anything to harm that bond."

Her panic receded, though her heart still pounded. "Thank you, Michael."

He nodded, his expression guarded. "I'm going to distract the wagon master. Have Auntie Vera stand watch while you open the wagon and release Badan and Aggie." He jumped down and placed his hand on Therese's shoulder. "And then both of us will pretend this never happened. Do you understand?"

She nodded, overcome with gratitude. She'd trust God that Michael hadn't completely lost his soul, though whether his intentions today had been to deliver them to harm or to safety, she would never know.

Once she got the hidden compartment door open, she whispered for Aggie to come out. When the woman shook her head, Therese added, "Mother has agreed to free you both. You'll be heading north tomorrow, but in a different way. A safer way." When Aggie still hesitated, Therese added, "This could be a *trap*, Aggie. Go to your room, and I'll come explain in a few minutes."

Eyes wide, Aggie wriggled out first and then slipped into the hospital through the back door. Badan emerged next, a scowl on his face.

"I'll explain everything to Aggie," she whispered. "For now, you'll just have to trust me. Go get Mother's buggy ready. She's almost ready for you to drive her back to the Corbetts' house."

Without a word, Badan headed for the stables, leaving only Auntie Vera on the loading dock. The poor woman hadn't been able to hear Therese's exchange with Michael, and now she was glaring at Therese with fury.

"Trust me," Therese again whispered. "I know what I'm doing."

Uncertainty flickered in Auntie Vera's still-angry eyes. But then she turned and went back into the hospital.

Therese waited by the wagon until Michael appeared, tipping his hat to the wagon master as he did.

When he saw her, he frowned. She returned the expression, not sure what to say to him. Perhaps the less she said the better. She curtsied and, without a farewell, retreated back to the hospital.

She passed Mother in the foyer and told her Badan was harnessing her horse.

"Wait." Mother pulled papers from her bag. "Give these to Aggie. I passed her on the stairs, but I think you should be the one to present them to her."

"Thank you, Mother."

"Well, you got your way, and hopefully we won't all starve. When we return to River Pines tomorrow afternoon, I expect you to come with us."

"Tomorrow afternoon? But you can't. Warner's in no condition to leave yet. You have to speak with Dr. Talbot—"

"Dr. Talbot," Mother snapped, "is the one who suggested it."

CHAPTER TWENTY-FIVE
Nicole

On the last Friday in May, at the end of the workday, I was in the stable and nearly out the door when it struck me that Hutch hadn't nickered his usual greeting.

"Well, hello to you too," I teased, backtracking to his stall to give him a pat. But then I hesitated when I noticed his demeanor. He seemed oddly restless, ears flat against his head, one hoof pawing tentatively at the ground. "You okay, buddy?"

Clearly uncomfortable, he kept shifting his weight, and as I glanced around his stall, I noticed that he'd barely touched his grain. Something was wrong. Brows furrowed, I went outside in search of a coworker, but none were in the area. I'd have to do this by myself.

Working quickly but smoothly, I retrieved the first aid kit and took out the supplies I would need to check Hutch's temperature and other vital signs. Then I grabbed his info card, clipped a lead rope to his bridle, and led him out to a hitching post. There I managed to calm him down enough to get some readings, and as I compared my numbers to the norms listed on his card, it was clear that the Arabian was in trouble.

I set him loose inside the nearby exercise ring then left him there to go in search of Nate. I found the man in his office in the main building, doing paperwork. As soon as I told him what was going on, he jumped up and came with me.

Back in the ring, as Nate examined the horse, I asked if the problem could be colic, which I knew was an obstruction in the bowels that was serious and sometimes even fatal.

"That's my guess," he replied. "We'll see what the vet says."

He dialed the veterinarian on his cell, spoke back and forth for a moment, and then hung up again, saying she'd be right over.

"You know," Nate added as he returned the phone to his pocket, "not everyone would have picked up on the signs at this stage, but with colic early identification is critical. You may have saved this horse's life."

My pulse surged at the praise, but I tried not to let it show. "So what happens now?"

Nate ran a hand down the animal's broad neck, trying to calm him. "The vet will check his temperature and pulse, probably confirm the diagnosis, and give him a dose of banamine to help remove the obstruction. Then I'll just have to keep an eye on him for the night, make sure he stays upright, walk him around the paddock every hour or so. I can't let him sit or lie down. He has to keep moving. Hopefully, the obstruction will pass by morning, and he'll be okay."

"You might have to stay up all night with him?"

Nate shrugged. "I've done it before. I'll be fine." Grasping the horse's lead rope, he thanked me again, told me to have a good weekend, and then turned to go.

Obviously, I'd been dismissed, but I hesitated, watching him lead Hutch away.

"Nate," I called after him, "why not let me take the first shift? My other work is almost done, and I don't have anything going on tonight."

He paused, turning back toward me. "Appreciate it, but this is a critical time. I need to be here myself. Plus, if it gets worse, Hutch could accidentally hurt you. He's going to get a lot more irritable and restless as the pain increases. Thanks, though."

After being dismissed a second time, I took the hint.

I finished out my last few duties in the stable and then skipped the showers to head straight for the parking lot. Except for my boots, I wasn't all that dirty today, and I didn't want it to look as if I was hanging around after Nate had made it clear I should leave. I climbed into my car and started it up, relieved to see the vet turning in the lot just as I was pulling out.

On the main road and headed for home, I didn't get far before I decided to go back. Something about leaving just didn't feel right, no matter what the boss had said. Not only was I worried about Hutch, but my gut told me Nate needed support during this time, whether he realized it or not.

I pulled in at a strip mall to make a U-turn, but as I did I spotted a pizza joint halfway down the row, so I parked instead. After going inside and placing an order, I headed to the grocery store next door to grab bottles of water, Cokes, chips, and a big bag of sunflower seeds. Nate ate them so much, the joke around the farm was that you could usually find him just by following the trail of seed shells.

Back in the pizza shop as I waited for my order to finish, I pulled out my phone and shot Maddee a text:

> Trouble with one of the horses. I'm going to stick around to help out. Don't wait up, could be super late.

She responded quickly:

> Okay, thanks for letting me know. Have fun with the handsome stallion...oh, and with the horse too.

With a chuckle, I put the phone away.

When I got back to the farm, I found Nate still at the smaller ring, only now he was standing on the outside of the fence and watching Hutch move around restlessly within.

"Hey, anybody hungry?" I called, and when he turned to look, I held up the pizza box and grocery bags. He seemed surprised to see me again, but not upset, which I was afraid he might be. Instead, I caught a glimpse of something else in his eyes, probably just relief that I'd come bearing food.

"The vet was here," he told me as I drew closer. "It's colic, all right."

"Oh, boy. Guess that means it's going to be a long night."

We just stood together at the fence for a few minutes, and though his attention was fully on the horse, I couldn't stop thinking about the man and how I could feel the heat of his body next to mine.

"So what have you got there?" he asked, turning to look. "Smells good."

"Yeah." Once again, I held the things up for him to see. "I brought a few snacks for myself. Not sure what you're going to have."

Nate gave an easy laugh, and I tried to ignore what a thrill it was to have been the source of that laughter. I'd heard him joke with others, but he and I had never shared a single moment of levity before.

"It was nice of you to come back," he said, gesturing toward a nearby picnic table. "I'm famished."

We carried the goods over to it, detouring past the antibacterial lotion dispenser on the way, and then spread everything out and dug in. Twice while we were eating, Nate returned to the ring to lead Hutch around some more, but otherwise we sat there in companionable silence, eyes on the patient as we shared the food.

I didn't know how long he'd let me stick around, but eventually we got to talking and the time passed. Every half hour or so, Nate would take Hutch for another walk around the ring as I watched from the fence, and the rhythm of the routine was pleasing somehow, despite the seriousness of the situation.

One of those times the sun was setting in the distance, and the beautiful orange-and-purple glow of the horizon created a striking silhouette of man and beast. I breathed deeply, taking it all in. For about the hundredth time since getting sober, I saw how deceptive drug use could be. As much as I'd always told myself that I had to be high to be happy, the truth was, the type of "happy" that came from drugs didn't begin to compare to the sheer bliss of moments like this. How I had gone for so long without any real joy in my life, I didn't know, but I thanked God for letting me find it again, and for feeling it now.

Time passed even less noticeably once it was fully dark, the hours blurring together into one long stretch of quiet talking and gentle laughter broken periodically by sounds from Hutch and the need to give him another walk. At one point, Nate left me alone while he ran off toward the main building. He returned about ten minutes later with a fresh can of bug spray, two thickly padded folding chairs, and a pop-up screen shelter. Soon we were ensconced inside the little structure, far more comfy and bug free but still with a full view of poor Hutch, who alternated between periods of quiet and bouts of huffing and whinnying, his stomach growling and groaning all the while.

More than once, Nate insisted I head home, but I politely declined. I could tell he was getting more worried about the horse with each passing hour, and I didn't want to leave him to deal with it by himself.

Late into the night, I finally brought up the racetrack ministry and the connection to Nana.

"Mrs. Talbot is your grandmother?" He broke into a broad grin. "I love that woman! She's a real kick. She always tells it like it is."

"Yeah, she's in your fan club too."

Nate shook his head, still smiling. "I can't believe I didn't make the connection."

"Talbot's a pretty common name around here."

"Yeah, but you're so much like her..."

My eyebrows raised, but I didn't reply.

"You are," he insisted. "She's strong, tough, no-nonsense, and she doesn't take smack from anybody."

We saw the horse trying to lie down in the ring, so Nate went to get him up and walk him some more. I stayed where I was, considering his words. I supposed it was a compliment in a way. I just hoped I could retain some of Nana's better qualities without also embodying some of her worst.

Despite talking most of the night, including telling Nate my story, it wasn't until the wee hours, as the black of the sky slowly turned blue, that he finally opened up in return. He told me how he'd grown up in Florida, migrating from track to track with his dad, and started drinking at just twelve years old. He didn't stop till he was seventeen.

"Sounds young, but you grow up pretty fast on the backside. I'm just lucky I didn't end up in prison or dead like some of my friends."

As he talked, all sorts of lightbulbs went on for me, including a better understanding of why he didn't trust addicts to stay on the straight and narrow. His mother had been clean and sober for three and a half years before she went back to heroin and accidentally overdosed when Nate was just five. Some of his friends had gone in and out of sobriety numerous times, some of them sobering up long enough to really seem as though they were going to make it, only to fall back into that life in the end.

I also understood now why Nate was so dedicated to the workers at Powhatan Downs, because he'd grown up living that way himself. He said he'd been sixteen, running wild, when he met the chaplain who would end up changing his life. I knew the odds against a kid that age getting—much less staying—sober, but according to Nate, he was transformed the moment he came face-to-face with Christ's love, with true grace.

"And that chaplain, man, he could see how badly I needed out of there. He's the one who arranged for a job for me here and vouched for my character. Can you imagine? The poor fool had so much faith in me that no way was I going to let him down. And I didn't. I worked hard, and after about two years I also started going to college at night, followed by seminary. My ultimate goal was to become a youth leader, maybe help out messed-up kids like me, but when I started looking around for a position, I realized there was one big problem."

"With your plans?"

"With the churches. Well, some of them anyway. They work hard at being polished and slick and entertaining, but that's not what Jesus had in mind. Why do we have to make Him neat and tidy? He was in the streets. He still is, doing miracles and delivering addicts from the gutter. He was a tough dude, the ultimate game changer, strong in body and mind to the end, when He showed the full extent of His strength by giving it all up for our sake."

He paused, flashing me a sheepish grin "Sorry. I didn't mean to preach a sermon here. I just get a little worked up sometimes."

"I think it's awesome," I replied softly, though by then he'd risen to go and check on Hutch, so I wasn't even sure if he heard me.

At my urging, Nate finished his story once he returned, telling me how three years ago he figured out where God had been leading him all along. When he was offered a part-time job as chaplain of Powhatan Downs, he negotiated his position here so that it would allow him the flexibility to do both. "The folks who own this place are really good people and strong Christians. If not for them, and for the chaplain who connected me with them in the first place, there's no telling where I'd be now."

Nate's passion was so clear, and as I'd been listening to him, it was as if I could literally feel myself falling in love. I knew those feelings weren't reciprocated—if anything, he made a point of never even brushing against me or standing too close or allowing his eyes to linger on mine. But I'd never met anyone like him, and I had felt my heart drawing nearer to his with every passing hour of the night.

"Thanks for sharing all that," I said into the quiet when he was finished, wishing I could reach out and take his hand.

"Thank you for sticking it out this long," he replied, flashing me a smile. As badly as I wanted to see some sort of feeling for me reflected there in return, all I could make out was a wall. This man was never going to see me as anything but an employee and an eventual relapser.

We heard a loud burst of gas from the horse, followed by some promising sounds, so we both jumped up and went to look. I never would have expected such a magical, intimate night between two people to conclude with a successful bowel movement, but there you go. Just as the horizon began to glow, Hutch passed the obstruction, and though I wanted to throw my arms around Nate in celebration, I had to be satisfied with the simple high five he offered me.

We stuck around to observe for another hour or so, during which Hutch continued to be happily, actively productive. Prancing around the ring now in a mix of relief and joy, he was starting to look like himself again.

When the sun was fully up, I knew I should go, so I helped fold away the screen tent and then just stood there, wishing desperately that Nate felt about me the way I did about him.

"You should come on Sunday—well, tomorrow now," Nate said easily as he topped off Hutch's water bucket. "To church at the racetrack, I mean. It's a secure area, but all I have to do is put your name on a list, and they'll let you through. I think you'd like it."

"All right," I said, looking forward to it.

The next morning I was there, eager to see the place for myself and especially to observe Nate in such a unique environment. When he'd said he was a chaplain, I'd had trouble picturing it, but once he was up front leading the group in song and prayer, it was easy to see that he was as perfect a fit there, caring for his flock, as he was at the farm, caring for the horses, not to mention the employees.

The place itself was dirty and gritty, the singing in several languages, boisterous children running free up and down the aisle the entire time. But I loved it. Every part of it. His sermon was excellent, about how faith conquers fear, and his words echoed in my mind long after the service was done.

"I see fear a lot where I work," he'd said. "Kids who meet horses for the first time, who touch their soft coats with shaking hands. The horses sense this fear, and they embody it. They become finicky, they huff and beat their hooves into the ground…"

He paused, looking around as many of the parishioners nodded their heads in agreement.

"But every day, I also see kids conquer their fears. They approach the horses. They climb on. Sure, there's risk. What if the horse rears and they fall off? What if they get their hand bitten? But here's the thing: The kids can't know the horse's love without first conquering their fear. And how is that done? Through faith and faith alone."

When I got home, I found Greg and Maddee cuddled on the couch and going through the Talbot photos. As soon as I walked in, my sister waved me over with a smile.

"Hey, remember the pic of Therese with the doctor named Talbot?" she asked, her eyes twinkling. "We figured he was the Talbot she ended up marrying?"

"Yeah?"

"Well, we found another photo of her with a completely different guy, also young and handsome, also a Talbot, only it's a *different* Talbot than the one before." She handed it over, adding, "So what do you think? Which of the two, if either, did she marry?"

I took a look at the picture. Though I'd seen it before, I hadn't read the names on the back, which listed the people as *M. Talbot, T. Jennings, and several unidentified soldiers*. The image had obviously been taken near the end of the war, and it featured Therese and a man standing in front of a wagon that was filled with ailing soldiers, three of whom had managed to sit up and pose for the photo.

Maddee was right. This Talbot was every bit as good looking as the other one, if not more so.

"'M. Talbot', huh?" I asked, handing the photo back to her. "You don't suppose that's *Michael* Talbot, do you? The one who was in France and brought home the illuminated manuscript?"

Maddee's eyes widened. "Oh! I don't know. I hadn't thought of that." She peered down at the picture for a long moment. "Could be. He is the right age."

"Are we direct descendants of Michael? Or is he just somewhere out there in our family tree, like a distant cousin or something?"

"I'm not sure," Maddee replied. "That whole story came from Detective Ortiz, not the family, so details like that weren't included. I never thought to ask. "

"Guess we have some new questions for Aunt Cissy the next time we see her, then," I replied.

Looking down at the pile of photos, I thought about Therese Jennings. I knew she had lived at a difficult time, and she'd had to endure much during the war. But if two men had been vying for her heart simultaneously, I realized now, that meant her love life had probably been even more complicated and confusing than mine.

CHAPTER TWENTY-SIX
Therese

A ggie listened as Therese quickly told her what was going on, her mouth open in disbelief. Then Therese handed her the papers. "Badan's are here too. Dr. Talbot and Ruth will take you on the train with them tomorrow. Let Badan know first thing in the morning when he brings Mother."

Nodding, Aggie embraced Therese. "It's more than I dreamed."

"Well," Therese said, hugging her friend, "Maine is cold in the winter—absolutely freezing with lots of snow. And there aren't many free blacks there, so it won't be an easy road. But if you stay here, Badan could be forced to fight soon, and I don't want you back at River Pines." She let go of Aggie and gazed down at her growing middle. "God willing, this baby will be free."

Aggie's smile dimmed. "So Mr. Michael was lying to us? It was a trap, like you said?"

Therese hesitated. She had to be honest with her friend. "I'm not entirely sure, Aggie. But even if it wasn't, you'll still be a lot safer leaving this way, with Alec and Ruth and your official papers, rather than being smuggled in the back of a wagon—and going through who knows what else in order to make your way north."

After telling her friend goodbye, Therese went looking for Alec. Surely the doctor hadn't been acting out of anger or betrayal when he told Mother she could take Warner home. Surely he wouldn't endanger Warner's life out of spite.

She was trying to find him when she ran into Ruth, who said, "There you are. I've been looking for you."

Ruth gestured toward a more private area in the hallway and led Therese there as she explained in a low voice that she wanted to make sure everything was in order for tomorrow morning's departure.

"Yes. Mother gave me the papers, and I passed them along to Aggie."

"Excellent. Then Alec and I will take it from here." Ruth cleared her throat. "There is one other matter I wanted to ask you about. I plan to return to New York eventually, to my work at the hospital there. I've invited Polly to join me. I'd like to extend the invitation to you as well."

Therese tried to hide her surprise. "Thank you." She smiled, wryly. "But I'm not cut from the same cloth as you and Polly. I'll be staying here and caring for my mother and brother."

"Ah. Well, I understand."

In return, Therese thanked Ruth for all of her care of the soldiers, including Warner. "You're a tremendously gifted nurse."

Ruth waved off the praise. "I'm grateful I could help. As for the...situation with Badan and Aggie...I just want to say that you've done a good thing, even if it was at such a high cost. I'm sorry for your sake, though, for how it all turned out. Truly I am."

Therese met Ruth's gaze. "No, you're not. You never wanted us to marry."

"I didn't want him to stay."

"That was never a possibility."

"You're mistaken. It was. But I talked him out of it. I emphasized how detrimental it would be for him—professionally, spiritually, and emotionally."

Therese's heart grew heavy with sadness, though she knew it didn't really matter now. All along she'd thought Alec was calm and pragmatic—but perhaps he was merely dispassionate, not to mention too easily swayed. That wasn't what she wanted in a husband.

"As for his relationship with you," Ruth continued, "I merely questioned whether a Southern belle could possess the temerity to survive the harsh realities of a life in Maine."

Therese's eyes widened. "Temerity? Please. Never mistake good manners and a gentle demeanor for weakness. I assure you, a true Southern belle can withstand almost anything—as this war has well proven."

"Point taken." Ruth smiled, and Therese could feel her harshness softening for the first time since they'd met.

"Ruth, may I ask you a question?"

"Yes?"

"Is everyone else in your family as, uh, direct as you are?"

Ruth surprised her by belting out a laugh. "Direct? You mean demanding? Snappish? Intrusive? Quick to anger?"

Therese's cheeks warmed even as she nodded.

"We all tend to speak our minds, but I suppose I take it further than most." She was quiet for a moment and then added, "Actually, from what I understand, I'm a lot like one of my forebears, Jeremiah Talbot, Emmanuel's youngest son. Family lore has it he was never one to mince words, not even harsh ones. Apparently, when he finally decided to leave Virginia and resettle in the northeast, the rest of his family wasn't all that sorry to see him go." Eyes twinkling, she added, "I'm sure you can relate to that. To not being sorry to see someone go."

It was Therese's turn to smile. Perhaps this was the marshmallow side of which Alec had spoken.

The two women parted, and Therese resumed her search, finally locating the doctor in his office. She paused in the open doorway.

"Why are you sending Warner home?" she asked, trying hard to keep her tone non-accusatory. "You know he's getting worse, not better."

Alec looked up, startled, and then he sat back and clasped his hands together in front of him. "Because the hospital is closing, Therese. For certain this time. The last of the patients will be transferred to Chimborazo this week. I gave your mother the option of sending him there or taking him home, and, no surprise, she chose the latter."

Therese exhaled slowly, flushed with guilt for her earlier assumptions.

Of course Alec would never endanger a patient out of spite. She stepped further into the room.

"What are Warner's chances of surviving? Please be honest." When he didn't reply, she added, "So, not good?"

He shook his head. "There's no way to know for sure. Hopefully, the gangrene won't return, but his stomach is still putrid. It could possibly heal, but I've rarely seen that before. We've done all we can for him. She should take him home."

"And keep him comfortable?"

Alec nodded. "Keep cleaning out the wound. Do you plan to go with them?"

"Yes."

"Good. He'll need you now more than ever."

Alec stood and walked around his desk, stopping a step from her.

"As for us," he added, seeming utterly miserable. "Therese. Please reconsider. Tell me you'll come to Maine eventually. That you still want to be my wife."

She met his eyes, and their gaze held for a long moment. Dr. Alec Talbot was a good, good man. He just wasn't the man for her.

"I'm sorry," she whispered, and she really meant it. She was sorry for hurting him. For not loving him the way he deserved to be loved.

Alec reached for her hand. "At least...may I walk you back to the Galloways' one last time?"

Therese shook her head and gave his hand a squeeze before pulling away. "The wagon master is giving me a ride."

"All right."

"Thank you for everything," she told him, truly meaning it. Then she hurried from the room before he could respond.

When Therese arrived back at the row house, Mr. Galloway was pacing in the hallway and the midwife was in the back room with Mrs. Galloway. "It's another girl—we've named her Lucy," Mr. Galloway said. "She's fine—small but doing all right. Delpha, on the other hand, is having a difficult time."

"Should I go help?"

Mr. Galloway nodded. "Would you?"

Therese hurried down the hall. The door was open, and she stepped into the room. Mrs. Galloway leaned against the headboard, holding the baby.

"If the bleeding starts up again," the midwife said, "send your husband to get me."

"I will." Mrs. Galloway spoke without taking her gaze from her new daughter. "Thank you."

The midwife turned to Therese. "She hemorrhaged. It's stopped, but she needs to take it easy. It's essential to her survival."

"I'll see that she does," Therese said, though her mind reeled. What about Warner? He needed her, but so did Delpha and the girls.

She spent the rest of the evening caring for the children, putting them to bed, and checking in on the mother and baby over and over. After she went up to her cold room and hunkered under the quilts, she prayed for Aggie and Badan and Ruth and Alec. Then for Mother and Warner. Finally, she prayed for Delpha, the baby, and the rest of the Galloway family. "I need a solution to being in two places at once, Lord," she whispered. "Or I'll have to choose between a very ill mother and her baby—or my own brother."

Eventually, she fell into a fitful sleep.

The next morning she awoke with an idea.

She dressed quickly, cared for the girls and the mother and baby, and then, once the midwife arrived to check on Delpha, she hurried to the hospital.

She found Polly beside Warner's cot. He was sound asleep and didn't stir.

Polly whispered that Alec and Ruth, along with Badan and Aggie, had already left. Therese let out a sigh of relief. The event she'd so desperately wanted to happen had—they were on their way. Aggie and Badan would soon be safe, and so would their baby.

After allowing herself to savor the moment, she explained to Polly what was going on with the Galloway family.

"My mother can help care for Warner until you or I get home," Polly said. "I'll send her a message."

Matron Webb was sorry to hear that Therese couldn't work this last week because of the situation at the Galloways, but at least she understood. Mother was harder to placate, though she did accept the idea of Miss Amanda's help. She hired a man to take the buggy to River Pines and another to drive a wagon with a bed in the back for Warner. Therese gave her the last of her earnings to pay for it all and met them at the hospital to tell them goodbye. "I'll come as soon as Mrs. Galloway is better."

Less than two weeks later, on February 24, the Institute Hospital finally closed its doors. Mr. Galloway told Therese when he got home that evening before heading on to the bedroom to see his wife.

As Therese dished up a thin vegetable soup for the girls, her thoughts drifted to Michael. The morning paper reported there had been little fighting around Petersburg, and she hadn't heard any artillery that day, but of course it only took one bullet to kill a person. She hadn't seen him since that horrible night when he'd tried to smuggle Badan and Aggie to who knew where. She shuddered at the thought of it as she dished up two bowls of soup, a small one for Mrs. Galloway and a larger one for her husband, who had begun taking his evening meal with his wife.

Therese started down the hall but then hesitated when she heard Mr. Galloway telling Delpha that the Union Army was getting closer. That fact was already common knowledge, no need to pass it along. Polly had told her that the spy network remained active despite Alec's departure, but Therese had a feeling her own spying days were over. This war was quickly coming to a close.

"I wish I could send you and the girls home to Louisiana. You'd all be safer there."

"We can't leave, not yet," Mrs. Galloway replied, her voice weak.

With a light knock, Therese entered the room and put the soup on the table beside the bed. At least Mrs. Galloway had been able to nurse the baby, even in her weakness. If she hadn't, Therese didn't know what they would have done.

The next morning, the cook was nowhere to be found. Apparently, she'd escaped too. Perhaps she overheard Mr. Galloway urging his wife to take the girls back to Louisiana and guessed her time left in Richmond, and closer to freedom, was short.

As the days passed, she devoted herself to Mrs. Galloway and tending to the children as best she could. She went to the market each day and scrounged for food. A few vegetables. An old squash. A half dozen eggs if she was lucky. She cooked and cleaned and cared for the baby, enlisting the older girls to help her. Once a week she tackled the laundry, and when she could come by enough flour, she would bake bread.

Mother wrote occasionally, begging Therese to return home. Auntie Vera was keeping up with the cooking, and having Miss Amanda stay at River Pines to help with Warner was an absolute blessing, but every day was difficult, and Mother longed to have Therese by her side. Old Joe was doing fine but slowing down. She feared Sonny had run off because no one had seen him for a few days, and Mr. Porter was as surly as ever. Warner grew weaker with each day.

"We need you," Mother wrote at the end of every letter.

Toward the middle of March, almost a month since the hospital closed down, Mr. Galloway came home from work seeming agitated. With barely a nod, he went straight down the hall to the sick room.

Therese had managed to make bread that day. They didn't have any butter, but she decided to slice pieces for the couple. When she neared the doorway, she stopped in the hall and listened.

"General Lee endorsed arming slaves," he said. "And the Confederate Congress passed the legislation. Black soldiers will be enlisted soon."

"Will it make a difference?" Mrs. Galloway asked.

"I doubt it. It's too late." He paused for a moment and then added, "The Confederate Army is turning west to flee the Union advance."

So much for Therese's spying days being over. Both facts seemed important enough to tell Polly. Therese waited until Mrs. Galloway changed the subject to the children before entering the room.

"Ah, thank you." Mr. Galloway took the plate of bread. "What would we do without you?"

Therese smiled and then asked if they minded, once she fed the girls, if she strolled around the corner to say hello to Polly. "I haven't seen her for more than a week."

"Yes, please go." Mr. Galloway gave his wife the largest slice. "The fresh air will do you good." He looked up at Therese. "Could you take the older girls?"

"Patrick," Mrs. Galloway said, "all she does is serve me and the girls all day. Let her have a few minutes of peace."

"Sorry." He nodded toward the door. "Go ahead and go now if you like. The bread will tide us over."

Therese made sure the three older girls were settled at the table with their bread, telling them she wouldn't be long, and then she hurried out the door and began walking toward the Baxter home. As she neared the house, she saw a driver pulling an army wagon to a stop out in front.

She froze, certain it was Michael. Polly ran out to greet him, and her smile broadened even more when she spotted Therese. She called out a hello.

Therese kept moving forward, knowing she couldn't turn around and leave now that she'd been seen. But she also couldn't tell Polly what she'd overheard in front of Michael.

He jumped down from the wagon. Therese's heart fluttered against her better judgment. Perhaps Michael Talbot would always make her feel as if she were still a schoolgirl.

He waved and asked, "How have you been?"

"Fine. And you?"

He shrugged. "I'll see. Rumor has it we're to be on the move soon."

"Oh? Do you know where?"

He shook his head. "I'm heading west tonight on a supply run. But after that I'm not sure. How's Warner?"

Therese patted the latest letter in her apron pocket. "Not well. Mother's worried about him."

Michael's brown eyes filled with compassion—genuinely, she was sure. He truly cared about Warner. "When can you go home?"

Tears stung Therese's eyes. "Hopefully soon, but Mrs. Galloway still isn't well enough to care for her family. Things are a bit of a mess all the way around."

"Not entirely," Polly said, stepping forward. "I can go to River Pines to help Mother and Auntie Vera care for Warner." Polly turned toward her brother. "Aren't you headed that way?"

He nodded. "I'd like to have you along."

"But what about the Baxters?" Therese asked.

"I just found out that Mrs. Baxter is leaving tomorrow with the children. I needed to find a ride out of here anyway. I may as well go with Michael."

Therese was glad for her friend, but she now felt more alone than ever. "May we speak privately for a moment?"

"All right." Polly's eyes sparkled as she stepped to the back of the wagon, leaving Michael on the bench.

Therese quickly whispered both things she'd overheard Mr. Galloway say. "Can you pass the information along?"

"Yes," Polly said. "On the way out of town, in fact."

"Without Michael knowing?"

Polly's eyes sparkled again. "Of course."

"What if I hear more information after you're gone?"

"It won't matter," Polly said. "I'm one of the last to leave Richmond. Most everyone else is already gone. You should go too. The Galloways will understand."

"I'll leave soon." Therese hugged her friend goodbye and thanked her for caring for Warner. Polly hurried into the house to pack her things, and Therese stepped back toward the wagon. Michael jumped down and tipped his hat to her.

"I've been hoping to talk with you, about that night at the hospital—"

"It's better if we don't discuss it," Therese said.

"No, I think we should."

Therese shook her head, not wanting to feel disappointed in Michael again. "Thank you for taking Polly to River Pines. Please tell Mother and Warner I'll be home as soon as I can."

"Of course," he answered.

She started to say goodbye, but the words stuck in her throat. Instead, she waved her hand and turned around quickly, rushing forward.

She could hear Michael's footsteps behind her. "Therese, wait!"

"I can't," she called out and kept going.

His footsteps stopped. "I'll find you when all of this is over." His voice was raw. "I promise."

She kept on going. It didn't matter. He wasn't the man she thought he was. Perhaps he would return to France to his sweetheart. Or take over the family's paper mill. If he stayed, she doubted she'd see him often, except maybe in passing at church.

Therese spent the next week wondering how she would get home. As the Union Army grew closer, droves of people fled Richmond, including Jefferson Davis's wife and children, who left on the train for North Carolina. Therese began packing the Galloways' belongings as best she could, readying them to leave too. Mrs. Galloway was up longer and longer each day, and it seemed perhaps she could make the trip back to their home in Louisiana.

On the first Sunday of April, Therese and Mr. Galloway took the three older girls to St. Paul's and sat in their usual pew, halfway toward the front. Not too long into the service, a messenger slipped down the side aisle and handed Jefferson Davis a note. Mr. Galloway craned his neck. A moment later, the president slipped up the aisle, and Mr. Galloway followed him out. The girls gave Therese alarmed looks. She smiled and pointed toward the priest, indicating they should concentrate on the sermon.

A few minutes later, Mr. Galloway returned and motioned for the girls and Therese to follow him. Once they reached the street, he whispered, "The Union Army is near. Anyone working for the Confederacy needs to leave. You should too."

A few blocks from the church, he hired a driver. Once they reached home, Therese tied hunks of cheese and bread in a cloth for the family and a portion for herself while Mr. and Mrs. Galloway chose what to take and what to leave. Soon they were all back in the hired wagon, bags and crates stacked around them. Therese had her two bags, including the books she'd brought with her and the two *cartes de visite,* the one of the black man with the lattice of scars across his back, and also the one of Alec, Polly, and Therese in the hospital. Both would forever remind her of the significance of her time in Richmond. As they pulled away from the row house and the linden trees, she imprinted the image on her mind.

She was sure her time in Richmond would be one of the most memorable periods of her life. She'd done everything from reveal state secrets to contribute to the survival of the Galloways, a family as staunchly Confederate as any she'd ever known. The two seemed contradictory—and yet they weren't, not at all. In the end, caring for the family had been no different than caring for the soldiers at the hospital. All of them had been swept up in a system of sin and oppression that forced them into roles that seemed unforgivable. And yet, God could still forgive them. Her family too. She hoped all would repent and seek reconciliation in the time to come.

She shivered, even though both Lydia and Florence were tucked next to her. Why was she willing to extend grace to everyone except Michael?

A lump formed in her throat.

Because she'd expected more from him.

For so long, she believed his character was similar to her father's. That was why her disappointment was so acute. She longed for the days at Box Tree Male Academy, for the simplicity of life before the war, and mostly for her friendship with Michael. For how he talked with her and encouraged her. Yes, she'd been young, but she had loved him. Her heart ached at the memory, torn in two by all she'd lost.

When they reached the train station, the driver stopped in the middle of Broad Street due to the traffic all around the block. Therese helped the older girls down and then loaded them with as much as they could carry, ushered them up the steps and into the station, and found a space against the wall in the lobby. Mr. and Mrs. Galloway soon joined them. She gave them all hugs and asked them to write and let her know when they arrived safely.

The family thanked her profusely.

"We'd better see to our tickets," Mr. Galloway said.

Therese nodded and hurried off toward the booths, hoping to be able to secure passage to Midlothian or perhaps farther, but the line was long, and soon word spread that all of the tickets were sold for that day, and for the next day too. She looked around for the Galloways but couldn't see them. She said a prayer they'd be able to secure a way out of the city and left the station. Not sure what to do, she decided to walk west and perhaps catch a ride with someone. As she crossed Eighth Street, she saw Jay Lewis, his camera pointed at the train station and the throngs of people milling about.

"Hello, Mr. Lewis!"

He stood straight and waved. As Therese reached him, a distant explosion caused her to turn toward the river. "Is it the Union Army already?"

Mr. Lewis shook his head. "No, ma'am. The Confederacy is blowing up munitions and other buildings."

"But that will start fires."

"It already has." He nodded toward the station. "Why aren't you in there?"

"I can't get a ticket."

"What do you plan to do?"

"Walk until I can find a ride."

"You can't do that, Miss Jennings. It isn't safe."

She glanced toward the river. "Staying here isn't either."

"That's true," he said. "Everyone's leaving. I heard Jeff Davis and his cabinet are all planning to take the train out of here tonight."

Therese doubted they'd have any trouble getting tickets.

Mr. Lewis stepped back to his camera. "Do you have time for me to get one last photo of you?"

"I suppose so." A few more minutes wouldn't make a difference.

Just as Mr. Lewis took the first picture, someone called out Therese's name. She turned. An army wagon without a cover came toward them. It was Michael.

"Therese!" he called out again. "Thank God! I've been looking for you." He pulled the wagon to a stop, set the brake, and jumped down. "I have a load of soldiers I'm taking to the Huguenot Springs Hospital. Can you help me?"

She stepped to the bed of the wagon. Seven injured soldiers were spread across it. She hadn't expected God to send Michael Talbot, but she wouldn't refuse the ride or the chance to help.

"Yes. Of course I will."

"One more photo?" Mr. Lewis asked. "Of the two of you beside the wagon." He dragged his camera so he could include the three soldiers in the back who had managed to sit up.

Michael stepped to Therese's side, and they all held still until Mr. Lewis said the image had been taken. He quickly started to unfasten his camera from the tripod.

"Where are you headed now?" she asked.

"Down to the river." He placed the camera in its case. "I want to photograph those fires before someone puts them out."

"I see. Well, be careful."

Mr. Lewis latched the case and then said, "Did the doctor give you and your friend your copies of the picture I took at the hospital?"

"Yes, thank you so much," she answered. "I have it in my bag."

"Nice fellow." Mr. Lewis glanced toward the hospital. "I can't believe he stayed all this time."

Therese shook her head. "He left for Maine a good while ago. In February."

"But you're still here. Weren't you two betrothed? That's what he said when he picked up the photos."

She wasn't sure what to say. She settled on, "Our circumstances changed."

"So you decided to stay?"

She nodded.

"Well, good," Mr. Lewis said. "It's going to take all of us to put this place back together again." He nodded to Michael. "You too. Thank you for all you've done. Sincerely." Then the two men shared an odd, knowing look.

Once she was on the wagon bench and Michael had turned the team of horses toward the west, she wondered exactly what Mr. Lewis meant in thanking Michael. He had done a lot—working in a field hospital, transporting and caring for soldiers, and procuring supplies. She couldn't help but wonder if there was more than that, though.

"Has Mr. Lewis been out to the front lines?"

"Yes. Several times. He's probably seen more of what's gone on in Virginia during the last few years than anyone else. His camera has given him an unusual perspective."

They rode in silence after that, past throngs of people carrying their belongings and shuffling along. Others drove wagons piled high with household goods—beds, crates, tools, tables, and chairs.

Finally, Michael broke the silence. "So, why didn't you go with Alec?"

Therese stared straight ahead.

"I shouldn't have asked."

"No, it's fine. It's just hard to explain."

He didn't respond, and she didn't attempt to elaborate.

A few times, Therese turned on the bench to watch the smoke rise over Richmond above the blooms of the dogwood trees and the tender green of the new leaves on the maples. Her heart grew sick at the damage done to the beautiful city. The acrid smell of the fires followed them as they fled, punctuated by explosions. Finally, Michael said, "Don't look back. Try to remember it the way it was."

Richmond had been a place of learning and adventure for her—both times she lived there. But now she was going home to River Pines. To her Mother and brother. "Dear God," she whispered low enough Michael couldn't hear her. "What do You have for me?"

Every few miles, he would stop so Therese could see to the soldiers. They pooled their food—Michael had some old apples to go with her cheese and bread—and tried to make it stretch for everyone, but all anyone got was a couple of bites.

They mostly rode in silence. One time Michael nodded off, and Therese gently took the reins from his hands. After about ten minutes, he awoke with a start.

"Don't tell me I fell asleep," he said, running a hand over his face while taking back the reins with the other.

"You did." Therese felt a pang of compassion for him. "You must be exhausted."

He sat up straighter. "I could use a night's sleep. That's certain."

Again they rode in silence until he asked, "So will you head up to Maine, in time?"

"Oh goodness, no," Therese said, surprised he thought that. "I'll stay at River Pines. Most likely I'll be in charge of the vegetable garden and the chickens." She tried to smile. "I think the future will mostly be about trying not to starve."

Michael glanced at her. "Your life would be so much easier if you'd go north."

"No," she responded, trying to ignore how his words tugged at her heart. He still cared for her in some way, even if he did think she should marry Alec. "It really wouldn't make anything easier." She would have had to ignore her promise to Father while pledging her life to a man she didn't really love. There would have been no point in doing that.

When they neared the turn for River Pines, Michael said he'd drop her off but wouldn't be able to stay. "I'll come see Warner when I can."

"Let's go on to the hospital." It was only a few more miles down the road. "Then you can bring me back and get some rest." She hoped food would be available too.

Michael agreed and thanked her. By the time they reached the Huguenot Springs Hospital, darkness had fallen, and only a couple of lights shone in the windows of the building. Michael pulled up front, set the brake, and jumped down. "I'll be right back."

It only took him a few minutes. "They're overwhelmed. The conditions aren't good, and they hardly have any nurses and not a single doctor."

Therese glanced back at the soldiers. "Let's take them to River Pines.

Polly and I will care for them. You can sleep tonight and then find your unit."

Michael exhaled, most likely in relief. "Thank you."

When they reached River Pines, Old Joe stepped out to meet the wagon and helped Therese down. "Welcome home, miss."

"Thank you," she answered, tears filling her eyes. It truly was all the home she had.

Chapter Twenty-Seven
Nicole

Between working full-time at the farm and volunteering on weekends at the racetrack, the next few weeks flew by. Before I knew it, it was nearly the end of June, and our cousins Renee and Danielle, along with Renee's boyfriend, Blake, would be arriving first thing in the morning. The plan was for the six of us to spend the day together, and then the reunion would officially kick off with dinner tomorrow night. Though I couldn't wait to see them, I was feeling some trepidation about the rest of the weekend, but for now I needed to put all of that out of my mind and focus on deworming some horses.

Not nearly as awful as it sounded, the deworming process basically involved giving a dose of medicine to every single horse in the place. My job was to check the chart and measure out the correct amount for each animal and then hand the syringe to Nate, who would squirt the medicine into the horse's mouth and get it swallowed—a task far easier said than done. The horse would shake its head and spit and sputter and generally fight him as best it could. But he had to be persistent until all of the medicine had gone down, a process that was necessary, if exhausting.

Nate and I chatted easily between battles, our relationship having moved to a new level after what we'd dubbed the "night of the logjam." We were still just friends, but we'd become good friends, especially on the weekends when we weren't so conscious of our status as boss and employee.

I'd been amazed at how easily I'd fallen into the role of youth helper at the track, and even more amazed at how many of the teens really seemed to have taken to me. Maddee was the one children usually flocked to, not me, but apparently when it came to teenagers, I was clutch. At least that's what they said, according to Nate, who was telling me all about it as we crossed between paddocks.

"You know why they like you, right?" he added, brushing a bug from his arm.

"You mean besides my abundance of charm and wit?"

He smiled. "That too. But I was going to say authenticity. The single most important quality for any youth leader is genuineness. Kids can smell a fake from miles away, but if you're real, they'll know it. And they'll respect you for it."

I considered his words as we reached the next horse, stopped, and launched into the dosing process yet again. If being real was the biggest requirement, I thought as I checked the numbers and pulled the liquid into a fresh syringe, then it was no wonder they liked me.

"Well, I'm nothing if not authentic. I am what I am, take it or leave it."

"I'll take it," Nate said.

I looked up quickly, astounded that he was finally going to flirt with me after all this time. But then I realized his hand was out, and he was talking about the syringe I'd just filled.

Heat rushing to my face, I passed it over and then busied myself with the medicine bottle, glad he was too distracted by the frisky gelding to notice the color in my cheeks. I don't know why I kept hoping things would change between us. He clearly saw me as just a friend and nothing more—and I feared he always would.

If only I didn't care about him so much in return! Some days, it was all I could do not to throw my arms around him or shout words of love across the paddock.

But I didn't. I wouldn't. For the first time in my life, I was determined to hold back, take things as they came, and leave my love life—or lack thereof—completely in God's hands.

Later, on my way home, I thought about that some more, about how utterly foreign this thing with Nate was for me. I'd been friends with guys before, but never with guys who looked like him. In the old days, whether he'd been my boss or not, I would've made a play for him on day one—and likely landed him too. That's just how I rolled.

But that wasn't really me. That was the Nicole whose life had been a train wreck. That was the Nicole I was still a little bit scared of—and had been since the early days of my sobriety.

Besides the drugs, there'd been other areas in my life that had needed work too. Lying was one of them, and I'd really made progress there. But men were another, and my efforts on that front had yet to begin. All I'd done thus far was avoid the male sex entirely. I hadn't had so much as a single date since the accident. I'd just been too scared to try, not to mention too focused on my recovery.

But I was ready now. I even knew what I wanted.

I thought back to my drive home at the beginning of the summer, when I'd worked through all the things I didn't want. I didn't want to end up with the kind of guy I'd always gone for before—the tough, sexy, dangerous type—but since then I'd learned that there was a third option, a man who was the tough, sexy, dangerous type, but who had stepped out of all that and aspired to a higher standard now.

Back then, I didn't want to end up sitting in a stuffy office working as a one-on-one counselor all day, but now I knew without a doubt that I wanted to be an equine therapist, which was still in my field but so much better suited to who I was. I'd already contacted my adviser at school, and though she said they didn't offer that specialty under my degree, she would see what she could do.

Even the investigation, as stagnant as it felt sometimes, had made progress since I first got home. I'd been scared to tell my big secret back then, but not only had getting it out been a tremendous relief, it had led to Nana sharing a secret of her own.

On the other hand, I was currently frustrated with Detective Ortiz, who had finally gotten back to us a few days ago about the Door of Freedom scholarship. She said she'd looked into the matter but had found no connection between it and my grandfather.

Maddee was willing to let the subject drop after that, but I wasn't. Ortiz had never even met Granddad, so she couldn't really understand the nuances of the situation. I just knew, deep in my gut, that he'd had something to do with the money that had funded the educations of Taavi Koenig's children.

That was why I had decided to shift my schedule for today, get off an hour earlier than usual, and take matters into my own hands. The investment firm I'd found online a few weeks ago was located inside a fancy sprawling office complex in downtown Richmond called the James Center. I went there now, located the suite, and stepped inside. From the looks of things—the expensive furniture, the polished floors, the marble-top counter ahead of me—it was obvious the company had done well through the years.

Trying not to feel self-conscious in my jeans and work shirt, I told the receptionist I needed to speak with someone about a transaction that had been handled by their firm back in the late 1990s. I thought the woman might ask for details, but instead she just told me to have a seat and she'd find out if one of their "long timers" was available.

I was perched on the edge of a fancy chair, looking around the room at the portraits of various executives and board members that hung on the walls, when one of the paintings caught my eye. I stopped and did a double take. It was the biggest one of all, in a gilded gold frame: a portrait of none other than Lev Sobol, Miss Vida's boyfriend.

I was still sitting there, just gaping at it, when a middle-aged man in an expensive suit came out and asked if he could help me.

I pointed to the portrait and blurted, "Who is that?"

The man looked at the picture. "Our founder. His name is Lev Sobol."

"Is he here now?" I asked, though a big part of me hoped he wasn't.

"No, I'm sorry. He retired a few years ago. But I'm sure someone else can help you."

Without replying, I jumped up and rushed for the door.

"Miss?" the man called out.

I kept going, my heart racing.

When I got home, I collapsed on the couch and breathlessly told Maddee what had happened. We tried to decide what it meant.

She sat down beside me. "Lev already admitted he knew Granddad when he was a kid, but he never said anything about them having done business together as adults, did he?"

I shook my head. "Do you think Lev has some connection with the Koenigs?" I asked. "And if not, did he at least know what the scholarship was about?"

We both sighed and then looked at each other. If my theory was correct, Granddad had arranged a scholarship for the Koenig children through Lev Sobol's investment firm. Now Lev just happened to be dating Maddee's landlady? Surely that was no coincidence. There was something fishy going on here—especially considering his story about how they met through a random "cold call" he'd made for business purposes. Since when did successful owners of well-established investment firms make cold calls—after they had retired, no less?

Maddee wrinkled her nose. "So what's next? Tell Ortiz? Go straight to Lev?"

I stood. "Let's talk to Miss Vida first. She needs to hear about this. For all we know, she could be in danger."

Maddee shook her head, reminding me that Miss Vida wasn't home because of her big women's getaway this weekend with the group from her synagogue. "I'll try and reach her," she added, "but at least she's not in any immediate danger. Let's call Ortiz first."

I sat back down, listening as Maddee dialed the detective and put her on speaker. After a quick hello, we cut to the chase and told her about Lev and his connection with the scholarship and our concerns that he was somehow using Miss Vida to get to us. Unlike last time, Ortiz seemed to take this new information seriously and promised to look into it right away.

"Don't worry about Vida," she added. "I'll send someone out to keep an eye on her."

Once we hung up, I felt relieved about Miss Vida, nervous about

Granddad's potential involvement, and excited about this new development. After all this time, maybe we were finally moving closer to the truth.

Maddee went upstairs to change, and I set about making dinner. According to the printout on the fridge, tonight's meal was to be a simple stir-fry, so I washed my hands and then began chopping and slicing the ingredients.

My mind went to the reunion as I worked. As excited as I was about our day with the cousins tomorrow, I had to admit that the rest of it I could do without. I thought I had wanted this, but the closer the reunion got, the more I realized I was dreading it. Maddee was super excited and had spent every evening this week over at Nana's, helping her get things ready. But I hadn't joined in with any of that. At this point, I couldn't think of anything I'd rather do less.

It wasn't so much the fact that Maddee was pushing for us to pay a return visit to the cabin that bothered me. True, I had no desire to go there, and I was hoping she'd be outvoted on that one, but she kept insisting that it looked totally different now that it had been partially dismantled by police in the course of their investigation. She felt that seeing it this way would give us all closure, so I would let majority rule once the cousins were here.

My problem with the reunion was that this was going to be the first one I had attended in three years. The last time I'd gone, Granddad was still alive. But he'd died a few months after, which had sent me into a terrible downward spiral, and by the time of the next reunion, I was "deep in the D's"—denial, depression, and drugs. I was living in Norfolk then, and I'd skipped the reunion weekend altogether, something no one in the immediate family had ever done.

At least I had come to Nana's place after it ended, at the request of my sister and two cousins, so that we could go to the old cabin together. They wanted to investigate it for blood residue and finally prove that a murder had taken place there. That hadn't been so bad, and I'd told myself then that I'd try not to miss another reunion ever again.

But by the time the next one rolled around, one year ago, I had been through my accident, recovery, and then months in rehab. I was still in rehab at that point and used it as my excuse not to attend—even though I was nearly done by then and easily could've gotten a pass if I'd wanted. But I was still in a pretty fragile state, emotionally speaking, and I'd been holding on to the secret Granddad said I must take to the grave. Just the thought of being there and having to interact and reminisce had been too much for me, and so I had declined.

Now here I was again, the same weekend at the end of June looming, but with no excuse in sight this time. I was sober, strong, and secret-free—and truly dreading the thought of all those relatives and how they probably viewed me by now. I couldn't bear the idea of all that small talk and gossip and whispering, even if I did deserve it. So not fun.

Besides that, there was still the messy, unfinished matter of the investigation. Somehow I'd assumed that revealing my big secret at the beginning of the summer would be the key to solving the questions that remained. But here it was almost two months later, and we still didn't know who killed Taavi Koenig or why, or where the body went, or what Granddad had to do with it. Somehow, the idea of spending the weekend with several hundred of my closest relatives only made those lingering questions that much more unbearable.

My thoughts were interrupted by Maddee, who showed up to help. The veggies were already sizzling in the pan, so I told her she could set the table—a habit of hers I had teased her about in the beginning but had eventually grown to appreciate.

As she worked, she chattered happily about how great it would be to see Renee and Danielle again, how Blake would be there too, and how he and Renee were doing so well together.

It'll all be fine, I told myself. Just hard.

As if reading my mind, Maddee paused and shot me a curious glance. "You okay, kid?"

"Meh." I gave the boiling rice a stir before re-covering it with the lid. "I'll survive."

"You know," she said as she neatly folded a napkin and placed it under knife and spoon just so, "if it's gossip and whispers you're worried about, just forget all of that. You have a secret weapon."

"A secret weapon?" I turned, eyebrows raised, a giant spoon in hand.

Maddee nodded. "Aunt Cissy. She's your biggest champion, you know. I guarantee you she won't put up with nothin' from nobody."

Smiling at my sister's attempt to sound tough, I turned back to the stove and thought about our aunt and how much I'd enjoyed getting to know her better this summer. I'd misjudged the woman for years, thinking she was just some foolish old biddy. But she was a sweetheart, not to mention an important family historian, and I knew that what Maddee was saying now was true. Aunt Cissy was in my corner, and she was a stand-up kind of gal.

"Trust me," Maddee added, stepping closer and putting a hand on my shoulder. "Between her and Nana and Renee and Blake and Danielle and Greg and me, we'll have your back for the whole weekend. Easy peasy. Okay?"

My stir-fry done, I shut off the burner and looked down at the steaming pan of vegetables, which began to blur. Setting the spoon aside, I wiped the tears from my eyes and then turned and wrapped my sister in a big hug.

"Stupid onions," I said when we finally pulled apart. I reached for a paper towel to dab at my eyes.

"Yeah, stupid onions," she agreed with a grin, grabbing one as well. "Amazing, isn't it, how they can burn this bad—even after they've been chopped and cooked?"

Chapter Twenty-Eight
Therese

Therese arrived home just in time to tell Warner she loved him and then goodbye. He passed the next morning with Polly, Michael, Mother, and her at his side. Polly said the gangrene hadn't returned, and that he'd actually been growing stronger. It seemed he might make it, but then a week ago he took a turn for the worse.

"Fever. Chills. Increased heart rate. Paler than usual. All signs of blood poisoning," Polly said, "most likely from his stomach wound. The last couple of days, I think he was only hanging on in hopes you would come home soon. He needed to know you were safe."

Michael and Old Joe dug a hole next to Grandfather's grave while Polly and Therese washed Warner's body, dressed him in his uniform, and wrapped him in a sheet. When Michael and Old Joe finished, they came into the house with a pine box Warner had asked Old Joe to make a few weeks before. Therese swiped her tears away at the thought. Poor Warner.

Mother rallied for the burial. She asked Michael to pray. He finished with, "Lead us, Lord. Heal us. Show us how to follow Your teachings."

Therese's heart swelled at his words. Yes, that was exactly what they needed. She was surprised he recognized it. After the short service, Michael headed west to find his unit. Therese was filled with emotion as she watched his battered army wagon roll down the lane away from her, feeling the old invisible thread give a tug. She said a prayer for his safety and that God would spare his life from the last of the fighting. She prayed for his soul, that he would come back to his boyhood ideals. She tried to shake away the thread, but she felt as if it was tangled around her feet, threatening to trip her.

During the next week, Auntie Vera, Therese, Polly, Old Joe, and even Mother worked to care for the soldiers. On Monday morning, Therese sent Old Joe, with a pass, to the Huguenot Springs Hospital in hopes of securing gauze for the dressings. When he returned, he found her in the dining room, tearing the last of the fabric she could find in the house into bandages. He seemed excited.

"What's the matter?" Therese asked.

"The Union has prevailed! No disrespect intended, miss, but hallelujah! It's over."

"Over," she echoed.

"The war. The nurses at Huguenot Springs said General Lee surrendered yesterday, out at Appomattox Courthouse."

Therese wrapped her arms around the man, tears streaming down her face. "It's over!"

"Miss Jennings," he said, pulling away.

"You're free!" She turned toward Polly, who stood under the archway into the parlor. "Old Joe is free! The war is finally over."

The girls hugged, as Therese called over her friend's shoulder to Auntie Vera. "You're free! You can go to Maine and live with Aggie."

A smile spread across the old woman's face.

Mother, who had been playing the piano, stopped. "It's over? Are you certain?"

"That's what everyone is saying," Old Joe affirmed. "I stopped by the flour mill on my way home just to hear what they knew. They said the same thing."

Over. Therese had never heard such a beautiful word. The fighting had stopped. The slaves had their freedom. Immediately, her thoughts fell to Michael. *God, keep him safe*, she prayed again. *And bring him home.*

Home. Perhaps River Pines was home after all for her, now that her family no longer owned others. Of course, only time would tell where home would be for Michael.

Auntie Vera said she'd stay at River Pines until Aggie and Badan sent for her, but Old Joe told them he'd probably stay for good. "Don't know where I'd go," he said. "I'm too old to leave."

Therese assured him they'd pay him for his labors as soon as they could. She wished Sonny had waited to leave so she could have helped him, but she guessed because they hadn't heard anything about him, that he'd made it to safety. Perhaps he'd joined up with the Union Army.

The next day, Therese confronted Mr. Porter without Mother's permission and told him it was time for him to leave. Regardless of her mother's fear that they didn't have enough help, Therese couldn't bear to have the man on the property any longer. He balked and said she couldn't force him to. She gave him until the next day. That evening when he came into the kitchen, drunk and slurring orders at Auntie Vera, Therese stood in front of the fireplace. It was a chilly evening, and she had her cloak on. She turned and imitated Polly's pistol trick in Richmond.

"I have Grandfather's revolver. I want you to get out now and be gone by morning."

He started to laugh. Therese held her hand higher just as a real gun cocked. Polly stood in the doorway of the kitchen with a Colt revolver pointed at Mr. Porter's head.

"Well, then," he said, turning slowly. "Just let me get to my cabin. I'll be gone by morning."

Therese couldn't help but admire Polly's courage. It turned out she'd been carrying the pistol around the last few days in case they needed protecting from marauders, but Therese also realized how much her own courage had grown. Life wasn't always black and white—but when she knew what the right thing to do was, she'd been able to do it.

The next morning, a knock fell on the front door. Therese opened it, with Mother behind her, to find the county sheriff, a man by the last name of Brown, and a deputy.

"Sorry to bother you, ma'am," Sheriff Brown said, "but we're looking for a Mr. Porter. I believe he's your overseer?"

"Was," I said quickly. "I fired him yesterday."

"Is he still around?"

"I'm not sure. What is this regarding?

"Just point us toward the overseer's cottage," the man said, ignoring her question, "We'll go take a look."

Rather than simply point the way, Therese led the men there herself, moving down the front steps, around the kitchen house, and then past the barn and stables. When they reached the cottage, Mr. Porter wasn't there, though his packed satchel was on the bed.

"He must still be around here somewhere," the deputy said. "I'll search the grounds."

He headed out while Sheriff Brown opened Mr. Porter's bag, dumped its contents onto the bed, and rustled through them, seeming dissatisfied.

"What's going on?" Mother demand, hovering in the doorway.

He turned and began to search the room as he explained. "Mr. Porter has been implicated in a crime. We arrested a local tavern owner yesterday for attempting to sell stolen merchandise and got a confession out of him this morning. He admitted this has been an ongoing scheme, and he fingered several people in the area who have been supplying him with stolen goods, including Porter. We're here to arrest him."

Mother put her hand to her throat.

As the sheriff continued to poke around, looking for a hiding place of some kind, he added that according to the fellow they had in custody, Porter had been stealing from this plantation for years. "He said that whenever the owner wasn't around, Porter would send the slaves, including the house slaves, out to the far field and then sneak into the home and rifle around. He wouldn't steal things that would be noticed missing right away, but he would take jewelry that was seldom worn, bills from a stack of money, a few pieces of silverware, that sort of thing. He didn't want Mr. LeFevre to get suspicious."

"All those things Father thought he'd misplaced," Mother said. Her hand went to her throat again. "And my brooch."

"Oh, dear," Therese said.

"The item we caught the guy trying to sell yesterday," Sheriff Brown told them, "was a fancy ring. A ruby surrounded by diamonds. It belonged to another family Porter works for sometimes, the Talbots? He was their handyman?"

Therese nodded as Mother gasped in dismay.

"Now we just need to find the guy so we can bring him in."

"I found him all right," the deputy called out from behind us. They all turned as he added, "But he's dead."

In shock, they followed him around the cottage and down past a stand of trees to the slave quarters, a row of five small clapboard buildings, only two of which were still in use. Sure enough, Mr. Porter was there, lying facedown on the ground.

Therese shuddered at the sight. "What do you think happened?"

The deputy walked over and pointed at Mr. Porter's hand, which was discolored and swollen and clearly bore two reddish-brown dots on the back. "Snakebite. Probably a copperhead."

The men loaded the body into the back of their wagon, saying they'd make sure he got a proper burial, and then they went about searching the other buildings, hoping to find some sort of hiding place. According to their prisoner, Mr. Porter had a "stash" where he hid items he'd stolen until he could get them to the seller. They found nothing, however, so they finally gave up.

Mother and Therese both thanked the men profusely, promising to continue the search on their own as time permitted and to let them know if they ever found anything. As the wagon rolled away, Therese's knees grew weak. Mother clutched her arm and said, "I'm sorry I didn't listen to you sooner."

Therese patted her Mother's hand. At least they would never have to worry about the man again.

Five days later, in the afternoon, Polly and Therese were walking from the kitchen to the back door of the house, each carrying a tray of porridge, when a neighbor arrived with the shocking and terrible news that President Lincoln had been shot the day before and then died that morning.

They thanked the neighbor for letting them know, and as he rode away, Therese asked Polly what this might mean for the Emancipation Proclamation.

"Will it be repealed, do you think?" Andrew Johnson, a Southern Unionist and former slaveholder, would now be president.

"No. It can't be. I'm sure of it," Polly answered as they stepped into the house.

After they'd shared the information with the others and fed the wounded, they headed back out to the kitchen.

"Isn't it interesting?" Therese held onto the empty tray with one hand and opened the back door with the other. "How differently people in the same family can think?"

Polly nodded and slipped through the open door. "Like you and your mother."

"Yes," Therese answered, following her friend. "And you and Michael."

"What?" Polly placed her tray onto the table.

Therese lowered her voice. "You were part of a spy network for the Union, while he was doing everything he could for the Confederacy."

Polly pursed her lips and then whispered, "Don't think because you knew a little, that you knew everything." With that she grabbed two of the bowls and hurried into the parlor.

As Therese fed a soldier who'd lost one arm and was left with a mangled second one, she thought about Polly's words. Michael had traveled in a thirty-mile radius around Richmond with no restrictions, often past Union encampments. He saw Polly frequently, and Alec too, along with others throughout the area. Most importantly, he wouldn't have let her know if he was part of a network, just as she wouldn't have let him know of her involvement. Not that she really was a spy, not like Polly. She'd simply passed on what she overheard or read. Perhaps his role wasn't as it appeared to her either.

Therese glanced at Polly, who was feeding another soldier. They both had justifiable worries about their neighbors finding out what they had done to aid the Union, Polly far more than Therese.

She hoped there would be no more secrets among family and friends. Perhaps Michael would return soon so Therese could ask him what his true thoughts and beliefs were.

Three days later he did return. Therese, followed by Polly, ran down the front steps of the house as the wheels of the wagon rattled up the drive. Michael waved from the bench. By the time he stopped the wagon, it was obvious he transported both Confederate and Union soldiers.

"Do you have room for a few more?" he called out.

"Yes." Therese wasn't sure how they'd feed everyone, but they'd do the best they could. And she'd make sure Mother minded her manners.

Michael hopped down, his haversack bouncing against his middle, and hugged Polly. Therese took a step backward, and he tipped his cap to her.

Later that evening, after the last of the work was completed, Therese found Michael on the veranda in a rocking chair, his head leaned back, his eyes closed. The evening was warm, and a full moon rose over the stables. She watched him for a moment, working up her nerve to confront him.

"Therese?"

"Yes."

"Do you have a minute?"

She stepped toward him.

"Come sit," he said.

She obliged and lowered herself onto the bench across from him.

"Is anyone around?" he whispered. "Your mother? Any of the wounded soldiers? Neighbors?"

She shook her head. Mother had gone to bed, Polly was on watch in the parlor, and no neighbors dared venture out after dark in such uncertain times.

They both spoke at once.

"I need to know what you really believe," she said.

"I need to explain some things to you," he said.

They both stopped for a moment and then smiled.

"May I go first?" He leaned forward in the rocking chair.

She nodded. The invisible thread between them tightened.

"I came back from France because I wanted to help—to do what I could to end the war as soon as possible for my family, for our neighbors, for the South, for the North. Nothing felt as if it were black and white—and as it turned out there were more shades of gray than there were different colors of Confederate uniforms. I met with—certain people in New York before I headed south." He paused a moment and then added, "Including Alec and Ruth."

"What?"

He nodded. "It was right before Alec came to Richmond. Contacts in France worked it out. We had it all planned from the beginning. Then, when I found out I could be part of the field hospital, I jumped at the chance. It made me more useful to Alec's spy network."

"What about Polly?" Therese asked. "Was she happy to have you spying?"

"No. In fact, she was against it."

"Why?"

"She didn't think both of us should be involved, not when our parents had already lost the twins. But she'd started spying for Alec before I could tell her not to. Between driving to the hospital, out into the country to find food, and near enemy camps, I was able to pass along information that Alec gave me. Sometimes I told other Southerners who passed it on. Other times I connected directly with Union spies, some who gave me money."

"Which you then used to buy the food for the Confederate troops?"

He nodded.

It was all beginning to make sense.

Michael continued. "And I was able to get slaves started on the Underground Railroad too."

"I had no idea," she managed to say. "Thank you." Her voice dropped to a whisper. "For trying to save Aggie and Badan."

"No, thank you. Your plan was much better. And thank you for all you did too."

From the look on his face, Therese knew he was talking about her efforts as a spy. "Polly told you?"

He shook his head. "I guessed from the information I received and knowing where you worked."

"I didn't guess any of it concerning you."

"Well, I purposefully misled you."

She nodded and looked away. Though she understood why he'd done it, it still hurt to hear him say the words. Didn't he know he could've been honest with her all along?

"I needed to appear as supportive of the Confederacy as possible."

"So the slavery thing, the 'what did we go to war for if not to protect our property' statement? You didn't really believe that?"

"No." He leaned back. "My family has always been opposed to slavery."

"I thought so," Therese said. "But you were so convincing."

"Besides, I couldn't be your father's student without believing in the abolitionist movement."

"But he didn't teach that. He would have been fired."

"He didn't teach it explicitly, but he taught us that God created humankind in His image. In history class he included the history of slavery back to the ancients and through to the present." Michael began rocking. "He didn't condone any of it, but the difference between then and now was that ours was based entirely on the color of a person's skin. He taught us to respect all people."

Therese swiped at a tear. That invisible thread between them was no longer in a tangle at her feet. Michael still was who he had been.

"He taught us to be empathetic. To turn the other cheek. To walk a mile in another person's shoes."

More tears trickled down Therese's face.

Michael stopped rocking. "I'm sorry. That wasn't very thoughtful of me—to speak about your father."

"No, it was." She swiped at the tears with both hands.

"You should have gone with Alec. Your life would be so much easier."

She shook her head. "You asked me why I didn't. Do you remember?"

"The day Richmond fell?"

"Yes, and I didn't answer, not directly. My priorities were to convince Mother to free Aggie and Badan, and to keep my promise to Father to care for Mother. But in making both of those things happen, I realized I didn't love Alec. At first I thought I did, but then…"

He leaned forward again. "What are you saying, Therese?"

She met his gaze. "You had a sweetheart in France. You planned to go back after the war."

"Why would you think that?"

"Polly said you brought home a porcelain box for your sweetheart. In France."

His brow furrowed. "A sweetheart?"

She nodded, feeling heat rush to her cheeks. "Polly saw…you had photographs. Of the two of you."

He stared at her blankly until she added, "She said the young woman in the pictures was quite beautiful."

Michael thought for another moment, and then to her surprise he burst into a laugh. "Eugenie? Are you kidding me? Oh, Therese. No. I'm so sorry. Shame on my sister for poking through my things. She completely misunderstood."

"She did?"

He nodded, his expression growing more serious as he looked into Therese's eyes.

"Those were advertisement photos to be used as samples of a new type of photographic paper my cousin and I were developing in France. The young woman was a paid model, and she was indeed quite beautiful, but she was a nightmare from beginning to end. The man we'd hired to pose with her didn't show, so they wrangled me into taking his place. The woman was nearly impossible to work with. The only reason I brought the pictures home was to show my father the new paper.

It's based on some of the ideas of Henry Fox Talbot, one of our English cousins who's become rather famous for his work in photography.
The paper uses a gelatine coating treated with potassium dichromate,
and, well..." His voice trailed off as he gave her a sheepish smile. "You
don't need to hear about all that right now. The important thing is that
I met the woman, worked with the woman, couldn't stand the woman,
and never saw the woman again. So much for my French sweetheart."

Therese sighed, wishing she had known that from the very beginning.

"I hoped *you* would be my sweetheart," he continued. "I know we
were young when I left Virginia, but I never stopped thinking of you
while I was in France. I bought the box for you the week before I left,
while I was in Paris, and I wanted to give it to you that very first day I
saw you after I returned." He pointed toward the front of the house.
"Right there."

Therese's heart began to race. So much had been different than what
she'd assumed. "But then my mother said those horrid things."

Michael grimaced. "It wasn't just that. It was bad timing on my part,
truly. Your grandfather had just died." He sighed. "I'd spoken to your
father about you before I left for France. He asked me not to say anything
or even to stay in touch with you, for that matter, because he wanted
you to focus on your studies. But he said if I felt the same way when I
returned, I should speak to him, and he would give me his blessing."

Tears stung Therese's eyes. If only she'd known that too.

"I was so anxious to say what I'd rehearsed all those years that I
rushed ahead, hoping I could say it to your mother when I should
have waited."

He reached down into the leather haversack he always carried with
him and pulled out a package wrapped in layers of paper. He began
to unpeel them, one by one as he spoke, placing each piece of paper
on the ground beside the chair. "I knew I'd offended your mother and
figured it would take time for me to win her favor. I intended to, first
chance I got, when I went off to join the 1st Infantry and you went to
Richmond. But Alec let me know early on he was interested in you. He
talked about how smart and caring you were, not to mention beautiful." He smiled. "I saw the way he looked at you."

Therese's face grew warm, but she stayed silent.

"I knew I didn't have a chance, for all sorts of reasons, including that you were mad at me. By then your mother felt better about me, compared to Alec." He smiled wryly. "But it was too late."

Therese shivered in the cool spring air.

"I'm sorry," Michael said. "I've kept you too long."

Therese shook her head. "Ask me again why I didn't go to Maine."

He exhaled. "All right. Why didn't you go to Maine?"

"It's true I realized I didn't love Alec, but the reason I knew I didn't love him was because I had loved you when I was young."

Michael's voice was raw. "Had?"

Tears filled her eyes. "And still did. But I was trying not to. I feared you were going to sell Badan and Aggie. I thought you believed in fighting to save the property of the South, meaning four million enslaved human beings. I thought you were doing everything you could to see that the South won. There are so many things I believed about you that were wrong."

He rocked forward again and put one hand on her shoulder. Finally, more than the thread connected them. Still holding the package, he whispered, "Shh. None of that was your fault. I needed you to believe those things for your safety and mine."

He tore away the last piece of paper, revealing the porcelain box with roses on the lid, and held it out to her. "This is what I intended for you all along, what I brought home—for you."

"Thank you." Blinking away tears, she studied it closely in the light of the nearly full moon. Then she opened it and was surprised to find a little folded piece of paper inside. She pulled it out and read the words written in Michael's own hand: *Therese, will you be my wife?*

Her heart pounding, she returned the note to the inside of the container, replaced the lid, and then cradled the box with both hands. She looked up at him, smiling, and softly whispered, "Yes. A million times, yes."

Beaming in return, Michael leaned toward her, and she raised her lips to his. He kissed her, at first softly and then with passion.

She'd always guessed Michael Talbot was a man of passion, and he was, intensely so.

She leaned into him, and he wrapped one arm around her, pulling her closer, off the bench and onto his lap. Rocking backward, they both laughed as Therese kept hold of the porcelain box. In the midst of loss and devastation, for a moment, joy bubbled up in both of them.

Chapter Twenty-Nine
Nicole

The next morning, Maddee, Greg, and I drove to our favorite local pancake house, where we met up with Danielle, who had driven in from Wilmington and was waiting for us at the door. We were still standing there talking excitedly when Renee and Blake showed up minutes later, straight off a red-eye from Seattle. After another round of squeals and hugs, followed by the introduction of Greg to the group, we all went inside and settled into a big corner booth amid the scents of coffee, bacon, and maple syrup.

All three out-of-towners looked great, especially Renee, who seemed aglow with happiness, in part thanks to the hunk at her side, I felt sure—not to mention the ring on her finger. I gasped when I saw it, which caused Maddee to look, and then everybody was talking at once. When things finally calmed down, Renee explained that they'd gotten engaged two weeks ago but had wanted to share the big news in person.

Of course, we were all thrilled, and we showered them with hugs and congratulations. Maddee was beyond ecstatic, and within moments the two couples were deep in discussion about wedding dates and logistics and all the other things of which my sister's dreams were made.

Ignoring the pang in my own heart, I turned to Danielle and quipped softly, "Guess that's two down, two to go, huh?"

From the shy smile she gave me in response, I realized I might be wrong.

"No way!" I cried. "Not you too."

Blushing furiously, she shook her head, explaining that no, she wasn't engaged, but yes, she had been seeing a very special man, one with whom she hoped to share a future.

"Not another starving artist, is he?" I teased, thinking of her penchant for men with ponytails and paint stains on their jeans.

Danielle shook her head, blond curls framing her pretty face. "No, but he is on the Arts Council. He owns a gallery on Front Street."

"Why didn't you bring him along? We don't bite, you know."

She smiled. "I wanted to, but he's in Europe right now on a buying trip."

I started to make another joke but thought better of it. Instead, I just gave her hand a squeeze and told her how happy I was for her. Smiling, the two of us focused on our menus as the others wrapped up their wedding talk.

We all placed our orders—corn berry pancakes, chicken and waffles, Big Daddy skillets, and more—and then Maddee got everyone's attention and shared her big idea about going out together as a group to see the cabin. "The police dismantled so much of it for their DNA testing that it's really quite different now," she explained. "It's a lot less scary and intimidating. It's given me such closure to see it this way. I think it would do the same for y'all too."

I'd been hoping the consensus would be to stay away, but her proposal was met with nods and yesses all the way around. Oh, well. At least we'd be there in the daylight, and all together.

"So other than that," Danielle asked, "what's up for today?"

We all naturally looked to Maddee, our activity director extraordinaire, who'd been gathering information and winnowing it down for weeks. She started by laying out a general overview of the timing, saying we would go from here to Nana's, get settled into the pool house, maybe swim a bit if anyone was interested, and go through the Civil

War family photos together. After that, we would hike to the cabin, have a late lunch, and then pick one activity for the afternoon.

She had narrowed down the dozens of options this area had to offer to a chosen few, custom tailored for these guys, and she passed out the info now. Not surprisingly, Blake took the page about kayak/raft/canoe/SUP rentals at James River Park, and Danielle reached for the one regarding a new outdoor sculpture exhibit at the botanical garden.

"We can wait and decide later," Maddee added. "Maybe play it by ear. If y'all are exhausted from your flight and just want to hang out at Nana's for the afternoon, that's fine too. This is our day, and we can spend it however we want."

The food arrived, so we paused the discussion until everyone had been served and Greg discreetly led us in a blessing. I'd gotten Southern pecan pancakes, which I dotted with butter and drizzled in syrup. Yum.

"One question." Renee looked to Maddee. "How can we hang out at Nana's today of all days? I can't see relaxing and swimming and stuff when we'll be surrounded by people working like crazy getting ready for the reunion."

I answered for my sister. "Not this year. Maddee's taken care of all that. She's been going over to Nana's all week, getting stuff ready ahead of time. She even arranged for an extra twenty-four hours on the rental stuff so that it could all be delivered and set up yesterday instead of today."

Everyone seemed pleased to hear it, and Maddee beamed as Danielle lifted her coffee cup in a toast, "To a guilt-free 'cousins' play day, compliments of our own personal superwoman."

Sure enough, things were relatively quiet at Nana's, considering. We parked our three cars together in a row near the garage and then headed into the main house first, just to say hello.

We found our grandmother at the big dining table with about ten local Talbot relatives, mostly older women whose job it was to put together the yearly "welcome packets" for the attendees. They did so in an assembly line fashion, chatting as they worked.

Once we'd finished with a general round of greetings, Nana excused herself to walk us back out. Before I went, however, I pulled Aunt Cissy aside and told her that we'd be going through the photos in the pool house in just a while if she'd like to come out and join us.

Eyes sparkling, she whispered, "More than you can imagine! If I have to hear one more time about Ethel's new grandbaby, apparently the single most brilliant child ever born, I'm afraid I might smack her with her own pile of manila envelopes."

Back outside, as the six of us rounded the garage, luggage in hand, I was amazed to see just how ready this place was for the big event, including several huge white tents gracing the lawn along with tons of chairs and tables, an entire outdoor cooking station, and more. In the distance, down by the tennis court, I even spotted the promised volleyball setup. Grinning at the sight, I challenged the group to a game later, girls against boys.

"Oh, you're going down, Talbots," Blake teased. "Get ready for total domination, even if we are outnumbered. Right, buddy?"

"Uh, sure," Greg replied, "though you probably should know their team has a secret weapon, a certain height-challenged individual with the musculature of a pole vaulter."

We all laughed, and he shot me a brotherly wink.

Fifteen minutes later, the two men were out swimming, and the women were settled into the pool house, sitting around the table and talking nonstop.

When Aunt Cissy showed up, we made room for her, ready to go through the photos. Before we did, however, Maddee opened the lid to the box, pulled out the two we'd left on top, and asked her the questions we'd been wondering about, starting with which of the two Talbots, if either, Therese ended up marrying. Maddee held out both images, the one of Therese with the doctor and the other of her with the soldier.

"That one," Aunt Cissy said with a grin, pointing to the latter, the image of Therese and the soldier, the man standing beside her in front of a wagon.

The four of us leaned in to study the image together, realizing that this was our great-great-great-grandfather. Warmth flooded through me at the thought.

"And is 'M. Talbot' Michael Talbot?" Maddee asked.

"Sure is."

"The same Michael Talbot who brought back the illuminated manuscript from France?" I added.

"One and the same."

My sister and I shared a grin, thrilled to learn that this clever and brave man had been our direct forebear.

We began passing around the photos, and our cousins seemed as charmed by them as Maddee and I had been. I'd gone through everything so many times now that I should've been bored, but of course I wasn't. The pictures still fascinated me, and it was particularly fun to share them with Renee and Danielle. Better yet, as we went through each one, the two of them asked questions that Maddee and I hadn't thought of, and that brought out even more new information from our family Civil War historian.

We'd been at it for a while when Danielle came to a photo I hadn't paid much attention to before. Something about it caught her eye, however, and after studying it for a long moment, she said, "That's the cabin."

Startled, I leaned in to look but didn't understand what she was talking about. The image featured five identical structures in a row, small and dingy clapboard buildings with brick chimneys.

"Where?" I asked.

Danielle pointed to the second building from the right. "There."

I was expecting Aunt Cissy to correct Danielle's mistake, but instead she nodded and said, "Good eye."

"What?" Maddee took the photo from Danielle and peered at it more closely. "How? That looks nothing like the cabin at all."

"That's because it was rebuilt," Aunt Cissy said, "back in the 1920s or '30s, for use as a hunting cabin. They gave it new walls and a new roof, but they retained the original framework, footings, and floor."

"The cabin doesn't have a chimney," I said, pointing to the one in the picture.

Aunt Cissy nodded. "By the time they did the rebuild, it was probably too damaged to use anymore, so they just took it out."

"But there are five buildings in the picture," Maddee said. "There's only one cabin."

"The others are long gone, though I imagine you could find traces of them if you looked."

Danielle nodded. "That's how I knew it was the cabin. Structurally it seemed about right, and the trees in the photo also work if you allow for time passed between then and now. But it was the brick piers that gave it away."

"What's a pier?" I asked.

Sliding the picture to the center of the table, she pointed at the base of the building, where each corner rested on a low square of bricks. "Most people call them footings, but the correct term is pier."

"And you recognized that was the cabin because of that little glimpse of bricks at the bottom?" Maddee asked, incredulous.

"Yeah." Danielle sat back in her chair and looked at each of us in turn. "Don't you guys remember the bricks from when we were kids? Other summers, before the incident? With the pine straw?"

The three of us looked at each other in confusion until Renee's face lit up.

"The brick squares. Of course." She looked from Maddee to me. "The area wasn't so overgrown back then, and we found these brick squares on the ground, a bunch of them. I guess they were sitting exactly where they are in this picture, minus the buildings."

"Our pine straw houses!" Maddee cried.

Then something clicked for me too. "That sounds so familiar, but I was really young then. Remind me."

Grinning, my sister explained that when we were kids, we loved going into the woods and playing in the cabin. But we also enjoyed playing *around* the cabin, building pretend houses by gathering pine straw into long piles that stretched from brick square to brick square. We usually worked together to create a single house, but one time we each made our own, and then we pretended we were all next-door neighbors.

The others pitched in as well, elaborating on those adventures and how fun they had been. I could barely recall what they were talking about, but somehow their memories gave me a warm feeling inside.

"Do you think those other squares are still out there now?" Maddee asked.

"I don't know why they wouldn't be," Danielle replied. "I can't imagine anyone ever went to the trouble to remove them. They're probably just so grown over that they're not noticeable anymore."

Suddenly, I found myself wanting to go out to the cabin after all. It would always be a place of trauma, but maybe these happy memories could help to temper that.

"One interesting architectural note about these buildings," Aunt Cissy said, pointing again at the photo. "Most slave quarters of that era were built flat on the ground, with packed dirt for floors. They only raised the buildings like these where drainage was poor."

I looked at her, confused. "What are you saying?"

She shrugged. "Just that the slaves who lived in these were lucky—well, not that any slave could be considered lucky, but you know what I mean. Dirt floors were awful, as you can imagine, so the fact that these slaves had wood floors, well, at least that was better than dirt."

The room fell silent as we all gaped at her.

"What's wrong?"

"We've always been told that no Talbot ever owned a slave," Renee said softly.

"That's true."

"But wasn't this Talbot land?"

Understanding filled Aunt Cissy's eyes, and she began to explain, saying that by the time Therese inherited this property, the Civil War had been over for a while, so the slaves were already free.

"Even so," she added, "Therese was reluctant to stay and raise a family here, knowing that the place had been built on the backs of slaves. She wanted to sell it so that she and Micael could start fresh somewhere else."

"But they didn't, obviously."

Aunt Cissy shook her head. "Michael talked her into staying. His family's paper mill was just across the river, so it worked out well. He was even able to provide jobs for several former slaves, including one from River Pines, a fellow named Old Joe."

"Sounds like Michael was a real man of character," Renee said.

"He was, not to mention a true romantic." She reached for the stack of love notes and held them up. "He'd brought a small porcelain box back with him from France, just for Therese, and when he gave it to her, he'd hidden a little note inside, asking her to marry him. I imagine that's where the tradition started, because, as you know, he continued to leave little love notes inside that same porcelain box for the rest of their lives."

"Wait, that's where she would find the love notes?" I asked.

Aunt Cissy nodded. "Every now and then she would peek into the box, and sometimes one would be there."

We all sighed, but by that point the guys had come back in from the pool and had overheard. They both groaned.

"Better watch out, Blake," Greg said. "Looks like someone's set a dangerous precedent for us."

"That's okay. I think our ladies are worth it."

"Amen to that."

They headed off down the hall to change clothes, and once they were out of earshot, Aunt Cissy let out a deep sigh. "Such handsome young men. You two ladies are very lucky indeed."

Before anyone could respond, she launched into song, trilling, "They broke the mold when they made you, my love..."

"So how about we all head to the cabin?" Danielle said quickly, cutting the woman off before she could get any further.

"Oh, wow," Renee said, the first to speak. We were all just standing there, side by side, staring at the cabin—or what was left of it.

Maddee was right. It had been significantly dismantled by the police for their investigation, leaving it open to the elements in places. The floorboards were mostly gone, as was the entire back wall. Somehow, it no longer looked menacing and evil. Just old and pathetic.

Besides, now that I knew this had originally been a slave quarter, that changed everything and really put our own experience into perspective. Far worse things had happened on this land back then than what happened to the four of us when we were children.

"I can't believe I'd forgotten about making the pine straw houses," Maddee said, stepping away from the cabin and looking around, into the brush, for the other brick piers.

"There's one," Renee said, joining her and pointing far into the weeds. Sure enough, she was right. Partially obscured by a bush and some thick vines sat a bricked square about two feet wide and eight inches high.

"Oh yeah, and another," Blake added. "Look there."

Soon we were poking around in the weeds and vines, searching for the brick piers. We couldn't get to all of them because of the brush, but we did find some, and though many had been reduced to rubble long ago, a lot of the ones we found were still intact. After a while, the ladies showed the guys how to build a pine straw house and soon they were all going to town on it together.

I stood back, not feeling quite so carefree. My mind filled with the image I'd seen at the museum of the man who'd been whipped, and I just couldn't get over the fact that these had been slave quarters.

"What a horrible legacy for this place," I said to Aunt Cissy, who was standing nearby.

"Michael didn't think so. To his mind, the legacy was redeemed, and I have to say that I agree." She went on to explain how the young couple worked to change the plantation in the years following the war. They picked a spot in the far field for a new house, just a simple structure at first, though subsequent generations would expand and enlarge it until it became the grand manse where Nana now lived. But back then, once they shifted over to their new home, they allowed this half of the property to grow wild, except for managing and harvesting the trees for the paper mill. During the construction of their house and later a barn, they dismantled much of the original mansion and other outbuildings, repurposing some of the materials and discarding the rest.

"But they left the slave quarters standing as they were," she concluded, "as a reminder of the past, lest it become our future."

I took in her words, thinking how wise our ancestors had been. I decided they were right. The sorrowful legacy of this place had been redeemed after all.

Standing in the heart of the woods, surrounded by loved ones and despite the presence of the cabin, I felt a growing sense of peace—until it was interrupted by a strange noise, like a bird being strangled or an animal with its leg in a trap. Turning, I realized the sound was coming from Aunt Cissy, who was standing with hands clasped and eyes closed, belting out her attempt at a soulful rendition of "Amazing Grace."

Oh, my.

I looked to see the rest of the gang in various states of surprise and muffled laughter. Overcome with a surge of protectiveness, I took in a deep breath, stepped over to her side, and joined in on the last two lines, our voices merging into a terrible, toe-curling cacophony:

"I once was lost, but now am found; was blind, but now I see."

The seven of us ended up staying out in the woods longer than we'd planned. It was such a beautiful day, and we were all having fun creating the world's biggest pine straw house as Aunt Cissy sat comfortably on a stump nearby and regaled us with tales of the Talbots. It had started after our song, when Danielle staved off a second verse by interrupting to ask Aunt Cissy how she knew so much about things that happened so long ago.

"We know Catherine's story from the 1600s because she left a journal," Danielle added. "And we know Celeste's story from the 1700s because she wrote about it in letters. But all we have for Therese are photos and love notes, right?"

Aunt Cissy had grinned. "Nope. For Therese we have what's known as an oral tradition. The stories I've been sharing with you girls were passed down to me verbally." Looking from one to the other of us, she added, "I've been hoping one of you might want to carry on the torch. Learn from me and someday take my place with the next generation." Wagging her eyebrows, she added, "The position does come with a prize."

"A prize?"

"The porcelain box Michael gave to Therese. It's in the museum exhibit right now, but ordinarily I keep it at home on the center of my mantel."

We all shared glances, knowing that what she was suggesting would be both an honor and a responsibility, one that none of us was exactly jumping up to claim. It was something to think about maybe, for when we were older.

The moment passed when Blake said he'd love to hear her account of the story of the missing illuminated manuscript if she felt like sharing. So there we were, gathering pine straw into mounds for walls and listening to the tale at a new level of detail. When Aunt Cissy was done sharing, we found ourselves so invested in the story that we began brainstorming about what could've possibly happened to the illuminated manuscript. We started with the facts as we knew them:

Mr. Porter stole some important valuables from the Talbots' safe, including the ruby ring and the illuminated manuscript.

For some reason, Porter then handed over the ring to the fence for him to sell, but not the manuscript.

The most logical reason Porter might have hung onto the manuscript was because he understood its full value and was planning to sell it on his own.

He had a secret place where he stashed his booty after stealing it, so considering that he'd not yet had a chance to sell it, the manuscript had probably still been in there when he died.

Considering there were no records of it ever having shown up, it was either hoarded away in someone's private collection or still in his old hiding place to this day.

So where was the hiding place? That question led us to some more conclusions:

If it had been in any of the buildings that were taken down by Michael and Therese, they more than likely would have run across it.

Porter was found dead on the grass behind the slave cabins, which could mean he was back there intending to dig it up from the ground. According to Aunt Cissy, many people buried their valuables during the war.

Then again, when he was found dead, he'd had no shovel with him nor any other indication of what he'd been doing there, so digging didn't seem likely.

"He could've been on his way to get a shovel," Maddee said, "and just cutting through here when he ran into the copperhead."

"No," Renee replied. "The snakebite was to the man's hand. If you're just walking along and get bitten, it's going to be on your leg or foot. More than likely, he was low to the ground when it happened." Ever the scientist, Renee continued, explaining that copperhead bites weren't usually fatal. "Which tells me he probably went into anaphylactic shock in reaction to the bite, and that's what killed him."

Blake stood and began pacing. "Okay, so he was found somewhere along here, behind the slave quarters, minus a shovel, low to the ground. Could his hiding place have been in a tree? Perhaps one with a hollow in it? I know it's been a hundred and fifty years since then, but a lot of these trees are at least that old."

Renee nodded, adding that the maximum lifespan for a white pine was something like 450 years.

Aunt Cissy had brought the photo of the old slave quarters with her, and suddenly everyone was crowding around looking at it, trying to figure out which of the trees that had been here back then were still here now. Before they got very far, however, Danielle seemed to have a different idea.

Stepping away from the group, she headed over to the cabin, walked around the back side, then called out for us.

"Hey, y'all. Come here!"

We rounded the corner to see her pointing at the cabin's back left brick pier.

"Look," she said. "This one is wider than the others—all the others, not just the ones with this building. Every intact pier out here is the same size, has the same number of bricks except for this one right here. See? It's wider, almost like someone added some extra length to create a little hiding space inside."

Sure enough, once she explained it, I understood what she meant—though only someone as extremely visual as she would ever have noticed such a thing. Curious, I stepped forward and knelt in front of the pier to get a closer look.

"Be careful, Nicole," Maddee scolded, sounding so much like her childhood self that we laughed.

From a safe enough distance, I poked at the pier until I found a chunk of two bricks, mortared together, that seemed to shift. Blake and Greg stepped in to help, and together the three of us managed to pull that chunk free from the wall. It fell to the ground, leaving behind an opening just large enough to use as a hidey-hole for all sorts of stolen treasures, including an illuminated manuscript.

Immediately, everyone whipped out their phones and turned on their flashlights to shine into the cavity that had been revealed.

"Watch out for snakes," Aunt Cissy warned again.

"Not to mention brown recluse spiders," Renee added.

None of us reached inside. All we could do was stare at what we were seeing, a bundle of some sort, just about the size and shape of a book.

"Well, what do you know?" I said softly.

Aunt Cissy gasped. "Is that—"

"We'll find out soon enough." My sister turned off the flashlight from her phone and dialed. "Detective Ortiz? It's Maddee Talbot. And, boy, do I have an interesting development for you."

Thanks to the excitement of our find, we were in top problem-solving form as we waited in the woods for police to arrive. If as a group we'd been able to use our collective reasoning to find a treasure that had been missing for one hundred fifty years, we decided, maybe we could figure out who killed Taavi as well. And so we began to brainstorm.

We all felt confident that Taavi had come here in search of Mr. Porter's hidey-hole. Like the old game of "you're getting colder, you're getting hotter," he'd probably been getting warmer and warmer, so to speak, in his search when he ran into someone who stabbed and killed him. That would have been a fairly straightforward crime save for the fact that they then somehow managed to get rid of his body and clean up a messy death in a short amount of time. That took the situation to a new level and made things infinitely more complicated. Heartsick, I couldn't help but wonder what Granddad's role in all of this might possibly have been.

"Okay," Maddee said, interrupting my thoughts, "let's walk through *our* day that day. Maybe something will come up that we haven't thought of before."

Such a blow-by-blow account ordinarily would've sent me into a spiral, but it wasn't so bad now. Being only six years old at the time, I had just a few memories from that day, and they were related to the moment of discovery and its aftermath. But the others had been older and recalled far more. As they launched in, starting with when we got up that morning, some of what they described sounded vaguely familiar, as if they were taking an old, half-erased sketch and coloring it in.

That's what I was thinking when something Danielle said caught Maddee's attention. "Wait, say that again."

"The double rainbow in the sky that morning, don't you remember? We saw it just before we set off into the woods, and it was so beautiful we all just stood there looking at it until it disappeared. Then we kept going."

Renee smiled. "Yeah, it's funny, Danielle was going on about the colors and the perfect arced shape and everything, and I was standing there thinking about how we'd used prisms in science class to study light refraction."

The others chuckled, but Maddee wasn't smiling.

"What is it?" I asked.

"The double rainbow," she said, her eyes wide. "The night Gabe came to Nana's, earlier this summer, he said something about there having been a double rainbow here the day his father died. Remember? He was real specific about all of it, the rain and the coolness and the rainbow and the warmth and the sunshine, like he knew what had happened step-by-step."

Now that she mentioned it, I did remember. "Yeah, but we all know the guy's obsessive. I'm sure he's studied every aspect of this case, including what the weather was like on the day his dad died."

"The temperature and the humidity, sure. But a rainbow? It just seems highly unlikely to me that any secondhand report would have included the fact that the same morning Taavi was killed, a double rainbow appeared in the sky."

We all gaped at her as she continued, articulating the obvious.

"Gabe must have been *here* that day and seen it for himself. He wasn't in Cleveland wondering where his dad had gone, but in Virginia. Maybe even here in the Dark Woods. Maybe even here at the cabin, hiding behind a tree and holding the knife he would use to kill his own father."

or the first time in memory, the annual Thursday night Talbot family reunion kickoff dinner was probably going to be delayed. As the afternoon wore on and people began to arrive, they were stopped from coming out back and sent to the main house instead. The pool house had become command central for Ortiz and her officers, though our little gang of seven had been allowed to stay. She had invited Nana to come out and join us as well, but the woman declined, saying she had guests to care for and we could fill her in later.

Officers had managed to extract the package from the pier, revealing a book-shaped bundle wrapped in canvas and coated with a shiny black substance. Blake and Renee had been reluctant for anyone to move the thing without Harold present, but they hadn't been able to reach him, so finally they'd compromised and allowed it to be put in a cooler, the kind used to transport organs between hospitals. Once that was done, the officers confirmed that the hiding place was otherwise empty, no stolen jewels or other exciting treasures to be found within, and we headed back with Ortiz.

Blake carried the cooler, walking carefully, all the way to the pool house, where he put it on the kitchen counter. Renee finally reached

Harold at that moment, and we were all so focused on her call that none of us noticed what Ortiz did next. She opened the cooler, removed the bundle, and set it on the table. She was about to unwrap the covering when Blake stopped her.

If this really was what we thought it was, he insisted, it had to be opened under the right conditions—light, humidity, and more. She couldn't just unwrap it even if she were careful about it. Renee hung up then and announced that Harold was about an hour away but that he was coming, so Ortiz agreed to wait and let him take charge of the unveiling.

In the meantime, Maddee shared our new realizations about Gabe with Ortiz—but her reaction was not what we'd expected. As it turned out, she already knew Gabe had been here the day his father died because he'd told her that right up front.

"Why didn't you tell us?" Maddee asked.

She shrugged. "Wasn't relevant, I guess. He's not a suspect. We ruled him out a long time ago for a number of reasons." She went on to tell us his story, how nineteen-year-old Gabe had come to Richmond on a hunch after his father disappeared, knowing this was probably where the man's never-ending quest for his holy grail had led him. The Talbots were the biggest connection Taavi had to the manuscript's disappearance, so Gabe camped out not far from the entrance to the estate with a pair of binoculars and watched everyone who came and went for a day and a half, hoping his dad would show up eventually.

He stuck it out until early afternoon on Saturday, when he was startled by the appearance of several police cars. Fearing he'd get in trouble for camping on private property, he waited until they were just out of sight up the driveway and then beat a hasty retreat. That was it. He headed back home to Cleveland, realizing the futility of his efforts. He never saw his father again and hadn't a clue that the man had been murdered that very morning less than a mile from where he'd been camping. In fact, no one knew what had happened to Taavi—until twenty years later, when Detective Ortiz contacted the Koenigs and told them about her investigation.

"What about Lev?" I asked. "Did you question him regarding his involvement?"

Ortiz nodded, a mysterious smile spreading on her face. "Sure did, and I have some new info you're going to want to hear. I was planning to fill you in later, but I might as well do it now while we're waiting for Harold."

Of course we all immediately gathered in front of her to listen, squeezing onto the couch and chairs, as Ortiz leaned against a kitchen stool and began to share what she'd discovered since Maddee and I called her about Lev Sobol the day before.

As it turned out, she said, Vida's boyfriend was not a bad guy as we'd feared, but someone who had in fact done us all a huge favor. That's because he managed to accomplish what Ortiz had not, thanks to threats from his high-powered lawyer and the efforts of several well-placed associates. The detective had questioned Lev not long after our phone call, she said, but in the face of her inquiry, rather than answer her questions, he had used his lawyer and insider contacts to convince the authorities to release information regarding Douglas Talbot's involvement with Operation Paper Trail. That, in turn, would serve to exonerate Lev.

And so we listened now, spellbound, as Ortiz told us the full story that she'd finally been given access to, starting back in June 1995, when our grandfather was approached by the Secret Service to enlist his help with an investigation.

With gasps and wide eyes, we all looked at one another. I could feel relief pulsing through my veins at the realization that my worst fears about Granddad's actions had not come true. He was an innocent man pulled into service by his government.

"The agents who contacted your grandfather told him they had it on good authority that 'the head of Talbot Paper and Printing' was soon going to hear from a representative of a bogus corporation, a 'small specialty printer just starting out,' that was going to try to convince him to serve as middleman in the purchase of a certain piece of printing equipment." Ortiz went on to explain that the rep would tell Granddad they wanted to buy the machine through his company so that they could get a better price on it, and in turn they would pay him a commission equal to half the amount saved. A win-win. In truth, price had nothing to do with it.

"They were in need of a specific kind of machine, one that would raise suspicions of counterfeiting if bought outright but that wouldn't seem questionable if ordered through an established paper and printing company. The agents told your grandfather that they wanted him to agree to help. He was to place that order, take delivery on it, and sell it to the rep in turn—all while being secretly recorded by them."

Picturing it, I tried to imagine being in poor Granddad's position. I'm sure he would rather not have gotten involved, but what choice did he have?

"As a good citizen," Ortiz said, "he eventually agreed to help, though he was reluctant, and none too happy when events unfolded as they did. He especially hated their conditions of confidentiality, but because this was a massive, ongoing investigation involving hundreds of people in a number of states and countries, he would have to keep his part of it completely confidential forever. He couldn't even tell his own wife, not then and not later, because the investigation was far from finished, and there were too many people at risk if they were found out. He stuck with the plan but had quite a shock when the rep who contacted him to discuss purchase of the machine, as predicted, was someone he already knew."

That rep was Harold Underwood, a local scholar Granddad had hired in the past to get advice about proper storage for the pamphlet. Granddad had also referred Taavi Koenig to Harold just a few weeks prior regarding the illuminated manuscript. Surely Underwood, he insisted later to the agents, wasn't involved with criminals. But the Secret Service told him to follow the course.

So he agreed to the deal and placed the order, the plan being for him to receive delivery at the company and then turn around and sell the machine to Harold while it was still on the truck.

"The machine was scheduled to arrive at Talbot headquarters on a Wednesday afternoon," Ortiz continued, "but then things got more complicated. In a completely unrelated matter, who showed up at his office that very day, without an appointment and asking to see him, but Taavi Koenig! They'd spoken on the phone before but never met in person, and now suddenly here he was. Taavi seemed stressed and disheveled, almost desperate in his pursuit of the old missing family heirloom he'd been looking for. He'd come to Richmond now, he explained, because he was following a hunch about a location where the manuscript might possibly be hidden. He'd brought a map with him, and he spread it out on your grandfather's desk and showed him where he wanted to explore on Talbot land. Then he started asking a bunch of questions about the original layout of what had once been the plantation known as River Pines."

She paused for a moment, glancing around as if to make sure we were still with her before continuing. "Well, the timing couldn't have been worse for your grandfather. Not only was he already stressed about the transaction that was supposed to take place just a short while later with Harold, but his big annual family reunion was to start the next evening. Now here Taavi was, talking about buried treasure and could he have permission to poke around in the woods at the estate and maybe bring in some digging equipment, and it was all just too much. Your granddad later admitted that he could've handled it better. But in the moment, all he could do was brusquely send the man away, telling him that this was a really bad time and he'd have to get in touch with him next week instead."

Apparently, that left Taavi worried and confused, not to mention paranoid, especially when he was about to drive away and spotted Harold Underwood—the man he'd hired to help find the manuscript a few weeks prior—walking into the building. Taavi had to wonder if Granddad had put him off so he could find the treasure himself first, especially now that it had been handed to him on a silver platter. Worse, it seemed he was conspiring with Harold Underwood."

"You're in cahoots!" I cried, startling everyone except Ortiz, who grinned.

"Exactly," she said. "Taavi didn't do anything at the time, but he stewed on the matter all night and then sought out your grandfather the next morning and confronted him."

I reminded the others of the words Taavi had said when he started yelling at Granddad outside the florist shop, including "You're in cahoots." He'd meant with Harold, that the two of them were working together to steal the manuscript out from under him.

"Of course," Ortiz continued, "your grandfather couldn't tell Taavi what was really going on with Harold, but he tried to assure him it was an entirely separate matter. He also explained in more detail about the size and scope of the reunion, hoping to make the man understand why he didn't want him poking around in the woods while all that was going on. Your grandfather even offered to foot the bill himself for the rental of any digging equipment as long as Taavi would wait until Monday, after the reunion was over, to get started."

According to Ortiz, Taavi finally calmed down and left, and that was the last Granddad ever saw of him.

"Then," she continued, her expression somber, "two days later, when you girls came running out of the woods screaming that someone had been killed inside the old hunting cabin, your grandfather's first thought was of Taavi, how maybe he'd decided to go ahead and start exploring anyway and had had some sort of fatal accident. Then again, he knew, his own involvement with the Secret Service had put him in a certain amount of danger, and this could have something to do with them or with the crime syndicate. That was why, before he called the police, he called the Secret Service."

"Which was the call Nana overheard," Maddee said in wonder.

Nodding, Ortiz continued, saying that the police came, hiked out to the cabin and took a look, but that there was nothing there. When they returned claiming it had all been a figment of our imagination, Granddad had known that probably wasn't true. If the syndicate was involved, chances were they had cleaned the mess up and gotten the body out of there in time, before the police arrived or the Secret Service afterward.

"Later, Nicole, after you realized nobody believed your story, you came over and told your grandfather that the dead man had been the same guy from the parking lot two days before. He couldn't fathom what might've happened, but something had gone seriously wrong out there. Because of the way things were cleaned up so quickly afterward, a larger entity had to be involved. Terrified for your safety, he made you promise you would never tell another soul, and then he got in touch with the Secret Service again and demanded some answers."

Their theory, in the end, was that the syndicate had gotten wind of Granddad's cooperation with the feds and in response had used the busyness of the reunion to place some bugs in the house and then set up a listening station in the cabin nearby. Later on, Secret Service agents had found a map and a shovel and other digging tools farther in the woods, which indicated to them that Taavi had probably been a victim of "wrong place, wrong time," happening upon the bad guys in his search for the manuscript and getting himself killed. It must have just happened when they heard us coming, so they ran out and hid nearby, watching and waiting and trying to decide what to do. When we ran off screaming, they probably rushed back inside, carted the body and their listening equipment away, cleaned up the blood, staged the fake scene with the stick and the blanket and the water, and then disappeared. I supposed we were all lucky that they hadn't decided just to kill us too!

So Granddad hadn't been involved in the murder after all, I realized, deeply relieved. When Nana heard him say, *We have a big problem here. You need to take care of it. Fast,* he wasn't calling someone to clean up a crime scene—he was worried the syndicate had murdered someone on his property, with his grandchildren around no less. Later, when he made me promise I wouldn't tell anyone what I knew, he'd done that for my own safety—for the safety of all of us. There were better ways he could've handled the situation, I felt sure, but he'd just been reacting in the moment, never realizing the impact that secret would end up having on me.

"When all was said and done," Ortiz continued, "and against your grandfather's strenuous objections, the Secret Service refused to let Taavi's family know what had happened, fearing that would impact their investigation. With no body to be found, they couldn't even be certain that the man you had seen had really been dead."

"So what happened to the body?" Renee asked softly.

"Considering it has never shown up, the assumption is that the syndicate disposed of it the same way they often did, by weighing it down and tossing it into the ocean far from shore."

Ortiz was quiet for a moment, and my mind went to poor Gabe and his family. At least they would have closure now, but without a body to bury, I had to wonder if they would ever really feel that this ordeal was over.

"Your grandfather had no choice but to comply with the Secret Service's gag order on Taavi's death," Ortiz continued, "but he did convince them to let him aid the man's family anonymously. Through Lev's finance company, they facilitated the scholarship fund, telling the Koenigs it was government administrated—"

"When in fact it was really created by Granddad, using his own money." Maddee gave me a meaningful glance.

"Correct," Ortiz replied. "Well, Harold Underwood pitched in too, though his contribution was smaller, of course. Not everyone has a hundred grand to give away at will. But Harold said he felt terrible about what had happened to his client, and he contributed ten thousand toward the total."

I thought of poor Harold and what an emotional burden he must have carried from all of that back then.

"As for Lev Sobel," Ortiz continued, "he'd worked with the government before on other financial matters and had enough security clearance to be told some of the facts, including that Douglas Talbot wanted to set up an anonymous fund for the children of a man who'd been killed on his property—even though the death was in no way Talbot's fault."

"So you're saying it was a coincidence that Lev and Miss Vida got together all these years later?" I asked skeptically.

"Nope," Ortiz replied with a smile. "You remember when the DNA report from the blood first came out, and she offered to spread the word that you were trying to track down a man of Jewish ancestry with brown hair and green eyes who'd gone missing in 1995?"

"Yes."

"Well, she put the word out among her Jewish friends and contacts and managed to come up with the name of Taavi Koenig. That story made the rounds for a good while afterward, and eventually Lev heard about it. He recognized the name of the missing man as the same name connected with the scholarships way back when, so he knew if it was the same person that he wasn't just missing but dead. He decided to see if, after all these years, the truth could finally come out. Thus his first phone call with Vida had been purely for information-gathering purposes. After that, he made the request to the Secret Service, but it was denied."

"How frustrating," Maddee said, "for all of us."

Ortiz nodded. "At least Lev's part of the story had a happy ending. As he put it, his first call with Vida had been under false pretenses, but by the end of that call his interest in her had been genuine, and so he ended up pursuing a relationship with her."

"So much for wondering if he was after her for her money," I said to Maddee, which caused Ortiz to laugh.

"Trust me, girls. The man has more money than he knows what to do with. I doubt he's after her for anything more than the pleasure of her company."

Maddee and I shared a smile, relieved and happy for Miss Vida.

"So do you think they'll ever figure out which member of the syndicate actually killed Taavi?" Renee asked. "Statistically speaking, that does narrow the field. How many people were at the cabin when it happened?"

"At a minimum, three—two to cart off the body and one to clean up—though given how quickly they got out of there, they think it was probably at least four. Regardless, the Secret Service has narrowed down the list of potential suspects, every one of which is already in custody for other crimes. At this point, they're just trying to get one of them to talk, and then it should all be downhill after that."

The detective sat back on the stool with a sigh, and I asked if her involvement was pretty much over at this point.

She shrugged. "Yeah. I'll be keeping tabs on things, and once the truth is out and the trials begin, I'll be involved there, of course, but that's about it." Biting her lip, she looked around at our little group and then added, "Speaking of which, the four of you will have to testify, you know."

If she was expecting us to balk, she was mistaken. Our response couldn't have been more emphatic—even mine. As traumatic as this situation had always been for me, I was eager to bring Taavi's killer to justice and put the entire matter behind me for good.

~

The moment Harold stepped into the room and spotted the bundle over on the table, he gasped. At the sound, everyone turned to look his way, and only then did he seem to catch himself. Continuing forward, he tried to gather his composure, but he wasn't fooling anyone. No matter how calm he pretended to be on the outside, he was obviously jumping up and down on the inside.

I couldn't blame him. This was an extremely significant find, especially in the field of diaspora. The fact that its history was so complex and fascinating made it even that much more valuable.

Harold set his things to the side and then stepped to the table and leaned in close, adjusting his glasses. As we all looked on, he studied the item from every angle, clearly enraptured by the sight. Danielle finally broke the silence by asking about the shiny black substance coating the exterior of the canvas.

"I'm pretty sure that's tar," he replied without taking his eyes from it. "Before shipping it out on the *Tycoon*, the owner probably had it waterproofed—to the extent they could in those days. During the Civil War, soldiers used to waterproof their haversacks by painting the bottoms with tar. My guess is that's essentially what was done here, just as a safeguard against exposure to rain or splashing waves while it was with the cargo aboard ship."

"So what do we need to unwrap this thing?" Ortiz asked. "I've been told that conditions must be perfect or we might damage it."

Harold took one last, long, lingering look and then let out a heavy sigh, straightened, and removed his glasses.

"Sadly, I should warn you that it's already quite damaged. There's no doubt of that, given where you found it." He went on to explain that the parchment and inks used in illuminated manuscripts were vulnerable to variances in temperature and humidity, not to mention mold and mildew, invasion by pests, and more. "If you're expecting to see a beautiful, perfect book emerge from this old bundle, you'll be sorely disappointed. We can only hope some fragments have survived."

His words were sobering, not to mention disappointing.

"It's still an important find, though," Renee said.

"Oh, yes. No question of that. This is a treasure, regardless of its condition. I just can't believe after all these years it's finally been found." He seemed almost spellbound as his eyes returned to the prize.

"So let's make this happen," Ortiz said, as eager as the rest of us to get a look. "What should we do? Close the drapes, maybe pump up the A/C?"

Harold's head whipped around, eyes wide. "No, ma'am! Not here. Not like this. It has to be done in a lab, under extremely controlled conditions, with just the right tools."

"I thought you came here to unwrap it for us."

"No, I came here to prepare it for transport."

She voiced her objections even as he retrieved from his equipment a container about the size and shape of a small cat carrier and set it on the table next to the bundle. Then he pulled on a pair of white cotton gloves and told everyone to please step back and give him room.

We all did as requested except for Renee and Blake, who were at the ready to assist.

"Do you have gloves?" Harold snapped, looking from one to the other.

"No."

"Well, there's not much you can do then, is there? Step back, please."

Wanting to get a good look, Danielle had positioned herself behind him, next to the fridge, but he wasn't tolerating that either.

"Don't hover. You'll make me nervous," he said, waving her around until she was standing with the rest of us.

We all glanced at each other, simultaneously irritated and amused.

At last Harold proceeded, slowly scooting a flat tray underneath the bundle and then picking that tray up by the side rims and carefully sliding it into the carrier from the back. His movements were so slow and precise, he looked like a scientist handling plutonium.

Securing the bundle once it was inside the carrier took a while as well, and eventually it became boring enough that both Aunt Cissy and Danielle decided to head up to the main house, touch base with Nana, and see everyone who'd arrived. Feeling antsy, Greg said he'd tag along, and though Maddee offered to join him, he told her to stay put. "I know you want to be in on this stuff. I'll go with them for now. Come find me when you're done."

Once they were gone, that left Maddee, Renee, Blake, Detective Ortiz, Harold, and me in the pool house. Harold was still fiddling with the carrier, and the longer it took, the more impatient Ortiz seemed to grow.

When he finally announced the bundle was secure and ready to roll, the two began butting heads over what was to happen next. Ortiz's intention was for the container to be brought to the lab by police, but Harold was insisting it would only be safe with someone who knew what they were doing. Renee volunteered Blake to help with the transport, saying he'd been the one to move and protect the pamphlet until it was safely in the hands of the Smithsonian. Ortiz thanked her but explained that this was about chain of custody, and that for now the manuscript had to be treated as evidence relating to the murder of Taavi Koenig.

"This priceless treasure isn't going into some evidence locker!" Harold cried. "Are you crazy?"

Watching him, something about his demeanor bothered me. It wasn't his words, because he was obviously correct. You couldn't store a priceless ancient artifact at a police station—and Ortiz knew it too. That wasn't what she was saying.

There was just something about his energy, his agitation level, his over-the-top arrogance that felt off somehow. Finally, I realized what it was: his eyes. In an instant, I recognized something all too familiar, a look I used to call, back in my drug days, "the sweet *almost*." In rehab, they referred to it as "the anticipatory surge of dopamine." Either way, I knew it when I saw it.

And I was seeing it now in Harold. His eyes had the look of a junkie just before a fix—the heroin user as he's thumping for a vein, or the meth head as she heats the pipe. It was the look some had while watching the ball spin at a roulette table or unwrapping a chocolate bar or stepping into a shopping mall. It was the crazed gleam of *addiction*, plain and simple.

But addiction to what?

To viewing precious artifacts?

To touching them?

To restoring them?

Whatever it was, Harold Underwood *needed* something in this moment no less strongly than any addict needed his next high. The display was unsettling, especially considering that he was only here as a consultant. It wasn't as though the item in question was going to end up as a part of his own collection.

It struck me that maybe I was making this more complicated than it needed to be. As their argument dragged on, I turned my attention to Renee and gestured toward the door. Eyes narrowing, she nodded in return.

"So what's up with him?" I asked as I stepped into the hot, muggy afternoon air and pulled the door closed behind me.

"I don't know. I guess he's just excited."

"That's not excited. That's frantic."

"I'm sure he'll calm down once we're in the lab, where things are more controlled."

"I don't know, Renee. I have to be honest. His behavior in there right now? He's exhibiting all the signs of an addict."

"What?" she cried with a laugh. "Yeah, right."

I put a hand on her arm and looked her in the eye. "I'm not kidding. I think Harold's using, and he's right on the verge of his next hit. Whatever he's on, he's about to be impaired. I don't want that man walking out of here with the manuscript."

Renee studied me for a long moment. "All right. I don't see it, and I don't want to believe it, but I trust you. What do you think we should do?"

My heart gave a thud at my cousin's words. *I trust you.* Who could have guessed I would ever hear her say that?

"Just follow my lead."

As we stepped back inside, it was obvious the situation had escalated.

"Fine!" Harold snapped, his face red with anger. "If that's how you want to handle it, then I don't want anything to do with this. I'm out of here."

With that, he stepped around to the back of the case, swung open the door, and reached inside. We could hear Velcro crackling free as he seemed to be undoing the straps he'd used to secure the bundle, followed by the sound of rustling fabric. Finally, with far less careful movements than before, he pulled out not the package but the contents from inside it, a bound stack of tattered and disintegrated parchment pages.

The illuminated manuscript.

Renee and Blake both cried out, but he just ignored them, set the ancient book on the table, and slammed the door of the case shut again.

"Let me know how things turn out," he snapped. "Or maybe I should say, let me know how badly you manage to ruin your priceless little treasure."

With that, he picked up the carrier, grabbed his other things, and headed for the door. I made a point of getting in his way as he tried to brush past. He hesitated for a moment, gave me a glare, and then sidestepped around me and kept walking.

Once he was gone, we gave a collective exhale, looking around at each other as if to say, *What just happened here?* Then everyone started talking at once—everyone except me. My mind was too busy trying to understand something.

The issue, again, was Harold's eyes. As he'd tried to get past me just now, I could clearly see that there'd been a change. The crazed look of an addict prior to a hit had been replaced with the satisfied, hopped-up gleam of the active user. Whatever drug he'd been craving before, he'd somehow managed to get it.

"Did he ever leave this room while he was here?" I asked.

They all looked at me as if I were nuts, but Blake and Ortiz both answered no. Then they went back to what they were doing, trying to find an expert who could take Harold's place so that the matter could proceed.

As Blake studied his iPad and Ortiz tapped at her phone, I moved over to the table to get a closer look at the manuscript. I peered at it, thinking, until I figured out what Harold's "fix" must have been: the real manuscript.

This one was a fake.

"What's wrong?" Renee stepped closer.

I looked up at her, my eyes wide. "You took pictures of the bundle earlier, once it was in the cooler, right?

She nodded.

"Did you text any of those photos to Harold before he got here?"

"Yeah, he said he needed as many as I had, plus the approximate dimensions and weight and stuff, so he'd be sure to bring the right equipment."

Meeting my cousin's eyes, I said, "I'm afraid equipment had nothing to do with it."

Rising, I cleared my throat and addressed the group. "Um, people? Big news. This isn't the manuscript. It's a fake. Harold pulled a switch on us. The real manuscript walked out that door in his carrying case."

Of course, the room erupted into pandemonium, Blake readying to go tackle Harold, Ortiz stopping him and whipping out her radio, Renee trying to figure out how he had pulled it off. Before they could panic too much, I reached into my pocket and pulled out a set of car keys, which I dangled from one finger.

"I'm sure he hasn't gotten too far without these."

"What?" Renee cried. "Why'd you do that?"

"Because Harold's an addict, and by the time he left this room, he'd gotten his fix. It was plain as day on his face." With a mischievous grin, I added, "What can I say? Friends don't let friends drive while intoxicated."

Ortiz and Blake both took off out the door in hot pursuit of Harold, who was probably still standing at his car, digging through his bags and pockets in a desperate search for the keys he just knew were there somewhere.

I was about to follow when Renee grabbed a pen and some paper from the kitchen drawer and started madly sketching.

"I know how he did it," she said finally, looking at me. "I've been to his lab and have seen the stacks of old documents that have accumulated there, too ruined by time to be of any real value but still too important to destroy. There must be hundreds of them. Once I called him and sent the info, all Harold had to do was dig through those piles until he found a document that could pass as an ancient Hebrew illuminated manuscript and then hide it in the bottom of his carrier. Remember how he insisted we all stand on that side of the table? That's because he didn't want us to see into the carrier and realize that there was already something in there."

She flipped around her drawing and pointed as she explained. "He slipped the tray with the real bundle into the track and secured it inside, but then when he gave the bundle back to us, he pulled out the fake one from underneath." Her expression grave, she added, "He probably didn't having anything on hand similar to the tar-coated canvas, so that's why he pretended to unwrap it first before he pulled it back out minus the covering. He argued with Ortiz on purpose, specifically so that he could leave the wrong one behind and storm out of here with the real bundle, unbeknownst to anyone but him."

The two of us went to see what was happening, and my mind raced as we walked. I thought of Aunt Cissy's words from earlier in the summer, about how some people wanted to own a piece of history whether they could share it with others or not. Was that Harold's driving need, to own pieces of history? To possess them, even if in secret?

Suddenly, I thought of his brother, the criminal, the artist talented enough to engrave plates used for manufacturing money. But money wasn't the only thing that could be counterfeited. Documents of all kinds—letters and journals and pamphlets and so much more—could be re-created convincingly if someone knew what they were doing.

What if, I wondered, Harold occasionally used his credentials to get people to hand over their most precious antique documents for authentication? Then, while the items were in his possession, his talented brother would create exact copies, counterfeit versions, and that's what Harold gave back to the owners when he was done, along with his authentication.

It could work. As long as the owner didn't seek a second opinion, they might go years without realizing they'd been duped. And in the meantime, Harold could slowly amass a collection of authentic, priceless, diaspora-related materials to love and treasure and possess—even if he had to keep it secret, even if it was something he could never share.

From the look in his eyes earlier, it was obvious now that he *had* to have this manuscript in his possession, just like an addict—and that he might do anything to make that happen.

As we rounded the garage, I thought of his history, his childhood, and it was easy to see the origins of such an addiction—not that that excused it. But I did understand it. I knew what could happen to a person when they were emotionally wounded at a young age and how that might create a need to numb the pain. I'd found my relief in drugs.

Coming upon the scene now, I just knew that his relief came from secretly acquiring and hoarding the relics of diaspora. The man who'd been forcibly removed from his home as a child found solace as an adult in accumulating the irrefutable evidence of the same travesty having been visited upon others.

Harold Underwood hadn't been an innocent pawn of his brother all those years ago. He'd been an active and willing participant, a criminal in his own right who'd been able to hide his nefarious activities under the veneer of a respected scholar. And it had worked too. The short, stout, balding little professor-type had seemed harmless and innocent to everyone—including the Secret Service. But there was nothing innocent about him.

That was obvious the moment we stepped past the garage and caught sight of the scene taking place in the driveway. Ortiz had Harold handcuffed and up against the car, her officers hovering at the ready nearby. On the lawn stood everyone who'd come out from the main house, though Danielle and Maddee gravitated back over to our side as soon as they saw us. We four stood there together, watching, astounded, as Dr. Harold Underwood was taken into police custody for the attempted theft of the priceless illuminated manuscript.

As Ortiz was walking him to the back of the police car, he glanced our way and then froze, sheer hatred radiating from his face.

"You stupid girls. If you just hadn't come to the cabin that day, I—" He stopped short, catching himself, suddenly looking like the proverbial deer in the headlights.

In that instant, we knew, as did Ortiz. Eyes wide, she gripped the man more firmly and said, "Guess what, Harold? You just became our primary person of interest in the murder of Taavi Koenig."

Chapter Thirty-One

Therese

A week later, after Therese and Michael declared their love for each other, the Union Army collected the Northern soldiers from River Pines and transferred them to Washington. Two weeks after that, the Huguenot Springs Hospital was able to take the rest of the Confederate soldiers.

Sadly, when Rabbi Elias Koenig returned from the fighting and finally came to retrieve his manuscript, Michael's father had to tell him the bad news about Mr. Porter and how the fellow had taken advantage of his position as a handyman to raid the family's safe, stealing several highly valuable items from inside, including the illuminated manuscript. The Talbots never even noticed anything was gone until the day the sheriff showed up, saying they'd caught a local criminal trying to sell a fancy ring someone recognized as having belonged to the Talbots. The sheriff managed to recover that plus a few other things that had been taken, but the manuscript had not been among them, and the fence denied ever having seen it or hearing anything about it. Thus, the illuminated manuscript that had already been stolen, sold, confiscated, bought, and brought all the way back home from France had now been stolen again.

The poor rabbi seemed heartbroken, though he didn't blame the Talbots. "Clearly," he said, "it is the will of HaShem that this book find a different home."

In other sad news, they learned that Box Tree Male Academy had been destroyed by fire and that the cottage had been taken over by soldiers and then also burned. All those books and papers of Father's that Mother insisted they leave behind were gone. However, Therese still had Rose O'Neal Greenhow's memoir. Even though she didn't agree with the woman's loyalties, God had used the book to give Therese courage to do the right thing. It would forever be a reminder of the work Polly, Michael, and she had done. In light of their safety however, they wouldn't ever share their own stories with others.

The first Saturday in June, Therese and Michael were married in a ceremony on the porch of the house at River Pines, where they would live, with only their families in attendance. Mother was thrilled to have Therese staying in Virginia, especially since her health had been declining since Warner passed. At first Therese believed it was grief, but soon after the wedding, as her cough grew worse, Polly diagnosed it as consumption.

By winter it was obvious Mother was dying. Therese and Polly did their best to care for her, but she joined Warner and Father on the other side in late February. But instead of being buried at River Pines, Mother had requested she be laid to rest beside Father in the churchyard cemetery. Therese found the gesture comforting. Mother seemed to have at last reconciled her fears. Love seemed to have won.

Therese had been fully embraced by the Talbot family, and she thanked God every day for their love and care. In April, Therese delivered her first baby, a girl. Michael insisted they name her Willa, in memory of Therese's father.

Polly cared for Therese and the baby into the early summer but then left to work in the hospital in New York, the position secured for her by Ruth. Auntie Vera went with her and then continued on to Maine, to Aggie and Badan and their baby boy. Michael worked nearly every day with his father and brother, Lance, at the Talbot paper mill on the James, and eventually they would be able to give Old Joe a job there as well. For now, the former slave was busy working alongside a couple of hired hands and doing his best to try to turn River Pines around. But the needed work was more than they could possibly manage.

In mid-August, while fireflies flitted around on the edge of the woods, Therese and Michael strolled along the banks of the James River. Michael carried their baby girl in his arms as the trees of River Pines swayed in the slight breeze to the south of them. They talked about the estate and what should be done about it.

"The old house is falling apart," Therese said, her right hand around the locket hanging from her neck, with the tintypes of her parents, and her other hand carrying a lantern. "Old Joe does his best, but the roof is leaking, and he found another crack in the foundation yesterday. And the hired hands can't seem to get anything to grow. Soon the woods will take over the entire property. Maybe we should sell it."

Michael shook his head. "No one local has the money to buy property right now. Besides, I don't think it's a bad thing if the woods do take over. We might as well use our own trees—the pines and firs and other softwoods—to help make paper. I'll figure out the best way to manage and harvest them."

"What about the house?" Although River Pines was the only home Therese had now, and she definitely felt more comfortable on the property than she had as a child, she didn't feel connected to it the way she had to Box Tree Male Academy. "Considering its history, shouldn't we try to sell it?"

Michael shook his head. "Don't you see? By staying, we're redeeming this place. Bit by bit. Maybe someday we'll build a new house, on a different part of the property altogether, or our children will. That will be our legacy." He lifted the baby into the air. Willa giggled as he did. "Just as your father left you and me a legacy, we'll leave one for our daughter and all of our future children. One of dignity and respect and faith, and, God willing, this property and the mill and the print shop." He pulled the baby close. "And we'll pray they'll pass the same legacy down to their children and their children's children."

Therese thought of the Box Tree Male Academy and the joy it had brought her. She wanted that for her children and someday her grandchildren. She leaned her head against Michael's shoulder and whispered, "Amen."

She hadn't yet told him another baby was on the way. That their legacy was already growing bigger, that her desire for a large family was one step closer. That in time, this new branch of the Talbot family would be as strong and sturdy as the branches that had come before.

She exhaled, putting the trauma of the war another small step behind her. Father used to say that faith wasn't a fix. Instead, he explained, it "helps us acknowledge our Creator as we trust Him to guide us through both the good and the bad." Funny how the good and the bad were often woven together. That was how her time in Richmond had seemed. She'd never endured such hardship, and yet she'd learned to draw on God's strength. She'd been tested and found that courage meant simply doing the right thing. She vowed to continue living that way, speaking up for those without a voice as she created a legacy that would impact generations to come.

She looked forward to her future with Michael and all the Talbots, and was eternally grateful for where God was leading her—where He was leading them all.

I stood in the kitchen looking at Maddee's whiteboard, barely believing that August 5 was finally here. No summer had ever passed so quickly for me as this one! It felt like about a week ago when I was sitting here listening to Maddee's rules and schedule—and laid out some rules of my own. By next summer she'd probably be married, which meant we'd likely never be roomies again, at least not for such an extended period of time.

My heart grew heavy at the thought, but I pushed it from my mind and headed for the living room area to pull the last of my things together and do some final cleaning. I'd be leaving in about an hour or so to head back to school for the fall semester.

At the moment, Maddee was next door with Miss Vida, who'd asked for her help in rounding up some goodies from her garden to send with me today. Thus, alone for now, I pumped up the music and wrestled with one bag and then the next, finally admitting that my new trophy wasn't going to fit in either. Instead, I rolled it in a blanket for protection and then slid that into a pillowcase. Perfect.

I'd received the trophy yesterday at the summer employees' farewell banquet, which was really just a pizza party with some awards given out at the end. The funny thing was, most everyone else would still be working there for at least another week or two. But Nate had given the party early so I could be included, and I understood why when I heard him call my name.

Up to that point, the awards had mostly been silly and just for fun, such as "Best Pooper Scooper" and "Most Likely to Sneak Sugar Cubes to the Horses." But then at the end, they gave out a couple of serious ones too, such as "Most Improved Rider" and "Best Groomer." Mine came last, the "Summer MVP" award. As everyone whooped and hollered, and I headed up front to claim my prize, Nate read from his little note card. "Not just for your consistent dedication and hard work, but also for saving the life of a horse through keen observation and quick action." I knew he was talking about Hutch, and though it seemed like a bit of a stretch to say I'd saved the animal's life, it still felt good to be honored.

As I accepted my trophy and envelope, I looked into Nate's eyes, needing to see here at the end, for just a moment, that he felt what we had even if he couldn't admit it to himself or to me. Once again, though, the only thing there was a wall. No matter how close we'd grown, or how wonderfully we got along, or how perfect we were for each other, this man was never going to admit to himself that I was worth the risk of loving. He would hold out for someone better, someone who'd never struggled with addiction, someone who wouldn't get his hopes up only to dash them on the rocks. Knowing his history, I couldn't really blame him.

When the party was over, I hadn't the heart for the kind of goodbye I knew he would give me, a simple handshake or maybe a quick side hug between friends, so I just caught his eye across the room, mouthed the words "Thank you," and gave him a wave. He waved in return, and for a moment he looked genuinely sad that I was leaving. But then someone interrupted on his end, so with that I slipped out the door and headed for my car.

The award had come with a fifty-dollar gift card, and I went straight from there to the store, where I spent it on a basket, tissue paper, and various engagement supplies, including a couple of thick, gorgeous bridal magazines, some nice thank-you stationery, a guide to wedding etiquette, and a little cake topper bride and groom just for fun. I put it all together and kept it hidden until this morning. When my sister headed over to Miss Vida's, I was able to slip upstairs and leave it on her bed along with a note thanking her for all she'd done for me this summer.

I'd never forgotten the little gift basket she made for me when I moved in after my accident. It hadn't been anything fancy. Just some candy bars and a couple of things like playing cards to help me pass the time. But it had touched me deeply in ways I hadn't even understood then, and my hope was that Maddee would see my love for her in this basket, as I had seen her love for me in that one.

Back downstairs, I finished the last of the packing and then turned my attention to cleaning. While I worked, my mind went to the investigation and Harold Underwood and all that had happened since the day at Nana's a little more than a month ago when Ortiz arrested him for the murder of Taavi Koenig.

According to Ortiz, after speaking with his lawyer, Harold ended up making a full confession about the murder, though he insisted on calling it "an accidental crime of passion." He explained how, on the day he went to Talbot headquarters to purchase the machine, Granddad mentioned the visit he'd just had from Taavi Koenig, including the fact that he'd brought a map with him showing the layout of the old plantation and the approximate location of the overseer's dead body. Wanting that map, Harold had gone to Taavi later and convinced him that Granddad was lying, and that the only reason he'd put him off for a week was because he wanted time to find the manuscript himself. Harold convinced Taavi that the two of them should go to the cabin first thing Saturday morning, while Granddad was busy with his reunion guests, and find that manuscript together instead.

What Taavi didn't know was that Harold had been out at the cabin several times recently, helping to facilitate the activities of his brother's crime syndicate. From the time Harold made first contact about purchasing the machine until that purchase was complete, the syndicate had been bugging the Talbots' home, with the cabin as their listening station, to make sure Granddad wasn't secretly cooperating with the feds. They were supposed to have closed up shop once the deal was done on Wednesday, which was why Harold was startled when he and Taavi got to the cabin Saturday morning to find three of the guys still out there. Unbeknownst to him, they'd been told to extend their watch for another week.

Taavi had seemed confused by the encounter, especially because Harold was clearly trying to prevent him from interacting with those men or seeing what they were doing inside the cabin. But he got a glimpse of their equipment and mistakenly assumed they were using high-tech means to search for the treasured manuscript. Furious, he pushed his way inside, where a scuffle ensued. Taavi kept yelling at the men about how they were stealing his hidden treasure, but that was the last thing Harold wanted these goons to hear, lest they insist on a piece of that action themselves. Before he knew it, Harold said, he had grabbed a big hunting knife from the sideboard and fatally stabbed Taavi in the chest.

Harold had been stunned, not to mention covered in blood, but lucky for him, the syndicate guys knew what to do from there. While two of them removed all the equipment and lugged it out to their vehicle, the third guy took Harold down the path that led to the river and cleaned him up as best he could. All four men got back to the cabin at about the same time, but just before they rounded the bend, they heard voices and stopped.

Peeking ahead, they saw a group of little girls inside the cabin at that very moment. The men hid and watched from the bushes, trying to decide what to do. None of them wanted to kill the kids, though that was an option. Instead, they waited till the girls took off, and then they moved into high gear, two of them wrapping the body in a tarp and carting it away while the other two cleaned up the blood as best they could. In a last-second burst of inspiration, finally snapping out of his stupor, Harold had been the one to set things up in such a way that it would cast suspicion on the children's story. They all left just in time, unseen, and later dumped Taavi's body into the Atlantic a few miles off the coast of Norfolk.

Of course, in time Harold would return to the cabin and continue his search, still pursuing Taavi's theory that Mr. Porter had hidden the manuscript somewhere in the vicinity of the old slave quarters. But despite coming back again and again, and looking as hard as he could, he'd never been able to find it.

Harold easily confessed all of this to Ortiz, though he didn't mention any other thievery—until police raided his home and office and discovered a secret collection, one with dozens of valuable diaspora-related documents, including the original version of Catherine Talbot Gillet's journal, which he'd kept several years ago, returning to the museum a faked version instead. The police were still in the process of tracing some of the other items back to their rightful owners, but so far it seemed Harold's basic technique had been as I'd guessed—that he used his reputation and authentication qualifications to keep originals and return fakes. Even his involvement with the pamphlet had been an attempt to steal it, apparently, but because it was being donated to the Smithsonian, he'd had to let that one go. It was too risky given that their own experts would be thoroughly checking it out soon after.

For now, Harold had been arraigned and was currently awaiting sentencing. With him behind bars and all his precious treasures gone, I had to wonder if he was going through withdrawals like a junkie. If so, at least prison would keep him on the straight and narrow. Convicts often managed to smuggle in drugs, but I highly doubted anyone was trading in diaspora-related historical documents.

As it turned out, the manuscript was in better shape than expected, though not by much. As Harold had said, years of vacillating temperatures and moisture and the like had wrought havoc with much of it. But some pages were intact, as well as numerous fragments. For now, it was with a restoration group, and we knew that once they were done, Gabe would be selling it, just as his father had planned to do—though he was hoping to keep one fragment as a remnant of the family heirloom. Museums all over the world had been putting out feelers since the day the story hit the news, so it wouldn't be hard to find buyers. Apparently, numbers were already being tossed about in the seven-to eight-figure range, not bad for a tattered and partially disintegrated old pile of parchment.

We never expected to share in the profits of our discovery, but to our surprise the Koenig family said that upon the final sale of the manuscript, they intended to give us a $100,000 reward, to be divided among the group of seven who were there the day it was found. We all knew they were simply paying back our family for the money Granddad had once given them now that they knew the true source of their scholarships, so after voicing some mild objections, we accepted their generosity.

And we did have fun deciding what we would each do with our share. I was going to put mine in the bank, earmarked for future horse-related expenses in my new career. Both couples would be using theirs toward down payments on their first homes, but Danielle surprised us all by saying she would like to invest hers in a nice video camera, professional lighting, and other equipment, which she would use to start a side business as a videographer. Her first project was to record Aunt Cissy sharing all the family stories she held in her head. Of course, Danielle would end up with the porcelain box for her efforts, which we all applauded.

In turn, Aunt Cissy was so pleased at the thought that she said she was going to spend her entire share on travel gift cards, which she would then give out to the four cousins. "They'll be for the sole purpose of visiting each other when you can. That's my legacy, to see that you girls always remain as close to one another as you are today."

Now, in the carriage house, as I gathered up the copies of Michael's love notes to put away with the Civil War photos, one of the pages fell out. I bent over and picked it up, reading the first line on the page, its words written in Michael's neat, masculine handwriting.

You are my vine and fig tree.

Maddee and Miss Vida came inside at just that moment, so I turned down the music and asked if they had any idea what he'd meant by that.

"I think it's from the Bible," Maddee offered, putting down the bags of produce she was carrying and pulling out her phone to google it. Meanwhile, Miss Vida used her phone to call her boyfriend.

"Okay, I was right," Maddee said, her eyes on the screen. "It comes up in the Old Testament. And, apparently, George Washington quoted the phrase often in his correspondence."

She read aloud the various interpretations of the verse, including something about peasant farmers living free of military oppression. But before she got to an explanation that made sense as an endearment, Miss Vida finished her call, hung up, and said, "Okay, I've got it."

We both gave her our attention.

"According to Lev, the phrase shows up three times in the Hebrew Scriptures in a slightly different context each time. He said if we're talking about a love letter from a man to a woman, more than likely it was referring to the version in Micah, which says, 'They will sit under their own vine and fig tree, and no one will make them afraid.' Or something like that."

As she went on to explain further, what she said made perfect sense, not just for Michael and Therese, but for Nate and me too. Listening to her words, I could feel my pulse surging, and I just kept thinking, yes. Yes!

"Thank you, Miss Vida!" When she was done, I threw my arms around the woman and gave her a big kiss on the cheek. Then I grabbed my purse and keys and headed for the door.

"Wait! Where are you going?" Maddee cried.

"To see a man about some figs. I'll be back."

When I arrived at Dover Creek Farms, I screeched to a halt in the first parking spot I saw and went in search of Nate. It took a while, but I found him in the far pasture repairing a broken section of the fence, several of the horses grazing contentedly nearby.

I marched quickly over to him and came to a stop about six feet away.

He didn't see me at first, but then Puzzles gave a loud nicker of hello, and Nate glanced up. When he saw me, he seemed surprised but obviously pleased.

"Nicole? What are you doing here?" he asked, setting down his tools and wiping his hands on his jeans as he rose. "Are you okay?"

I let out a breath and locked my eyes on his. "You are my vine and fig tree, Nate."

"What?"

"It's a verse from the Bible. The words were also in a love note one of my ancestors wrote to his wife."

"Okay..."

"In Micah, the term 'vine and fig tree' means a place of rest, of safety, of peace. Understand, these two people had gone through the Civil War. I think what my great-great-great-grandfather was saying was that after all the craziness and pain and destruction and devastation of that, he was going to be okay because *she* was his place of rest. My great-great-great-grandmother was his vine and fig tree."

Nate's eyes narrowed. Clearly, he was trying to figure out where I was going with this.

"I've had craziness too, and pain," I continued, "and I've left behind plenty of destruction and devastation. But that isn't me anymore. I came out the other side, Nate. I don't want the craziness. I don't need it. I just want peace and rest."

"Why are you telling me this?"

"Because I know that's what scares you about me. You've been let down so many times that I'm sure you told yourself you would never, ever get involved with an addict, even one in recovery."

To my surprise, his eyes grew shiny with tears, though he blinked them away.

"All summer," I continued, the sight making me tear up as well, "you've kept me at arm's length because you're so afraid of that part of me. You're terrified it's still in there somewhere, just waiting to come back out again. It scares you to death. It's what keeps you from—"

I stopped, feeling a sob threaten at the back of my throat.

"It's what keeps me from taking you in my arms?" he asked softly, moving a step closer. "From telling you that I love you?"

"Yes." My heart pounded. "And I understand. I really do. You can't know for certain that all that stuff is behind me. No addict can, Nate. You can't even say that for sure about yourself."

He nodded. "I know. So how can I take that risk with someone else? Even if that someone is you?"

I looked over at the horses, grasping for the right words to say. Then they came to me. "Maybe as a wise chaplain once told me, you have to let faith conquer fear."

Nate blinked, this time sending twin tracks of tears down his handsome, chiseled face.

"Sure, there's risk, just like with horses," I said, paraphrasing the sermon he'd given that first time I visited the racetrack. "You could fall off, or get your hand bitten, or whatever. The problem is, Nate, you can't know a horse's love without first conquering your fear. And how do you do that?"

We spoke in unison, "Through faith and faith alone."

Nate wiped impatiently at his cheeks and then groaned, his eyes to the sky. Whether he was wrestling with God or himself, I wasn't sure, but finally he moved closer toward me across the grass.

"Do you know how tough it's been to spend every day with you and not say anything about how I really feel?" he demanded, coming to a stop just inches away. "About how I probably fell for you the moment I first saw you? How I did everything I could to keep you at arm's length because I just knew you were trouble on wheels, but you got under my skin anyway? How you ended up being this amazing person I just wanted to get to know better, to spend time with. To love."

Heart pounding, I reached up and placed a hand on his cheek. It was warm and rough and felt like home.

"So be my vine and fig tree, Nate," I whispered. "Be my place of rest. And I'll be yours."

He closed his eyes, as if in one last futile attempt to resist. But when he opened them again, I could see that the wall between us had come down.

With a deep sigh, he took me in his arms, and then slowly, ever so slowly, he brought his lips to mine.

We fit together perfectly, beautifully, like nothing I had ever known before. Despite all the guys in my past, every stupid mistake I had ever made, somehow this felt like the first real kiss of my life. When it ended, I laid my head against his chest and we just stood there, wrapped in each other's arms and rocking side to side in the pasture with the horses looking on. I could have stayed like that for the next fifty years.

"I'm so in love with you," he whispered.

"I'm so in love with you," I replied.

Then it was my turn to kiss him, which I did long and hard and with all the passion that had been building up inside of me since the day we met. When we pulled apart again, he didn't let me get far.

"So this is going to be a long-distance relationship for now, huh?" he asked, gently brushing a lock of hair from my face. "I can do that, I guess. If I have to."

"We'll see," I replied, thinking there might come a point where I would decide to transfer closer, not just to be near Nate and my family, but to learn at a university that offered a full program in equine therapy. I would miss my friends and the team and everything, but most of them were older and would be graduating at the end of this year anyway. Besides, Silver Lake University had been the right choice at the time just for the seclusion and the protection. But I was beyond that now. I was stronger than I'd ever known I could be.

"Can I ask you a question?" He stepped back and took me by the hand, interlacing his fingers with mine.

"Anything."

"What if I told you I can see spending the rest of my life with you? That when I look at you, I can imagine all of it—marriage, kids, rocking chairs on the porch when we're old." His cheeks flushing, he added, "I mean, we'll take our time getting there, but I'm not interested in just a passing romance, Nicole, not with you. I see us ending up as something much, much bigger."

My pulse surged. "Okay."

"That doesn't scare you?"

Looking out across the rolling fields, I thought of Maddee and Renee and Danielle and how they'd all found their true loves. I thought of Nana and Aunt Cissy and the whole Talbot family, especially those who had come before. I thought of Therese and Michael Talbot, who had endured the unspeakable horrors of war but had somehow managed to find peace—and each other—on the other side. I thought, generations prior, of Emmanuel and Celeste and Berta Talbot, siblings who had come to the New World in search of a better life. I thought of their parents, Catherine and Pierre Talbot, who had escaped France, leaving everything they knew and loved behind for the sake of their beliefs. These people weren't just my forebears. They were my heroes.

Breathing in deeply, I met Nate's gaze. "Doesn't scare me in the least," I told him, unable to hold in my smile. "But even if it did, not to worry. I come from a long line of women who know a thing or two about courage."

DISCUSSION QUESTIONS

1. Nicole has a secret she's carried since childhood. How has it affected her throughout her growing-up years? What finally makes her decide to disclose it? What are the results of her sharing her secret with those she loves?

2. Therese's mother, Helene, veers away from her late husband's beliefs about abolition and instead embraces the lifestyle of her childhood, which includes the owning of slaves, after her father dies. What changes for Helene? What is her motivation? Were you sympathetic toward her or, like Therese, frustrated by her?

3. Nate is afraid to get close to Nicole because of her history as an addict. What's behind his fear? What makes him finally decide to take a chance on her? Do you think it is hypocritical of him, as a former addict, to fear a relationship with her?

4. The *carte des visite* from 1863 of the former slave with the web of scar tissue across his back has been referred to as the "viral photo that changed America." According to Frank Goodyear, codirector of the Bowdoin College Museum of Art, "It suggests that the Southern idea that slavery was a benign institution was in fact a lie." What impact do images have on your emotions? Is there a particular photo that has changed your thinking? If so, what is it and how did it affect you?

5. After much thought, Therese decides to spy for the enemy. What process does she go through to come to this decision as a Southern belle? Whose story helps convince her to do it? What was your response to Therese spying?

6. At the beginning of the novel, Therese is firm in her ideals but fairly compliant. By the end of the story, she is able to stand up for herself and those she loves. What are some of the steps to independence Therese goes through?

7. Therese volunteers as a nurse at the Institute Hospital and then is hired to work there. Her experience caring for her father doesn't prepare her for the work in the hospital. How is caring for soldiers different? If you had been alive during the Civil War, could you have volunteered to work as a nurse?

8. The night Maddee and Greg get engaged, Nicole decides that even if their union was the only good thing to come out of all of the pain and suffering of her accident, it still would have been worth it. Have you ever had something wonderful come from something awful? In the end, was the suffering you were forced to endure worth it?

9. Each of the four cousins contributes her own unique skill to the solving of the mystery—Renee with her knowledge of science, Danielle with her artist's eye and understanding of architecture, and Maddee with her ability to organize and administrate. What is Nicole's contribution, and how does her own history allow her to recognize addiction in others?

10. In all three novels of the Cousins of the Dove series, the cousins in the modern thread learn about themselves from their ancestors' trials and triumphs. What have you learned from your ancestors? Have any of their stories helped you navigate your own life?

Acknowledgments

Mindy thanks

John Clark, my husband of nearly 30 years and my hero in ways too many to count.

Emily and Lauren Clark, my amazingly helpful and supportive daughters.

Tara Kenny, Amanda Luedeke, and Madeira James, the best behind-the-scenes team a writer could ask for.

David Clark, my resource for all things automotive.

Suzanne Scannell and Gabriella Clark, who helped bring the horses in this story to life.

Leslie thanks

My husband, Peter Gould, for all of your encouragement in both life and writing. I couldn't do this without you.

My children—Kaleb, Taylor, Hana, and Thao—for supporting my storytelling.

Jaylun Lewis, photographer extraordinaire, for inspiring me with his vision.

Dr. Ann Woodlief, Huguenot Society of Manakin national librarian; Bryan S. Godfrey, Huguenot Society of Manakin library assistant; and the Huguenot Society of the Founders of Manakin in the Colony of Virginia, for their help on the history of Huguenots in Virginia.

The staff at the following Richmond sites: the Virginia Historical Society, the White House and Museum of the Confederacy, the Valentine, the Linden Row Inn, and the American Civil War Museum.

Any mistakes in the story are ours.

Mindy and Leslie thank

Chip MacGregor, our ever-helpful agent.

Kim Moore, our always-supportive editor.

All the wonderful folks at Harvest House Publishers.

ABOUT THE AUTHORS

Mindy Starns Clark is the bestselling author of almost 30 books, both fiction and nonfiction (over 1 million copies sold) including coauthoring the Christy Award–winning *The Amish Midwife* with Leslie Gould. Mindy and her husband, John, have two adult children and live in Pennsylvania.

Leslie Gould is the bestselling and award-winning author of 24 novels. She received her master of fine arts degree from Portland State University and lives in Oregon. She and her husband, Peter, are the parents of four children.

To connect with the authors,
visit Mindy's and Leslie's websites at
www.mindystarnsclark.com and www.lesliegould.com

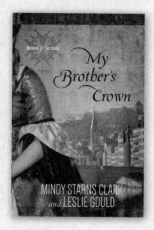

Women of Uncommon Courage

France, 1685

Catherine Gillet knows her brother, Jules, wants to protect her from the sinister threats of the French crown. But Jules is involved in a potentially deadly enterprise, one connected with an encoded document. When his actions put the whole family at risk, will Catherine find a way to save them?

Virginia, present day

Renee Talbot, a direct descendant of Catherine's, is fascinated by the document that's been part of her family legacy for more than three centuries. Certain its pages hold hidden secrets, she takes a closer look—and makes a shocking discovery. But when memories of a childhood trauma are rekindled, she's forced to seek answers of a different kind. Inspired by the faith and bravery of Catherine, can Renee find the truth and face her deepest fears at last?

From the authors of the Christy Award–winning *The Amish Midwife* comes an epic story of two women, centuries apart, each discovering her own hidden bravery, standing for what she believes in, and finding love in unexpected places.

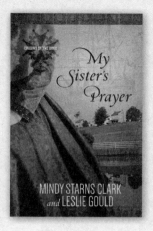

Women of Fearless Devotion

Virginia, 1704

Celeste Talbot is usually such a sensible young woman—until she falls for an English soldier reassigned to the Colonies. Leaving her Huguenot family behind, she sets sail for America, only to realize that her younger sister, Berta, has been kidnapped and forced on board the very same ship. Whom can Celeste trust? The dashing soldier? Or the vigilant carpenter who remains by their side in the perilous New World?

Virginia, present day

Madeline "Maddee" Talbot has her hands full when she agrees to take in her younger sister, Nicole, following a serious car accident. The young women grew apart when Nicole fell into drug addiction, and Maddee prays this will be the start of a better life for her sister. But as they investigate a trauma from their childhood, Maddee must keep a diligent eye on Nicole—and the shadowy figure watching them from afar.

From the Christy Award–winning team of Mindy Starns Clark and Leslie Gould, *My Sister's Prayer* tells an epic tale of two women compelled to protect their sisters, confront their fears, and navigate the muddy waters of betrayal to find true love.

To learn more about Harvest House books and
to read sample chapters, visit our website:

www.harvesthousepublishers.com

HARVEST HOUSE PUBLISHERS
EUGENE, OREGON